Beloved Avenger

"Are you awake?" he asked softly.

She could not remain silent. "Have you ever slept chained to a bed?"

"As a matter of fact, I have."

"Doubtless you deserved it!"

Lucian smiled in the blackness. What a sassy wench she was. Chained to a bed, carried she knew not where, yet able to give him an answer like that. By God, she was braver than a lot of men he knew.

He had never expected to find the most beautiful woman he had ever seen aboard the *Stargazer*. She was Guinevere and Isolde and Aurora, Queen of the Dawn, all combined in one delectable body . . .

Beloved Avenger

Joan Van Nuys

AVON BOOKS ◆ NEW YORK

BELOVED AVENGER is an original publication of Avon Books. This work has never before appeared in book form. This work is a novel. Any similarity to actual persons or events is purely coincidental.

AVON BOOKS
A division of
The Hearst Corporation
1350 Avenue of the Americas
New York, New York 10019

Special Printing: June 1993
First Avon Books Printing: December 1989

AVON TRADEMARK REG. U.S. PAT. OFF. AND IN OTHER COUNTRIES, MARCA REGISTRADA, HECHO EN U.S.A.

Printed in the U.S.A.

RA 10 9 8 7 6 5 4 3 2

This book is dedicated with great admiration to my friend and teacher, Sylvie Sommerfield

When in disgrace with fortune and men's eyes
I all alone beweep my outcast state,
And trouble deaf heaven with my bootless cries,
And look upon myself and curse my fate,
Wishing me like to one more rich in hope,
Featur'd like him, like him with friends possess'd,
Desiring this man's art, and that man's scope,
With what I most enjoy contented least;
Yet in these thoughts myself almost despising,
Haply I think on thee, —and then my state,
Like to the lark at break of day arising
From sullen earth, sings hymns at heaven's gate;
   For thy sweet love remember'd such wealth brings
   That then I scorn to change my state with kings.

—William Shakespeare

Prologue

September, 1787

"**M**an-of-war off our stern, Captain, and coming full sail." Lt. Donal Fleming stared through his telescope long and hard before adding, "It's one of our own, sir, I am happy to say."

"And I'm happy to hear it. Thank you, Mr. Fleming."

Lucian Thorne, captain of HMS *Peacekeeper*, studied the speck on the horizon with thoughtful blue eyes. The *Peacekeeper* should have been the only Royal Navy ship patroling these smuggler- and pirate-infested southern waters, so what was this ship? Lucian took the telescope himself and inspected more closely the fast-moving vessel.

"It's the *Gull*, Mr. Fleming," he finally said. "Her boarding flag just went up. Trim our sails and let's see what she wants."

"Aye, sir."

When the *Peacekeeper*, herself a tall, gleaming man-of-war, came within hailing distance of the *Gull*, a longboat was rapidly lowered from the latter and rowed across the dark, heaving gulf between them.

Lucian waited amidships, his hands clasped behind his back and his long, powerful legs braced against the constant roll of the vessel. With the sun striking diamond glints in his blue-black hair and intensifying the cobalt blue of his eyes, he was an impressive figure,

1

even clad in a cropped, sleeveless white shirt and faded blue breeches. His unruly hair, which barely touched his collar, was tamed by a scarlet band. Only his knee-high black boots showed his naval discipline in their suppleness and mirrorlike gleam.

At twenty-six, Lucian Thorne was tall and darkly handsome: six feet two inches of lean, broad-shouldered, sun-bronzed hardness, with a look of power and responsibility and calm, unquestioned authority; a brash, fearless seagoing prince who dearly loved his watery kingdom. But he kept such emotion well-hidden. His broad mouth, usually so quick to smile, was now compressed to firmness. His face showed no sign of his sensitivity, humor, or compassion, only his keen interest in the business at hand.

As the *Gull*'s captain and a contingent of officers were piped aboard, he stepped forward and saluted.

"Captain Lucian Thorne commanding, sir. Welcome aboard the *Peacekeeper*."

"Captain John Pomeroy, sir."

John Pomeroy appeared so stiff and unfriendly that Lucian studied him curiously. He was a slight, small-boned man, fastidiously groomed; gray-haired and gray-eyed, with a coldly handsome face. Lucian sensed instantly that he was a gloater, a strutter, a proud little peacock. And why was he rigged out in full regalia? Smart three-cornered reefer's hat, blue silk tailcoat, white breeches. It was damned odd.

"To what do we owe this visit, sir?"

Captain Pomeroy cleared his throat. "Admiralty orders, sir. I am to seize and search this vessel."

Lucian loosed a peal of laughter. "I think there has been some mistake."

"None that I know of, Captain. We have reason to suspect you are carrying illegal cargo."

Lucian's deeply tanned face flushed dusky red. As a second load of men boarded from the *Gull*, his stance turned openly hostile: legs apart, shoulders squared, powerful hands resting on his hipbones.

"Just what is it we are supposed to be carrying?" His voice was soft but menacing.

Pomeroy looked from the *Peacekeeper*'s closed-face crew to the nervous-looking men of the *Gull*.

"I would rather we spoke in private."

Lucian spun wordlessly and strode to his cabin, a wood-paneled room that ran the width of the vessel.

Pomeroy followed, noting with disapproval the man's casual attire and dark neatly-trimmed beard. Both violated regulations. The fellow looked no better than his crew, a motley lot at best and certainly not befitting a Royal Navy man-of-war.

It was too bad, all of it, he thought. Fine old family, the Thornes, father a former commander, mother a gentlewoman. Pomeroy shook his head. As the heavy oaken door closed behind them, a shiver crossed his slight shoulders. Damned fellow made him nervous— his height, all that black hair, the arrogant nose and stubborn mouth. Why, he could have been a Spaniard but for those fiercely blue eyes. Doubtless some renegade Black Irish that had crept in. A bad lot, the Black Irish . . .

"Now, then—" Lucian's blue eyes burned with a fury that he made no attempt to hide. "What the bloody hell is this all about?"

"Sir, I regret . . ." Pomeroy's high forehead glowed with sweat, but he held his ground with dignity. "You are accused of procuring and secreting on this vessel the Pearls of Naipoor."

Lucian stared at him. The Pearls of Naipoor? The Admiralty thought he had stolen and hidden the bloody Pearls of Naipoor on the *Peacekeeper*? Good God! He wanted to bellow with laughter, with outrage. More than that, he wanted to deck this dandy. Instead, he kept his hot temper in check. He shook his head. The Pearls of Naipoor. God. It was one more instance of government bungling.

"Sir, with all respect," he said carefully, "it has been my job these past two years to catch smugglers, not be one."

"Yes, so it was thought," said Pomeroy crisply.

Lucian commanded himself to remain calm. Soon this farce would play itself out. They would search the *Peacekeeper*, find nothing, and leave.

"Just what do you suppose I would do with the pearls if I did have them, which I do not?" His mouth curved with sarcasm. "Where would I sell them when everyone in the world is on the lookout for them?"

"That I cannot begin to contemplate, sir."

"Nor can I, sir." Lucian began to pace, his narrowed eyes drilling the older man. "Who has accused me?"

"I know only that the Lords of the Admiralty have accurate information which lists names, dates, and places which connect the theft with you. There was no choice but to investigate."

Lucian looked disgusted. "What names? What dates and places? Accurate in what way?"

"Among other things, you were in Naipoor in May of this year, at the exact time the theft took place."

Lucian snorted. "So were hundreds of other travelers. In fact, we helped search dozens of ships for the pearls."

"Indeed."

Of course he would have helped in the search, thought Pomeroy. What better camouflage? Now, at long last, the Admiralty was cracking down on the many cocky young devils who thought they were above the law, growing rich on custom duties that rightly belonged to the British crown. In addition, this Naipoor affair could well cause an international incident. Well, he hoped to heaven his men found the pearls. It would be a decided feather in his cap. And if they were found, an example would be made of this man. He was all for it.

Lucian stopped pacing and glared at the older man. The pompous ass didn't believe him. And what was this information they had? What in God's name was going on? His racing heart pumped his blood through his taut body faster and faster.

"Sir"—he spoke through clenched teeth in an effort

to remain civil—"when you have this Admiralty 'information' in hand for me to examine, then you may search my ship. Not before." He knew he was within his rights.

"Captain Thorne, sir?" There was a sharp rap on his cabin door.

"Aye, Mr. Yates?"

A frightened-looking young seaman entered. "I—I think they found what they were looking for, sir."

"The hell you say, mister! That is impossible!"

Lucian pushed them both aside and stormed on deck, where his men still stood at attention. The men of the *Gull* were hovering about a moldy-looking pouch lying on the planks.

"We found it abaft of the back hatch, sir," one was saying. "None would've seen it without looking . . ."

"Good, Mr. Cubbage."

"What in the—?" Lucian made to pick it up, but Pomeroy stayed his hand.

"One moment, sir," he said sharply. "Mr. Cubbage . . ."

Cubbage retrieved the pouch, loosened the stiff bindings, and gingerly lifted out what seemed to be a large cream-colored marble. It was a huge pearl. They watched, all of them grimly silent, as pearl after pearl was removed and held up for inspection, each more luminous and beautiful than the one preceding it. The Pearls of Naipoor.

Lucian was thunderstruck. As God was his witness, he had not taken the damned things. But someone had. One of his crew. None but crew ever set foot on his vessel.

Pomeroy's dry voice interrupted Lucian's chaotic thoughts. "You understand, Captain Thorne, that we must question you and your brother?"

Lucian stiffened, his hands tensing to fists. "What has my brother to do with this?"

"Was he not in Naipoor with you?" Pomeroy turned to his officer. "Call Seaman Shane Thorne to step forward, Mr. Cubbage."

"Aye, sir."

"Now, wait just a damned minute," Lucian demanded. "This is not what it seems—"

"Seaman Shane Thorne, step forward," Cubbage bellowed.

Shane, looking young and thin and white-faced, moved out of the ranks and stood at attention. Lucian felt an icy finger of fear brush his spine. The situation was quickly moving out of his control. He himself they could accuse of anything they damned well pleased—he would fight them and win—but Shane, Shane was just a slim boy of sixteen with the tender heart of a poet. He did not belong in the harsh world of men taking ships to sea. Against his better judgment, Lucian had given in to his coaxing and taken the lad on as a seaman for one year. After this cruise, his duty was ended.

"Now then, men," Pomeroy commanded briskly, "escort these two to the *Gull* on the double."

Lucian opened his mouth to protest but closed it. Thirteen years of naval discipline demanded that he obey, but it did not mean he had to like it. His angry eyes caught those of his best friend.

"Take over, Lieutenant Fleming. I will soon be back."

"Aye, Captain. I've nary a doubt of it." Donal Fleming's black eyes blazed with outrage as Lucian and Shane climbed over the side and descended the rope ladder to the waiting longboat. "Ye'll be back afore nightfall easy," he called after them.

Pomeroy regarded him coldly. "I would not count on that, Lieutenant. Indeed, I would not. It may be necessary for our two ships to rendezvous with the *Coronet* tomorrow."

Donal felt as though he had just taken a cannonball in his gut. Holy hell, the *Coronet* was the Fleet Commander's ship.

"Sir, the *Coronet*'s farr from our sector." He was painfully aware that his Scot's burr had returned in his fury. "Ye'd leave this area unpatrolled then?"

"That is so, Lieutenant Fleming. We will therefore hope a rendezvous is unnecessary."

John Pomeroy himself hoped it would be unnecessary. Shane Thorne's youth and apparent innocence had given him pause, and Lucian Thorne, despite his bold looks, seemed an honest man. But then, the pearls had been aboard. He shook his head. He did not like it.

Drenched with sweat, Lucian sat hunched and shivering on a bunk in a small dim cell below deck. Between his chained hands he held half a loaf of hard bread and a chunk of jerky. It was the first he had sat or eaten since he and Shane had boarded the *Gull* yesterday afternoon. They had been separated immediately and then the questioning had begun, an interrogation that had gone on all day and all night.

He chewed his food without enthusiasm and sipped tepid water from a tin cup. It did not ease the gnawing in his belly or the dryness of his mouth. What of Shane? he wondered. How was he faring? He groaned and lay back painfully on the bunk, his shins and calf muscles aching and his feet sore and swollen. It had been torture to stand motionless hour after endless hour.

He knew now that he had been set up, as cleverly and thoroughly as ever a man could be set up—an unknown crewman bribed, the pearls planted, and the Admiralty informed. But by whom? Who was this deadly enemy who wanted him destroyed? For there was no doubt he was headed for a court-martial. Shane, also.

This was a nasty business. England had been negotiating an alliance with Hyderabad for some time, and now it seemed the British themselves were the culprits who had stolen part of that country's royal treasury. And no less than a captain in the Royal Navy.

The events in Naipoor on that tenth day of May had been altered so diabolically that the accusations looked plausible. His most innocent activities, even his most

intimate ones, had been twisted to make himself and
Shane look guilty. Even the girl, lovely little Rajeen
whom he always visited when he was in port in Hyderabad, even Rajeen had been implicated and was
now languishing in some black hole of a prison.

Lucian twisted on his bunk but could not get comfortable, not with his hands chained and his body aching. Cold sweat oozed from his pores as he worried
about Shane for the hundredth time, worried about his
parents, worried about Rajeen . . . He got to his feet
angrily. This was no time for softness. He needed all
of his wits, all of his strength now. He began pacing,
remembering names, places, faces, times.

He had been captain of one vessel or another since
he was twenty-two years old. In four years since then—
hell, in this past year alone—he had made dozens of
enemies. No ship's captain alive was ever without enemies, no matter how well-liked he was. Men had been
pressed into service on his ships; men had been disci-
plined, sometimes harshly; pirates had been taken,
smugglers caught.

It was all part of the sea game, and Lucian was forever on the alert. He was no trusting beardless boy.
None would ever catch him in a dark alley without a
strong and loyal mate by his side. But treachery from
a crew that he thought loyal . . . that he was not prepared for.

He thought of one who *was* loyal: Donal Fleming. If
things went from bad to worse, and they no doubt
would, Donal would spread his nets and discover the
identity of Lucian's blood-enemy. And when this dastardly business was all over, Lucian could lay his finger
right on the bastard responsible. But that was for the
future.

His thoughts returned to Shane. Shane confused and
frightened: Shane chained like the worst criminal:
Shane fighting to be brave: Shane so young and innocent . . .

Lucian sank to his bunk and put his throbbing head
in his hands. The chains clanked and his pounding

heart sounded like the drums that beat for the poor devils who were flogged through the fleet—rowed from ship to ship so that all might witness their punishment.

The lash. He stiffened as he thought of it. Himself they could flog—they could kill him with the cat and probably would—but not Shane! Shane had his whole life ahead of him. Lucian's hope soared briefly at the idea of offering himself for double the lashes if only Shane were spared. Maybe it would work.

Lucian Thorne was not a religious man, but he dropped to his knees and prayed . . .

Chapter 1

April, 1790

As the setting sun turned London to gold and gentle shadows, a stately parade of gleaming horse-drawn carriages began arriving at a great red-brick town house in Mayfair, the city's most fashionable district. Within the glowing candle-lit drawing room, the young hostess moved about warmly greeting her guests: the women in their elegant gowns like brightly colored butterflies; the men resplendent in satin and ruffles. The hum of voices and laughter drifted through tall windows thrown open to the spring night, and the air held the tinkle of a pianoforte and the aroma of exquisite cuisine. It was one of the soirees for which the young mistress of Kenley Gables was famous.

But it was not that which drew men to Sarina Fairburn as bees were inexorably drawn to nectar. They enjoyed her warmth and quick humor and basked in her sunny temperament. And she was beautiful—tall and willow-slender, with a creamy throat, a full pink mouth, and green eyes shimmering in a face like a flower. This evening her eyes exactly matched her satin sea-foam gown, a delicious contrast to the mass of rippling red-gold hair caught atop her head in a diamond and emerald circlet. She was the object of every masculine eye and was soon pressed in by a crowd of admiring young men.

"Come sailing with me Sunday afternoon, Sarina," said one.

"Ian, I am not quite sure that I—"

"You're bothering the lady, Ian," said another, taking her hand. "My love, you promised me we would sail this weekend."

"Men, let an expert take over." A third dropped to one knee and took her other hand, which he kissed. "Sarina, say you will come to the Hunt Ball with me."

Sarina threw back her head and laughed. Every masculine heart beat harder as they noted her swanlike throat with the emerald drop at its center and the coppery coils of hair clinging so temptingly to her soft white shoulders.

"Geoff, you idiot, get up off the floor."

"Not until you promise, my beauty."

Sarina gently freed her hands from both men. "Gentlemen, I know you will forgive me, but can we not discuss it a bit later? I really must welcome my other guests." She gave each of them an affectionate pat on the arm. "Now have a wonderful evening, all of you . . ." She moved to the drawing room where her father stood at one of the buffets.

"You've outdone yourself this time, young lady." George Fairburn sampled a dainty cheese and onion tart from a silver platter. "Marvelous," he said. "And what is this other?"

"A new kind of savory pie."

He tasted it. "Superb. I see why everyone is raving." He gave his daughter a hug. "Never forget how grateful I am for all the work you put into these affairs, Sarina."

"But Father, I love doing it."

"Nevertheless, it is greatly appreciated." His eyes moved over the room where London's most eminent citizens were heaping their Wedgwood plates to overflowing with Sarina's exquisite fare. "You have the same wonderful talent and enthusiasm for entertaining that your dear mother had."

"Good evening, Mr. Fairburn."

"Ginelle! Good evening, child. How nice you look."

"Thank you." The young woman stood on tiptoe to kiss his cheek. "What a wonderful party it is."

"Tell it to the lady who did the work, my dear, and now I will get back to our guests."

Ginelle gave her best friend a hug. "It's absolutely marvelous, Rina. I knew it would be and you look gorgeous, as usual, and I think I hate you."

Sarina laughed. "I don't know whether to thank you or scold you. And whether or not you believe it, you look lovely."

"I don't believe it."

But she was lovely, Sarina thought. Ginelle Crandall was a true beauty, with flawless white skin, cornflower-blue eyes, and fine wheaten hair caught back in an elegant chignon. Yet that very morning she had wept in Sarina's arms, saying she was too plump to fit into any of her gowns.

"Your dress is perfect," said Sarina. "It matches your eyes exactly. Where on earth did you find it?"

"Sadlers, and my pater will doubtless make me pay for it by scrubbing floors."

Sarina smiled. "Oh, doubtless. How long have you been here?"

"For eons." Ginelle pouted prettily. "I could not get near you, you were so swamped with hot-eyed beaux."

"You too could be swamped with hot-eyed beaux, and you know it. There are several men here begging to meet you."

Ginelle sniffed. "Oh? I must say, I cannot get too excited."

Sarina did not press the subject. Ginelle was still hurting over a broken engagement.

"Speaking of beaux," Ginelle said, "whatever will your pater do for a hostess if, or should I say when, you marry that gorgeous Ryan Douglas?"

"Marry Ryan? Ginelle Crandall, what could possibly make you think such a ridiculous thing?" Sarina whispered fiercely.

"I have eyes, love, and I can see how you look at each other. Which reminds me, I was standing near him when Ian and Geoffrey and the others were practically fighting over you. He got livid, absolutely positively livid with jealousy. I think he was ready to duel."

"I have never seen him jealous."

"I tell you he was jealous. It would not surprise me one bit if he proposed tonight just to keep some other young knave from getting you."

Sarina laughed to cover her confusion. "Well, if he does, which I assure you he will not, I am simply not ready to marry."

She liked Ryan Douglas. She liked him more than any man she had ever met, and her heart did strange things when he stood close to her. A woman could not ask for a more dashing and handsome escort. But marry him? She had never even considered it.

"I'm glad to hear it," Ginelle answered, "because I'm not ready to lose you to the colonies just yet, and I'm sure your father is not."

Nor was Sarina herself ready to give up all of those things dear to her: her father, her friends, the comfortable home in which she had been born. Marrying a man who lived in England or Scotland was one thing, but for six months out of the year, Ryan lived thousands of miles across the sea in the American colonies.

After his wife had died, George Fairburn had had no heart for giving any large parties at Kenley Gables. And then Sarina, possessing a wisdom and a gentle maturity far beyond her seventeen years, had seen his need and taken the difficult matter in hand. Now, five years later, he had come to depend upon her. And then there was Ginelle. Where would Sarina ever find another friend as dear as Ginelle Crandall? The answer was, nowhere else in the world. No, Sarina was not ready to leave home just yet . . .

Ginelle was inspecting the desserts with hungry eyes. "Rina, what are these dear little white squares with the sugar sheep grazing on top?"

"It's called Floating Island," said a deep voice behind them. "Please allow me, Miss Crandall—you must not miss this treat. I first tasted it at the British embassy in Bombay."

Ryan Douglas expertly maneuvered a square of custard and sponge cake onto a small flowered plate and placed it in Ginelle's eager hands.

"Why, Mr. Douglas, thank you kindly."

"My pleasure."

Sarina's heart gave a skip. "I'm so glad you could come, Ryan."

"I've looked forward to it for days."

As his hot brown eyes captured and held hers, Ryan vowed she would be his. She would not escape him. She was the essence, the absolute epitome of feminine beauty with her innocently sensuous look, her soft white skin, her shimmering, rippling hair. God, but she drove him crazy.

Sarina's heart had begun to race. Ryan Douglas was more handsome in the shadows and candlelight than she had ever before seen him: tall and extremely masculine despite the satin and ruffles of his formal attire. What if Ginelle were right? she wondered. What if he proposed to her tonight? She had received proposals of marriage before, but could she, dared she, turn down Ryan? Would anyone she liked as well ever come her way again, or would she be doomed forever to the Ians and Geoffreys of the world?

She sighed. Perhaps she had answered her own question. She liked Ryan, yes, but she wanted to experience more than liking for the man she took as her husband. She wanted love, in addition to passion and excitement. But perhaps what she felt for Ryan *was* love. Oh, how on earth could one tell?

Watching them, Ginelle said wistfully, "Well, I must toddle along now. It was delightful to see you again, Mr. Douglas."

Ryan's dark eyes flickered over her, studying her briefly. "It has been my pleasure entirely, Miss Crandall. May I say you are looking quite lovely this evening? That dress suits you perfectly."

"Why, how sweet of you." Ginelle's pretty face was glowing with pleasure as she left them.

Sarina's glow was inside. Ryan Douglas had just revealed himself as a warm, compassionate man. He had sensed Ginelle's need and responded instantly, bringing a blush to her cheeks. Sarina liked that. She allowed him to take her hand.

"I hope you did not mind my praising her beauty?"

"Don't be silly . . ."

"Ginelle is lovely, but you—have you any idea how exquisite you are tonight?" He pressed his lips to her palm.

"You are being gallant, but do look around you. Every woman here is exquisite tonight."

Ryan shook his dark head. "You alone are the prize."

"Come now." She laughed, but she was blooming, warming under his burning gaze. Perhaps she was in love. He made her feel so precious, so desirable, and yet—there was something about him that sometimes worried her. She could not quite put her finger on it.

She *was* the prize, Ryan thought. Every powerful man in London was tempted by her, but it was he who would possess her, just as he possessed the finest of everything. Not only did her beauty take his breath away, but she was vastly wealthy, heiress to the Fairburn shipping fortune. And he had her in his net. She melted when he so much as looked at her.

"Never doubt you are the prize, Sarina," he murmured, and took her other hand.

The unexpected intimacy of his warm lips on both her palms sent Sarina's blood pulsing, bubbling through her body like hot wine. It was intoxicating. This was no boy, no silly Ian or Geoffrey begging for outings and kisses. She had recognized Ryan's sophistication immediately and known he was a man of culture and taste. Now, for the first time, she glimpsed the passion, the animal maleness, he had chosen to hide from her. Sensing he was a man who could make her forget all caution, she trembled. His hands were so big and strong, imprisoning her own like two small white lilies . . .

"Do you not think it is quite warm in here?" she asked. "I—I must tell Manley to open more windows."

Ryan smiled down at her. Her pink cheeks and rapid breathing told him that she was practically his.

"I think it is quite comfortable," he said, his voice low. "Perhaps you need a breath of cool air. May I suggest a stroll in the garden?"

He took her arm and magically, a path opened for them. Smiling gazes followed them. Her father, watching from across the room, winked. He approved. But approved of what? Sarina wondered, her heart racing. Walking in the garden with Ryan? The kisses she knew they were going to share before the evening was over?

The walled garden of Kenley Gables was lush and green and quiet in the moonlight, the night air perfumed with flowers: the pink blossoms on the lone apple tree, the massed lilies of the valley gleaming palely, lilacs turning the west wall to lavender.

"This was a lovely idea." Sarina drew the sweet, cool air into her lungs. "I can only take so much chatter."

Ryan laughed. "You? London's most sought-after hostess?"

"You flatter me."

"Never." His eyes were gently mocking. "But I thought you thrived on these affairs."

"On the challenge, yes, and I love seeing everyone having a good time. But it is noisy, you have to admit."

They strolled lazily toward the clipped yews at the back of the garden, his nearness making Sarina pleasantly light-headed.

"Have you ever seen our maze?" she asked.

"No." He took her hand. "Show me."

Within the high shadowy walls of green, the only sounds were their breathing and the rustlings of silk and satin. Sarina was floating in a dream world, until Ryan's eyes went to the creamy swells of her half-

exposed breasts and lingered there. She realized then—
it was that aspect of him which made her uneasy, the
possessive way he sometimes looked at her body.

"I love it here," she whispered, as his arm slipped
around her waist. "It seems enchanted, don't you
think?"

Her question went unanswered as she was pulled
roughly into his arms. She had only a glimpse of his
eyes before closing her own, but their hunger startled
her. So did the savagery of his kiss. But almost immediately he grew gentle.

"You are so beautiful," he murmured against her
mouth. "So beautiful . . ."

The many kisses he pressed on her face and throat
remained gentle, and his hands, searching over her
heated flesh, never once approached her breasts or her
thighs. She felt safe in his arms, soft and yielding. She
brushed gossamer kisses over his face, his lips, his
hands. Oh, she did like him—and would she want a
man who did not yearn to touch her or who did not
hunger for her?

"Mistress Fairburn, mum?"

It was her butler's voice coming unexpectedly from
beyond the maze. Sarina was about to answer when
Ryan lay a warning finger across her lips.

"Mistress Fairburn, are you in there, mum?"

Ryan scowled so horribly that her laughter bubbled
out. She could not help it. "I am here, Manley, what
is it?"

"Is Mr. Douglas there, mum, begging your pardon. . . ?"

Ryan threw up his hands in exasperation. "I am
here, Manley. Miss Fairburn was just showing me the
maze."

"Of course, sir."

"Damn it, Manley, what is it?" The old coot was too
smart by half.

"There is a gentleman here from your office, sir. He
says it is quite urgent or I would never have intruded,
sir."

"Mr. Douglas?" It was his office manager bawling from the other side of the yews.

"I'm coming, Atkins, I'm coming." Ryan caught Sarina's hand and kissed it. "Be assured we will continue, my sweet," he whispered, "but in the meantime, get me out of here."

Atkins, his face anxious, was waiting as they emerged from the maze. "Sir, the *Marilee* just docked . . ."

Ryan's brows pulled together. "You interrupted me for that?" When Atkins shot a cautious look at Sarina, Ryan said, "It is perfectly all right. Talk, man."

"It's pirates, sir."

"What?"

Damn, he thought. First the Crown's outrageous custom duties had forced him into smuggling, now pirates again. Always some bloody thieves wanting what was his.

"I'm happy to say your ship and crew are safe, sir."

Ryan stared at him, uncomprehending. "What do you mean, my ship and crew are safe? Pirates either take a ship or sink it. They kill the crew or press them." His ships had encountered several pirate vessels over the years.

"Sir, it's your cargo."

Atkins swallowed hard and looked so woebegone that Ryan wanted to smash him. Lily-livered cringing sort of fellow. He never could abide him except the man was good with figures.

"For God's sake, get it out. What happened?"

"The cargo was dumped, sir. The rogues didn't want it."

"Dumped?"

"Dumped!" Sarina exclaimed, as astonished as Ryan. Her father, too, had had trouble with pirates upon occasion, but never had she heard of a cargo being dumped.

"Are you telling me"—Ryan's eyes narrowed—"that my precious cargo was simply tossed overboard like so much garbage?"

"I fear so, sir."

Ryan looked at Sarina. "I have never heard of such a damnable thing."

Sarina caught his hands in hers. "I am so sorry . . ."

"Have they any idea who did it?" His stomach had twisted into one huge knot.

"This crew's Manx and Scots, sir, and you know how superstitious they are. They're talking about a ghost ship."

Sarina felt a thrill of horror.

"That's damned nonsense," Ryan said.

"She was gray colored and looked abandoned, and when they boarded her to investigate, they were overpowered by hooded men, their faces half-covered."

"Hooded? Cowards, by God!"

"Yes, sir."

Ryan was hugely relieved that it was not the *Stargazer* which had been attacked. She was commanded by his uncle and was his only ship now carrying contraband—precious gems in the wine kegs and vials of rare perfumes in the chests of tea. God, what a catastrophe if it had been the *Stargazer*. Nonetheless, cargo was cargo. He wanted to go down to the dock and throw the *Marilee*'s entire crew of clowns into chains, but Sarina's sorrowful green eyes were on him. He straightened his shoulders.

"It seems to be bad luck for me, Atkins. Damned bad luck."

"Yes, sir, the men feel something awful about this. They're waiting now to see you."

Ryan turned to Sarina. "I must go, my sweet. I am sorry. Please make my apologies to your father."

"I will, and I'm sorry, Ryan."

"I know you are."

She stood on tiptoe and kissed his cheek, relieved that he was so much calmer now. "You're taking this very well . . ."

He shrugged satin-clad shoulders. "There is nothing much that can be done tonight. Remember, *ma pe-*

tite''—he lowered his voice—''I expect to see the rest of your maze . . .''

''You will,'' she whispered. ''I shall look forward to it.''

Sarina stayed in the garden for a while after he had gone. It was too beautiful to return to her noisy house and besides, her imagination was soaring. She was thinking of a gray ship in a gray sea, drifting, seemingly abandoned, a ghost ship filled with dangerous hooded men. What a clever ruse, and how daring . . .

Chapter 2

May, 1790

Sarina and Ginelle had spent the entire afternoon shopping and visiting friends, and had returned to Kenley Gables in time for tea. Ginelle buttered a scone, kicked off her shoes, and curled up on the settle, her curious gaze fastened on Sarina. Sarina, perched at the settle's other end, sipped her tea and gazed out the open window to where the sun bathed a garden filled with spring flowers.

"What ails you, love?" Ginelle asked. "Spring fever? You've been daydreaming all day long and I will wager you have not heard a single word I've just said."

Sarina gave her an affectionate smile. "You lose that wager. You played cards with Bert yesterday, and you are going to the Whitehouse Ball with Martin." She was relieved that Ginelle had recovered so well from her broken engagement.

"Sarina Fairburn, what are you hiding from me?" Ginelle took a bite of scone and jam, and studied her friend with narrowed eyes. Seeing Sarina's cheeks turn pink, she cried, "Ryan proposed!"

Sarina nodded, her eyes starry.

"You dickens. I knew it all along, and you denied it!"

"I was about to tell you." She had been in agony wondering how to give Ginelle the news that was going to break her heart.

"Did Ryan speak with your pater?"

"Yes, and would you believe, it is what father has had in mind all along? In fact, he asked why it took so long."

"I declare, I don't know whether to laugh or cry."

"You are allowed to do both, you know. In fact, I may join you." They went into each other's arms laughing, but their eyes were soon brimming.

"Really, I am happy for you, Rina, you know I am, so pay no attention to me." Ginelle blew her nose daintily. "And you know I absolutely adore weddings, and yours especially, except they always make me cry. When is it to be?"

Sarina forced herself to meet Ginelle's wet eyes.

"In two weeks. May fifteenth."

"Two weeks!"

"Ryan does not want to wait. He has urgent business in the colonies and wants us to make the crossing as soon as possible. We will be staying in New York until early next summer."

"Next summer!" Ginelle's face puckered. "And no church wedding? Rina, I can scarcely believe it."

"I hope you can understand that there just would not be time." Sarina added softly, "I am also hoping that you will help me plan a small ceremony here in the drawing room. And be my maid of honor."

Ginelle was crushed, but seeing the concern in Sarina's beautiful eyes, she forced herself to rally. She would not spoil her friend's happiness out of selfishness. She would not!

"Forgive me, my pet, I am being frightfully silly. Of course I will help, and—and yes, I will be your maid of honor. Of course I will. My goodness, we will have to get busy right away, won't we? How many will be coming?" She was glad to hear how bright she sounded. "And there are the gowns to think about. Oh, dear, I really should lose five pounds before then."

Manley knocked and entered. "Mr. Douglas to see you, mum."

"Thank you, Manley, show him—"

Ryan strode in. "Never mind, Manley, I am here."

Sarina saw instantly that he was angry. He did not embrace her. "Ryan, what is it?"

Ginelle murmured, "Perhaps I should run along."

"No, you may stay. This is not private." He flung himself into a wing chair. "Another of my ships has been attacked."

"How absolutely awful!" Ginelle cried.

"And your crew?" It was Sarina's first thought. "Were any of them hurt or seized?"

"No, the ship and crew are intact."

"Then it was the Ghost again," Sarina whispered.

Ryan gave her a sharp look. Damned if it was not a good name for a coward who hid his face and sailed a ghost ship. "Yes, it was the Ghost again."

He smashed a fist against his palm and felt a murderous rage beating inside his head and chest. Who was this bloody bastard of a Ghost who had gotten away scot-free both times? It was intolerable. Outrageous.

"Were your men tricked again?" Sarina asked as calmly as she could. "Did the vessel appear abandoned?" Her heart ached for Ryan. He worked so hard . . .

"Fortunately for their miserable hides, no. Otherwise, I would have lashed the whole bloody lot of them."

She knelt and smoothed his disheveled brown hair. "Ryan, you would not. You know you would not."

"No, I suppose not . . ."

But he damned well would have. If the idiots had allowed themselves to be fooled again by a seemingly abandoned ship, despite the alert given his fleet, he would have used the lash with pleasure. But he must watch his tongue with Sarina. He stroked her hand.

"I'm sorry if I have upset you, my sweet. It's just that I'm ready to kill this fellow. The *Canute* was chased down and grapneled. She didn't have a chance."

"And the cargo was dumped?"

"All dumped." He twisted the ruby ring on his forefinger, wishing it were a garrote around the Ghost's neck. "Tea, tapestries, silks, perfumes, the finest brasswork."

"The man sounds demented," Ginelle exclaimed. "How are other merchants dealing with the problem? I trust you have all banded together?"

"No one else has been attacked by the crazy bastard," Ryan muttered.

Sarina's hand went to her breast, her eyes green pools of concern, angry pink staining her cheeks. "You mean—you are being singled out?"

"So it seems. It is a damned vendetta."

"Oh, Ryan!"

The thought of an unknown, vicious criminal lurking in the deep and waiting for Ryan alone terrified and infuriated her. She yearned to strike back, to protect him in some way.

"What man would do such a thing?" she cried.

"I wish to God I knew." He had had enemies aplenty over the years, but he had always struck them down before they could destroy him. This was something new.

"Wh—what are you going to do?" Sarina asked. She was almost afraid to know, his eyes burned so fiercely.

"I have posted a reward, of course, but more important, I am going after the devil myself."

"My love, you could be hurt!"

Ryan laughed. "The Ghost is the one who will be hurt, *ma petite*. I am outfitting the *Manxman* with cannons and giving my men firelocks. We sail tomorrow evening."

Sarina stared at him, disbelieving. He had been pressed into the navy as a young boy, and he hated the sea with a vengeance. She told herself to stay calm and not make a fuss. She said quietly: "Sail to where, my love?"

"Florida. The bastard's days are numbered, Sarina. I will see him hanged."

The day was warm, but Sarina shivered, thinking of

the gray ship and its dangerous gray-clad men. She could not let him do it.

"Ryan, such talk frightens me. Is it not better to lose an occasional cargo than your life?"

Ryan's mouth tightened. "It seems you think the fellow can best me."

"Not at all. It is just that—"

"Ryan Douglas," Ginelle flared, "you are Sarina's fiancé now, or have you forgotten? And have you forgotten you are to be married in two weeks?"

"It's all right," Sarina said hurriedly, seeing the black look Ryan shot her friend. "We will simply postpone it."

She had forgotten what a lioness Ginelle could be. And in her own concern for Ryan, she had forgotten how proud men were of their strength and power and possessions, and of their ability to defend them. She poured tea for him from the fresh pot Manley had brought and soothed him with a small plate of his favorite pastries.

Ryan's mood changed abruptly. He chuckled and drew Sarina closer, to perch on the arm of the chair. She was the most important thing, after all, and he still had her. With Sarina Fairburn as his wife, his future was assured, even were the Ghost to sink every damned one of his cargos, including the contraband. And what a future it would be, he thought, his arms tightening around her soft body. He lifted her silky mane of red-blonde hair, pressed a kiss on the back of her neck, and inhaled her delicious lily scent.

"Not for one instant have I forgotten that I am an affianced man. Know that, my love," he whispered huskily.

"I do know it."

But Sarina was hurt. After pursuing her so hotly these past few months, he was now willing, on the instant, to postpone their wedding and go chasing off to sea.

"Not only have I not forgotten, but I have made other wedding arrangements for us. In my anger I neglected to mention them.'' He kissed her slender white finger bearing his diamond and emerald band. ''You will leave for New York in three weeks, Sarina, and we will be married there. What do you think of that, my precious?''

''What!'' She could not believe it. ''And have my father miss our wedding?''

Ryan laughed. ''It was your father who suggested it. He understands my need to catch this bastard.''

Sarina rose, her eyes flashing. ''And just what other grandiose plans does my father have for us, pray?''

''Well, now''—Ryan's own dark eyes were dancing—''for one, he wants Ginelle to accompany you.''

''What?'' It was a squeal from Ginelle. ''Oh, the darling! Oh, Rina, oh, do say yes. How exciting! I never thought I would see the colonies!''

Ryan chuckled. ''What do you think now, my love? Are you willing?''

Sarina saw that she was outnumbered. Ginelle was hopping with excitement; it was what Ryan wanted; even her own father seemed to want it. She laughed and shrugged.

''The matter seems to be settled.''

''Oh, Rina! Oh, you love! Oh, fabulous day!'' Ginelle gave her a fierce hug.

''I admit, Ginny, that having you along will make all the difference, and if my father truly does not mind—'' The enormity of it hit Sarina suddenly. A wedding in New York!

''And knowing you, Ryan,'' Ginelle bubbled, ''it will be an absolutely fabulous affair. Oh, Rina, it will be such fun!''

Sarina's eyes began to shimmer. ''I suppose I cannot believe it, it is so sudden and unexpected. It takes my breath away even to think of it.''

Ryan rose and smiled down on her. ''Good. And now I will make all the travel preparations. Naturally I'll send a woman along to maid you both.''

Sarina laughed. ''Darling, really, I certainly won't be

fussing with my hair or wardrobe in the middle of the
Atlantic.''

He gave her a possessive kiss. "But you will. Not for
one instant will my men forget your position as my
future bride.''

"Silly," she said softly, but she was pleased. "Of
course they will not forget.''

"Pay her no attention, Ryan," said Ginelle. "A maid
sounds lovely. I thank you, but I, uh, do have one
small question . . .''

"I will be happy to answer.''

"What if you do not catch your Ghost? What if he
catches us instead while you are waiting for him in
Florida?''

Ryan's handsome face darkened. "Do you really believe I would leave the safety of such precious cargo to
chance?''

Little did the cocky wench know just how precious
a cargo it was. Not only would the *Stargazer* be carrying
his future bride to New York, it would also be carrying contraband. French perfume, gems from Algiers,
pearls from Japan, and all under the watchful eye of
his uncle. Jon Gray, who did his dealing in foreign
ports, was the only one aboard who knew the vessel
carried the illegal goods.

Ginelle flushed. She had asked the question half in
jest, and now Ryan was angry. "I—actually, I was only
teasing . . .''

"My ships have made countless trips to the colonies
without incident," Ryan continued coolly. "I guarantee the Ghost will be in Florida waters where it is warm
and where he has easy access to fresh water and supplies and hidden anchorage. He has attacked me twice
there, and it is where the coward will meet his doom.
Sarina, I trust you are not concerned about this also?''

Sarina shook her head, seeing how sensitive he was
on the subject. "If you say there is no danger, Ryan, I
am satisfied. I am sure Ginelle is, too.''

"Oh, I am, I am. Really, I—I was just teasing,

Ryan." She hurried on: "Rina, let us begin shopping for your trousseau tomorrow."

But Ryan was still annoyed. Ignoring Ginelle, he gave his bride-to-be a passionate kiss.

"By all means, my love, assemble your trousseau. I am counting the days until I see you in it."

Three weeks later, George Fairburn escorted the women to Coates Harbor, where they boarded the *Stargazer*, a Douglas merchantman. Ginelle was agog over those commonplace things that Sarina had seen her entire life: broad scrubbed decks, polished brass, coils of rope, webs of rope, ropes everywhere connecting the flapping sails to the towering masts.

"Oh, I cannot believe this is actually happening! We are actually going to New York!"

"Ye'll have my cabin for the voyage, ladies," said the captain, Jon Gray.

"But that is surely an imposition," Sarina protested.

Her father laughed. "Now, pet, there is no other place aboard suitable for two ladies for a five-week voyage, believe me. I thank you, Jon. I will not forget your kindness."

"Do ye need help wi' the trunks, Mr. Fairburn?" offered Jon Gray. "I can rout up a pair o' men quick."

"Thank you, but I brought my own." Just then two seamen came aboard bearing a large metal-bound black trunk between them.

"Put it in the captain's cabin," Jon Gray ordered, "and now, young ladies, if ye'll follow me . . ."

Sarina's first sight of their cabin was cause for dismay. The room was clean, certainly, and large enough for their needs, but it was a dreary gray-brown and smelled faintly of sweat and sour beer.

"It is—very nice," she offered. "Very nice."

"Lovely," Ginelle added, her eyes meeting her friend's in silent distress.

"Aye, that it is. Ye'll find it private an' the beds good. The other lady will be in the cabin next to this one."

"That is most convenient. Thank you so much, Captain."

He touched two tanned fingers to his cap. "My pleasure, mistress Fairburn, an' now I'd best get back to my work."

"I, too, had better be going, ladies," George Fairburn said. "You two will want to settle in and I have a meeting to attend, besides which"—his voice was gruff—"long good-byes never accomplish anything."

"I'll check the other room," Ginelle murmured.

After she left, Sarina threw her arms around her father. This was the moment she had been dreading, and all of her concerns for him returned. How was he ever going to get along without her? She would have a new happy life to occupy her time whereas he would be alone with no one who loved him to tend to his needs.

"Are you all right, pet?"

"I am—worried about you, Father."

He kissed the fragrant cloud of her hair and her white forehead. "You were there when I needed you, my darling, and now it is time you made a life for yourself. Ryan is a good man. I could not be happier for you."

"I am happy too, Father."

"And when I see you next year, you will be an old married lady." He laughed and cupped her chin in his hand. "Perhaps you'll have a little one for me to dandle on my knee!"

"Perhaps." She held him tight. "Oh, Father!"

"Now, now, no tears," he said brusquely.

Miraculously, Sarina was able to obey. She held close the anticipation of a wonderful life with Ryan, the excitement of New York, the adventures that awaited her and Ginelle, and goodness, they were not separating forever. One year was not all that long. They kissed again, Ginelle returned, thanked him again profusely, was hugged, and all three went on deck.

" 'Till next year then, Sarina," George Fairburn said. He descended the gangplank without looking back.

" 'Till next year, Father," Sarina called firmly after him.

Not until his carriage, pulled by two matched grays, was out of sight did the women turn toward their cabin.

"M-my goodness," Ginelle whispered.

The deck was filled with crew who had just come up from their work in the hold. Sweating, half-naked, and silent, they lounged against spars and rails gazing at the women.

"We are perfectly safe," Sarina murmured, taking her arm. "Have you forgotten that this is Ryan's ship? Come along now. Step briskly and hold your head up."

"Yoo hoo!" a feminine voice called suddenly from the dock. "I'd be grateful for help wi' me trunk, boys."

The men swarmed to the rail to stare at the young woman in green who was ascending the gangplank. She was young and pretty, with big brown eyes, rosy cheeks, and long brown hair. When they saw her shapeliness and full bosom, there was rowdy applause and cheering. She stepped on deck with easy aplomb, grinned, and dropped her admirers a curtsy.

"Sorry, boys, I've got me a man, an' Joe Ward'll blow the head off any who dares touch me, but like I said, I'd be grateful for help wi' me trunk." There was a stampede to her carriage.

The girl readjusted her perky green hat and dropped a curtsy to Sarina and Ginelle. "I'm Rosie Coggins, ladies, an' I'm to be your ladies' maid. I can be with you jist as soon as I gets me gear stowed. Where's me bunk?"

Rosie Coggins was nineteen years old, the eldest of a fisherman's great brood of children, and there seemed nothing she could not do or did not know. She brewed their tea, fixed their meals, dressed their hair, kept them scrubbed and their clothing spotless, cleaned their cabin daily—and she was a tyrant.

"Mum!" she scolded Sarina on the third day out.

"You must never, never git out o' bed on the left again!"

"Why ever not, Rosie?"

"Everyone knows it's unlucky, same as Friday's unlucky."

Sarina kept a grave face. "I see."

"An' with all these pirates around, I say why tempt fate."

Sarina smiled. "There is no danger whatsoever. Mr. Douglas himself assured us that pirates stay in warmer waters."

Rosie snorted. "Meanin' no disrespect, mum, but I'm more inclined to believe my Joe, who's on the sea more days o' the year than your Mr. Douglas. Joe says pirates is everywhere, 'specially in summer, an' there's some what's real lusty devils, expecially them Caribbean ones what sells women into harems after they rapes them. But then, this bein' the Atlantic, the men's blood's no doubt cooler an' we needn't worry quite so much. Yet it don't hurt none to plan ahead, I always say."

Sarina, who had not been worried at all, felt as though she had just fallen into icy black water over her head.

"Plan for what?" she asked quietly.

"Joe's gi' me me orders, mum. He says if we're boarded, I'm to fling meself at the biggest, toughest-looking bruiser there an' gi' meself to him."

Ginelle gave a little cry. "Give yourself to him?"

Sarina took the girl's shoulders and gave her a little shake. "Do not clown, Rosie! You are trying to entertain us and there really is no need, you know."

Rosie looked insulted. "Mum, if I was to clown about sich a thing, may God strike me dead! My Joe says it's better to be taken by one man an' be protected by him than raped by the whole crew. An' beggin' your pardon, mums, but I think if it ever comes to that, ye'd best do the same, you both bein' so purty."

Sarina's eyes glittered. "I absolutely do not believe this."

"Nor do I." Ginelle giggled nervously. "Why, I would die first."

"I would jump overboard," Sarina said stiffly.

Rosie regarded them pityingly. "Joe says pirates has their code o' honor. Most don't mistreat women, but they're hungry for female bodies, it bein' a long time between, er . . .''

"That is enough, Rosie," Sarina said crisply.

"Yes'm. But don't forget, mum, the sea's awful deep an' wet an' dark . . . an' final."

Four days into their voyage, the *Stargazer* was plowing through a smothering cloak of mist when a bell began to clang insistently. Ginelle ran to a portal and looked out.

"I cannot see a thing. What is it, do you suppose?"

When Sarina opened the door to investigate, Rosie flew in, her dark eyes huge in her white face. "Oh, mum, I thinks it's pirates!"

"Rosie, calm yourself. We do not know that."

"But we do, mum. I was on deck an' it's some boat what's chasin' us! The men says it's pirates."

"Sarina, what are you doing?" Ginelle gasped as Sarina caught up her shawl. "Don't go out there!"

"I must! I have to know what is happening."

Gathering the soft lavender wool about her shoulders, Sarina stepped cautiously on deck. It was as though she had walked into a cloud, the fog was so thick. Clinging to the rail, she made her way to the stern. Surely, she thought, there was a reasonable explanation for a ship "chasing" them without its being pirates. Rosie always exaggerated so.

As the fog wisped and thinned for an instant, Sarina froze. A ship was out there and practically on top of them, a mist-gray sloop with a rapierlike bowsprit as long as the vessel herself. She bristled with cannons and carried such a large parade of gray canvas, Sarina knew instantly that she was one of the fleetest vessels afloat. And one of the most beautiful—sleek, graceful, her great sails blossoming with wind. Sarina's throat suddenly tightened. A gray ship with gray sails. Dear God, the ghost ship! She fled to the cabin.

"Did you see anything?" Ginelle cried.

Sarina shot home the great bolt on the cabin door, removed her engagement ring, and buried it deep in one of her trunks.

"Close and lock the portals," she commanded. "Hurry."

"Oh, mum, it's pirates, ain't it? Jist like I said!"

There was a grinding, crunching noise just then, and the *Stargazer* shuddered. Ginelle and Rosie screamed. All three women were hurled to the floor as the vessel came to a stop in the gently rocking waves. The three stared at each other, horrified, as they heard thumps and scrapes.

"It's grapnels, I bet," Rosie gasped. "They'll board us!"

There were hoarse shouts and deep male laughter as the women huddled, trembling, in a corner of the locked cabin.

"I hear drums—an' horns! For sure it's pirates! Oh!" Rosie exclaimed.

"Rina! Sh-should we do as Rosie said? Give ourself to—to—"

"Ginelle!"

Rosie's pretty face was white. "Oh, why din't I mind my Joe, what din't want me to come in the first place!"

"Hush, both of you!" Sarina's heart was pounding. "If we are quiet, they might not find us."

"Oh, mum, I ain't as brave as you."

"Rosie, please, love, do hush—"

"Oh, Rina, should we. . . ?" Ginelle wept. "Oh, God!"

Sarina pulled Rosie into her arms and held out a hand to Ginelle.

"It is the Ghost," she whispered. "It is a gray ship . . ."

"What?" Ginelle's eyes popped. "Oh, Rina, Ryan will be absolutely furious if it's the Ghost."

Sarina managed a smile. "Remember now, this man always dumps the cargo and leaves, and he will do the same today. I just know he will. We will all be left safe and sound. Hush, now! Shhh, hush, dears. Everything is going to be fine . . ."

Chapter 3

L ucian Thorne felt his blood run faster. A merchant-man had suddenly crossed the bow of the *Vengeance* in the milky mist and, if it was the *Stargazer* as he hoped, that meant his spies had been right for the third time. He went to the hatch and called down softly.

"Donal, up here on the double."

Donal Fleming took the steps three at a time. "Did you spot her?"

"Could be. A square-rigger just crossed our bow, headed west. Give me speed, Mr. Fleming, and I want quiet. Let us see who she is."

"Aye, sir."

As his gray-clad men moved silently into action, Lucian scanned the haze for the familiar outline—three masts, square-rigged, long fine lines, low in the water . . . There! There she was, and she had not yet seen the *Vengeance*. He held the telescope to his eye, focused on the bow, and felt his heart jump. It was the *Stargazer*. He met Donal's watchful eyes and nodded. Seconds later, a blood-red pennant was hoisted.

Swiftly, silently, the only sound the snap of canvas and the slap of oars against water, the *Vengeance* drew closer. She was big, a hundred-tonner, and she carried seventy-five men and fourteen cannon. Lucian watched, waiting for that moment when his prey would realize her jeopardy. When at long last her alarm sounded, it was too late for her to respond. He laughed. He had her, by God.

He'd taken the *Marilee* in retaliation for Rajeen, still held in a nameless prison. The *Canute* had been for the tears his mother shed and would shed forever. Now the *Stargazer*. Would she be for Shane? Perhaps, although her cargo would have to be priceless to make up for his loss. Again Lucian laughed. And this, old friend, old shipmate, was only the beginning. As his crew pulled on the gray hoods that covered the upper half of their faces, he pulled on his own hood and turned to Donal.

"Grapnels," he said.

"Grapnels!" Donal shouted.

Lucian watched the hooks sail over the water and attach themselves to the enemy bow with a thud. The vessels crunched together.

"Board," he said quietly.

"Board!" Donal bellowed.

The pipers and drummers unleashed a sudden frenzy of sound as Lucian, sword drawn, led his men over the rails to swarm, howling, across the *Stargazer*'s decks. Her quaking crew was easily subdued and her every seam, nook, and cranny searched. When it was over, her cargo, both legal and contraband, lay at the bottom of the sea.

"I have saved your cabin until last, Captain," Lucian courteously addressed his smoldering counterpart.

"I've nothing to hide," Jon Gray lied. "Why waste your time?" The damned devil unknowingly had tossed a fortune overboard in gems and perfumes, and now he was about to find his nephew's lady. Was there no justice in the world?

Lucian tried the cabin door. "Well, well. Locked from the inside. Lieutenant, fetch the ram."

Four hooded men carried the beam to the cabin and soon the air rang with the thud of oak on oak.

Jon Gray's face was ashen. He and Ryan had already lost a fortune with the cargo thrown overboard, and now there was no telling what this bastard would do to his fiancée. To all the women . . . "Captain, for the love of God . . ." The thudding continued; the door began to give, splintered finally, and fell. "Sir, if you have any mercy in your heart . . ."

Lucian strode into the dim room, noting that it smelled like a flower garden. Roses, gardenias, lillies . . . He stopped abruptly. Good God, women! His first thought was to back out and get his crew off the ship immediately. They would go wild. But even as he thought it, it was too late. The men were jamming into the cabin.

Two of the women were huddled on the floor. A third guarding them, her slender arms outspread and protective. When Lucian's eyes adjusted to the dimness, he saw that she was beautiful—a young mermaid, white-skinned and slender in her green dress, with a fall of shimmering red hair rippling almost to her waist. Her eyes matched the sea, and her soft, mutinous mouth reminded him of a ripe plum.

"Holy heaven!" Donal's own eyes were fastened on the trembling blonde.

The men whistled and howled, and a shout went up: "Women! There's women in here, mates! Beauties!" More men pushed into the room, jostling and staring hungrily.

"Pigs!" the mermaid cried, her eyes flashing green fire. "Don't you dare touch us! We are under the protection of Mr. Ryan Douglas. This is his ship!"

Lucian chortled. Well, well, was this another sort of goods Douglas was dealing in now? But then, why should it surprise him if the bastard now sold the sort of women he had always favored in the past? What other sort would dare travel such a distance without their own men to protect them—or be allowed to travel alone, for that matter? His eyes slid insolently over them.

"It seems Mr. Douglas is unavailable to protect you at the moment, madam," he drawled.

"Lucky for you!" she cried.

"Yes, lucky for us. Not so lucky for you."

The men sniggered and then the inevitable happened. One of them seized Sarina roughly in his arms.

"That's enough talk," he growled. "I'm takin' this 'un."

"Indeed you will not, you animal! Let me go!" Sarina pounded him with her fists.

"The lady's right." Another laughed and gave his mate a staggering punch on the arm. "Ye're an animal. Why should ye have 'er? I'll take 'er first."

"Just try it, mate!"

"This 'un's for me." Ginelle was lifted, screaming, and hurled over a broad gray shoulder.

"Stop!" At the command in Lucian's voice, his men fell quiet. "This ship is under my command and you will—"

"Oh, sir, awooo . . ."

The third woman, a pretty dark-haired little thing, suddenly ran forward and threw herself at his feet. She wrapped her arms around his legs in a death grip.

"I'm yours!" she cried. "Ye can do anythin' ye likes wi' me, sir, anythin', jist don't let the others have me. I'm yours!"

Lucian blinked down at her, astonished. What the devil? His men howled with laughter as he tried to disentangle himself.

"Rosie Coggins, get on your feet!" the mermaid cried from her captor's arms, whereupon he kissed her on her soft pink mouth.

She smacked his face, squirmed free, and kicked Ginelle's tormentor on the shin with her small pointed shoe. The men hooted.

"Put her down, I said!" Sarina demanded.

He smirked. She kicked his other shin. When he dropped the shrieking Ginelle to nurse his injuries, his mates roared their approval, delighted by the beautiful firebrand in their midst.

Sarina yanked Rosie to her feet, took Ginelle's hand, and faced Lucian like a steaming volcano.

"How dare you, all of you! And you call yourselves men!"

She was tall, but standing beside the captain of the ghost ship, she felt small and fragile, the top of her head barely reaching his well-muscled gray-clad shoulder. She raised defiant eyes to his hooded face, noting grudgingly that what she could see of it was not unpleasing: a deep square clean-shaven jaw, darkly tanned skin, a sharply etched mouth, his throat a powerful teak-colored column rising from a broad chest.

She lifted her chin, seeing that he was laughing at her, laughing at their misery. She wanted to fly at him, fly at them all. She wanted to slay them!

"I have never known men who would terrorize helpless women," she cried, "or hide under hoods. You are nothing but cowards."

Even as she spoke, Sarina knew she was pushing him dangerously. The slightest pressure from one of those big dark hands could force her to her knees.

Lucian stood transfixed. She was the most beautiful thing he had ever seen. And he was not fooled by her bravado. He saw her soft lips trembling and the fright flickering in her large green eyes, saw the rapid breaths that thrust her white breasts so temptingly against the low neckline of her gown. She was ready to drop from terror, yet she was a lioness. He felt a hot stirring inside.

"Men, back off," he demanded. "Clear out of here."

Obeying, they crowded into the corridor and milled about, watching. Lucian and Donal remained in the cabin.

"Thank you," Sarina said stiffly. She wished Rosie would not gulp and wail so when she wept, and that Ginelle could control her chattering teeth.

"There now, lass." Donal gently patted the arm of the small, trembling blonde. "Ye needna worra now."

She started at his touch, blinked up at him with her big wet eyes, and he found himself moved to the core. She was so white and soft and tender-looking—and plump. Dear God, how he loved a woman to have soft white flesh on her bones and be rounded all over. And all of that long shining spun-gold hair . . . He drew in a great sigh. She was the loveliest lass he had seen in a long, long time.

Sarina addressed the captain with ice in her voice. "I would greatly appreciate your mending our door before you take your leave . . ."

Lucian threw back his head and laughed again, deep easy laughter that was taken up by his men. He had not had such a good laugh in a long time. Joy, amusement, laughter, none of them played much of a part in his life any more. Not since the Pearls of Naipoor had been discovered aboard the *Peacekeeper*.

There had been a rapid court-martial, with overwhelming evidence against himself and Shane. They had been flogged around the fleet. Shane had died. Lucian had gone to prison for a year, where he burned for revenge and lived on stubbornly in his broken body. He had suspected everyone, even lashing out at old friends who wanted only to comfort him. After prison, he had bought a parcel of wooded islands off the Virginia coast.

Malaga was a paradise with good anchorage and lush, wild vegetation. Lucian had been content to build a house there and live quietly, content to recover his strength and his health while he waited for Donal to find the traitor. And Donal had. Lucian was not surprised to learn who it was. He had suspected Ryan Douglas from the beginning, but there had been no proof.

Lucian had been on his initial sea voyage when he first met and befriended Ryan, a frightened lad pressed into the Royal Navy aboard Lucian's own frigate. For six months they were best friends, and then Lucian was transferred. Years later when Lucian stopped a Douglas Trader for a routine check, he discovered a fortune in contraband and Ryan Douglas offering him an exorbitant bribe to look the other way. He was saddened to see the arrogant man Ryan had become— condescending, above the law.

Honor-bound to the British crown, whose man-of-war he commanded, Lucian refused the bribe and impounded the valuable illegal cargo. Ryan was heavily fined, but Lucian knew he would not be deterred for long by such a slap on the wrist. He also suspected that Ryan would be vengeful. He had not known how much so.

Lucian himself was not above vengeance. On the day he learned who had betrayed him, Ryan Douglas' doom was sealed. Lucian and Donal planned their scheme to the last detail. And now, here was this delicious little tart arrogantly informing him she and the other two were under the bastard's protection. And he was to fix her door . . .

"Madam, you have more courage than sense," he muttered.

Sarina's gaze was frigid. "And you have no courage at all, preying on people who must work hard for a living. Have you not the least speck of honor in you?"

"Honor?" Lucian's deep laughter filled the room. "God's blood, no. I have no honor. When there is deceit and betrayal to be dealt with, there can only be revenge."

Despite her bravado, Sarina was atremble. A man without honor who was bent on vengeance was a man capable of anything. Yet to her knowledge, the Ghost had never harmed anyone. Still, his words chilled her. Hoping to draw his mind away from their helplessness, and to seem unafraid, she said icily:

"I insist you repair our door before you take your leave."

"I think not," Lucian said quietly.

Through the slits in his hood Sarina saw the sudden glint of his eyes. They were blue, the bluest blue she had ever seen, like chips of ice under a winter sky. They frightened her more than the cruel lines of his mouth.

Lucian watched her pink tongue tip dart across her lips, saw the leaping pulse in her soft throat, smelled her warm, fragrant scent. Lilies. His men wanted her. They wanted all three women. They were jostling each other, clamoring, more restless than he had ever seen them. She was right. At a time like this, they were animals. He himself felt the wild call, but he was not about to harken to it or give his men permission to do so.

"I remind you again"—Sarina's voice was firm and high with only the slightest tremor in it—"that we are under Mr. Douglas' protection. If you harm us, never doubt that you will answer to him."

Lucian gave a snort. "That fills me with terror."

If she thought so highly of the bastard, maybe she was not worth saving. He was convinced of their calling—English beauty commanded a high price in New York brothels—but being ravished by a shipload of men was another matter entirely. He had seen enough of it to know. No, Douglas' tarts or not, they would never suffer such a fate on any vessel under his command.

"Come on, Cap'n, give us the women!" a crewman yelled.

"We want the women! We want the women!" A chant began.

Lucian's eyes met Donal's, and he saw they were of one accord. Wordlessly they moved shoulder to shoulder to bar the cabin door, swords still in their scabbards. Lucian's voice rang out:

"You will follow my rules, the ones you agreed to when you signed on with me."

"Aw, Cap'n, come on! This is different. Give us the women!"

"They're booty, same as the stuff we dumped."

"We've a right to booty, ye can't deny it!"

"I do deny it. You have waived all rights to booty. You are paid fair and square for every cargo, and don't forget it."

There was angry murmuring, and Lucian lay his hand atop his sword hilt, his heart thumping. He could see it all too clearly. The women struggling, begging for mercy as they were stripped and their clothing tossed overboard; dark, hard bodies thrusting into soft white ones; grunts, laughter, screams. Screams that went on and on as the three women were carried endlessly from man to man. He gave his head a violent shake to dispel the image.

Looking over his shoulder, he saw the blonde and the brunette weeping in each other's arms in the farthest corner. The mermaid stood facing him, her arms akimbo, fright and defiance in her big green eyes, that wonderful hair falling over her breasts, rosy lips parted to show her small white teeth.

His sword hissed as he unsheathed it. "I have never allowed killing or raping under my command," he said harshly, "and you will not start now."

"I stand with 'im," Donal said with quiet menace.

Seeing the uncertainty on his men's faces, Lucian knew there was yet hope. He had been good to this crew, all of them mercenaries except Donal and Sky Braden, his old friends and shipmates from years long gone. He had fed, clothed, and armed the lot of them and paid them fairly and promptly for each cargo dumped. But now, as it always did, came the reckoning. How much had it meant to them? Did their loyalty to him outweigh the temptation these women offered or did he have a mutiny on his hands?

"No killin', no rapin', an' ye bastards all agreed," Donal said softly. "An' now ye see these pretty helpless lassies an' the rules can go to bloody hell, is that it?"

Sarina moved quietly to the dim corner of the cabin where Ginelle and Rosie continued to weep softly. She stroked their hair and patted their shoulders, for there was nothing to be said, nothing to be done but wait. She knew one thing for a certainty—she would fight. Until her last breath was drawn, if it came to that, she would fight.

She watched the tall captain, his vibrant voice lowered, coaxing and reasoning with his men. Despite her loathing for who he was and what he was doing to Ryan, he seemed to have at least a speck of honor in him, despite his denial of it. It surprised her. She held her breath as he turned and walked toward her, the muscles of his long legs flexing under his gray leggings.

"You will have nothing to fear from my crew," he said gruffly. "They will not touch you."

Ginelle burst into fresh tears. "Oh! Oh, thank you, thank you! Oh, thank you so much!"

"Oh, sir," Rosie gushed, adoration on her tear-stained face. "I knew yer was a good man the minute I laid eyes on yer!"

"Thank you," Sarina managed through stiff lips. She could have shaken Rosie, the silly thing, except that she was shaking so badly herself.

Obviously the Ghost was not "a good man." Good men did not hide their faces and lurk about sinking the cargos of honorable, hardworking men like her fiancé. Nonetheless she was weak with relief as she watched the sailors depart. She could hardly wait for them to be on their way. It was then that she noticed the Ghost's eyes glittering over her. The soft hairs rose on her arms and the back of her neck. She did not at all like the way he was looking at her . . .

Chapter 4

L ucian tried to suppress the desire growing within him, but it would not be damped. He should leave; he should walk away from her and never think of her again. Yes, he thought blackly, and be tortured by the memory of her beauty for the rest of his life—wondering what she would have felt and tasted like, wondering what she was doing here in the first place.

"I have some questions for you," he said. "Come with me."

Sarina looked at his partially hooded face with distaste. "Indeed I will not."

He shrugged. "So be it." He lifted her in his arms.

She shrieked. She saw Ginelle's and Rosie's shocked faces as she was carried from the room to the next cabin. As he slid the bolt shut, she bit her lip and suppressed a second shriek. She would never let him see how frightened she was.

Lucian did not release her immediately but held her in his arms close against him, his face buried in her fragrant hair. She was warm and soft and smelled like springtime. He ached with wanting her.

"Put me down," she said crisply.

He stood her on her feet, and when he met her green eyes, he was reminded of the inner core of a hurricane, still but deadly. He watched her retreat to the farthest corner of the cabin.

"So"—Sarina forced her voice to remain quiet—"we

have nothing to fear from the crew. It is the noble captain himself we must fear.''

Lucian removed his sword belt and made himself comfortable in the only chair.

"How are you three connected with Douglas?" he asked. "Are you working for him?"

Sarina was amazed by the question. She laughed. "Working for him? I cannot imagine what you mean nor why such a thing should concern you."

Lucian smiled. Not only was the wench ravishing, but she also had a streak of daring that he admired.

"Is New York your final destination?" When she made no answer, just glared down at him, he said softly, "Madam, I am asking you politely for answers and I expect you to give them."

"And I will not. It is none of your concern!" Her beautiful face flushed a deep pink.

Lucian had his answer. Tarts, he thought, with genuine regret. What else could they be? He shook his head, musing that the bastard's taste had improved vastly over what he had seen in the past. In fact, this mermaid was so delicious that his desire for her had grown painful. He stood. He would leave before he did something he regretted, but first . . .

"Wh-what are you doing?" Sarina cried, her indignation turning suddenly to fright as the Ghost closed the distance between them with two long strides. She was taken into his arms, her own pinned behind her. "How d-dare you!"

"Don't be afraid," he said. "I am just going to kiss you . . ."

It was all he had intended, one kiss, but tasting her freshness, he could not let her go. He took her mouth hungrily, and then took it again and again, probing, searching its hot sweetness with his tongue. Her lily-scented skin inflamed him further.

"P-pirate dog!" Sarina choked.

Lucian saw that her full lips were bruised from his kisses, and the delicate skin of her face was pinkened by his own rough skin. As his hand moved gently but insistently over her breasts, he wondered if she would make love with him.

"I will not harm you."

"Y-you have a strange way of showing it!" He had nearly smothered her with kisses. "Release me this instant!"

"I want you . . ."

"No!"

Terror swam over Sarina, dizzying her. He was going to rape her. She opened her mouth to beg for mercy, but the hateful words would not pass her lips. She would never beg a man for anything, not even her honor. She would fight. She would bite, kick, scratch . . . She tried desperately then to free her hands, but he gripped her wrists all the tighter, one big hand still stroking her breasts.

"You are very beautiful."

Lucian's admiration for his enemy's unexpectedly fine taste in women was matched by his bafflement at the women themselves. Silly wenches, putting their lives into such greedy, uncaring hands. Douglas was a taker, not a giver. He would work them without mercy.

"Scum!" Sarina cried. "Now I understand why your crew was not allowed to rape us. You want us for yourself!"

Unsmiling, Lucian said, "Madam, my crew was not permitted to rape you because their ardor would have killed you."

"Whereas you, of course, rape gently!"

He chuckled. "I don't rape women, I make love to them. You will enjoy my lovemaking, I promise you."

Before Sarina could protest, his mouth sealed hers. The next thing she knew, they were on the bunk, his tall body pressing against every inch of her. He pulled up her skirts and threw one muscular gray-clad leg over her own silk-covered legs, pinning them down. She was helpless, but no, he was no longer holding her hands. She twisted her head, at last freeing her mouth from his endless kiss, and gave his face a stinging slap. He chuckled.

"Little hellion." He captured both her hands and forced them above her head.

"Bastard!" She was about to scream, then thought better of it. What if his crew came and overpowered him? She could not risk it. Oh, God . . .

Lucian's long, dark fingers slipped around her throat, caressing it, stroking her full lips before tasting them again. His kiss was gentle, questing, seeming to treasure her even as he savored her. Without warning, his hand slid between her thighs. His kiss deepened.

Sarina drew in a sharp breath, shocked by the gesture and the dizzying sensation that swept over her. In her humiliation she wanted to die. Ryan had never touched her there, no man had, nor would she have permitted it, yet this man did it as if he owned her.

She tried to twist away from his teasing fingers, tried desperately to wrench her hands from the iron grip above her head and free her mouth from his plunging tongue, but he was too strong. And the way her body felt frightened her. It no longer seemed her own, but belonged to a hot, throbbing stranger melting beneath him.

Lucian raised his head and gazed down at her, his smile mocking. "I knew you would like it—and I see you like to struggle. Fine, if it increases your pleasure."

Sarina was outraged. "You disgust me."

He kissed the soft hollow at the base of her throat. "And you delight me, sweetheart. You will be well-compensated, believe me."

She could scarcely believe her ears. Compensated? "I will kill you. I swear it."

His smile was a dazzle of white in his dark face. "You'll have to stand in line. Or you might even change your mind."

"Never!" She shuddered as his fingers slipped beneath the neckline of her gown to explore the soft skin there. Suddenly, roughly, he tugged it downward, fully exposing her breasts.

"Please—stop. I beg of you . . ." Her face flamed as

she heard herself begging. "I—I will kill you. I swear I will."

"Shhh."

His mouth found the wild pulse in her throat. He touched his lips and tongue to it, inhaled her fragrance, let his eyes feast on those white rose-tipped mounds before he took one in his mouth. She gave a little cry, writhed, and Lucian felt his manhood swelling, thrusting against his breeches. He could not hold back much longer, but he was uneasy.

He had spoken the truth. He had never raped a woman and never would. He prided himself on the pleasure he gave women. But this one had him confused. She said no, but her lips were soft and hungry, and her breathing was coming in shallow gasps. She had mewed like a kitten and arched against him when he had touched her between her soft thighs. And damn it, this was her business, after all, pleasing men. But then, she probably had never been with a pirate before and doubtless she had heard some harrowing tales. He would be more gentle with her than usual.

"You are beautiful. Very beautiful." He stroked her hair. What color was it? It was neither red nor gold, yet it was both. He had never seen its like before.

"You are h-hateful and cruel."

"Never."

He gently smoothed her hair back on the pillow, dipped his mouth to one rosy nipple and kissed it, heard her gasp of shock, took the other in his mouth, nipped it gently, saw her writhe again. By God, she did like it, even though she tried to hide the fact. His breathing came harder and faster as he struggled to remove her layers of lacy silk undergarments. Why did females wear so many clothes? They were a damned nuisance, and her feigned resistance was beginning to annoy him. It was not easy, keeping her pinned down and trying to get her clothes off with her squirming and trying to bite him. The little witch.

"I have had enough of your teasing, madam," he whispered, his voice husky.

"If I do not succeed in killing you, my fiancé will,"
Sarina cried softly. "Do not think for one minute you
will get away with this dastardly act, because you will
not. Ryan Douglas is a very important man. He knows
all kinds of important men and—"

He released her so quickly that Sarina stared at him
in amazement. It was as though he had been scorched.
She realized then, delighted, that he was afraid. The
Ghost was afraid of Ryan! She leaped to her feet,
quickly restoring herself to decency and smoothing her
wildly tumbled hair. She was furious with herself. How
stupid, not saying sooner that she was promised to
Ryan. She could have saved them all so much agony.

Seeing his frigid gaze behind the slits of his hood,
and his mouth compressed into a thin line, Sarina gave
him her sweetest smile. She felt vindictive, giddy with
triumph.

"I trust I am free to go now, and I trust you will—"

"Shut up."

She blinked. The hands that seconds ago had been
caressing her breasts so hungrily were now clenching
and unclenching at his sides, as though he wanted to
break her in half. He strode to the door, slid the bolt,
and flung the door open. She tried to slip past him,
but he caught her.

"Really, I must insist that you release me. I—oh!
What are you doing?" He swooped her up, carried her
to the bunk, and dumped her onto it in an inglorious
sprawl.

"Stay here 'til I say otherwise," he ordered. "I do
not want to hear a sound out of you." He stepped out
into the corridor. "Lieutenant!"

Sarina's fear returned in a sick rush. Something was
very wrong. She watched, wide-eyed and silent, as the
lieutenant entered the room, the man who had spoken
kindly to Ginelle.

"We can sail any time, sir."

"Good. There is a change in plans, Lieutenant. We
are taking the women with us."

"Sir?"

"You heard me."

"No!" It was a cry from Sarina. "You—you cannot!" Ryan himself had said the Ghost never took anyone from the ships he attacked.

Lucian was by her side in two steps, his big hand fastened on her throat. The pressure of his fingers, though gentle, frightened Sarina horribly. She knew he could snuff out her life without even trying . . .

"Do you understand English?" he asked. When she nodded, her eyes fear-filled, he said, "Good. Then I will say it again. I want quiet from you. No talking, no crying, no squeals, howls, or yowls. Nothing unless you are spoken to. Do you think you can manage that?"

Again Sarina nodded, her heart pounding as she watched him strap on his sword and leave. She did not move. She did not dare. But what had happened? He had been obsessed with her and then—then he had become a different man entirely. Cold, brusque, brutal. She put a hand to her throat. He had not hurt her, not really, but his control had been close to its limit.

Lucian was quietly jubilant. This was his day. Not in his wildest dreams had he ever imagined a windfall like this—having the bastard's woman in his hands. If Douglas was proud of his conquest of her, and what man would not be, her loss would devastate him like nothing else ever could. All the dumped cargos in the world would not compare with one passionate look from those fiery green eyes, one passionate kiss from those soft rosy lips . . .

After warning his men not to use any of their names henceforth, Lucian returned to the cabin where Sarina still sat on the bunk, wide-eyed and mouse-quiet. She was not a high-priced little piece at all, he thought, his eyes sliding over her. In a way, it was too bad. He could respect a tart who did her job well, but for this one, he could have no respect. Not ever. Not for a woman who had given herself to the world's most heartless bastard.

The image of his brother's broken body filled Lucian's mind. Shane. A young boy, a good boy who had not even begun to live, had had his back laid open with the lash because of Ryan Douglas' greed. After three years, it still tortured Lucian to think of it. But then, he needed to remember, wanted to remember until every gold coin was squeezed out of the man, and after the gold was gone, every drop of blood . . .

Lucian's calculating eyes glittered over the exquisite woman sitting on the bunk as though it were her throne, her small chin held high. This cargo, he decided suddenly, was for Shane. What booty was more valuable to a man than the woman he intended to marry? And now he himself would have her first. Many times. And she was going to enjoy it. She was going to beg him for it. And that was going to hurt his old friend and shipmate more than anything else ever could. Lucian smiled, well-satisfied.

"Up!" he said gruffly.

Sarina looked down her small, perfect nose at him.

"Up." Lucian jerked a thumb toward the ceiling. "We are leaving."

"I—I refuse!"

He grasped her arms and lifted her roughly to her feet. He towered over her, lean, muscular, silent, a gray menace with dangerous eyes.

Very well, Sarina thought, she would obey, but his hour would come. She was shaking, but she straightened her shoulders and followed him on deck where the *Stargazer*'s crew, their hands bound behind them, gazed sullenly at the planking. Hearing shrieks, she turned to see Ginelle and Rosie being carried from the cabin. Oh, no. Her best friend, who would never have been here but for her, and poor little Rosie. Oh, God.

She confronted the Ghost. "Why are you taking them? Since I am the one you seem to hate so much, leave them. I will go with you willingly."

He made no answer. He motioned his men to continue and watched as the two women were handed across the rails of the two wallowing vessels. When a hooded seaman attempted to lift Sarina, she gave him a smart blow to the head.

"Keep your filthy hands off me! I will manage on my own."

As soon as she said it, she was sorry. The railings were high, slippery, and uneven; dark waves slapped hungrily between the two ships. She commanded herself not to look at them, not to think about falling, but the possibility was foremost in her mind. When her heel caught in one of her skirts, she panicked and lost her balance. She screamed, felt herself going, and then a pair of strong arms went around her. She caught back a sob.

"Do you want to kill yourself?" the Ghost muttered. "Let the man help you."

Sarina was relinquished to the strong arms of the seaman she had struck, and then she was aboard the ghost ship in another pair of arms. Seeing that Rosie and Ginelle were suffering the same fate, she tried desperately to hold on to one last hope—that Captain Gray would follow them in the *Stargazer* and somehow succeed in rescuing them.

When his prize was safe aboard his vessel, Lucian commanded his men:

"Fetch their trunks and then slash these sails."

He detested wanton destruction, but in this instance he was taking no chance of pursuit, however remote it might be. Once his orders had been carried out and his men were back on the *Vengeance*, Lucian freed the *Stargazer* of the grapnels and leaped aboard his own vessel. He found his men clustered around the women.

"Now hear this," he barked. "These women are not aboard for any man's pleasure. For now, I want them in the brig under guard."

Having witnessed the unconscionable destruction of the *Stargazer*'s mainsails, Sarina cried: "And who is to protect us from our 'guard,' pray, and from our noble captain?"

The Ghost gave no indication that he had heard her.

They were carried below deck immediately and thrust into one of several small, damp, windowless cells with a barred opening on the door. The glow from a lantern in the corridor dimly illuminated the space, empty except for one bench. Rosie sobbed at the sight of it.

"Oh, mum, this'll be the end o' us! What if they fergets we're here? We'll starve fer sure!"

Sarina clenched her teeth to prevent their chattering. "They will not forget us, I assure you, Rosie, nor will we starve." She knew the animals would fight amongst themselves over who would get to guard them and touch them . . .

Ginelle dusted the bench with her handkerchief and sat on it gingerly. "Did you see how they looked at us?" she whispered, shivering. "Oh, Rina, do you think they might—they might . . ." She covered her mouth, unable even to utter the horrible word.

"If yer mean might they rape us after all, mum," Rosie said, "I say it's likely. These seems as bad as any I've heard Joe tell of. The one what carried me was the devil hisself, slobberin' all over me an' his big ugly hands everywhere. Ugh!"

"And I was squeezed and kissed." Ginelle's voice was faint. "Oh, dear!"

"And you are here because of me . . ." Sarina said dully.

"Sarina Fairburn, do not dare to blame yourself!"

"How can I not?"

"Now see here," Ginelle flared with her old spunk, "we could not let you sail off to New York all alone."

Sarina shook her head. "What I mean is, the Ghost would have left us on the *Stargazer* had I not mentioned I was Ryan's fiancée. I—I am certain of it."

"Rina, you cannot know that." Ginelle took her hand and lowered her voice. "My pet, what on earth happened after he—carried you off? Oh, dear, I am afraid to hear. What a coward I am."

"Indeed you are not a coward, and—and nothing happened," Sarina lied. It would be cruel to frighten them further. "He merely questioned me."

Ginelle got up, wrung her hands, peeked through the bars of the door, and collapsed onto the bunk again. "The wretch out there threw a kiss at me. Oh, Rina, I wonder, should we do as Rosie suggested after all? I mean, we are completely at their mercy."

"Ginelle Crandall, I will not allow you to disgrace yourself that way."

"But that Scotsman . . ." Ginelle blushed. "He seemed so gentle, and he never stopped staring at me."

"Do as you wish, certainly," Sarina said crisply. "I cannot stop you. But you will never catch me doing such a thing."

"Oh, mum," said Rosie, "we two ain't as brave as you. In fact, mebbe I'll drop another little hint to that Ghost feller."

Sarina's lip curled. "Like the first little hint, you mean?" Actually wrapping herself around the man's legs and tripping him? Really.

"He's got sich nice laigs an' brawny arms an' a nice hard narrer bottom—an' that mouth o' his . . ." Rosie rolled her big brown eyes. "I'll bet he's a real good kisser, mum, Ghost er no."

Sarina felt her face flame, but Ginelle was preoccupied and Rosie's mouth was running on and on.

"Mum, I knows it sounds traitorous, but my goodness, he do make my Joe look like a reg'lar scarecrow!"

Sarina grasped Rosie's arm and lowered her voice to a fierce whisper. "Now you listen to me, Rosie Coggins. Your Joe may look like a scarecrow, but he is not out dumping the cargos of hardworking men or terrorizing helpless women."

Rosie's tears gushed anew. "Oh, mum, yer right. I'm a wicked woman, I am."

Their door was suddenly unbarred and thrown open. They all jumped.

"You." A seaman pointed at Sarina. "Come wi' me."

"Indeed I will not!" Sarina planted her feet on the wooden floorboards, her hands on her hips.

He laughed. "Good. I'll carry ye then."

She stiffened. ''No! I—I will come.''

Ginelle hugged her. ''Oh, love, you are so brave . . .'' She added softly, ''Here, slip this inside your bodice.'' It was a small dagger.

Sarina hid it between her breasts and gave Ginelle a kiss. ''Do not tell them our names, please, either of you,'' she whispered. ''It could put us in even greater danger . . .''

Chapter 5

The dagger lay as cold as a viper against Sarina's skin, and her heart tapped out a wild beat as she followed the seaman up steep stairs and down narrow passageways. The ship's floor lifted and lowered constantly beneath her unsteady feet, and several times she was thrown against the man or the walls. Once, she was hurled to the deck.

"Ye'll be gettin' your sea legs soon," he said with a laugh, "unless, o' course, the cap'n has other plans for ye. Like keepin' ye in his bed most o' the time . . ."

Holding back her hot retort, she stepped past him with icy dignity into the cabin.

"Yer to wait here, lady, an' I warn ye"—his gaze undressed her—"the cap'n won't hesitate to break 'is own door down."

After he left, Sarina withdrew Ginelle's tiny dagger, warmed from lying between her breasts. Not more than six inches long, it nonetheless had an evil-looking stiletto-thin blade. It could kill, but not in her hands, she decided instantly. While she had spoken hotly to the Ghost of killing him, she would not; she couldn't even step on a spider. Besides, if she harmed him, what would happen to the three of them? The Ghost alone could protect them from his crew. At this point, she wondered if she dared refuse anything he demanded of her. How unfair it was!

She returned the weapon to its hiding place and looked around her for the first time. The cabin was spacious and smelled of pine. Its cleanliness astonished Sarina. Even her own room in Kenley Gables did not sparkle so. Her wide gaze moved over two bunks, neatly made with burgundy-colored covers; polished brass lanterns; two armchairs with thick orange cushions; a big maple desk with a chart above it; a chessboard set up with exotic jade chessmen; bookcases . . . Bookcases? What sort of books would a criminal like the Ghost possibly be interested in? She drifted to the shelves, ready to spring away if he should enter. She peered at the titles in the fading light: *The Decline and Fall of the Roman Empire; Motion of the Solar System;* Kant's *Critique of Pure Reason;* Goethe's *Iphigenie and Tauris; A Treatise on Mechanically Driven Boats; The Table of Thirty-One Chemical Elements; New Theory of the Earth.* What in the world! She could not believe it.

"You are welcome to read anything you like." The deep voice behind her was gruff but polite.

Sarina had been so absorbed she had not heard the door open. She jumped, shocked at the sight of him, for he had discarded his ghost-gray hood and clothing for dark-blue breeches belted with a scarlet sash. They were tucked into his boots and topped by a blue sleeveless shirt. His midriff, visible between the scarlet and blue, was as teak-colored and muscular as his long arms.

But it was not at his clothing that she stared like a frightened doe. His dark-skinned face with its broad cheekbones and square jaw was a terrifying study in hard, unyielding maleness. Straight jet-black hair hung to his shoulders, and his black brows arced above icy blue eyes. His nose was straight, aristocratic; his mouth broad with full sensual lips, yet Sarina saw the cruelty in them.

She forced her gaze away. How could she be thinking of Rosie's silly words—that he would be a good kisser—at a time like this? Remembering, Sarina trembled. He had, indeed, known how to kiss, and as frightened as she had been, her body had responded. But now it was responding in a different way. Seeing the aura of power that clung to him and the proud way he carried himself, his arrogant, possessive assessment of her, she felt afraid.

"You might like this book," he said, surprising her. He reached for a small red one that made his hands seem stronger and darker than ever. The sonnets of Shakespeare.

While she truly loved the sonnets, Sarina's only answer was a look of loathing. She moved to the other side of the cabin. She heard the book being returned to its slot and the sharp click of his gleaming black boots on the floorboards, then felt his warm presence close behind her. She spun. She would as soon offer her unprotected back to a wild boar.

"You will be staying in this cabin," he said. "You have probably already noticed that your trunks are here."

She looked around, startled. She had not noticed, and yes, there they were, side by side along one wall.

"I think you will find your stay aboard comfortable," he said crisply. "There is a private privy in the stern, the bed is good, the food is fair, and you can—"

"I insist"—she fought to keep her breathing even and her voice calm—"that you return us to the *Stargazer*. If you—"

"—you can read anything here, providing you are capable of reading, of course . . ."

She was growing hotter by the second. "—if you know what is good for you, you will return us immediately!"

"And you will be happy to know," he continued coolly, as though she had not said a word, "that you are permitted to walk on deck for exercise. My men will not touch you. I suggest you—"

"Did you not hear me?" Sarina cried.

"—change into more practical clothing. And there is no high tea aboard this vessel. You will come to the mess with the rest of us."

"And whose fault is it that I am aboard this miserable tub in the first place?"

When he did not answer, she began to shake with anger. The wretch! The miserable, unspeakable, cowardly wretch.

"I—I insist my friend be here with me and not in that awful cell. And my maid must be close by. I will have need of her."

"Ah, your maid."

Lucian's face did not reveal his contempt. If he had given it any thought, he would have realized the girl called Rosie was a serving woman for the other two. He allowed his gaze to slide suggestively over his captive, knowing it would frighten her. He wanted to frighten her, the pampered, spoiled little witch. Her green gown was torn and soiled now, but he was aware of its worth, and for the first time he saw the glitter of green on her shapely earlobes. Emeralds, by God. Emeralds as green as her eyes. Douglas had kept her well. He was also going to pay well to have her back in his bed again . . .

Lucian imagined her in his own bed, a delight he had contemplated ever since he had first set eyes on her. He thought of that satiny white skin beneath his fingers, beneath his own body, her red-gold hair fanned out on his pillow, his mouth pressed to her pomegranate lips and the delicate rosy buds of her nipples, the lily fragrance of her soft flesh. He sucked in a ragged breath and picked up a jade chesspiece.

"You will do without your maid for now," he said, "and as for having your friend with you, the answer is no. I am quartering her elsewhere." Seeing her beautiful face crumple in disappointment, he was torn between satisfaction and compassion. He was turning into as mean a bastard as Douglas himself.

"You are separating us so your men can torment us, so we cannot help each other!"

"I said you would be safe," he replied brusquely.

"I don't believe you!" Sarina put her hands to her damp cheeks, having failed to hold back her angry tears. "Why are you doing this? I don't understand. I know you don't take captives. And why do you harass only Ryan?"

His eyes narrowed. "Why do you think that?"

"Because he said so." When he made no reply, she gave him a look of scorn. "This is ridiculous, you know. If you risk the danger of seizing a vessel and stealing its cargo, why dump it? Why not get some pleasure from it? You are going to be hanged anyway."

Lucian carefully replaced the chesspiece on the polished board and picked up a bishop, testing its weight and smoothness in his hand. His gaze flickered over her.

"Perhaps things are about to change," he said quietly.

Sarina stepped back, her face suddenly burning. "I knew you never meant it when you said we would not be harmed."

"I have told you, you will not be—harmed. You will be returned safely to your fiancé after he pays the ransom I will ask for you." He returned the bishop to its proper place and moved a pawn forward.

"Ransom?"

Sarina sank onto a chair. It was exactly what she had feared. Of course Ryan would try to pay whatever was demanded, but if this man—this looting coward—discovered who she was, if he learned of the great fortune to which she was heir . . . Oh, God, her father would surrender everything for which he had worked his entire life to ensure her safe return. She could not let that happen. She rose swiftly to her feet, the dagger suddenly in her hand and the Ghost, moving an opposing pawn on his chessboard, completely unaware of his danger.

Where should she strike? she thought, frantic, moving up behind him, her eyes on his broad back. His back? Never! His heart? His throat? Oh, God, she could not! But neither could she allow him to abuse her!

She flew at him then, flailing blindly at his left arm

with the deadly little weapon before his fingers closed around her wrist like a steel band.

Lucian tried to pry the dagger from her hand, but her fingers were bonded to its pearl handle. She broke free and, crouching low, her arm outstretched, held him at bay.

"By God"—he laughed—"I may sign you on when this is over."

"You may be dead before then."

She slashed. He retreated. She advanced, emboldened by his apparent fear. All she had to do, she thought, astonished, was to wave this little thing in front of her to keep him away. But how long could she hold him off? And then what would happen?

Lucian was enjoying himself. She had caught him unawares, which was damned stupid of him, but she had not struck to kill. Nevertheless, she could have accidentally hit a vital spot that would have left him just as dead. It was a good lesson to have learned. She was dangerous.

He laughed and retreated, allowing her to think she was besting him while he relished the ludicrousness of the situation, and her spirit. Just looking at her, pink-cheeked with fury in her eyes, her white teeth showing, stirred his passions. But enough of this. She had had her fun. He reached out with one long arm, seized her wrist, and easily disarmed her. He slipped the dagger into his belt.

"That is a dangerous toy for you to play with, Madam."

She was breathing fast, and his eyes feasted on the rise and fall of her lovely breasts. He pulled her into his arms. Instantly her hand shot out and before he could prevent it, her palm cracked against his cheek like a pistol shot. He sucked in a painful breath.

Silently, furiously, he forced her arms behind her and pulled her so close against his chest that she cried out. He bent his dark head, pressed a hot kiss to the valley between her breasts, and inhaled her scent.

"Y-you craven!"

Lucian felt himself rising, hungering to thrust into her, but no, he would leave before that could happen. He sought her mouth. She bit him on the lip. That angered him. Still imprisoning her with his one arm, he grasped her chin roughly between his fingers and thumb and jerked her head upward. He felt her shudder.

"Y-you're hurting me!"

"Madam"—his voice was filled with menace—"don't ever bite me. Not ever. Is that understood?"

"You were hurting me, p-pawing me. And you are holding me for ransom." Her voice was high and childlike. "Am I expected to dance and sing for joy?"

Her words stung. Pawing? For him it had been a heady experience. His senses reeled with the taste and feel of her. Certainly other women had never complained. But then, no woman had ever been terrified of him before. He had never taken one captive or thrown one in the brig. Certainly no woman had seen him hooded or had needed to defend herself against him. Not until now.

The flicker of compassion he felt for her faded as quickly as it had come. This was Douglas' woman, with her maid and her jewels and her expensive gowns, her beautiful body already sullied by Douglas' dirty hands. Lucian released her.

"You are loathsome," Sarina snapped. She made a great pretense of brushing his touch from her clothing and flesh with her small lacy handkerchief. "Ugh!"

Lucian laughed at her childishness. "I'm leaving now, but when I return, I want this door to be unbarred."

Her answer was a sullen glare. She continued to scrub the damp imprints of his mouth from her lips and bosom.

"Do I make myself clear? Don't bar this door or I will knock it down." She did not answer. "We eat at eight bells. I will stop by for you."

"You need not bother. I will not be hungry."

"Suit yourself."

After he left Sarina paced the room. How long could she hold him off? She thought then of her father and Ryan, of how frantic and enraged they would be when they heard of her capture. And to think, they would not know for weeks yet. Travel was so slow, it would take forever and ever before the three of them could leave this horrible ship. Thinking of Ginelle and Rosie in their grim prison, Sarina paced faster. She could hardly wait until the beast was caught and punished for all the grief he was causing everyone. Oh, she could hardly wait . . .

A while later she hurried to the stern, performed a hasty toilette, and rushed back to the cabin. Against the Ghost's orders, she barred the door while she changed into a pale-blue muslin nightgown. She unbarred the door before crawling into one of the beds. She sighed. The pillow was clean and fluffy, the burgundy blanket surprisingly soft. She pulled it up under her chin, sighed again, and yawned. He was right, the bed was good. She had not realized how exhausted she was until now . . .

Sarina was sleeping, lulled by the ship's rocking motion, when a noise awakened her. Hearing a thump and a soft oath, she sat up and held her breath. Someone was in her room moving about in the dark! She screamed.

"There is no need to screech," said a deep voice. "It's only me."

"You!"

There was a click as a port window was opened, and then another. In the moonlight that flooded the room, Sarina saw that he was naked. Bronzed arms and legs, broad shoulders, a hard muscular chest with a vee of black hair on it, his— Oh, God. She pulled the blanket over her head.

"What are you doing here?" Her voice was muffled.

"What am I doing here? Hell, this is my cabin."

"But—"

"No buts."

She sat there, furious, before finally lowering the

blanket just enough to peek at him. She found him glaring at her. He had donned a loose blue nightshirt that stopped at mid-thigh.

"You dare to tell me we are—sharing this room?"

"You dare to tell me you thought I was sleeping on deck?"

"I—I will not have it! It is simply impossible." She remembered his hungry mouth and hands moving over her earlier.

He nodded. "You're right. I wouldn't sleep a damn, wondering if you had another toy hidden away somewhere." He went to his desk and rummaged in a drawer, finally finding what he wanted. "This won't hurt . . ."

Her eyes flew open. "Don't come near me with that thing." She scrambled from the bed and put a chair between them. "Don't you dare!"

"Shhh. Remember, the ports are open. What will my crew think if they hear you squawking? Be good now." He put the chair aside.

"You brute!" There was nowhere for her to run or hide. She faced him with smoldering eyes. She hated him.

"If you don't let me put this on nicely, I will put it on roughly. I don't want my head bashed in during the night . . ."

Sarina's tears flowed freely in the darkness as she fingered the thin gold bracelet around her wrist that chained her to a post on the bunk. The Ghost's uneven breathing coming from the second bunk on the other side of the room told her that he was as wakeful as she was. She did not intend to sleep, for what if he came to her in the night?

"Are you awake?" he asked softly.

She could not remain silent. "Have you ever slept chained to a bed?"

"As a matter of fact, I have."

"Doubtless you deserved it!"

Lucian smiled in the blackness. What a sassy little

wench she was, chained to a bed, carried she knew not where, yet able to give him an answer like that. By God, she was braver than a lot of men he knew.

"What is your name?" he asked gently.

"You have taken my freedom, my friends, and now this, this final humility . . ." She fingered the bracelet and chain again. "I will die before I tell you my name."

His chuckle was deep and easy. "There is hardly need for so drastic a measure since I much prefer you alive."

Sarina pressed the pillow against her ears and pulled the blanket over her head.

"I will call you Aurora. If you have no objection, that is."

When there was no answer, not even an outraged sputter, Lucian took a deep breath. He had never expected to find the most beautiful woman he had ever seen aboard the *Stargazer*. She was Guinevere and Isolde and Aurora, Queen of the Dawn, all combined in one delectable body, but she would not appreciate hearing such praise from him. She detested him. And all he felt for her was hunger and hostility—and admiration for her bravery. Hell, he had thought of the little wench enough for one night; it was time to get some sleep. He turned onto his side, his eyes barely making out the humped form on the other bunk.

"Good night, Aurora," he said softly.

Sarina did not know he had spoken. She was weeping silently, the pillow and blanket still pulled over her head.

Chapter 6

The night was warm and clear, with strong easterly winds, and the watch, perched a hundred feet up a mast thrust into the starry blackness, could see for miles across the moon-gilded sea. It was the kind of night when men stayed on deck. Some slept on hammocks strung between mast and rail; others talked or played dice or cards while they quaffed their day's ration of grog.

Earlier, Lucian had moved among them questioning them, as he always did at nightfall, for he took good care of his men. None lacked for anything that was his to provide: warm dry boots and clothing, good food and grog, advice if they asked for it. Many evenings he was up talking and gaming along with them, but not this night. Tonight he had gone to his cabin shortly after darkness fell, and every man aboard knew a woman was there.

Donal Fleming and Skylar Braden sprawled glumly on adjacent coils of rope, sipping grog and speaking softly.

"The lad's off 'is bloomin' head, takin' captives," Sky muttered.

"The 'lad' is master of this ship, old man," Donal whispered back. "Don't ever let him or the crew hear you call him that."

"But I'm quartermaster, damn it. He should've consulted me, and I'd've said no and saved us a shipload o' trouble."

"If it comes to that," Donal grumbled, "he should have asked me too, as second in command. But what does he do? He bellows for me, says there's a change in plans and we're taking the women. Just like that." He snapped his fingers. "And let me tell you, man, when I see that icy look he has in his eyes nowadays, I don't argue."

"Nor I." Sky took another sip of grog.

"We should have sat on him first thing and reminded him of the damned pirate code."

"Aye. Article Six," Sky intoned morosely. "If any man be found seducin' a woman or carryin' her to sea, he shall suffer death."

"Aye."

Donal sighed, sipped his grog, and felt it seeping through his tired body. His own thoughts of the little blonde had bedeviled him for hours: how soft and white and plump she was, and how that golden hair of hers would look streaming down over her full white breasts with the pink nipples peeking through. Ah, holy heaven.

"I wouldn't mind havin' that sassy little brown-haired wench myself," Sky confessed, his voice low. "When we took in the cots and blankets for them, it set fire in my guts just to look at her. An' that performance o' hers with Luc—" His handsome face broke into a grin. "Whew, I'll take her under my protection any time. Any time."

Donal's teeth shone white in the moonglow. "Protection, eh? Come on, man, this is Donal you're talking to."

But Sky had grown serious again. "I thought I heard a scream earlier—from Luc's cabin. Did you hear it?"

"No. It had to be the wind."

"I was close by. It wasn't wind . . ."

They rose and walked to the stern, where they gazed stonily at the luminous wake left by the *Vengeance*.

"Don't jump to conclusions," Donal said. "Lucian's above hurting a woman. We both know that . . ."

He had known his friend since they were lads aboard

their first vessel. Even then Lucian Thorne had been too much of a gentleman to hurt a woman in any way, or to cross swords with an inferior. If the wench had screamed, it was for some reason other than his hurting her. But what it was, Donal could not imagine.

Sky drained the last drop of grog from his tin mug. "First thing tomorrow we're goin' to have a talk with the lad."

"And say what?"

"That this won't work. That a pirate ship's no place for women who look like those three, especially when he takes one himself and leaves the rest of us starving and empty-handed. Mark my words, there'll be trouble. If this was a typical pirate outfit, the crew would've booted him off the bridge as soon as she was brought to his cabin."

"But this isn't a typical pirate outfit," Donal said harshly, "and he has their allegiance. He can command them to do anything. He proved that this afternoon."

Sky leaned against the rail, gray eyes narrowed, blond hair silvered with moonlight, a tall figure wearing the ghost-gray clothing he preferred to any other.

"I hope you're right, but the fact remains, ship life's no life for women."

"With that I have to agree."

"Good. So how about this—instead o' goin' to Florida for careening, we head back to England tomorrow and put the ladies ashore in some safe fishing village. Fisher-folk are always kindly, and they'll see that the three o' them get back to London. Our repairs aren't so extensive that they can't wait until we reach the Irish coast."

Donal scowled. "Lucian won't like it. The women can identify us."

Sky laughed. "God, man, we can't keep them with us forever—they can identify us later as well as sooner. But then, maybe they'll not remember our faces well enough to describe us."

Donal's black eyes danced. "Maybe not your face, old man, but women don't forget me all that easily."

"Well, now, they don't forget Sky Braden that easily either, youngster. I'm what's considered a catch. I have all my hair and teeth, both eyes, four sturdy limbs . . ."

They grinned at each other, and Donal gave Sky's arm a hefty punch. "As do I, friend, and mine are ten years younger."

"Ah, but I have ten years more practice and expertise in the fine art of lovemaking, lad."

"No lass has held that against me yet, Braden. . . ."

Ginelle could not sleep. If this dreadful experience ever did end, the memory of it alone would keep her awake for the rest of her life. She still wore the pink silk gown she had donned that morning aboard the *Stargazer*, and now it was twisted and wrapped about her legs so that she could scarcely move. In addition, the cot was hard, the blanket scratchy, and her pillow lumpy. And they were in darkness. The cell's only illumination came dimly from the guard's lantern beyond the door. Too often she saw his bearded face peering at them through the barred opening, and each time she shuddered. He was built like an ox, and his eyes were little and hot and cruel-looking.

What worried Ginelle even more was that Sarina had not returned. What terrible fate had befallen her? she brooded. Would the two of them be next? It was an absolutely hideous situation, and Ginelle felt a growing fury toward Ryan Douglas. She had been absolutely right to question him about their safety.

She yearned to untangle her gown, stand up, and stretch her legs, but the ship was rolling so much that she knew she would be pitched about. The last thing she wanted was to call attention to herself.

"Girlie . . ."

Ginelle froze. The guard was looking in. She squeezed her eyes shut in a pretense of sleep, but her heart had jumped to her throat. As the bolt slid back and the door creaked open, a silent scream tore through her body. When a rough hand stroked her shoulder, she leaped to her feet. Tangled in her skirts, she fell immediately to the damp plank floor. The man laughed and hung his lantern from a hook overhead.

"G-go away!" Ginelle gasped, then cried, "Rosie! Rosie, wake up!"

"Yes 'm?" Rosie sat up, sleepy-eyed. "What kin I get ye, mum?" Suddenly seeing the bearded intruder, she shrieked and flew to Ginelle's side.

"Now, girlies," he whispered, "let's not get all fussed over a little kiss or two, an' a feel." He grabbed Ginelle around the waist and clamped her to his chest. "I'll start with you, sweetie. I likes a meaty female best, an' blondes has the sweetest, softest flesh of all."

"Meaty!" Ginelle cried.

Her fears were completely forgotten in the wave of outrage that swirled over her. Her palm cracked against his hairy cheek at the same instant that Rosie pounded her heavy shoe against his skull.

"Insult me mistress, will ye? Take that, dastard!"

"Leave this instant," Ginelle commanded, fiery-eyed, bosom heaving, "and if you know what's good for you, you will never touch me again!"

Meaty, she thought again, crushed. She would kill him! She gave his shin a fearsome kick as Rosie continued to hammer his head with her shoe. It was then that she saw the two tall men in the doorway, one dark, the other fair. Seeing that both were laughing, she grew even angrier.

"It's funny, is it?" she demanded. "Abducting us, keeping us in this hideous prison, and now this—this cur . . ." She knew she would burst into tears if she went on. She flew at the dark one like a small tornado, kicking, punching, scratching.

"Whoa, there." Donal caught her wrists and held her at bay. "I'm not going to hurt you."

"We don't believe yer, mister," Rosie cried. "All the men on this here boat is animals. Slobberin' all over us an' pinchin', an' now it seems we ain't safe even here

in jail. That dastard''—she pointed at the glowering
guard—''was maulin' me mistress.''

''Mister, what exactly were you doing in here?''
Donal's black eyes narrowed on the man.

''I was invited in,'' he muttered.

''Hah! Liar!'' Rosie threw her shoe at him.

''She's right,'' Ginelle murmured, her legs feeling
suddenly weak as her fury ebbed and she realized what
might have happened. ''I was trying to sleep and suddenly he was standing over me. H-he grabbed me . . .''
And he said she was meaty and she wanted to die . . .

''I am sorry,'' the dark man said.

Ginelle stared at him in the flickering candlelight. It
was the lieutenant. With his hood gone, and clad in a
red shirt and black pants, he looked very different. His
hair was black and curly, framing a handsome youthful
face, and his eyes gleamed like jet under fierce black
brows that nearly met over his narrow high-bridged
nose. He was magnificent.

She wondered suddenly, astonishingly, if he was
tender when he kissed a woman, wondered if his long,
strong fingers would be gentle . . . She blinked and
shook her head to dispel the image. How could she be
thinking such preposterous thoughts? This man was a
criminal, a pirate, and she absolutely would not respond to the way his bold gaze was roving over her.

''Mister,'' Donal growled to the guard, ''take yourself to the next cell.''

He glowered back. ''Sir, this little bitch—''

''On the double, mister! Quartermaster, lock him
in.''

''Aye, sir.''

When Sky returned, he shot an appreciative glance
at the feisty brunette and found her gazing at him
with big brown eyes. Well, well. She liked him, it
seemed. He willed her to throw her curvy little body
at his feet . . .

''Ladies, I am making a change here and now,''
Donal said crisply. ''You will be in my cabin for the
remainder of the voyage.''

"Hah! An' then you'll be the one doin' the squee-zin'!" Rosie snapped. "We'll be at your mercy."

"Nor do I trust you." Ginelle eyed him suspiciously.

Donal bowed stiffly. "I am giving you a choice. Be in my cabin and at my mercy, which is considerable, or remain here at the mercy of the guards."

Sky snorted. Since when was Donal Fleming's mercy considerable when it came to females? The man was a lady-killer—but then he himself wanted the little fox so bad he could feel and taste her already.

"Awooo, mum." Rosie's soft eyes brimmed with tears. "It ain't fair." She ran the back of her hand under her small wet nose. "Wot'll we do? I don't want ta be at any man's mercy."

"We will leave you to consider it, ladies." Donal turned toward the door. "In the meantime, I must post another guard."

"Wait!" Ginelle cried. "I—I—" Oh, she didn't know what to do. If only Sarina were here. She chewed her lower lip and blinked at him. "Where is my friend? What have you done with her?"

"She is quite safe," said Donal, hoping to God it was true. "Just as you ladies will be safe from now on."

"Give me one good reason why I should believe you," Ginelle said, but then, looking around her at the tiny, dark, damp cell, she sighed, "Oh, never mind. Oh, dear, I suppose we should accept your offer."

"An' jist where'll you be bunkin', mister?" Rosie demanded.

Donal scowled down at the brunette. She was too damned sassy a baggage to suit his taste. He liked his women soft and pliable.

"You will stay here, I think, unless you watch your tongue." His statement had the precise effect he intended. The women flew into each other's arms, and the baggage set up a howl.

"Then we will both stay," said Ginelle stiffly.

"Oh, mum, no! Oh, sir," Rosie blubbered, "I'll be-have meself, I promise I will. Jist take me, too."

They both looked so woebegone that Donal felt ashamed of himself. Manipulating them had been child's play. As he grasped the blonde's soft upper arm and led her from the cell, he promised himself she would be safe in his cabin. Of course, if she should ever want to crawl into his bed for further protection, so be it . . .

Lucian had gone on deck several times during the night, prowling among his sprawled and sleeping men, and exchanging words with the watches at either end of his vessel and in the crow's nest. All had been well. And all had been well in his cabin. His hotheaded mermaid had calmed down sufficiently to fall asleep.

Now it was dawn and she still slept. He stood gazing down at her, thinking how soft and dewy-looking she was, how incredibly beautiful and impossibly vulnerable. How could someone who looked so fragile, so tender, live and breathe in a world as harsh as this one? Contemplating then that she belonged to a man like Ryan Douglas gave him such a pang in his gut that it was like a knife twisting there. He put the idea from his head, released the chain from her wrist, and went out on deck.

Too many important matters claimed his attention to allow him to think of her further. The damned worms, for instance. In another few days they would bore so far into the planking that his ship would need extensive repair. And then there was the dwindling supply of lemons to consider. His was one of the few vessels afloat whose men were not scurvy-ridden. He gave full credit to the lemon juice he insisted they drink daily.

He stopped a crewman. "Purser, how is the lemon supply?"

"Four days, sir, that bein' if the women don't need them yet."

"They don't, not yet."

It meant they could make it to Florida easily. There they could stock up on supplies, including lemons, careen the ship, and replace the bad planking. Afterward, they could look for the armed *Manxman* that he'd heard was in Florida waters, carrying Douglas himself.

Just thinking of the bastard made Lucian's blood simmer. Why could his spies not locate the damned cache where Douglas hid his contraband? For until they did, and Douglas was caught red-handed, the *Vengeance* must continue to harass his merchantmen—and to do that cost money. The prospect put Lucian in a mood for battle.

"Luc—"

Lucian turned. It was Sky.

"We have to talk, Luc."

He saw that Donal was there, too.

"It's about the women," Sky said.

Already Lucian felt defensive. "All right, let's hear it."

"Since the death penalty does not faze you, I'll not mention it—" Sky began.

"Good."

"But it does bother the rest o' us somewhat."

"I trust you prepared papers for each sailor to sign, stating that he took part in the abduction under duress?"

"I did."

"Then the responsibility is mine alone. Anything else?"

Sky's gaze went to Donal, who took over. "We think the women should be released," he said quietly.

Lucian stood taller. "Do you now?"

"Well, why not, man?" Donal, too, stood taller. "What's the purpose of keeping them? Women aboard are nothing but trouble. We found Garrick in their cell, molesting the blonde. The brunette would've been next, and I haven't a doubt he'd've threatened to kill them if they told. That would be a fine thing going, now wouldn't it?"

Lucian's face darkened. "The bastard. Is he in the brig?" When Sky nodded, Lucian snapped, "Seven lashes, mister. Trice him to the gangway jeers. I want an example made of him."

"Aye, sir." As quartermaster, it was Sky's duty to mete out discipline.

"I've put the women in my cabin," Donal continued. "Sky and I will bunk together." He pulled in a long, fortifying breath. "But having the redhead in with you—" He shook his head, not sure how to continue.

"Now hear this," Lucian said low, "and hear it well. I am master of this vessel, and if I want fifteen redheads in my cabin, I will have them. Is that understood? This is my ship, my money, my men, bought and paid for, and I will do as I bloody well please."

Donal clapped his old friend on the shoulder. "You don't want these women hurt, man, you know you don't. Think of the volatile situation we had back on the *Stargazer*. The men were wild—and now we find Garrick in with the women and God only knows how many others will try, and there are only the three of us to protect them."

"She stays, mister, and that's the end of it."

"No, lad, it's not the end of it," Sky insisted. "I signed on because o' what Douglas did to you, not to take helpless women hostage. I say take them back to England, leave them in a safe place, and do our repairs in Ireland."

"No." Lucian saw that he was turning into a bona fide bastard.

"Hell, Luc."

"Mister, even if we had enough lemons to get us across the Atlantic, which we do not, and even if we did not need repairs within the week, which we do, the answer would still be no." Lucian lowered his voice further. "I am going to ask for ransom for the redhead."

"Ransom!" Donal bellowed.

Lucian glared at him. "Shout it to the whole ship, why don't you, Mr. Fleming?"

Donal glared back. "You're way out o' line now, Lucian! This is bad. Bad."

Lucian's smile was icy. "On the contrary, it is good. It is very good. She is Douglas' woman. His fiancée."

Sky whistled.

Donal's eyes went wide in surprise, then began to twinkle. He grinned. "Damn me!" he said softly.

No one wanted Ryan Douglas punished more than Donal Fleming. Holy heaven, had he himself not suffered from that devil's doings? He would never forget young Shane Thorne's flogging, nor the broken man Lucian had been when he'd been hauled aboard the *Peacekeeper* to be delivered to prison for a crime he had never committed. Holy heaven, Donal's whole life had been altered and colored by it.

He had vowed to find the man responsible, and he had found him. He had vowed to make the scum pay, and his goal was within reach. And now the bastard's woman had fallen into their hands. Donal Fleming made another vow: He was not going to tell his friend what to do with her . . .

Chapter 7

When Sarina awoke, she despaired to discover
that she had not been dreaming. The nightmare
had happened. The three of them had indeed been stolen from the *Stargazer* by pirates. Her hands went to
her bare wrist. She was no longer chained to the bed
and was free to move about. Her eyes went to the other
bed. It was neatly and tightly made, not a wrinkle in
sight. There was no evidence anywhere that the Ghost
had slept there the night before.

She rose, hurriedly donned her green gown, and
slipped her bare feet into her shoes. It would be just
like him to barge in without knocking. Her worried
thoughts centered on Ginelle and Rosie—were they still
in that awful cell? She was crushed by guilt, having
slept like a baby in a lovely clean bed, and in relative
safety, for the Ghost had not touched her. Despite the
fury she felt toward him, she had to admit he had not
come near her. Hearing a noise, she spun.

The Ghost stood in the doorway, filling it. He wore
faded blue breeches, a cropped sleeveless shirt, and
the now-familiar scarlet band around his black hair. As
his mocking blue gaze drilled through her, Sarina returned it with disdain. Pirate dog! she thought heat-
edly. Greedy, lawless renegade! And then she
remembered the night before—his long-limbed, powerful body; his polished skin gleaming in the moonlight and shadows, and contrasting with the black mat
of hair on his chest; his swollen manhood right there

for her to see. She blushed. She had never seen a naked, aroused male before, and it was a sight she would not soon forget.

"Come and eat," he said without preamble. "The mess is on."

Sarina rebelled at the command in his voice. "Do you never say please? And can you not knock before entering?"

She still looked like a sea nymph, Lucian thought. The shimmering green dress; her wide gold-lashed eyes the color of a blue-green cavern in the sea; that mane of hair falling to her waist, the color of dawn on a stormy day, a glowing sun-gilded red.

He caught his breath. Her wrist, which had been so white, so soft and slender, was now red and raw from the metal bracelet he had forced on her. He felt like a damned brute. But only for an instant.

"Most of the men are below so I suggest you use the facilities now. I will wait here for you." She left without a word, her eyes hurling green fury at him. She returned shortly.

"Am I ever to have bathwater?"

His gaze trailed insolently over her. "I suppose I can spare it—it should rain before the day is out. Now let's get going." She stayed planted to the floorboards, arms akimbo. "Look," he said, "either you eat now or you wait until the next mess."

"I am quite sure that is exactly what it is—a mess." She lifted her chin. "I will forgo the pleasure, thank you."

Chuckling, he folded his arms, lounged against the door frame, and studied her furious face.

"You're starving. Hell, your stomach sounds like a jungle in full cry. I can hear it from here. Never say no when you mean yes, madam."

Sarina blinked, taken aback by his crudeness. Her stomach most certainly was not growling, but he had caught her off guard with his last words. As a child, she had learned the hard way never to say no when she meant yes. It had been one of her father's rules.

But this was different. How could she possibly face all those leering men merely to soothe her empty stomach? They would believe that the very worst had happened to her during the night.

"Make up your mind. Are you coming?"

She gave him a quelling look. "You cannot imagine how much I detest you."

Seeing that she was yielding, Lucian grinned down at her. "I'll let you show me sometime. Maybe tonight . . ."

Sarina lagged behind him to where the whole crew sat eating at tables. To a man, their avid eyes bored into her.

"I—I've changed my mind. I want to go back to the cabin."

Lucian grasped her arm and forced her across the room. "You're going to eat."

The whistling and applause were deafening, and Sarina's whole body burned with shame. It was as she had known it would be: they thought he had taken her in the night . . .

Lucian seated his captive and held up a hand for quiet. Seeing his angry eyes, his crew hushed, waited.

"There will be a flogging at four bells," he said. "Be there."

Sarina lifted frightened eyes to his face and tried to suppress the terrible panic rising inside her, threatening to smother her, to stop the very beating of her heart.

"I'm—to be flogged?" Her choked whisper didn't sound like her own voice. "I knew you hated me, but I didn't realize how much. Why? Will you at least tell me that?"

Lucian was astonished. He looked down at her white, pinched face, then threw back his head and laughed, turning every head in the mess.

"Flogged? You?"

Sarina's lips quivered. "I don't find it amusing."

"Madam, madam . . ."

He shook his head at the thought of a cat-o'-nine

lashing her tender woman's body. No, it was not at all amusing. It had been bad enough for himself and for Shane, both of them lean and hard and strong, but for a woman . . .

"I would never have you flogged," he muttered. "Why would you even think it?"

"Because you hate me." Her voice was faint. "And y-you are cruel. It would make a fine sh-show for your men." She stared at the table, white-faced.

"God's death!" An ugly heaviness was spreading through him. That she could think him capable of such a thing! He leaned forward, his voice intense. "I do not hate you, and I have not meant to be cruel."

"You have taken our freedom and separated us. What have you done with my friends anyway?"

"They are safe." No thanks to him, he thought with a pang of guilt. It was a damned lucky thing that Donal and Sky had heard their screams. "They are in comfortable quarters, and you will see them soon. They have the freedom of the upper deck just as you do."

"Then why are they not here eating with us?"

"Because they ate earlier." Lucian smiled, seeing that she was calmer and was looking about the room with curious eyes. "I hear the two of them nearly emptied the larder."

Sarina stared. He had a dimple in one corner of his mouth and seemed a different man entirely when he smiled.

"Here ya go, ma'am, Cap'n . . ." A seaman deposited two heaping platters before them. "Ya both needs to keep up yer strength, I figger." Pinned suddenly by Lucian's icy eyes, he added hurriedly, "Rigors o' the sea, Cap'n. Rigors o' the voyage is all I means. No offense, sir . . ."

"Move on, mister."

Sarina pretended she hadn't heard the rogue's uncouth words. She focused her attention on the delicious-looking fare on her plate and proceeded to disgrace herself by eating everything in sight. When a second helping was brought to the table, she ate that, too. She was so absorbed, she did not realize the Ghost was watching her.

"I'm glad it was edible," he drawled, seeing that she had polished off every scrap.

She wiped her mouth on her handkerchief and gave him a cool gaze.

"It was quite adequate." She simply could not thank him, even though it had been excellent.

Adequate? Lucian thought. The little liar. The food on Douglas' tub was as bad as that on most sailing vessels—moldy and infested with weevils—while he himself made sure his men had only the best. He got to his feet.

"Let us go."

Sarina rose in silence and shook the crumbs from her skirts. This time there were no shouts or whistles, for the mess was empty. The men were on deck. She disregarded their insolent stares and concentrated on staying upright as the *Vengeance* plunged through choppy seas. She could well imagine the howls and hoots if she were thrown into the Ghost's arms.

"You said I would see my friends—where are they?" She was not sure she could believe anything he told her. "You said they have comfortable quarters. Where?"

"My first lieutenant has given them his cabin."

The lieutenant? That Scotsman who could not keep his eyes off Ginelle? Doubtless it was a ruse so he could have her in his power. Before Sarina could voice a protest, the wind rose, whipping her long hair into her eyes and mouth. One violent gust lifted her skirt above her head, and there was laughter and applause as she struggled, pink-faced, to tame it.

Lucian feasted his eyes on the sight. What a luscious little wench she was. A veritable sea sprite with her red mane streaming and her silky green dress plastered to her body, the skirt floating out behind her. When it ballooned upward, he was surprised to see that her legs were naked. And they were beautiful, the sort of legs men dreamed of—long, white, soft, slender yet curvaceous, the knees dimpled, the silky skin covered with a fine pale down. His heart quickened. Soon he would run his hands over them, and he would kiss her from head to toe and then back up to that tempting treasure waiting for him between her thighs.

"If you changed into something more suitable, you would not have this problem," he commented.

"My only problem in this world is you!" she snapped.

"Ah, so you had no wind on the *Stargazer*?"

She gave him a withering gaze. There was absolutely no need for him to know that on the *Stargazer* she had never been on deck in wind like this. Rosie had always brought their meals to them.

"Awooo, mum!"

"Rosie!"

The women flew into each other's arms, and then Ginelle joined them with much hugging and weeping. Lucian waited for several minutes before interrupting the joyous reunion.

"I have a few things to say before I leave you to yourselves."

"Oh, sir, there ain't no need, really!" Rosie protested. "To leave, that is. Do stay."

"Rosie!" Sarina protested.

Lucian hid his amusement. The little trollop was thrusting her tempting bosom at him and batting her eyelashes while Aurora was bent on saving her from his lust.

He said gravely: "I have work to do, Rosie, but first, for your own safety, I expect you all to obey some simple rules while you are aboard my vessel."

Sarina folded her arms over her breasts and stared at the sky in outright defiance. Ginelle and Rosie gave him their rapt attention.

"We eat at four bells, seven bells, and two bells," he said. "Be prompt or you won't eat. Do not go below deck except for meals, and stay in the cabins during the night." His eyes roved over them. "Questions?"

Sarina tapped her foot. As if she could leave the cabin at night, chained as she was to the bed!

"Aboard the *Stargazer* there was no question of our safety," she pointed out.

Lucian ignored her. "Aside from that, ladies, you are free to come and go at will." He gave them a polite bow and strode away.

Sarina ran after him. "Wait!"

He stopped, scowling down at her. "Yes?"

"I really do need some bathwater. We all do. I mean, look at me." He did. He looked at her with such insolence that she could have slapped his face. She lowered her voice. "That was uncalled for."

"My men will bring your bathwater," he said coolly.

"Good," Sarina answered, equally cool and more determined than ever not to thank him for anything.

After a short conference with Ginelle and Rosie, during which they planned to meet again at eight bells, Sarina hurried to the cabin. How wonderful to luxuriate in a tub of lovely warm, fragrant, bubbly water. While she waited for it, she would make her bed, decide what to wear, and—

Noticing a bucket standing inside her door, she went over and peered into it. It was half full of ice-cold water. Her bathwater? she wondered, horrified. It was. Such disappointment rushed over her that she wanted to take the bucket on deck and douse the first man she saw, preferably the Ghost. Of course, she did no such thing. She knew that, unpleasant as it would be, she could get herself just as clean with a cupful of ice water as with a tubful of hot water. But damn the man! He had done this on purpose.

Sarina lifted the bucket to a chair, barred the door, collected her soap, sponge, and towel, and began stripping off her filthy dress and underthings. Oh, that horrible man was going to pay dearly for her discomfort!

Lucian and Donal stood at the rail scanning the horizon.

"Strange," Lucian said, his eyes narrowed against

the glare on the water. "Not a cloud in sight, but I still don't like it. I smell trouble."

"Your nose must be damned good, man," Donal replied. "There is nothing out there that I can see but a slight shift in current. Any changes you want me to make?" As second in command, he was navigator and in charge of setting the sails.

"Keep her as is for now, but I want an alternate route plotted. At this time of year, the weather can change fast." They were headed for his cabin for the charts when Lucian stopped, remembering. "Damn! The wench is taking her bath."

Donal whistled. "I wonder if she closed the ports."

Lucian grinned. "They're closed." He rapped on his door. No answer. He rapped again. Still no answer. Damn.

"I need to come in for a minute," he shouted.

"No." Her voice was small and muffled. "You absolutely cannot come in."

"Damn it, woman, I need my charts. I will count to five and then I'm coming in. Cover yourself with a blanket." At her small shriek he exchanged a grin with Donal. "One . . . two . . ."

"Dastard!"

". . . three . . . this door had better be unlocked . . . four . . ." There were scurrying sounds, and the bolt was slid back. ". . . five . . . ah, very good. Wait here, lieutenant," he told Donal.

As Lucian entered the cabin, the aroma of her lily-scented soap and damp female flesh filled his nostrils. She was sitting on her bunk swathed in a blanket, doubtless glaring at him. He did not look to find out. He needed a clear head for plotting this new course, and her scent alone was a powerful aphrodisiac. At that instant, he knew he was going to have her. Within the hour he would have her. He had waited long enough. He tucked the roll of charts under his arm and made for the door, eyes straight ahead.

"Thank you," he said crisply.

"You are not welcome," Sarina snapped.

She finished her cold, unsatisfying bath in a high temper, thinking that the Ghost was the most demanding, arrogant, bold, high-and-mighty man she had ever encountered. And the handsomest. At the thought, she felt a warm stirring within her. But she would not let herself be attracted. She would not. The man was a criminal, handsome or not, and she, for one, was looking forward to his capture and punishment. Oh, he had so far to fall . . .

She searched wildly through both her trunks for something suitable to wear on the windswept decks of the *Vengeance*, but found absolutely nothing. All of her gowns were fragile, with voluminous skirts. Ryan had insisted. He had never meant for her to climb up and down narrow stairways or be buffeted by gale-force winds. She eventually chose a pink muslin gown and donned it without petticoats. She thrust her bare feet into comfortable old slippers and was brushing her hair, unable to see clearly how she looked in the tiny mirror, when her door opened. She glared at the tall intruder.

"Will you never learn to knock?"

The Ghost went back out, closed the door, and knocked.

Sarina felt foolish. "Now you're being silly. You have already barged in, after all.'

He came in. "You're mighty hard to please."

"You will never please me." Her eyes widened as he closed and barred the door. "Wh-why are you doing that?"

He did not answer. The blue eyes moving over her held a look she had never seen before. Her heart began to race.

"I—I am going on deck . . ." When he shook his head and closed the ports, she cried, "Indeed I am!"

"No."

Sarina flew to the door, but she was too late to slide back the bar. His arms went around her; his lips pressed against the side of her throat. She struggled, trying to prevent his big hands from possessing her. He forced her arms behind her.

"Ten minutes ago you were furious with me."

"This is now." His voice was husky.

Lucian kissed the delectable curves of her breasts heaped above the neckline of her pink gown, ran his fingers over her rounded white arms, and traced the outline of her swanlike throat. His breathing quickened. God, there was nothing more delicious than a soft, newly bathed sweet-smelling woman.

Sarina yearned to kick him and bite his mouth, but remembering his white-faced fury the last time she had resisted, she dared not. This was a man who thought nothing of seizing ships, of abducting women, of flogging men.

"You tempting little wench."

She twisted her head sideways as his lips sought hers, her thoughts bordering on the hysterical. He was going to rape her. This time there would be no escape.

"Please . . ."

Her mouth was taken in a harsh kiss. As she was lifted off her feet and crushed brutally against the steely length of his body, he plundered her mouth again and again, his manhood thrusting hard against her as he carried her to his bunk. He tumbled her onto it, tore the scarlet band from his black hair, and stripped off his shirt. Her horrified eyes could not help but see the muscles moving smoothly and powerfully beneath his dark skin, the broad shoulders tapering to a narrow waist, his chest covered with an inviting mat of silky dark hair. He was an Apollo. But he was also a selfish, uncaring, lustful savage, and she hated him.

"You said you had never raped a woman and never would!" she cried. "What do you call this, pray?"

"It will certainly not be rape. Now be quiet."

"I will not be quiet," she exclaimed as he stretched out beside her. "Rogue! Dastard!" He pulled her into his arms. "Dog! Dog of a pirate! Miserable pigeon-livered hound!"

Laughing, he took her luscious mouth again, but

Sarina was shaking. She was furious and more frightened than she could ever remember being, for all was lost. Everything that mattered in her life was about to be stolen—her honor, her future, Ryan . . . For how could she go to him, a used, dishonored woman?

The answer was that she could not.

Chapter 8

Lucian's eyes burned over the trembling woman he held in his arms. He saw that she was terrified and was hiding it beneath her fury, but he knew her terror would not last. He had not missed her earlier stolen glances at him that left her pink-cheeked and bright-eyed, and already he could taste the delights awaiting him. And he would return them in full measure. Women enjoyed his lovemaking. This little vixen especially would revel in it, having belonged to a crude bastard like Douglas. Cradling her firmly in one arm with her head on his shoulder, he ran a gentle hand across both her breasts.

"Let us see what we have here." He undid the top button of her gown.

"Don't you dare!" She dealt his hand a stinging swat and refastened the button.

Sealing her mouth with a long kiss, he undid the same button. Again she slapped his hand. He laughed, his gaze kindling as it moved over her. "You do it then."

"I will not!"

She struggled to sit up, but he held her fast beside him. Taking one full breast in his hand, he cupped and caressed it. With his other hand, he tilted her face toward his.

"Unspeakable cur! Detestable dastard!" He tasted her rosy lips even as she sputtered outrages at him. "Y-you miserable, horrible—"

"—pigeon-livered hound," he added. "Where did you learn such language, my little cosset? On the docks?"

Lucian took her mouth easily, lazily, kissing the corners, gently exploring its sweet cavern with his tongue, and all the while kneading the full white breast in his hand, kneading the other, stroking her hair, tracing the delicate lines of her exquisitely carved ears and her long, lovely throat.

She was delicious. She tasted and smelled and felt just as he had known she would, and by and by she no longer trembled. Fast, hot gasps of her sweet breath warmed his face and throat. When she kicked his shin suddenly with the toe of her slipper, he was neither surprised nor perturbed. She was spirited and unpredictable, qualities he admired in a woman.

Not interrupting his probing of her mouth and lips, nor stilling his roaming hands, Lucian threw one heavy leg over hers, effectively pinning hers down. She was helpless. He continued to take his time kissing and fondling her, savoring her sweet, soft mouth and the fluttering lids over her glazed eyes, savoring the way her body arched under his gentle stroking. She wanted him, no doubt about it. She was ready to yield. He trailed kisses down to the soft hollow at the base of her throat, then raised his head.

"Unbutton your dress and take it off."

She gasped. "I refuse."

Fine. If she wanted to fight to the last instant, that was all right with him. He pressed his mouth to one hard nipple peaked against the pink fabric of her gown and circled it sensuously with his tongue. He nipped it, sucked on it.

Sarina whimpered, her body writhing of its own volition beneath his mouth as a scalding wave of pleasure swept through her. The bastard! He was doing things to her that no man had ever dared to do, making her feel things she had never felt before, and she hated him for it. She stiffened, steeling herself against such dangerous sensations.

Lucian laughed at the mutinous look on her beautiful face.

"Why pretend you don't like it when you do? I can see you do. Come, Aurora, take off your dress." He touched one dark finger to her pink mouth. "Take everything off."

"I will not!" It had taken great effort not to bite his finger. "And I am not Aurora. Do not call me that."

"What would you prefer I call you?"

"I would prefer to be a thousand miles from here!"

Lucian released her. Enough was enough. He rose abruptly, wordlessly, and strode to a chair where he removed his boots and breeches. He stood naked, gazing down at her, his eyes hooded and dangerous.

Entangled in her long hair and her dress, Sarina had struggled to a sitting position, her back to the wall. Now she glared at him, her breath coming in gasps, her eyes flashing green fire. She would fight him. She would fight until she could fight no more, no matter how furious or abusive he became. She would scratch and kick and yes, bite and— Her head swam as the full impact of his nakedness struck her.

How tall he was. And how long and hard and strong were his tanned arms and legs, sinewy, shadowed with soft dark fur. And those wide shoulders and his hard-muscled chest; his blue eyes hungry, no tenderness in them; his thrusting manhood . . .

Sarina trembled. But it was not the sight of his nakedness or his obvious lust that frightened her; it was the shocking response of her own body, the stream of fire rushing through her veins and consuming her. What was happening to her? She must fight him and fight this passion flaming through her . . .

"Take off your clothes or I will take them off for you," the Ghost said softly, "and I won't bother with buttons . . ."

"I will not!" she exclaimed, but she knew she was going to obey him.

With shaking fingers, she undid the many buttons on her gown, coolly submitting when he slipped it down over her shoulders and hips and then stripped off her linen chemise. Her face burned with shame even as her body burned with desire at the touch of his dark hands. When nothing remained to cover her nakedness from his hot gaze but the cloud of soft red-gold hair veiling her breasts, he lifted the curls gently so that they fell down her back. He then lowered his head and took one upthrust nipple in his mouth. Sarina moaned. Heat seared her breasts, her entire body, though she told herself she hated the way she felt, and hated him. Hated her body for betraying her.

Lucian was ready, and by the looks of the wench, so was she, eyes glazed and hooded, lips parted, nipples as taut and full as rosebuds, breath coming in little pants. His own breathing was short and ragged. He touched his shaft to her, positioning it, feasting his eyes on her.

He thought again that she was the most beautiful woman he had ever seen. But more important, she belonged to his enemy. Holding that dark thought in his mind, savoring it, Lucian smoothed and kissed and stroked her once more and then, as gently as his raging passion would allow, he took her.

Until that moment, Sarina had been winning her battle against those delicious sensations forced upon her. Struggling to think of other things, she had fought the fire fed by the Ghost's searing lips, his hands that branded her flesh, his hot shaft teasing, and titillating her as he gently searched for entry.

When at last he thrust within her, she gave a cry that was half astonishment, half pain, and saw the disbelief in his eyes. Then fury leapt within her. Fury at herself for yielding so easily and fury at him for hurting her so. Why had she not fought harder? Oh, she despised him. She could kill him! Instinctively, she lashed out, her nails leaving four ugly gashes on his cheek. It did not deter him. Her tears mingled with his kisses as he pinned her hands above her head and began moving heavily, rhythmically, pushing ever more deeply within her.

He had conquered her, Sarina thought bitterly, but he would pay for it. He was going to be caught and hanged. Either that or Ryan would kill him, or her father—or she herself would do the deed. And she would be glad; oh, she would be glad. She lay like a board beneath him, an unresponsive hate-filled aching board, her mouth and face stiff, not even aware that the pain had faded until a strange, invading warmth began seeping into her consciousness.

At first one small burning bud of sweetness, it was soon flowering and swelling, filling her whole body with its nectar as she was carried along by the man above her to a place, a height so wondrous that she could scarcely bear it. In the end, there was such wild release, such an ecstatic explosion, that she was left limp and weeping. But almost instantly, the stark reality of what had happened overwhelmed her. Her honor was gone, as was her future with Ryan, both gone, stolen from her because this criminal could not control his animal lust.

Tears of bitterness replaced her tears of release. In addition to her shame, she was frightened and confused. What was this terrible passion that had caused her to yield when she had vowed to fight? Even now, she was glowing from head to toe in its aftermath. Oh, it was hideous. Never in her worst nightmares had she dreamed that such a thing could be. She continued to sob, her face buried in the wet pillow as the Ghost rose from the bed, silently clothed himself, and just as silently left the cabin.

Lucian's mood was dangerous as he strode onto the pitching deck of the *Vengeance*. He had done as he had intended, easily and thoroughly seducing his captive until she became warm and submissive, but damn it all to hell, now he felt consumed with guilt. She was not at all what he had expected. When had Ryan Douglas ever left a woman a virgin? His thoughts tossed, whirled, a morass of confusion and regret with only one thing clear: his hatred for his enemy had blinded him to the truth. She was not a wanton, not the coy, teasing sort of female Douglas preferred. She had not been playing games. She had meant it when she said no . . .

He angrily dabbed his bloodied cheek with his sash before knotting it around his head to tame his hair. He ground his teeth in helpless fury. She had softened and yielded, yes, but what else in bloody hell could she have done? Doubtless she thought he would give her to his crew or beat or kill her if she refused. He was six feet two inches of powerful male whereas she was only a soft, slender woman, a frail dove trying desperately not to show her terror. And he had taken her. Now he had to get his damned face cleaned up, the blood stanched so his crew would not smirk behind his back. He gave a disgusted growl. They would see the scratches anyway, and he would deserve their derision.

"Sir"—it was Donal—"there is a slight wind from the southwest but little change in current." Not once did his black eyes stray to Lucian's cheek, where the bloody stripes were stinging like fire.

"Good, lieutenant. Keep her steady as she is."

"Aye, sir. Ah, here are Sky and the ladies."

Lucian's temper went from hot to sizzling. Why didn't the whole damned crew parade by before he could sponge off the blood?

"Awooo, sir, whatever happint ta your poor cheek?" Rosie exclaimed. " 'Tis a right wicked-lookin' wound ye have. Almost like ye'd been clawed by some beast." Her brown eyes were wide and sympathetic. "Ye'd best warsh it off good so's not to get the putred fever, sir."

Lucian ignored her and gave Sky a black scowl. "Well, mister, what is it? I'm in a hurry."

"The lady is right, sir," Sky drawled, his silvery eyes resting with languid curiosity on his friend's face. "Ye'd best slather some o' my special ointment on it. Cleanse it first with the fever wash. They're both in the cabinet in my—"

"I know where they are," Lucian snapped.

Sky blinked. "Aside from that, sir, my only question is for the ladies—they're lookin' for their friend. She was to meet them on the bow at eight bells, but she didn't turn up. I told them you might—"

"She is indisposed at the present," Lucian said, barely moving his tight lips. "You may take the ladies back to their cabin, Mister."

Rosie squawked. "But sir, yer said—" Her protest was stilled by the ice in Lucian's eyes.

"Now," he said.

"What have you done to Sarina?" Ginelle cried. "I want to see her."

"Men, get these females out of my sight and keep them out."

"Ay, sir." Donal took the blonde's plump white elbow. "Now then, Guinevere," he said softly, "let me get you a tasty little tidbit to tide you over 'til dinner . . ."

"I do not want a tasty tidbit." Ginelle whimpered, trying to pull free. "I want my friend."

Donal promptly released her elbow and slipped a possessive arm around her waist instead. "Hush now, little one, she's foine, I'm sure. She'll have a headache, I wager. Come, fondling, aren't ye a foine brave lassie now?"

Lucian stared after his second in command. Guinevere? What in the blazing hell was that all about? Had she actually told him her name? And that Scottish burr. Only the deepest of emotions ever stirred Donal Fleming to the Scotch burr he had worked so hard to lose. Lucian glanced at Sky Braden, but Sky's gray eyes were roving over the brunette's luscious body.

"Come along, girl." His voice was firm but kindly. "If the cap'n says you're to go to the cabin, the cabin it is. You're sure to find something of interest to do there." His dark hand slipped around her upper arm.

"Oh, sir, yer so helpful."

Lucian strode to Sky's cabin, found the wash and ointment, then strained to see what damage had been done to him. Sky's mirror was as bad as his own, but it was clear the wench had done some damage. He sponged the deep scratches with the fever wash, cringed when it stung, then used the ointment sparingly.

But he was at fault, and there was no way he could make it up to her. What was done was done. He could still see the shock in her eyes when he took her. Great God almighty, what devil had ever possessed him to bring those three aboard in the first place? He shook his head, disgusted with himself.

He was weary beyond words, and Sky's bunk was a temptation he could not resist. From what he had just seen, Sky was going to be busy for a while anyway, and Donal was feeding the little blonde her tidbit. He would stretch out and close his eyes just for a minute.

"Lucian, wake up, man!"

Donal was shaking his arm. Sky, too, was there, his face grim. It took Lucian only an instant to spring to his feet.

"Trouble?"

"Aye."

He headed for the deck. "How long?"

"It just started."

"Withdraw cannons and close all ports."

"Aye."

On deck, Lucian looked out upon sullen, oily swells and a rapidly darkening sky. He immediately noted the change in wind. It was from the south now, not the southwest, and even as he reckoned the situation, the tide turned against them and a squall came screaming over the horizon, bringing heavy mist and churning the water to thick white froth. Almost instantly, the seas grew mountainous and the air cold. Lucian sent men up on the yard to try and control the main topsail, but the bolt rope broke.

"She's goin'!" Donal cried. "God in heaven, she's splittin' to ribbons already."

"Luc, the yard's sprung!" Sky shouted.

Lucian's eyes, narrowed against the stinging wind-driven sleet, studied the splintered spar. There was no way it could be lowered for repair and a new sail bent now, and he dared not lose his ability to maneuver his vessel. His mind clicked rapidly over various solutions and settled on the best.

"Trim the yards and sheets to get the wind abeam, and then I want men in the shrouds," he shouted to Donal above the howling wind.

"The shrouds!" Sky goggled at him.

"Man, you're crazy!" Donal yelled.

"We've got to act as a wind vane to keep her head off the wind," he yelled. "Damn it to hell, move!"

"We're with you, lad," agreed Sky.

As his orders were followed, Lucian himself made for the shrouds and rapidly ascended the mast, whose ropes converged on the bowsprit.

As the wind blew more ferociously than ever and shredded the split mainsail to threads, the startled crew was ordered to follow Lucian's lead. Soon, twenty-four men, Sky and Donal among them, were clinging to the shrouds, those ropes and wires which held steady the long, graceful snout of the *Vengeance*'s bowsprit. Beneath them was nothing but empty space and snarling wind and frothing seas.

Lucian clung to the topmost rigging, his body taking the full force of the wind and icy rain. His hands, gripping the taut rope and wires, seemed frozen already. But if he was right, and he had seen many such capricious squalls before, this one would die as quickly as it was born.

Suddenly, far below on the gleaming wave-washed deck, he saw a small pink-clad figure with flying red hair. It flitted to the rail and clung there, swaying. Aurora! Lucian's heart gave a terrible thump, stopped, and then roared in his ears. At any moment she could be swept overboard and swallowed by the hungry sea. He knew terror at the thought, and sadness. Never to hold her sweet, soft body in his arms again; never to say he was sorry. God, the fool, could she not see her terrible danger? He shouted down at her, knowing she could not hear him above the storm's fury.

"Go back! Back!"

She looked up, and he made a desperate gesture toward the cabin, imperiling his own life by letting go of the ropes. She stared wide-eyed for just an instant and then obeyed. Lucian held his breath as she made her way to safety and the door closed after her. He was weak with relief, his near-frozen arms and hands aching as if they had been laid to fire, but he had to hold on. Just a little longer . . .

Sarina had cried herself to sleep and been awakened when she was tumbled out of bed onto the floor by the storm. Deathly afraid of being trapped in the cabin of a sinking ship, she had fled on deck. Now she was back on her bunk trembling, the awful memory of what she had just seen impressed on her mind: bare spars, reefed sails, a suffocating wall of ghostly mist and spray enveloping the ship as the bow plunged and rose, plunged and rose. The mainsail was nothing but strings, and the seas were so black and steep and raging that she knew the *Vengeance* would go to the bottom if a wave hit them broadside. But the most frightening thing of all, above the bowsprit and hanging onto the shrouds, had been the Ghost and his men.

Sarina did not understand why he—why any of them—should be in such a precarious place. She only knew that he could fall into the sea and be gone in an instant. And if he did fall, if the Ghost's strong arms faltered, they would all be lost . . .

Chapter 9

The squall behaved as Lucian thought it might, roaring over them like a thousand devils straight from hell and then leaving in an hour's time. The wind still battered them with its icy breath, but the sleet and the black skies were gone and the sun came out. He ordered his men down from the shrouds. They descended, shaking with weariness and terror, grateful to be on solid deck once more. Lucian clasped the shoulders of one lad, as brawny as a young bull but as tender in years as Lucian himself had been on his own first sea voyage.

"I'm proud to have you aboard, Mister."

The boy gulped, blinked. "An' I'm proud to be aboard, sir. What a caper!"

"See how they are doing with the pumps, man."

"Aye, sir."

They were lucky, Lucian thought, looking around him. Damned lucky. He had seen ships capsized during such storms, and men swept overboard or killed outright, their backs or necks broken. Although the *Vengeance* had had her yard split and the mainsail was gone, his men were safe. It was all that mattered.

"Lieutenant," he called to Donal, "check our bearings and report immediately. We will lie to under bare poles for the next several hours."

"Aye, sir."

Lucian knew that a sudden letup in a squall could be followed by disaster, the winds returning with such renewed violence that all sails could be torn from the yards.

"Woodings, take several men and check the upper works for looseness. Brown, have your men check every seam."

He issued command after command. There was work to be done and done fast. The yard was lowered and repaired, the riggings mended, a new sail bent. Without her mainsail the *Vengeance* was a sitting duck. Lucian himself began emptying the water troughs into the giant earthenware jars fastened in the shrouds. As he worked, his mind drifted back to what had happened in his cabin before the storm. Regret weighed heavily on him. How was Aurora now? Was she still crying? He emptied a trough and replaced it under the collection mat. He had to know. He started for his cabin.

"Sir—"

"Aye, Mister?" His eyes met Donal's and he wondered, had his old friend treated the little blonde as badly? And Sky, the pretty little Rosie? He doubted it. "Have you looked in on the two in your cabin?" he asked Donal.

"Aye. They're fine."

"Good."

"Sir, we've been blown north so far that we may as well head for Malaga," Donal said. "The wind is from the south and the current's gone crazy. With no mainsail, we can only follow it."

Lucian considered the other alternatives and found no good reason not to head for his island home off the Virginia coast. In fact, there was every reason *for* doing so. When he encountered his enemy on the armed *Manxman*, he wanted the *Vengeance* to be in top condition. He gave Donal a slap on the back.

"Malaga it is, man."

"Shall I set us a double reef course?"

"Aye, after an hour or so. I want to make sure the strong wind does not return."

It was a wonderful idea, going home, he thought. The women would be much better off on Malaga. His thoughts returned to the sea nymph in his cabin. He had to know how she was . . .

Sarina sat on her bunk, knees pulled up to her tensed body and her head pressed to them. Her eyes were closed. The ship was still pitching wildly, but at least she no longer heard the wind screaming or the sleet hitting the port side. She could not erase from her mind the terrible sight she had seen such a short time ago, those white-faced men hanging in the shrouds. She realized now that they had been replacing the shredded sail. What strength and courage it had taken to climb the riggings and cling there at the height of the storm. Without them, criminals or not, she suspected the *Vengeance* might now be lying at the bottom of the Atlantic.

She remembered the Ghost clinging to the highest point where the wind was whipping its hardest. When lightning had slashed nearby, she had seen his dark handsome face etched in fiery blue. He had looked so unafraid, his eyes filled with such unholy excitement, that even now she shivered at the memory. What sort of man was he to thrive on such danger?

She knew already. He was a man who feared no one, a man who would stop at nothing to get what he wanted. And he wanted her . . .

Sarina opened her eyes and gazed beyond the port. Seeing that the sky was blue again, she rose and looked out at the steep, frothing waves. Was the worst over? She yearned to go on deck to see what was happening, to look for Ginelle and Rosie, but she was sure to encounter the Ghost there. If only she never had to see him again!

She sighed. It was wishful thinking. He ruled this ship with an iron hand, and she could well imagine his plans for her from now on. She would be chained to the bed during the days as well as the nights so as to be readily available for him. The bastard. It stung her that no other man, not even Ryan, had ever excited her as he had. Of course they had not, she told herself.

The men she knew were all gentlemen. They had never even touched her, let alone dishonored her. And how shameful that she had allowed herself to melt, to—to positively wallow in sensations against which she should have fought.

She angrily thrust away the memory, only to have it return more vividly than ever, his teasing and kissing and stroking and licking her. Ryan had never licked her! She jumped to her feet and paced, her hands pressed to her burning cheeks. Oh, she was so confused. She should have hated it, all of it, so why had she not? Was she growing wanton?

Another thought jolted her so that she had to sit down. Had the Ghost fallen into that black, raging sea and drowned? Would she never see him again? Never see his face or feel his kisses or his arms around her again? The possibility numbed her. She buried her face in her hands. And if, God forbid, that were so, it meant the three of them were at the mercy of the crew . . .

Sarina started at the soft knock on her door. When it opened to reveal the Ghost, her relief was so great that her knees began to shake. He was safe! Oh, thank God, he was safe. She saw that he was drenched and utterly weary. Rivulets of water streamed down his face from his black hair, and his clothing was plastered to his strong frame. Then, seeing the red gashes on his cheek, and remembering how they came there, Sarina grew angry all over again.

"Are you all right?" His voice was low.

She gave a bitter laugh. "It is a trifle late to ask, don't you think? And now I suppose you have come to chain me to the bed again."

A muscle clenched in his jaw. "Hardly. Not until bedtime." He went to his trunk, yanked out several articles of clothing, and tossed them over his shoulder. "You may not realize what a storm we just came through."

"I have been to sea before and I am not stupid."

"Don't you know you could have been killed out there? Swept overboard?"

"How kind of you to be concerned." She moved to the port and gazed out stonily, arms folded across her breasts, head held high.

Every time Lucian looked at her, he wanted her. He wanted to entice and beguile and seduce her again, to have her soft and squirming in his arms. He knew her slender, sensuous body would yield to him long before her will surrendered. But was he hardened enough to take advantage of it and not concern himself with her feelings? For three years now, vengeance had been all that mattered to him. Night and day, he had lived and breathed and slept vengeance, and now, to have her in his power, to have the ultimate weapon with which to shame and humiliate and enrage his enemy . . . But how far to go? It was a thing he must weigh and consider very carefully. He closed the trunk and moved to the door.

"Dinner will be late," he said. He did not look at her or wait for any sassy answer. He left.

Sarina was not hungry, but she had to get out of the cabin. And she wanted desperately to see Ginelle and Rosie. When she grew brave enough to steal down the companionway to the mess, she found her friends already seated at one of the oak-plank tables which were lowered from overhead at mealtimes. Ginelle waved wildly, motioning her over. Strangely, the men paid them little heed. They were wolfing down their food and discussing the storm and the repairs that were under way.

Ginelle embraced her. "Oh, Rina, are you all right? We were so worried, what with that hideous storm and all, and why did you not meet us? The Ghost said you were 'indisposed'—what does that mean?—and he looked so furious. Oh, love, did he hurt you?"

"I told 'er yer musta give the handsome devil a thing er two ta think about, mum, seein' them bloody gashes on 'is face. 'Tweren't no beast what give 'im those, I said, for I knows fingernail scratches when I sees them, havin' give out plenty o' me own. But oh, mum, are yer all right?"

"I'm fine," Sarina assured them both. Now was certainly not the time or the place to tell them the truth, or even hint at it, and start them worrying. In fact, she was not sure she could ever tell them.

"But them scratches . . ." Rosie persisted.

"Frankly, I had not noticed. I scarcely ever look at the man, and I would rather not talk about him if you do not mind." She dug briskly into the food that had been brought to her. "I want to hear about you both. Were you as terrified as I was during the squall? And how did you come to be quartered in the lieutenant's cabin?"

Ginelle answered all of her questions, adding in a whisper, "And now the lieutenant says we can stay there for the whole voyage. He's quite nice actually, Rina, a real gentleman, and he has told the men he will not tolerate any rudeness toward us."

Sarina stared at the rising color in her friend's fair complexion.

"You—like him!"

"As a matter of fact I do. I like him very much."

"An' my Mr. Quartermaster's a dear, too, mum. I'm under his complete protection. He says any man what touches me will taste the cat, an' he arter know as he's the one what wields it."

Seeing that Rosie was completely smitten with the man, Sarina asked, "But what about your Joe?"

Rosie blinked, innocent as a spring lamb. "Joe who, mum?"

Sarina almost felt ill. What had happened for all three of them to yield to the flattery and the wiles of criminals? She was certain that when they reached land, the madness would end, but when would that be? And until that time, it was clear they needed each other's support and protection. After a hasty discussion, it was agreed that they would confront the Ghost and demand, absolutely demand, that they share quarters.

They found him in the bow, his watchful blue eyes noting everything: his men working on repairs in the twilight, how the current was running, each small change in the wind's direction. Sarina nervously cleared her throat and straightened her back. It brought the top of her coppery head to his breastbone.

"Captain?"

He looked down at her, his expression remote. "Yes?"

She was determined to be polite, for what she wanted meant a great deal to all of them.

"I—I would like very much to be with my friends. As I said before, we want to be quartered together. May I move to their cabin?" She held her breath.

"No."

Her anger flared. "No?"

"No." His eyes, strangely empty, flickered over her before returning to the horizon.

Sarina looked to Rosie and Ginelle for support and found them like statues, too terrified to speak. She opened her mouth to argue but did not. What was the use? She would succeed only in angering him. His power over her, over them all, was so complete that he could do whatever he wanted and she could not do a thing about it. With great effort, she kept her temper as the three of them walked to the waist of the ship.

"Well, I suppose that is that," she said, hiding her fury and disappointment.

"Rina, I am so ashamed," Ginelle began faintly.

"An' me, mum. Beggin' your pardon, but me mouth jist wun't open. Awooo, he's a scary bugger when his eyes is icy like that." Rosie shuddered.

"Perhaps tomorrow he will be more amenable," Sarina murmured. "I—I'm tired now, dears. I think I'll go to bed." Seeing the distress on Ginelle's face, she whispered, "It's all right. Please don't worry. We'll meet at breakfast then?" Ginelle nodded.

Back in her cabin, Sarina threw herself onto the bunk. She wanted to cry and scream and rage and throw his books and his chessmen. Yes, and perhaps be bound and gagged for her trouble. No, it would not do. She would have to behave herself and bide her time. But somehow, someway, someday she would pay

him back for all of the humiliation he was heaping upon
her.

Her fear during the storm had drained her body, yet
her mind was still alert and filled with angry thoughts.
She would not be able to sleep. She decided to soothe
herself with Shakespeare. Taking the small book of
sonnets from the bookcase, Sarina crawled into bed
fully clothed in the pink muslin gown that the Ghost
had stripped from her that morning. From now on, she
vowed hotly, she would go to bed dressed in the clothing she wore during the day. She was not going to
make things easy for him!

She ran her fingers gently over the book's fine leather
binding, thinking once more how strange it was that
the captain of the ghost ship would have so many
books. She opened the volume and gazed at the in-
scription penned in a firm, boyish hand. *From Shane
with admiration*, it said.

Shane . . . Sarina's curiosity was forgotten as the
book fell open to the very page she wanted to read.
How remarkable. Did it mean that the Ghost, too,
loved this sonnet, perhaps even drawing strength from
it as she herself did? The page was badly soiled and
dog-eared, and she stared at the suspicious-looking
smears on it. She sniffed in distaste. Doubtless they
were bloodstains, considering the wild and reckless life
he lived. And doubtless they were well-deserved. With
that, she forgot them and began eagerly to read: *When
in disgrace with fortune and men's eyes* . . .

Sarina had finished her reading and lain sleepless for
what seemed like hours when the door opened and the
Ghost came in. In the moonglow filtering through the
port, she watched him come to her. Her heart pounded
so hard that she thought she might faint, but she kept
her breathing deep and regular, pretending sleep.

"Aurora?" When she made no answer, he sat down
on the bunk beside her. "I know you're not asleep,"
he said, his voice soft and so deep that it set up a vi-
bration inside her.

"Go away."

"Not until I put this on you . . ."

Feeling the hated bracelet go around her wrist, Sarina cried, "Again? You mean to tell me I am to be chained every night?"

"Every night." The tiny key clicked in the lock.

"What kind of man are you to be afraid of a woman?"

"A man who wants to wake up in one piece in the morning."

"If I were on the *Stargazer*, you would have no problem," she said. "Or if I were with my friends . . ." The chain clanked as he attached it to her bunk.

"That is not possible," he said gruffly. "I'm sorry."

He went to a port and breathed the night air into his lungs. Being near her for even that short a time had intoxicated him. His nostrils were filled with her scent and the fragrance of her warm breath, and his mind reeled with the remembered taste of her flesh and mouth, the feel of her full breasts in his hands.

"You are heartless. Merciless . . ."

"Yes."

Was he going to make love to her tonight or not? he brooded, then caught himself abruptly. Bastard. Had he forgotten so soon what he had done to her? His thoughts were a jumble of contrasting images: Aurora weeping, scratching him, and then warm and yielding, arching against him, whimpering, giving him her hungry kisses, her yearning body, and then more weeping.

Hell. For certain, he meant to enjoy unprecedented pleasure in the coming weeks, followed by more unprecedented pleasure when Douglas learned of what he'd done. The devil would be wild with fury. But uneasiness nagged Lucian, a vague feeling that he might destroy this woman as easily as he seduced her. He shook his head. He was growing addled on the subject, making her out to be some impossibly fragile flower when it was clear she had enjoyed herself, at least part of the time. He drew another deep breath and began stripping off his clothing.

In the pale light streaming through the port, Sarina gazed resentfully at the Ghost's tall, naked body, the moonlight turning it into a harshly beautiful study in shadow and silver. She resisted the memory of their lovemaking until finally it overwhelmed her: the salty male taste of him, his long hard body pressing her into the bed, squeezing the breath out of her and taking her strength, her will, her very being for his own. Oh, she loathed him. She loathed his strength and his power. No one should have such power over another human being as he had over her.

"You are unfeeling and ruthless and contemptible," she cried.

"All of that," Lucian agreed quietly, getting into his own bunk.

Was there nothing that she could do or say to hurt him? she wondered, seething. How she yearned to pull him down and trample him, crush his pride and his arrogance.

Lucian lay staring at the silver-drenched night beyond the port, but all of his senses were focused on the woman in the other bed. He was taut, heart roaring, blood racing, manhood erect. He wanted to stretch out beside her and pull her close. He wanted to feel every inch of her soft, smooth body pressed hard against him; wanted to kiss her everywhere, on her long sweeping lashes, the tip of her adorable nose, her saucy pink nipples, her soft rounded belly, even the pink soles of her feet. He wanted to be inside her.

Damn it, why should he not have her? She was booty. Any other sea wolf would have had her many times over by now and been sharing her with his men. Why should he be softhearted just because she was not the tart he had expected? She was Douglas' woman, wasn't she? Any female who chose that bastard for a husband had to be a wrong one, either that or dim-witted.

He sighed and turned over. Dim-witted she was not. She was bright, and she was gently bred and sensitive and brave and high-spirited. Somehow, God alone knew how, Douglas had gotten himself a woman whom any man would be proud of. And Lucian wanted her for himself.

"Aurora .."

"I refuse to speak to you as long as this chain is on me."

His breathing was uneven and his thoughts lustful. He cursed his hunger and forced himself to dwell on her weakness, her helplessness. She was completely at his mercy.

"Aurora, I want to make love."

Sarina pulled the blanket over her head and curled up into a ball. Was it all the man ever thought of? Suddenly she knew how to hurt him. Men were such vain creatures. She lowered her blanket.

"You realize," she said, forcing her voice to icy loathing, "that I will never let you touch me of my own free will. Your touch nauseates me. You make me feel dirty."

He said nothing. The only sounds she heard were the ever-present creaking and groaning of the ship, the wash of waves against her plunging bow, and the sigh of wind in the sails. Frantic to goad him, Sarina raised her voice.

"I would willingly sleep with anyone but you. Anyone. Not only do you make me feel dirty, but you are completely inadequate."

Inadequate? Lucian chuckled softly. "Is that so?"

"It—it certainly is," she said.

When he rose from his bunk and closed the ports, Sarina's heart sank. She had made a dreadful blunder thinking that he would react as any normal man might to such an insult. He was too confident, too assured to sink into a deep dolor over something he knew was not true. The chain clanked as she hurriedly sat up, her back against the wall.

"Stay away from me!"

"It seems I must try harder, my cosset."

"If you so much as t-touch me," Sarina said from

between clenched teeth, "I will strangle you with this chain. I swear it!"

Lucian laughed softly. He pulled off her blanket and tossed it to the floor.

"I am going to make love to you, Aurora."

"It takes two to make love," she cried.

"I think this time you will find me more than— adequate." He got into her bunk, caught her around the waist, and pulled her close. "Little tease . . ."

"I swear you will regret this—" She struggled, pushing against his chest. "I will pay you back, pirate dog!"

"Shhh." His lips sought hers.

"I swear it," she cried as he took her mouth in a deep kiss.

Sarina twisted her face from his and tried to pull free, but he was too powerful. With one arm, he held her easily against him, and though she tried to prevent it, he unbuttoned her gown, all the while kissing her lips, her face, her throat. Once again the familiar magic that she had experienced in his arms began flowing through her, burning her, melting her, making her so soft, so lacking in strength, that she could not have snapped her fingers, let alone resisted him . . .

Chapter 10

The next morning Sarina was agonizing over how she was going to bear the remainder of the journey when two seamen appeared at her door.

"Yes?" She gave them an icy look.

"Yer to be wi' t'other ladies from now on," said one.

"What?"

"Cap'n's orders." Without waiting for her reply, they lifted one of her trunks and ordered her to follow them.

Sarina obeyed, bewildered but grateful to escape a situation that had become intolerable. She could no longer deny the strange magic that existed between herself and the captain of the *Vengeance*, a magic that had placed her on a precarious border between heaven and hell, between ecstasy and disaster.

She was a woman about to be married, yet last night another man had lifted her to a rapture she had never known existed. When he had returned to his own bunk, she had lain awake for hours, tormented by guilt and confusion and resentful that he could sleep.

And now he was tired of her, she thought, marching behind his men to the lieutenant's cabin. Fine. He had gotten what he wanted and was ready to forget her. Good, good! She was just as ready to forget him. The day would come when he would discover he could not use women so cavalierly. At least not this woman.

Sarina spent the following days with Ginelle and Rosie. She chattered with them endlessly, played card games, and laughed gaily at anything and everything. She was not happy. She doubted she could ever be truly happy again. But she was pleased that their lives had become relatively uncomplicated. They were protected from the crew, the Ghost now kept his distance, and they were headed for land, a place called Malaga.

They did not know what or where it was, but it mattered little. It would be solid earth inhabited by other people. Even if they were guarded, Sarina meant to find a means of escape. She could not sit by helplessly awaiting rescue. And in Malaga they could bathe properly, wash their hair and clothes, and walk without falling down. Oh, it would be wonderful.

It was sunset on June 15 when Sarina saw mist on the horizon. Ginelle smelled earth and grass and the perfume of blossoms.

"Could that be it?" She gasped, pointing to the low-lying mist.

"Why, mum, that ain't nothink but an island," Rosie said, peering harder as they drew closer. "An island out in the middle o' nowhere. That surely ain't it."

"I agree," Sarina murmured. "That surely cannot be it. Of what possible value would such a place be to the Ghost?"

She tried to stem her growing unease, but common sense told her that it was a perfect hiding place for a criminal. It was isolated and looked forbidding, with sheer cliffs on one side, breakers crashing on the boulder-strewn shore and behind it, a junglelike terrain of impenetrable trees and brush. Ginelle flew to the lieutenant.

"Sir . . ."

"Aye, lovely lady?" His black eyes danced.

"I trust that very ominous-looking island is not Malaga?"

Donal grinned. "As a matter of fact, it is. I can't talk now, lass, but later I will show you around."

"But it is a—an awful-looking place," Ginelle said.

"We thought, we hoped, we were going to a town! Oh, Lieutenant . . ."

He patted her shoulder, and Sarina was shocked by the affection she saw in his eyes.

"There, there, lass, ye'll like it, I promise. An' now, we've got work to do."

The three women stood in a forlorn huddle at the rail as every man did his job. Sails were furled and oars were brought into play as the *Vengeance* drew perilously close to where the breakers were crashing onto the beach.

"We're going to run aground!" Ginelle shrieked.

"Awooo, I'm too young to die!" Rosie wailed.

"Look," Sarina cried.

She had been watching in horror as they drew closer and closer to what had seemed a green cliff. Now she saw that it moved and swayed in the wind. They were going through a thick curtain of vines, some of which snapped off and became entangled in the spars and yards as the *Vengeance* passed through them and into a quiet inlet.

Sarina watched gloomily as the oars dipped and rose, dipped and rose in perfect unison to carry them deeper into the green recesses of what seemed to be a cluster of islands. It was breathtakingly beautiful, but here they would be every bit as captive as they had been at sea. And they would never be found. Deep waterways lay between the islands, and above them was a canopy of leaves. At last the *Vengeance* came to rest in a bay whose white sandy shore stretched almost to the house that stood there.

Sarina stared at it, never having seen anything so exotic. It was low and rambling, made of wood, with a thatch roof. A covered porch wrapped around the three sides she could see.

"Ladies, welcome to Malaga," the lieutenant said, his smile white in his handsome face. "We will get you ashore in just a bit . . ."

The day after they arrived on Malaga, even Sarina admitted, grudgingly, that Malaga was a paradise. It was blessed with blue skies, white sand, soft winds, and flowering fruit trees and berry bushes. Vegetables grew wild, fish and fowl begged to be caught, and there was an abundance of sweet rainwater to drink.

"I have never seen anything so beautiful," Ginelle said softly as the two women plucked berries for dessert. "And the lieutenant says the adjacent islands are equally beautiful. He will show them to me, to all of us if we wish, tomorrow." Seeing Sarina's compressed lips, she gasped, "Oh, Rina, oh dear, I am sorry. It is dreadful, I know, your not having Ryan here with you."

"Is that not rather beside the point?" Sarina asked coolly. "We have been abducted, brought here by force, Ryan's cargo sunk, his sails slashed, ransom being asked for my return . . ." And she had been raped, not once but twice.

But it had not been rape, she reminded herself bitterly. Had she truly been raped, she would not have responded as she had. If she had absolutely refused him and not wilted so ridiculously in his arms, the Ghost would have withdrawn his attentions, she was certain of it. He was far too proud a man to have forced her. With his romantic good looks and commanding presence, he had no need to force any woman. No, it was not rape, but rather seduction. He had coaxed and teased and caressed and kissed her until she was wild with need for him. He was a master of seduction, she thought angrily, and weak fool that she was, she had surrendered to him.

Ginelle's cornflower-blue eyes swam. "I'm a thoughtless, empty-headed beast." She sank to the grass, as did Sarina. "All of what you say is true, yet none of it changes the fact that the lieutenant is wonderful. He says there is a good reason for what they are doing."

"Oh, doubtless," Sarina snapped. "Does the man not have a name?"

Ginelle blinked. "I did not ask. I just assumed he wouldn't tell me." She peered up at the canopy of dark shiny leaves where brightly colored birds were fluttering from branch to branch, chirping and twittering. "He calls me Guinevere . . ." When Sarina gave no answer, she blurted, "Oh, Rina, I know it's awful of me, but I love it here. And he is the sweetest man I have ever known. I'm sorry, but it's true . . ." When Sarina emitted a small snort, Ginelle asked, "Was the Ghost not the least bit nice with you when you shared his cabin?"

"Nice?" She looked at her friend askance.

"I mean, he's so handsome and virile and—"

Sarina flushed. As Ginelle's eyes widened in astonishment, Sarina remembered her naked body sealed to his, his tongue expertly coaxing hers to dance and flicker with his, his hungry mouth seeking her throat, her lips, her eyes, everywhere, and his—his . . . No! She was determined to forget the way she had felt.

"Sarina Fairburn," Ginelle whispered, "so he was nice to you. Did you kiss him? Did he kiss you?"

Sarina shot her a hurt gaze. How innocent she was. As innocent as she herself had been when their voyage first began. She got to her feet.

"Are you not forgetting something—such as the fact that I was on my way to be married and that you were to be my maid of honor?"

Ginelle, always impetuous, flung her arms around her friend's neck. "Oh, Rina! Oh, I hate myself! I would not blame you a bit if you hated me, too." She fell into a shamed silence as they made their way back to the Ghost's bungalow.

Ryan Douglas paced the floor of his office in Bolting Street. He had just returned from Florida to face a desk piled high with work. In addition, the damned Ghost was still at large; he had found neither hide nor hair of the bastard during his week in southern waters. And as if that were not enough, Sarina would be arriving within a week or two, and there were a thousand things undone. At least the ice-blue gown had been ordered. He raised a golden pomander to his nostrils, inhaled deeply of its scent, and returned to his desk.

"Mr. Douglas, sir."

Ryan scowled at the loud rapping. "Come in, come in. What is it, Hastings? You know I am never to be disturbed when I do the accounts."

"Sir, there is dreadful news!"

"Indeed?" Ryan frowned at the grim-faced stranger following close on Hastings' heels.

"I'm Captain Quirk o' the *Graybill*, sir, and I'll get right to the point. We come on your *Stargazer* wallowing and helpless the morning o' the twenty-eighth. She'd been attacked by pirates the day before an' her cargo dumped. Th' ladies was carried off."

Ryan leaped to his feet so abruptly that his chair was knocked over. "What? Carried off?"

"Aye. Carried off to God knows what fate."

Ryan was so incensed, he could not speak.

"Your men made mention of a ghost," Quirk continued, "though it made no sense to us then nor does it now. At any rate, we laid to alongside o' her for a day an' helped mend her sails. I told Captain Gray I'd stop by an' tell you. He wasn't sure when they'd get here . . ."

As Ryan's wits returned, he realized this was news that George Fairburn must not hear. Not yet.

"I would appreciate it, sir," he said, lowering his voice, "if you kept your crew quiet about this matter for now. It will be worth their while."

Robert Quirk's curious eyes moved over the elegantly dressed owner of Douglas Traders. "Well, now, sir, fancy that. I thought that might be the case, an' I already warned them to keep their mouths shut."

And he must warn Jon Gray, Ryan thought angrily, and the *Stargazer* crew, and that fool, Hastings, and anyone else who had overheard. The news must go no further.

Ryan returned to Douglas Hall immediately. He told Gilmore he did not want to be disturbed, went to the drawing room, poured himself some gin, and flung himself onto the settee. By the gods, how he yearned to get his hands around the cowardly neck of the brute who had been harassing him, who had now had the consummate gall to abduct his fiancée. He groaned from rage and frustration. Damn the bastard. Who was he and how had he known that Sarina would be aboard the *Stargazer*, unless he had spies all over?

Ryan dragged in a deep breath and worried the golden pomander on the golden chain around his neck. The brute would have taken his pleasure of her by now, God only knew how many times. But then, what did it matter after the first? The very thought of the faceless enemy he hated so much tasting and enjoying what should have been his alone made his rage turn murderous. He mopped his flushed face with a fine cambric handkerchief and tortured himself further by recalling his uneventful sail from Florida to New York while the dastardly crime was being committed just east of him.

It was almost more than he could bear. But he would see the bastard hanged, he promised himself. Preferably by his own hand, but failing that, through the authorities. It did not matter which; the fellow would be just as dead one way as the other. There would be a ransom letter, of course, but all he could do now was wait for it to arrive. He could do nothing until the Ghost made his next move.

In anticipation, he ordered several men to watch his office, the docks, and his home so that when the message was delivered, the messenger himself would be apprehended. The blackguard would talk, Ryan thought darkly. He personally would see to that. He rather hoped it would take the lash to persuade the fellow.

Sarina . . . the Ghost . . . For the hundredth time he thought of them together and got to his feet and paced. That beautiful body of hers, those luscious breasts he had never seen or felt, enjoyed by a lawless sea wolf. Damn it, she was his. It was his right alone to deflower that delectable pink blossom sealed so tightly between her thighs. But no more was it sweetly intact and waiting for him.

An even worse thought struck him then. What if she had liked it—the rape . . . ? He had found, to his amazement and delight, that the more roughly he treated women, the softer and more yielding some of them became. Was that Sarina's way? When the wench was finally in his bed, and he had not the slightest doubt she would be, it would be an intriguing path to explore. Using gentle force on her, an iron hand in a velvet glove, so to speak. It could well move her to the very pinnacle of excitement, he decided, his mouth curving at the prospect. It would be only right for him to teach her who was master . . .

Ryan sighed and closed his eyes. He should feel guilty, having such thoughts at a time like this, but he did not. It would be just retribution. Sarina Fairburn was the most independent female he had ever come across. He deeply resented having to treat her with kid gloves, but he had hidden his resentment well. It would not do to come a cropper with her father and jeopardize his future position as son-in-law of the owner of Fairburn Shipping, prince consort to the heiress of a vast fortune. Prince consort, hell. He would be heir apparent, and one day he would be king. He had only to keep up this damned groveling facade until the old man was in his grave.

At the thought of George Fairburn, Ryan groaned again. Why had he himself not taken Sarina directly to New York on the armed *Manxman* and gone ghost hunting another time? But he had not, and now she was God only knew where, and her father would have his hide. He touched his tongue to the gin, sniffed his pomander, and commanded himself to calm down. He did not intend to send word to the old man just yet. With a bit of luck, he could have his sweet treasure, tarnished though she might now be, safe in his own bed before her damned old crotchet of a father ever knew she had been missing.

* * *

Lucian had worked day and night, the three days they had been on Malaga. They had careened the vessel, replaced the rotten wood, scraped and caulked her, and set up a forge on the shore to repair the loose ironwork. Now she was being scrubbed from bow to stern and her water jars filled. He reckoned departure the next evening, but for now, he thought, yawning, it was time to rest.

The night was almost tropical, with a hot fragrant breeze blowing out of the south, and the moon full and golden, a luminous silver piece in a diamond-studded sky. The men of the *Vengeance* had gone to the lagoon to cool off, but their captain found refreshment only in the breaking waves on the outer edge of the island.

Lucian removed his clothing, climbed easily over the boulders dotting the shoreline, and felt the soft sand and cool frothing water healing his tired feet. He dove in, swam out to sea with several powerful strokes, and then turned over onto his back. He lay gazing upward, the slow, easy swells like a bed gently supporting and caressing his weary body. He needed only one other thing to complete the perfection of the moment: Aurora. Aurora unafraid and wanting him. He imagined her floating beside him, her pink-tipped white breasts thrusting up out of the water, gleaming in the moonlight . . . He pushed the temptation abruptly from his mind.

Had she been a different kind of woman, one more fickle and less innocent, she might have wanted him, but she was not. Unless she was a damned skillful actress, she was loving and faithful. The sort of woman who would give her heart to only one man. And she had, the silly wench. She had given it to Douglas.

But if he, Lucian, wanted the ultimate revenge, if he wanted her to desire and yearn for him rather than his enemy, he would do well to lure her love away from the bastard and win her complete surrender—her will and her soul in addition to her body. But that would be more of her than he wanted or needed. And if he made her love him, and gave her nothing in return, he might destroy her.

He pulled in a long breath, turned over, and swam toward the open sea. He had wanted to put distance between them until he had had time to think things through, and now, in the space of a heartbeat, he made his decision. He would hold her for ransom, yes, and he would squeeze every bloody coin he could from Douglas' greedy pockets before he released her. But he would not touch her again.

It concerned him that already he may have hurt her. He had been so sure of himself, so sure she would enjoy his lovemaking, and she had, damn it, except . . . He reversed direction abruptly. She was like no woman he had ever known before, and he would never be able to figure her out; so forget it, he commanded himself. Forget it, man. It was done.

Anger drove his arms through the water like pistons as he headed for the breakers and shore. Once there, he retrieved his clothing, forced his wet legs into his breeches, and plowed through the sand toward home. He would turn in and get up at dawn to finish the work that remained.

Lucian slowed his step as a feminine form stepped from the woods onto the beach. He watched, unseen, as she bent, removed her shoes, and walked to where the waves rushed between the boulders and foamed across the sand. She raised her skirts, allowing the water to wash over her feet, and even in the dimness, he saw that the mane of hair falling down her back was long and red-gold. It was Aurora.

Not wanting to frighten her, he stopped where he was and called softly: "Hello."

Sarina started, but immediately regained her poise. "Hello . . ." It was like a whisper of wind.

"It's a beautiful night."

"I was just thinking that."

She had come there in a terrible temper, having seen both Ginelle and Rosie being courted by men they obviously adored, whereas she was alone. And the terrible thing, the thing that had wrenched her ever since they had reached Malaga, was that she had expected, had actually hoped, the Ghost would continue his pursuit of her. Thankfully, he had not, but that she wanted him made her furious with herself.

And now here he was, his dark face and arms gleaming with water droplets that sparkled in his black hair and in the hair on his chest. His breeches molded to his powerful legs, and moonlight shone in his grave blue eyes. Her own eyes regarded him coolly. She meant him to know that she was unafraid and unconquered, despite everything.

"It seems you have been swimming," she said crisply.

"The water is usually good, not too cold. You should try it sometime, but in the lagoon perhaps. The current is tricky here."

"I will sometime."

She sensed instantly that there was a change in him, which made him more of a mystery than ever. He was no longer the brusque, angry man of that first day, and he had not come near her since their second lovemaking several days ago. Since then his eyes had rarely met hers. They were distant, thoughtful. And his allowing her to be with her friends was a favor of some magnitude. While she had vowed never to thank him for anything, she wondered if perhaps it was time to relent.

Lucian was astonished that she was not running from him, and good God, how could she be more beautiful than she had been before? But she was. The moon's rays slanted across her face, softening it, emphasizing her high cheekbones, small rounded chin, and the rosy succulence of her mouth. He tensed, reminding himself that he was not going to touch her, not going to make the same mistake a third time.

He heard her soft sigh. Her eyes seemed sad, their green depths moon-silvered and quiet. He watched her pink tongue flicker across her upper lip and was tempted to catch it gently between his teeth and kiss it. He felt sweat starting at his temples, the first hot stirrings of desire.

"Well, enjoy yourself," he said gruffly. "I'm ready to turn in." He moved off.

"Captain."

He turned and felt pure pleasure at the sight of her: the moon and the waves breaking behind her, wind tumbling her hair in a wild cloud around her face, her eyes wide and wistful, her pink lips parted, her white feet and slim ankles peeking from beneath her skirt as she struggled through the deep sand to reach him.

"Captain, I—have been meaning to—thank you."

He laughed. "Thank me? For what?" For stealing her from her fiancé? For raping and ransoming her?

"You were kind to let me be with my friends, both on board ship and now here. I appreciate it."

"Kind?" The last he had heard, she had thought him heartless, ruthless, and uncaring.

She nodded. She was so small and looked so vulnerable that he wanted to cradle her in his arms, tell her that everything was going to be all right. But he could not. He did not know what the outcome of this caper would be. Up until tonight he had not even been sure he would return her to Douglas. The thought of her in the devil's arms, in his bed, his mouth on her breasts and lips, his senses dizzied by her perfume, had driven Lucian crazy. It still did.

"I have hardly been kind." His voice was harsh with suppressed emotion.

"Perhaps not at first . . ."

Sarina saw the glow in his eyes as they flickered over her. The fire in her own veins was spreading through her like a fever, making her tingle as it blended with the heat of her shame. For she was so very ashamed of her strange hunger for this man. How could she give in to it again? Yet how could she not? It was a restlessness that pulsed through her body with each surge of her heart. Confused, she turned to flee, but her foot found a deep hole in the sand. She was falling when the Ghost's arms went around her.

She gasped. "How stupid of me."

"Aurora . . ."

Passion kindled in Lucian like wildfire, swiftly overwhelming his decision not to touch her again. Her eyes were wide and startled, beseeching. But beseeching him to do what? he wondered angrily. His arms tightened, pressing her closer. Damn it, he had no control over himself where she was concerned. If she did not resist him, did not try to escape, there would be no turning back. He watched her tongue dart across her lips again, her eyes no longer wide but half-closed and dreamy. Was the little vixen teasing him, or was she so damned innocent and inexperienced that she did not realize what she was doing to him?

Cautiously, he brushed his lips over her eyelids and her soft lashes. He slipped his fingers beneath the neck of her gown and gently stroked the satiny skin there.

Sarina shivered, although his mouth and fingers were like flames on her body. She tried to think of Ryan worrying about her and waiting for her. Even so, her lips parted for the Ghost, and her breathing quickened as his tongue began a delicate, sensuous exploration of her mouth. In a distant part of her mind, she knew she should fight what she was doing and the way she felt, but she could not. She thrilled to the Ghost's low growl as his hot lips scorched her breasts. Oh, he filled her with the most incredible delight. As in a dream, she slowly unbuttoned her violet gown, allowed his dark hands, ever so gentle, to remove it and her lacy underthings.

Lucian drew in a long breath, seeing her body in the moonlight: her slender waist flaring out to softly rounded hips, her breasts full and high and made to fill the palms of his hungry hands. Quickly he removed his breeches and drew her down to the powder-soft sand. He kissed her mouth, touched his tongue to her nipples and gently nipped them, turning them into hard rubies. He trailed kisses over the white mound of her belly, the silken skin of her thighs and calves before turning her onto her side.

He spooned her tightly against him, her back to his chest, his swollen shaft cradled in the deep cleft between her buttocks. Kissing the nape of her neck, he slipped his arms under hers and claimed a breast in each hand. Sarina twisted her head from side to side, offering her mouth for his kisses, offering her shoulders, her throat, anything he chose to take. By the time he turned her onto her back and sat astride her, she was all his, desire having sapped her of her strength as well as her reason.

How magnificent he was—lean, hard, dark, and strong. She caught his hand and pressed her lips to his palm. It smelled of the sea. Shyly she put the tip of her tongue to it, tasting and licking its saltiness, kissing it, shivering with the delight such a small thing gave her. How very good it felt, how wonderful, not pretending, doing exactly what she wanted, running her curious hands over his arms and thighs, shadowy with crisp black hair.

"You are beautiful," Lucian murmured, his voice husky.

"And your hair is filled with diamonds," Sarina whispered, laughing, reaching up and touching its gleaming blackness. "Or perhaps they are moondrops . . ."

Lucian's hungry eyes adored her breasts and belly. She was perfection. He stroked her skin, tenderly cupped her breasts in his hands to kiss each rosy-peaked nipple, and then his long fingers were searching, teasing the cleft between her legs. He could wait no longer.

Sarina heard his breathing quicken, heard her own gasp at his deep, delicious probing, at his exposing to his burning eyes the taut peak that awaited him, and then he was steering himself into her, gently at first, and then, unable to contain his fierce passion, thrusting himself inside her in one swift motion.

Sarina stifled a cry. She was blossoming wide open for him as he plunged deeper and deeper. He filled her so completely that the fire that had been smoldering within her flared instantly. She wept softly, joyously as she began moving beneath him, trying to match the fierce beat of his manhood within her. It was a sensation almost too sweet to bear until, seconds later, he touched the very center of her being and she knew ecstasy.

She was drawn inward, inward, all of her bearing down on that one thick shaft moving so sensuously, so deliciously within her. And then their desires, like two stars flaming, racing side by side, met and burst as one, exploding into thousands of fiery sparks and illuminating what before had been only darkness.

Sarina felt inexpressibly weary, empty now that the delight of being so hotly consumed by the man at her side was over. How she wished she could remain in his arms to experience those last sweet sensations she had learned to expect, to sleep there even. But she could not. Her sanity had returned. The Ghost had been about to leave—he would not have touched her—but she had gone after him and actually given herself to him.

At that moment she so loathed herself and her weakness that she wanted to throw herself into the sea. She sat up, clutching her discarded gown to her breasts. She had to dress, but how could she with him lying there and gazing at her?

"You had better wash off that sand before you dress," he said softly.

"Yes . . ." Still she sat there, numb, staring at nothing, unable to move.

Seeing her despair, Lucian got to his feet and took her hand.

"Come," he coaxed. "Let us both wash the sand off."

Sarina shook her head, still trying to hide her nakedness, her eyes brimming. Gently Lucian pulled her to her feet.

"Come, little one, it's all right. Come." His voice was deep and easy, but as he led her to a small tidal pool, he cursed himself.

Why in God's name had he done exactly what he had decided against? The beauty of Malaga had overcome her inhibitions, and she was hungry to be loved. That was all it was. She was no tart. But in the eyes of a one-man woman like Aurora, their lovemaking was a shameful, unforgivable act. He knew that, had seen how she was, so why in hell had he not just patted her on the head and gone to bed as he had planned?

He filled his cupped hands with the moon-glittered azure water and poured it over her back and shoulders, cleansing her of the powdery white sand that clung to her. Afterward, he patted her dry with his shirt and helped tug her resistant dress down over her damp body.

"There now." He gave her wet head a pat. "You are almost as good as new."

Sarina lifted her chin, but she could not meet his eyes. "Yes, almost," she whispered. She fled without another word.

Chapter 11

~~~OC~~~

It was dawn. Alone aboard the *Vengeance*, Lucian was giving her a thorough inspection. She was repaired, her gray paint freshened, and when the scrubbing was completed, she would gleam from stem to stern, as handsome and seaworthy a vessel as she had been on that first day he got her. Afterward, they need wait only for the tide and sunset before weighing anchor for New York.

They would not berth there. They would row up a certain river in New Jersey that Lucian knew of, and from there, he would send a man into the city with the ransom message for Douglas. What would happen afterward was unclear. The bastard might actually be in his office and get the message immediately, or he might not receive it for weeks. Lucian wondered if he knew yet of his devastating loss of the *Stargazer*'s cargo and female passengers, for the ship would have been delayed as her crew struggled to make repairs.

In any case, as soon as his messenger was back on board, Lucian intended to return to sea and search for more Douglas merchantmen to harass. He had men in New York who would watch for Douglas' newspaper reply, an insertion which was to say, simply: *I understand. I await your instructions.*

It was all going to take time, he thought, checking the fastenings on the water jars that hung, already filled, in the shrouds. Early on in the game, he'd had all the time in the world. After his release from a year

131

in gaol, he had needed time to heal, to plan. Then he
had bought his ship, hired his men and moved to Malaga. He had stretched a net of spies across the land
and the waters so that he knew Douglas' plans almost
as soon as they were made.

Now things were different. Time was the enemy. He
had never worried about the capital to finance his vengeance; the source of his family's wealth was secure.
But now he was hungry, greedy for the devil to pay
for his treachery. Never had Lucian thought it would
take so long for his men to locate the damned cache
where Douglas hid his loot. But then, he should have
known better than to underestimate the fellow's cleverness.

Suddenly it was as if Lucian was back on the *Gull*
three years ago, his sick terror undiminished. He could
still hear Shane's screams, still hear his own cries and
curses, still taste his own blood and sweat as the two
of them were drummed around the hastily gathered
fleet for lashing. The torment raged through his body
still. Shane, Rajeen, his ship, his honor—all taken from
him. Now it was Douglas' turn . . .

Lucian's gaze was distant under frowning brows as
he remembered Douglas' woman in his arms the night
before. This time she had come to him. It still had been
against her will, against her heart, he knew, and he
was a bastard to have taken advantage. But was he?

Why was it his responsibility to protect her from her
hunger when she had practically fainted in his arms
from need of him? Recalling her later despair, he
weighed it against the pleasure he had given her. Why
should he not teach her the things Douglas had not?
Give her excitement and pleasure she had never
known, give himself pleasure and, at the same time,
inflict on his enemy the sweetest revenge known to
man. In the light of day, it seemed natural and reasonable. All the uncertainties that had nagged him in the
night were gone.

Once more he toyed with the idea of not returning
her to the bastard after all, but of keeping her at Ma-

laga for himself—at least for now. His decisions were not carved in stone. He moved with the tide and did what was appropriate for the moment. Maybe he would just send a message stating that the women were captive and would remain so, no ransom asked. His smile was cruel as he considered Douglas' reaction to that. And then there was the equally intriguing possibility of taking the ransom and not living up to his end of the bargain. Not an honorable thing, but then neither was abduction honorable. Neither was the treachery Douglas had perpetrated. Lucian was dealing with scum now.

"Excuse me . . ."

Lucian turned, his eyes widening briefly in surprise. He had not heard Sarina come on board. She was barefoot, and her hair trailed down her back in one long thick red-gold braid. What in God's name was she wearing? He saw then that it was something fashioned from her green gown: loose-fitting breeches and a low-necked shirt that had once been the bodice. Her slender arms were exposed to the elbows and her shapely legs to the calves. The sight stirred memories of his kissing every soft, delectable inch of them the night before. It also brought to mind her despair afterward. Yet it seemed she had recovered nicely . . .

"Good morning," he said gravely. "Did you want something?"

"I—must talk with you."

Noting the twinkle in his blue eyes, Sarina lifted her chin and regarded him coolly.

"I see my clothing amuses you."

"Not at all."

"And while you may think it looks ridiculous, I intend to wear it anyway." She grew warm as his appreciative gaze roved over her. "My gowns are simply too cumbersome and elaborate for—for captivity on Malaga."

He nodded, grave once more. "I understand. I think it shows—great creativity."

His words annoyed her hugely. She had not come

to him to show off her creativity. She had come to him for her freedom, freedom for the three of them. She wanted it more than ever. She had been brooding for hours, gathering the courage to face and reason with him. Now, standing so close to him, all she could think of was his lovemaking: the fierceness of his passion and his astonishing tenderness. She bit her lip. She must not think of last night, not if she was going to convince him that things could not go on as they were now.

"Actually, you look quite fetching."

"It was not my intention to look fetching. And do not forget that two of my best gowns have been ruined during this debacle. I fully expect you to replace them."

Lucian gave a little bow. "I would be happy to. Provide me with your measurements and the colors you prefer, and I will see to it when I am in New York." His mouth tilted at the thought of how much easier it would be to undress her from now on. No camisoles or petticoats or stockings; no endless unbuttoning.

"We are—going to New York?"

Seeing her eyes light up, Lucian was reminded of sunbeams dancing on the sea in summer. He said quietly: "I'm sorry—not you."

Of course. He was dressed in gray, which meant the ghost ship was about to strike again. The only time the crew wore gray was before they went on a hunt. But if their destination were New York, it was surely to deliver the ransom note!

Sarina's heart hammered at the thought of going along. Oh, he had to take the three of them with him, he simply had to. She opened her mouth to beg then snapped it shut. No. She would not beg nor would she let him see how eager she was. At least that much about her had not changed.

"You realize, of course, that you will be hanged when my fiancé catches you?" she said matter-of-factly.

Lucian laughed. "It will freeze in Hell before that day ever comes."

"I should not count on that. His whole fleet is on

the lookout for you and he is arming them." No sooner had she said it than she died inside. How stupid. Ryan certainly had not meant for his enemy to know that.

"God's wounds, you are right." Lucian's eyes were mocking. "I had clean forgotten those tin cannon he has stuck on the *Manxman.*"

She did not show her concern, but his words frightened her. How did he know so much about Ryan and his business?

"I wish I knew why you hate him so. If only I understood . . ."

"Someday I may tell you."

"But I want to hear now."

"No. And now if you will excuse me." He started down the companionway.

Sarina followed close behind him. "My fiancé knows many men in high places. If I tell him you did not harm me, that you wanted only the money—" She shivered as he stopped abruptly, his blue eyes raking her. "If y-you take us with you to New York and free us," she persisted, "it is possible he will tell the authorities to— to be merciful."

Again Lucian laughed.

"I mean it!" she cried, dogging his heels. "I personally will—will vouch for your own mercy."

"Of which I have none. You, of all people, know that."

"Shall I beg for my freedom then?" she asked stiffly, remembering Rosie's embarrassing performance. "Is that what you want? Shall I throw myself at your feet? If you want to humiliate me, and that is what it takes, I will do it."

"I have no desire to humiliate you," he said gruffly. He gave the hold a brief but careful inspection, followed by the galley and the mess. He went back up the companionway.

"I do not believe you. And I wonder if you have ever considered there is more than just myself to think about. There are my friends—"

"—who have completely addled two of my officers."

"—who have families that will be frantic about them. My own father will be beside himself with worry. It is clear you detest my fiancé and want to hurt him as much as possible for some insane reason, but my father"—her eyes brimmed—"is old and alone. M-my mother is gone. I am all he has." Seeing his grave face, Sarina thought surely she had touched his icy heart.

Lucian had completed his inspection and strode down the gangway, making every effort to close his mind to her words. It was struggle enough not to think about his own family, who now grieved over him as much as they did Shane.

"Well? Have you nothing to say?" she cried, her calm rapidly disappearing. "Would you have my father sicken and die?"

Sarina floundered after him through the deep sand, across the veranda into his house, and to the very door of his bedchamber. He gazed down at her, dark-faced and silent, his hand on the brass handle.

She was breathless from keeping pace with his long strides. "I promise that if it is money you want, you will have it. I promise! Just take us with you and free us in New York."

She trembled in her eagerness. If he relented, perhaps she would be back with Ryan before her father even knew she was missing. She and Ginelle could plan the wedding and she would never see the Ghost again. It was exactly what she wanted, never to see him again.

Why then did she feel so empty? Why was she comparing the feel of his arms around her and the taste of his mouth on hers to sunrises and sunsets? Why could she not separate the fragrance of the night-blooming jasmine and the warm sea breezes from the sensations he alone had aroused in her? Having just discovered there were such things, could she bear to lose them?

Yes, yes, yes, she told herself. Ryan would have made her feel the same way had she given him the smallest chance. And she *would* give him the chance. She would. It was Malaga, not this man, that was bewitching her. Malaga madness. All three of them had succumbed to it.

"I'm sorry about your father," Lucian said quietly.

"Sorry?" Seeing his set jaw, she knew she had failed to convince him. Damn him. "That makes everything all right, I suppose? You can do anything you choose so long as you are sorry."

"I regret that he must be hurt. Hell, my own parents—" He bit off the words in mid-sentence.

Sarina was astonished. Never once had she thought of him as having parents who might cry in the night over him. Sensing his sudden vulnerability, she said softly: "Please, tell me about them. Where do they—"

He held up his hand. "The subject is not one we will discuss."

She studied him curiously, realizing how much about him she did not know. This was the man who had abducted her and made her weep with pain and humiliation; who had tenderly washed the sand from her body and helped her to dress; who had comforted her. And he had parents for whom he cared deeply; she had seen it on his face. But the man who looked at her now, a warning in his icy eyes, was the Ghost, a man she did not like.

"We sail at dusk," he said. "You three will remain. I trust you will be comfortable here while we are gone."

"You dare to tell me you are leaving us alone?" she flared.

"Malaga is never left untended. Two men are always here to watch over things. I assumed you knew that."

"Yes, but—"

Her anger left in a rush; her skin crawled. Any men he left would be after them as soon as the *Vengeance* was out of sight.

Seeing the fear in her beautiful eyes, Lucian said softly, "My first lieutenant will remain also. Did you really think I would leave you unprotected?"

"I—did not know." She blushed as his eyes moved over her body. He was remembering, just as she was.

"Rest assured, no harm will befall you with him here."

"Then I can only regret I was not under the lieutenant's protection earlier," she said quietly and left, her head high.

Donal Fleming's heart thumped against his rib cage as he watched the departure of the *Vengeance*. He had not requested that he be left behind to guard the women. Lucian simply had chosen him, and it was the grandest thing that ever could have happened. He was in love. He had been in love with the fair lass he called Guinevere ever since he had first clapped eyes on her.

He had been raised in an orphanage, gone to sea at twelve, and had adored and been adored by women in every port in the world. Never had he bedded a wench he did not care for. It was a fact that he liked women too well and they liked him back. But now it was different. Now he wanted only this angel-lass. He wanted to give her the world.

What a darling she was. What a blessed treasure. Sassy yet shy, bold but innocent, and pure as snow. And she trusted him. From the very first, she had looked to him for protection. Not least, she was beautiful. The most beautiful wench he had ever seen. A lushly plump little body—dear God, how he loved for a woman to have flesh on her bones!—and white skin and long thick yellow hair, her lips and cheeks full and red, and her bosom . . . Ah, holy heaven, but it was marvelous to look upon. It was so deep and full and sweet it fair took his breath away every time he gazed at it. It was almost as if the Almighty Himself had fashioned the wench especially for him.

And she liked him. He saw it in her eyes and in the way she blushed when he so much as looked at her. And while the others were gone, he meant to bed her. Up until now he had been patient. Aye, when in God's name had he ever been such a perfect gentleman? But soon he would bed her. Maybe even tonight . . .

* * *

Ginelle studied Sarina with silent admiration. How very attractive she looked in those boy's clothes she had fashioned from her torn gown, and what a good idea it was. She wished she could try them on, but she was certain to pop out of them. The food here was so tasty, she knew she had put on extra pounds while Sarina, on the other hand, looked as though she had lost weight. And how sad she looked. Ginelle put down her playing cards and gazed at her friend sadly.

"Rina, love, are you not afraid you will ruin your eyes, doing all that embroidering by lamplight?"

"It's something I want to do," Sarina answered quietly.

"But you've been at it for hours and hours. It's not as though there's any rush. Do save your eyes, pet."

"My eyes will be fine."

Ginelle sighed. Poor little thing. She was embroidering a ruffle for one of the fine linen shirts she had brought for Ryan, one of her wedding gifts to him. She was doing all the fancy work herself—to make it more special, she said—but now she was doing it to feel closer to her beloved. Ginelle's eyes misted at the thought. That dreadful rogue of a Ghost! That cur, disrupting their lives so, especially Sarina's. It was not fair and if she were a man, what she would not do to him!

"How about taking a little walk?" she asked gently, as though Sarina were a grieving child. "The night is so lovely."

"You go ahead."

"You're sure?"

"I'll be fine," Sarina's voice was soft but firm. "I will work a bit longer and then it is bed for me. Will you please send Rosie to me?"

"Of course." Ginelle turned to go.

"Ginny—"

"Yes, love?"

"I know you will be seeing the lieutenant, and I know it's none of my concern"—Sarina rested her hoop on her lap and gazed at her friend with worried eyes—

"but I could not bear for you and Rosie to be hurt more than you have been already." She feared the men were merely using them.

Ginelle gave her a hug. "It's my turn to say I'll be fine."

Sarina stared at her friend's calm, glowing face. "It sounds as if you really mean it."

"Indeed I do. I'm not the frightened child I was when this all began." She kissed Sarina's cheek. "And now, darling, if you are sure you do not mind, I will go now."

Ginelle had been sitting on the veranda for only a moment when Donal appeared. At the sight of him, a thrill shivered up her spine and radiated into her arms and legs. He was dressed in white, making his hair and eyes and skin seem more dangerously dark than ever.

"Would you care to walk?" he asked.

"I would love it," Ginelle murmured.

He always held her arm when they walked and, silly thing that she was, it was her main reason for wanting to walk. She loved feeling his strong hand grasping her arm or touching her waist, and oh, if only he would kiss her again! He had twice, or rather, they had almost been kisses . . .

Really, she simply did not understand the man. At times, he seemed dazzled by her, but then if he really were, why on earth did he not do something about it? Oh, dear, doubtless she had misconstrued the situation and he did not like her as much as she imagined, which was exactly why she had broken her engagement. Such a sad thought . . .

"Where are ye, lovely lady?" Donal laughed and snapped his fingers in front of her nose. "Come back to me."

Ginelle blinked, startled. "Pardon? Were you speaking?"

"I was merely sayin' how lovely ye look in this moonlight, Guinevere. All pale gold an' ivory. Ah, 'swounds, maybe I should call ye Diana instead. She's the—''

"Moon goddess," Ginelle whispered, stars in her eyes.

Oh, fabulous day, he was dazzled after all! And he was so handsome and gentle and—and flattering. And was it her imagination, or did he acquire that enchanting burr in his speech only when he was with her?

"Aye, the moon goddess, but let me tell ye, my lovely fondling, Diana in all her glory couldna hold a candle to your beauty."

Ginelle caught her breath. She lay a hand on her wildly beating heart as a terrible boldness stole over her.

"Please, do call me Ginelle . . ."

She knew Rina would worry because she'd told him her real name, but why should she tell her friend? Besides, how could his knowing her Christian name possibly hurt anything?

"Ah, Ginelle, is it?" His black eyes burned over her. "It is a beautiful name for a beautiful woman."

They were near a rosebush, and as Ginelle watched entranced, Donal snipped off a red rose with his dagger and removed its thorns. He inhaled its fragrance, pressed it to his lips, and boldly kissed it before tucking it between her curvaceous breasts.

"Roses should bloom together," he murmured.

For the first time in her life, Ginelle was speechless.

Donal wasted no time. He took her trembling body into his arms and pressed his lips to hers, gently at first but soon, unable to contain his ardor, he rained kisses over her snowy throat and bosom and berrystained lips. His hands, gently, cautiously, began to explore her voluptuous secrets. They were yielded to him, unopposed. The only sounds she made were joyous cries and murmurs of pleasure.

Holy God, he thought, he had died and gone to heaven. Holy God, he had to have her.

The moon, streaming through the canopy of leaves, made a silvery pattern of lacework on the dark green dell in which they found themselves. Donal sank to the deep grass and pulled Ginelle down beside him.

"My precious lass . . ." His eyes and hands moved, worshipful and adoring, over her beautiful breasts. Gently he pushed her onto her back and began undoing the buttons of her gown, his lips fastened on her sweet mouth. She resisted not a whit. Her soft hands were atop his as he parted her gown to reveal the dazzling whiteness of her body and the lushness of her breasts . . .

Ginelle lay quietly in the crook of Donal Fleming's dark arm, her head on his shoulder. She had not dreamed such a wonderful thing was possible. And now the darling was sleeping, his thick black lashes brushing his tanned cheeks, his lips slightly parted so that his warm breath stirred her hair swirled across the black mat of curls on his chest. He had been playing with it when he dozed off. She took one of his big hands between hers and kissed the back of it, felt the crisp black hairs with the tip of her tongue, tasted his salty flesh, inhaled his wonderful male scent. She laughed softly. Goodness, whoever would have thought? She loved him. A pirate. She absolutely adored him. How marvelous, but how awful. Rina would never understand.

"Ginelle . . ." His deep voice vibrated through her body. He caressed her shoulder and kissed the top of her blonde head. " 'Tis a lovely name, lass. Thank ye for tellin' me."

She gazed up at him. Shyly she ran her fingers over his jaw and down his throat. He needed a shave . . .

"Could we keep it secret?" she murmured. "That I told you, I mean? My—my friend will worry if—"

Donal lay a finger on her lips, tracing their perfect outline. "She will never know, I promise."

"She wants to be freed so desperately—"

And how very ironic that now she herself wanted to stay, Ginelle thought. She wanted to be with him. She nipped his finger between her teeth, at the same time chiding herself. Her loyalty to Sarina came first, and what would her poor parents think? Why, they would be frantic. If only they knew how safe and happy she was.

"When do you think we will be allowed to leave?" she murmured.

"I couldna say, lass. It's entirely up to the captain."

She stiffened. "The man is a brute."

"Nay, lass," Donal said, softly. "Dinna say such a thing until ye've walked in his shoes."

Once again, his hands were roving over her skin, testing its softness and texture, and then he was tasting her mouth again, kissing it and her breasts, pulling her closer and closer, their breath and tongues meeting. Wondrously, he felt her guiding him into her, wrapping her shapely white legs around his dark form, urging him into her sheath more deeply than ever.

Ah, God, how delicious she was, Donal thought afterward. He would never find another like her, nor would he ever want to. And it was clear to him now that she felt the same about him. She was as good as his. In fact, he would make sure of that right here and now.

"Darlin', I want ye with me both day and night." When she sighed and did not answer, he kissed the top of her golden head. "Share my bed with me."

Ginelle was flushed with joy. He wanted her as much as she wanted him. "That is very nice—"

Nice? he thought. God's wounds! Nice?

"—but I—I could not. I—simply do not do that sort of thing."

Donal raised himself on one elbow and gazed down at her in puzzled distress. "My sweet cosset, ye just did."

Her gaze was wide and innocent. "Lieutenant, your ardor and your—your masculinity simply carried me away, but I—I could not share your bed. I just could not . . ." Her heart raced.

Donal scowled. "Is that so? And why not, pray?"

He caught himself then. What was he thinking? He was so out of his head with wanting her that he had forgotten she was no tart but a respectable upper-class Englishwoman. His face darkened.

"If I insulted ye, I'm sorry. What I meant to say was—will ye share not only my bed but my life with me?" Holy God, what was he doing? He really was out of his head. "Will ye marry me, Ginelle?"

"Yes!" she cried instantly. She threw her white arms around his neck and pressed her naked body against his. "Oh, yes! Oh, Lieutenant, it would give me the greatest pleasure to marry you!"

Dazed with delight and shock at his own audacity, Donal took her lips again. "My sweet, sweet lass," he whispered against them. "Call me Donal."

"Oh, how beautiful! Donal . . . Oh, I love it!"

"Let us marry now, lass. Let us marry ourselves with our own vows before God." He felt his manhood rising again, drained and exhausted though he was. 'Swounds, he could not believe he wanted the little wench again already.

"Oh, dear, you will hate me, but I—I must not. I dare not think of my own happiness until my friend is safe and happy—until she is safely married to Ryan. And though you say your captain is not a brute, Donal, truthfully now, can you not see that he is?"

"Now, lass . . ." Donal could barely think of anything save her rounded breasts pressed against his chest.

"She may not be safe for weeks to come. Months, even. Such a dreadful thought . . ."

Donal gave a groan, half-passion, half-despair. He agreed. It was indeed a dreadful thought, and for sure, something had to be done about it.

"Lass, listen to me now," he muttered, stroking her buttocks and bosom. "No harm will come to your friend, I assure ye. She's safe as a babe in its cradle"—and he would damn well make sure of it—"for the cap'n is a good man, a good good man, believe me. An' now, lass, can we exchange vows?"

Ginelle batted her long golden lashes at him. "You would not just say that to take advantage of a helpless woman? A woman completely at your mercy?"

"God in heaven, no! Great God in heaven!" Donal gathered her closer and smothered her sweet bare flesh with passionate kisses. "My cap'n is a wronged man, lass. A good man who is only doin' what he has to do to make his life bearable. We're helpin' him, is all."

Ginelle blinked. "My goodness, whatever happened?"

"I canna talk of it now, my little white blossom," he said, kissing her deeply, "but someday ye'll know, I promise."

Ryan Douglas raised his head as his butler tapped on his drawing room door and entered. "Yes, Gilmore?"

"Sir, there is a man from your office. He says it is urgent."

"Yes? Yes? Damn it, Gilmore, don't just stand there! Send him in." Ryan rose, straightening the ruffles at his neck and wrists. He touched his handkerchief to his damp face again. "Ah, Clements, what have you there?"

"I trust it is what you have been awaiting, sir, but I fear we have been somewhat remiss."

Ryan took the packet, his brown eyes pinning the man where he stood. "Remiss? Was the messenger not apprehended?"

"Sir, the only untoward thing that occurred all day was when a young lad blundered in, thinking we were a solicitor's office—"

Ryan stared at him, feeling his blood heat and pound through his veins. God's death! Not only had he a bunch of asses working for him in London and at sea, but he was surrounded by fools in New York.

"A lad?" he rasped.

"Yes, sir. He came in for just an instant, inquiring after his mother. That was this afternoon, and it was not until later that we . . . discovered the packet on the floor . . ." Clements took a step backward and stumbled over his own feet. "Sir, we were expecting a sinister-looking gent."

Ryan pointed to the double doors that led to the entrance hall. "Out!" It was like the crack of a whip. "Out of my sight! Out!"

Ryan's hands shook so that he could hardly undo the packet and unroll the paper. He carried it to the window, the better to see the bold black printing.

Your woman is in my hands, he read, and gave a violent shudder. *2,000 pieces of gold for her.*

Two thousand pieces of gold? His temples began to throb. It was absurd. Outrageous. Even if he had two thousand pieces of gold which, because of the Ghost, he did not, the bastard would never lay one greedy finger on them. Seething, he read on:

Insert in the Clarion: I understand. I await your Instructions.

Ryan hurled the offensive message onto the Persian rug and dropped into an elaborate gilt and brocade chair. After a while, his thoughts, shadowy before the note had arrived, began to take substance. He would agree to pay, certainly, but in reality, he would not pay a farthing. Instead, he was going to net the bastard and see him hanged by his miserable neck until he was dead. He rubbed his hands together. Yes, the Ghost, whoever he was, would rue the day he had ever tangled with Ryan Douglas.

But first things first. He sat down at his desk, quickly put pen to paper, and scratched out his response. He understood . . . he awaited instructions . . .

"Gilmore!" he shouted.

The man appeared at his elbow. "Sir?"

"Run this down to the *Clarion* instantly."

"Begging your pardon, sir, but the offices are not open at this late hour."

"Damn the hour. Break the door down if need be. Old Stokes is always in the back. I want this message to go in immediately."

Chapter 12

After the *Vengeance* departed, Sarina could not sustain her blue mood for long. The days were too beautiful, and there were too many things to enjoy for her to stay gloomy. She and Ginelle and Rosie paddled in the lagoon. The lieutenant taught them to fish—Sarina and Ginelle threw theirs back—and he even taught them to swim a bit. When Sarina wore the breeches and shirt made from her green gown, she was as agile and graceful as a fish.

When all three of their "guards" proved to be gentlemen, Sarina found herself warming to them, especially the lieutenant. But unlike Ginelle and Rosie, she was careful never to become too friendly or to act too grateful for the care and good food given them. She had not asked to be kept as a captive, after all.

Often she thought of the Ghost and of the man's strange power over her. But each time that she was certain everything was going to work out all right, and that she had recovered from her passion for the tall dark-haired captain of the *Vengeance*, a man whose name she did not even know, then a fragrance, or a birdcall, perhaps the ocean at dusk, would remind her of him all over again.

She commanded herself to think only of his arrogance and cruelty and his hot, blinding hatred for Ryan. But instead she would remember the way he looked at her; his small kindnesses; the fiery yet tender way he made love; his dark handsome face and tall strong body. She would pace again, wondering if she would be returned to Ryan soon and allowing herself to dream that even now the Ghost might be coming to fetch the three of them.

After five days, the *Vengeance* was home. The sky was darkening and the wind beginning to gust as the ship slipped past the thick veil of vines hiding the great rift in the face of Malaga's cliffs and slid into calm deep-green waterways. Lucian leaned on the rail, gazed at the dipping oars, and thought back on his journey. It had been a good one, with fair weather, and he had accomplished all he had set out to do. He had taken another fat Douglas Trader, and he had taken secret anchorage near the city and sent a message to Douglas' office on the wharf. He had then steeled himself and gone into New York to seek out a dress-seller's shop.

He shook his head at the memory of what had been the most annoying part of the voyage: wading through mountains of fabric and lace and ribbons, and squeezing past giggling perfumed females to a room the size of a broom closet where the ready-made gowns were hung. That he actually found two dresses that looked the right size and colors for Aurora was a miracle. He smiled, thinking of the other item he had bought her, a filmy peach-colored nightdress that most women would adore.

It would stay in its silken wrapper in his trunk for the present. Lucian had not forgotten Sarina's sizzling fury at being left behind, and were he to give the gift to her now, she would no doubt fling it in his face. He chuckled. No, he had not forgotten her temper or anything else about her, the feisty little wench.

His thoughts were diverted by a shout from Donal as he and the other two men hurried down to the pier. "Ahoy there, Captain! How was she? Did she behave for you?"

Lucian grinned. The *Vengeance* would always be Donal's sweetheart.

"She moved as swift as a dolphin," he called back,

"and now, get that skiff out here for our gear before it blows."

"Aye."

As the three men rowed out to the *Vengeance*, her anchors were lowered. The skiff was then hastily loaded with the crew's boots, clothing, and two very large boxes. The wind was rising as Lucian and his men went over the side and swam ashore. He hoisted his long, glistening body onto the pier, his eyes searching for one who was not there.

"How are the women? Any problems?"

"None. They were happy as larks the whole while."

Lucian gave him a skeptical look. "All three?"

Donal grinned. "Well—at least two of them all of the time, and three of them part of the time."

It was something, Lucian thought. He did not purposely try to make her unhappy; too often it just worked out that way. Seeing the mist and black clouds closing in on them, he called to his men:

"The house is open to all of you. Come in and get dry, but first let's batten down the shutters. Mr. Wilding," he said, singling out his cook, "break out that keg of Benicarlo." A cheer went up.

Wine was the only thing that they never dumped from Douglas Traders, and the Benicarlo was a fine Spanish red they had seized two days ago. Lucian was in the mood for a celebration.

"Can you manage salmagundi for grub in this blow, Mr. Wilding?"

"Can I manage! Hah!" Wilding crowed. "When have I ever not managed, sir, blow or no? I'll need help though, an' don't count on eatin' 'till moonrise, if there be a moon. Mister," he called to the Malaga cook, "fetch me whatever ye have o' fish, chicken, duck, pigeon, an' turtle, and get me a fire blazin' i' th' fireplace i' the kitchen-house. We'll be roastin', which means I'll need me some crew lads for skipjacks—no whinin' now, lads. Ye'll take turns at the spit. An' I wants all ye has o' cabbage, anchovies, an' pickled herring, mister, an' mangoes, eggs—get them boilin'—palm hearts, onions, grapes, an' anything ye got what's pickled . . .''

Satisfied, Lucian went to his bedchamber. He toweled himself dry and was donning fresh clothing when the first raindrops slashed across the shutters. Outside, the trees would be bending and the *Vengeance* straining at her chains on the choppy water. He smiled, knowing his crew would be ecstatic. To a man, they believed that rain on weddings, births, and homecomings was the luckiest of omens. Lucian did not. He had never trusted in luck to give him what he wanted in life. He worked for what he desired, took what he wanted. He thought then of the woman in the next room. He was looking forward to seeing her again . . .

Sarina was reading when the sky began to darken. She hurried to the window and was looking out just as the *Vengeance* raised her great bank of oars in unison and the lieutenant called out a greeting. What news had the Ghost brought her? she wondered, her heart pounding. Had Ryan responded instantly and would they be leaving for New York soon? She yearned to fly down to the dock and hurl a hundred questions at the Ghost, but seeing they were racing the storm, she held back.

She watched, fascinated, as the anchors were lowered, the ports closed, and the men began swimming ashore. She forced herself back to her book and tried to remain calm. Why should she show her vulnerability by letting him see she was dying for the merest scrap of news? She would not. Let him come to her.

"Rina! Rina, are you there?" Hearing the frantic rapping on her door, Sarina unlocked it. Ginelle entered, her cheeks pink. "They're here! They have just arrived!"

"I know, I saw."

"Oh, I'm so excited! Rosie and I were berry-picking, and when we came back, they were all jumping off the boat and swimming ashore. Oh, do come, Rina, and let us hear what the Ghost has to say!"

Sarina lifted her chin. "He can come to me, I think."

"But aren't you eager to hear his news?" Seeing her friend's stubborn face, Ginelle understood. Sarina was proud. And since the news might be bad, they might as well wait a while longer to hear it. She replied softly, "Whatever you say, love. My goodness, just listen to that thunder—they got here just in time. Do you think we should close the shutters?"

There were bangs and thumps just then as shutters all over the house were closed and barricaded. Their room was plunged into shadow.

"Well, I suppose that answers my question." Ginelle laughed. "My, how exciting it is. This certainly isn't London!"

Sarina was always stirred by any show of nature, but now her thoughts were on one thing only. Would they be freed?

"One of us had best get a spill to light our lanterns," she said.

"I'll do it," Ginelle offered. "I'll ask Donal."

Seeing Sarina's eyes widen, Ginelle stilled her hand on the door-latch. Until this instant, she had had wits enough not to utter his name, for she feared if she confessed one thing, she would confess all. Like Sarina, she was an atrocious liar. And if Rina were to know that she had given herself body and soul to Donal that one night—oh, dear! She blushed and tried to slip out the door.

"Ginelle!"

"I know you didn't want us to reveal our names, but I had to," Ginelle whispered, as the house exploded with the laughter and shouts of the arriving crew. "And then he told me his. Donal. Guinevere seemed so silly, Rina, and he—likes Ginelle. Oh, I hope you're not too upset."

Sarina felt a sharp stab of remorse for having caused her friend such uneasiness. It was unthinkable that she criticize Ginelle after what she herself had done with the Ghost.

"And well he should like the name Ginelle," she

said quietly. "It is a lovely name. And no, I am not upset."

Ginelle stared. "You don't mind my telling him?"

"I don't mind. And if we're lucky, we will soon be released and our names won't matter."

Ginelle gave a little squeal. "Do you really think that's possible?"

"I'm hoping."

"Oh, wouldn't it be heavenly!"

Ginelle had withstood Donal's tempting offer to exchange vows, but now she was imagining a real marriage to her hot-eyed lieutenant. But then what? Would she sail the seas with him, or would she be forever waiting for him here at Malaga? Would he go to prison, or would he be hanged? She could not bear the thought, for he was not a criminal. None of them were.

Ginelle jumped as thunder boomed and rolled overhead, followed by a rowdy cheer from the throats of seventy-five brawny men. She felt the soft hairs rise on her arms.

"Wh-why are they cheering, do you suppose?"

"Doubtless they have just opened a keg," Sarina answered. "Or perhaps they have taken some cargo this time and are dividing it." The thought made her furious. "But you had best run along and fetch the light. It's getting darker." And Donal would have heard the Ghost's news by now. Ginelle could get it from him.

Donal, however, chatted amiably about the weather as he lit Sarina's two lanterns.

"There now, little lady, that's cozier, I'll venture." He flashed her a friendly grin. "The food will be a bit late tonight, but I guarantee it will be worth your wait, being salmagundi. Can I fetch you a small sip of Benicarlo in the meantime? It's a rare red wine from Spain that will—"

"Thank you, no," Sarina said coolly, then immediately regretted the words. She clenched her hands at her sides and ordered herself to ask him. Ask him! But she could not. She would not. She was too proud to reveal her eagerness to know if Ryan had agreed to the ransom demand.

Ginelle's glowing face said that, no matter what the outcome, she would stay with Donal. While Sarina was glad for her happiness, her own loneliness and confusion overwhelmed her. Was it possible that she herself wanted to stay too? The answer came instantly. No, absolutely and positively. She had willingly given her body to the Ghost—she would never understand why—but there was a part of her he would never claim—her heart. That belonged to Ryan. It would always belong to Ryan.

Ginelle was regarding her curiously. "Shall I stay here with you a while, love?"

Sarina shook her head. "There's no need."

"Very well, but I'm bringing you a glass of Benicarlo. I absolutely refuse to take no for an answer."

Lucian had been dozing in an armchair. Now he stretched and yawned, content. The fire still danced and flickered, he was warm and dry, and he had had a good voyage, a good meal, and good drink. And he had a damned fine crew, he mused, gazing at them, sprawled sleeping on the floor of the great room. Normally they lived aboard the *Vengeance* or slung hammocks ashore when it was balmy, but with the storm still howling like a banshee, they were curled up in corners and under trestle tables, their boots cushioning their heads. They had gone through a whole vat of salmagundi, drunk two kegs of Benicarlo, and now they slept like the dead.

Looking about for Donal and Sky, Lucian remembered they had gone off hours ago with their wenches. He smiled. The sassy brown-eyed baggage had hardly torn herself from Sky long enough to take dinner to her mistress, and as for Donal—it seemed he had done well for himself while they were gone. He had the look of a man who had discovered treasure. As for Aurora . . .

Lucian shook his head. The little vixen had chosen

not to show her face all evening. She was as proud as a peacock and as stubborn as a mule, and even at this late hour he knew she would be pacing the floor, waiting for him to come to her. Never would she seek him out, the silly wench. No, she would suffer rather than let him see she was perishing from anxiety. Too bad. He could have assuaged her curiosity hours ago.

He downed the last of his wine and stood, stretching, his long shadow leaping across the room in the fire's glow while outside, thunder still rolled and rain poured down. He moved to his own bedchamber, hoisted two large rectangular boxes to his shoulder, and went to Aurora's room, tapping lightly on her door.

"Yes?"

Her voice was muffled and so icy that Lucian grinned. She was as mad as a hornet. "Don't you want to see what I've brought you?"

"Not particularly." Sarina unlocked the door and gazed coolly up at him. She ignored the boxes. "It would have been thoughtful of you to tell me any news sooner than this."

"I figured if you were interested, you would ask."

Her lily scent filled his nostrils in the warm dampness, and he saw that she wore a royal-blue gown with dozens of tiny buttons up the front. Imagining her in the flowing gossamer bedgown he had bought her, he felt his hunger stir.

"If I were interested!" Sarina cried, and threw up her hands. "Did you really expect me to appear in the same room with all your rowdy ruffians?"

"Your friends enjoyed themselves."

She glowered at him, wishing with all her heart that he were not so wonderful-looking. His coal-black hair hung freely to his shoulders, and he was dressed in white: loose white trousers cut off at the knees and a sleeveless white shirt. In the lamplight, he seemed taller and darker than she remembered. As he gazed at her with mocking eyes, Sarina was horrified to feel

what she had dreaded, the fading of her earlier resolve. She could have wept. Instead she flared:

"Well? Did my fiancé agree to the ransom?" Her
heart was fluttering like a bird in her throat.

"I didn't wait to find out," Lucian said easily, plac-
ing the boxes on the bed. "We will return in two weeks
or so to see what he has decided."

Sarina gasped. "Two weeks! Why, that's impossible! That's completely unacceptable." She knew now
that she could scarcely withstand her attraction for the
Ghost for one minute let alone two weeks. "I cannot
believe this. How could you be so callous after—" A
vivid image of their lovemaking filled her mind, and
she could not finish. She grew furiously pink as his
gaze moved over her.

"These things take time," Lucian said.

As she walked nervously around the room, he
opened first one box and then the other, spilling sea-
green and dawn-pink silk and satin and lace onto the
four-poster bed. He saw the brief widening of her eyes,
the flicker of a pink tongue-tip across her lips, but she
kept on pacing.

"These are for you," he said quietly.

"You can keep them," she cried.

The rise and fall of her breasts caught his gaze. How
white and silken was her skin against that deep blue.
By the gods, she was magnificent. He felt the stirring
of a dim memory . . . the black hellhole where he had
lain for a year . . . a random verse . . . "Haply I think
on thee,—and then my state, like to the lark at break
of day arising . . ."

He shook his head. In gaol the poem had meant a
lot to him even though he had had no woman then to
think on happily. He had had only the thought of vengeance to sustain him.

"Come, Aurora, you will look beautiful in these
gowns," he coaxed, seeing the hurt in her eyes. "I told
you before I left that I would replace the ones that were
destroyed."

"If you think your fancy gowns will make me forget

I am your prisoner, you are more unfeeling than I thought. Two weeks! How could it take two weeks? Was Ryan not there? And what of my poor father?'' She was trembling even before his arm slid around her waist. His flesh felt like fire through her clothing. She tried to twist free.

"Remember how it was, Aurora?'' he said softly.

Now that he was home, his men and his ship in safe harbor, he allowed himself to remember how she had come to him on the beach, how they had made love.

Lucian pulled her slender body close, his fingers sinking into her arms. He was angry, almost wanting to hurt her because the little witch was resisting him when he desired her so desperately. Had she forgotten the delight they had given each other?

"Remember how it was?'' he asked again, a whisper against her temple.

Sarina tried to free herself. "It cannot happen again . . .''

Determined to keep a close rein on his temper, he coaxed: "Come now, cosset, you were made to make love.'' His voice was husky, soothing. His mouth sought hers. "Such silken skin . . .'' He stroked her swanlike throat and slipped his fingers between her breasts. "Such silken hair . . . silken lips . . . silken breasts . . .'' He kissed one taut nipple thrusting against the fabric of the gown.

Sarina tried to prevent his hungry mouth from taking hers, but her strength was ebbing. He was holding her so tightly against him, his lips brushing across her flesh so hotly, that she trembled. Her lips parted, her breathing quickened. It was what always happened when she was in his arms. She had grown as weak as a kitten, and deep inside were those delicious stirrings she experienced only with him. But did he stir such passions in other women while he was gone from her? she wondered suddenly, wildly. Oh, you fool, of course he did. She felt such fury at the thought that she lashed out:

"You knave, how can any woman bear you!''

Lucian's own anger had reached a crisis point. She had been softening, melting against him, and now this stupid outburst.

"I think we have talked enough," he said harshly.

Forcing her arms behind her, he took her mouth, plundering it so deeply and hungrily that she whimpered. Instantly, he grew gentle, caressing her, smoothing back her tumbled hair with his big hands, brushing zephyr-soft kisses over her face and breasts and shoulders.

"Aurora, oh, God . . ."

Sarina moved against him, not certain whether she was struggling to escape or frantic to get closer. Feeling his lips teasing her breast, she knew. She wanted him. More now than ever. In a torment, she tried to imagine it was Ryan in whose arms she was cradled so closely, Ryan whose sweet, hot mouth was claiming and consuming her. She could not. He was a pale shadow. She could scarcely remember how he looked.

"Aurora, I want you . . ."

The Ghost's voice was thick with passion, but it was his grave face and haunted eyes that touched her heart. He needed her. She could not imagine why, but suddenly he needed her strength and comforting, and she doubted he even knew it. She took his hand, pressed it to her lips, and led him to her bed. Gently she drew him down beside her.

Chapter 13

⌒◦◦⌒

The days following that stormy night when Sarina and the Ghost made love, she kept a cool and wary distance from him. But she knew they would make love again. As surely as the tides changed and the moon and the sun rose and set, she knew they would be drawn together. There was a strange, irresistible link between them, an attraction that they could not deny. To keep her sanity, Sarina told herself over and over that Malaga madness was responsible, and when she returned to Ryan, it would all seem like a dream.

Ryan . . . Sometimes it was he who seemed like a dream as she waited endlessly, fruitlessly to hear from him. Each time the Ghost returned from a short absence, her heart filled with the renewed hope that he would have news for her. It was always dashed. One such time she was waiting for him at the dock when he disembarked.

"Well?" she demanded.

"Good morning," he said, his dark face telling her nothing.

Sarina ignored the greeting. "Have you any word for me?"

"No."

"Have you even tried to get word?"

"No."

She wanted to fly at him. She took a deep breath and dug her nails into her palms.

"I don't understand you. You said you would return

in two weeks! This is July and we have been here since June. Why did you ask for ransom if you never intended to take it?"

His eyes shuttered. He moved past her. "You will excuse me . . ."

Sarina plodded behind him through the deep sand and onto the veranda of the house. Her eyes flashed dangerously.

"It seems you want us to live here forever!"

"God forbid."

"Well, at least we agree on something. It would be hideous, being cooped up here in the winter with all of you."

Amusement flickered across his face. "No fear of that, Your Highness. I will be home by winter."

Home. How odd the word sounded on his lips. She could not imagine him anywhere but commanding the *Vengeance* or ruling Malaga. Was home where his parents lived? she wondered. Was it where a young wife waited for him? She doubted it, but her cheeks warmed. She knew his body so well, yet she knew nothing at all about the man himself. Not even his name.

"Where, pray, is your home?" she asked crisply.

"England."

"Of course, England, but where in England?"

He sprawled in a wicker lounge chair. "Someday I may tell you."

Sarina's green eyes narrowed. Was that yearning she heard in his voice? Always alert to a chance to press an advantage, she perched on the steps at his feet.

"I think you miss England and your home," she said quietly.

"I think you have an active imagination. England is just one of my homes. Malaga is another. I am quite content wherever I happen to be."

But she was right, and her perceptiveness annoyed him. He did miss his home, his birthplace in the green English downs at Kirkbridge. His mother and father were growing old there, their only reasons for living gone—Shane and himself. He had promised he would be there for Christmas, which would mean leaving Malaga no later than mid-October.

"Say what you will," Sarina said, "but I know you want to go home. Surely you can see that my friends and I feel the same way. We want to go home and have our lives return to normal."

"I would say your friends have already decided that Malaga is 'normal'," he drawled.

"My friends," she said, giving him a level look, "are not particularly farseeing."

"Ah. And you are."

"Yes." She looked down at her hands. "Enough to see the three of you at the end of a rope."

Lucian gave no answer. His own eyes were on the *Vengeance*, on his men moving about the deck, working, laughing, talking. They would be safe from the gallows; he had seen to that by insisting they sign letters declaring that he had forced them into piracy. Everyone except Donal and Sky had signed.

"How can you not see it?" Sarina whispered. "It is—inevitable."

He laughed, and all the sunshine, all the warm winds and blue skies and white sands of Malaga, were in the sound. Suddenly, Sarina wanted desperately to be caught up by them, by him.

"Oh, you are impossible!"

He raised lean, bronzed arms above his head, stretched, and gave her a mocking smile. "And you are beautiful."

"Captain, listen to me." She spoke as calmly as she could. "You will be caught. I want you caught. I pray you will be caught—" She met his dancing blue eyes but refused to return their hot message. "For no one should be so above the law that he can go about terrorizing hardworking merchants and abducting women. But I do not want you to be hanged." Her voice dropped to a whisper. "I simply could not bear for you to be hanged . . ."

Her hands were caught suddenly, trapped in his, her eyes held by him.

"My cosset, you are not to worry."

"If only you would free us," she said, her heart soaring at his touch, "I would vouch for you. All three of us would vouch that we were unharmed and—"

"Cap'n!" It was a shout from the *Vengeance*. "The *Bluebell*'s just come. She's waitin' offshore to talk wi' ye!"

"Thanks, mister," Lucian called back. He still held Sarina's hands, still held her wide-eyed green gaze. "Remember, you are not to worry . . ."

Sarina jumped up, her thoughts racing. "What ship is it?" she cried. "Is she carrying word from Ryan?" She followed him down to the dock. "I'm coming, too!"

"No."

"Please, may I come?"

"I'm sorry."

He boarded the skiff with two crewmen, and seconds later it was skimming toward the open sea. Sarina raced to the back of the house and through the junglelike woods on a path she had come to know well. Reaching the boulder-dotted outer bank, she saw the skiff, like a small gray minnow, approaching a sloop in full sail. The larger vessel, her waist across the buffeting wind, moved sideways, wave-dancing, biding her time. The Ghost did not board her. Greetings were exchanged, followed by a discussion in lowered voices. It was word from Ryan, Sarina thought breathlessly. What else could it be?

As his men rowed back through the emerald-green channels of Malaga, Lucian thought over what he had just learned. Ryan Douglas had agreed to the ransom, two thousand pieces of gold which Lucian knew he did not have—which meant it was a trick. Douglas meant to trap him. But the devil would never get the chance. There would be no exchange of gold and captives because Lucian was going to keep the women. He had delivered the ransom note with every intention of following through with it, but now he had changed his mind. He was going to keep Sarina.

It was the deadliest blow he could strike against Douglas, yet part of him recoiled from it. He had never kept a woman in his power before or used one as he was using Aurora, practically forcing her to love him when he had no intention of ever loving her back. It was wrong. Worse, knowing it was wrong, he was going to go on doing it.

He wasn't ready to think ahead as to how long he would keep her. Perhaps if he didn't surrender her by the time he left Malaga in mid-October, he would take her back to England with him and do as Donal had suggested—leave her, leave them all, in some fishing village.

Lucian shook his head and ran long fingers through his hair. Ah, God, but vengeance had darkened his soul. Seeing Aurora waiting for him at the dock, pink-cheeked with anticipation, he wondered what to tell her. It seemed he had thought of everything except that.

"Was there an answer this time?" she cried, no longer trying to hide her eagerness. She could hardly believe it when he gave her no answer but started for the house.

"Captain!" she called sharply after him. "Did you not hear me? How dare you walk away and not tell me what was said!"

Lucian took a deep breath, knowing he was going to break her heart. "There was no answer."

The angry pink drained from Sarina's face. "Are you saying there was—no message at all?"

"None. I'm sorry."

"Then clearly he did not receive your demand."

"He got it, all right." Bastard, he lashed himself, look at her. The poor little bird, trying so hard to be brave.

"Then there has been a misunderstanding." Her voice was high and tight.

"I think not."

Sarina was crushed, humiliated. How could Ryan not have responded? Why, if she were in his place, she would have armed the entire Douglas fleet and enlisted the whole Royal Navy to search for the three of them until they were found!

"I'm sorry," Lucian repeated, his face grave.

"Oh, I'm sure you are."

Men! What beasts they were, all of them, she thought, marching toward the house with her head high. She hated them all. The only thing the Ghost wanted out of this debacle was gold. He didn't care a whit for her.

She spun, facing Lucian, wanting to cry out that her father would pay for her return. The words hovered on her trembling lips, but she knew she couldn't let the Ghost know who she was. He would bleed George Fairburn of his entire fortune, and even then might not release her.

Sarina resumed her march to the house. She held back her tears until she was safely in her room, whereupon she locked the door, flung herself onto her bed, and wept a storm of absolute fury. It was hopeless. Her father was unaware of her plight, and it was perfectly clear that Ryan no longer wanted her—not if he had to pay for her.

For two days, Sarina wallowed in self-pity and frustration, her low mood not helped by the departure of the *Vengeance* and her gray-clad crew. She knew they had not gone off merely to replenish the meat and dairy supplies. Once again they were on the prowl for Ryan's ships.

On the third day her anger returned, but there was nothing on the surface to show that she was smoldering like a volcano deep inside. She was gazing out the window of her darkening room, wondering when the *Vengeance* would return, when Ginelle rapped on her door.

"Rina?"

"Just a moment . . ." She unlocked the door.

Ginelle entered with a spill and a tray bearing two small cups. She put down the tray and lit Sarina's lamp.

"I thought you might want to play cards."

"I fear I'm not in much of a mood for anything but murder," Sarina said. She went to the window again.

Seeing the fire in her eyes, Ginelle gave a prayer of thanks. She had been worried sick when Sarina sat in her room, staring out the window and not talking.

"I know it hurts," she said gently, "but I'm certain there's a good explanation." She fetched the small cups from the tray. "Rosie has made us a bedtime drink. Perhaps it will help you relax. I'll just leave yours with you and toddle off to bed, I think."

"Ginny, I'm sorry I'm such bad company . . ."

"Indeed you are not. I would be a complete shrew in your place." She kissed her friend on the cheek and bid her good night.

Sarina had just dropped off to sleep when there was a banging on her door.

"Rina! Wake up! Oh, please wake up!"

Hearing the urgency in Ginelle's voice, she flew to the door and opened it. "What is it? What's wrong?"

"Th-the Ghost . . ."

Sarina put a comforting arm around Ginelle's shoulders. "Pet, you've had a bad dream."

"Oh, Rina, it is no dream. Please come."

Her heart thundering in her ears, Sarina donned a wrapper and followed Ginelle to the Ghost's bedchamber. Two lamps burned low, and in the flickering light, she saw his tall figure sprawled on the bed. He was naked to the waist, and his eyes were closed. Sweat shone on his white brow. Sky stood at the foot of the bed, Rosie clinging to his arm, as Donal led Sarina to the bedside. She gasped at the sight of the large bloodstained bandage plastered to the Ghost's lean ribs.

"He was askin' for ye," Donal said in a low voice, "but now he's gone off again. Would ye be kind enough to wait a while?"

Sarina nodded and sat on the chair that was brought to the bedside for her. Her wide eyes never left the sleeping man—or perhaps he was not sleeping, but unconscious. She commanded herself to appear calm. There must be no weeping, no frantic scene.

"Wh-what happened?"

Her anxious eyes drank in the Ghost's pale face and parted lips, his black lashes lying on waxen cheeks.

"He's had a smidgen o' bad luck, that's all. He'll be fine."

"I'm glad to hear it." But Sarina found that impossible to believe. She yearned to catch his hand and press it to her lips, press life into it.

"Aye. It takes more than a dagger in the hands of a fool to keep down such a man."

"The fool seems to have done a fairly good job."

Her gaze held no more than cool interest as she studied the Ghost, but her heart was shriveling. How still and pale he looked with that awful glistening sheen on his skin. If only she could breathe her own breath into his cold body to warm him.

"A good job? Ha!" Donal snorted. "It was the barest scratch until he ignored th' wound and it got infected. But he'll be as good as new in a few days."

Sarina's relief was so great that it instantly turned to anger. "I would certainly hope so! We have much to discuss." She shot an accusatory look at Donal. "I suppose you were attacking another Douglas Trader?"

"That would be for the cap'n himself to tell ye, ma'am."

"If you were," Sarina said softly, "he got what he deserved."

Donal regarded her sternly. "Ma'am, if ye'd rather not stay 'til he wakes, it's understood."

"No, I—I will stay. If he called for me, of course I

will stay. I'm sorry, I did not mean I wanted him hurt. It is just that—"

"Say no more," Donal replied.

The little vixen. He had already seen that she had fallen head over heels in love with Lucian, but it was clear she would never show or admit it. And probably just as well, for little good would it do her.

"We'll leave ye with him now," Donal said. "I'll grab some sleep and be back later to spell ye."

"She's wonderful at nursing," Ginelle offered eagerly.

Sky did not look convinced. "Give 'im half a cup of my fever water every hour," he muttered. "It's on the washstand."

Sarina nodded. "A half-cup every hour."

After they left, Sarina gently pulled the sheet over the Ghost's sweat-glistened body and sat down. She listened to his quiet breathing, marveled at the thickness of the black lashes that lay on his cheeks, the perfection of the winged brows curving above his closed eyes. How very beautiful he was. She took one dark hand from beneath the sheet and held it to her lips. She kissed it. But no, she must not . . .

She rose and walked about the room, gazing at the large bookcase filled with books; the desk holding yet more books and papers and a newspaper; the large wall map above it.

"Aurora . . ." The Ghost was sitting up, flushed, his blue eyes wide and unseeing.

"I'm here. It's all right." She hurried to his side and gave him a sip of water. "Go back to sleep now. Go to sleep."

He obeyed, but she grew concerned, for he was delirious. She had heard Ryan say there were good doctors in New York, but how far from New York were they? If the Ghost worsened rapidly, could they get there in time? Studying the map, she saw a black dot off the Virginia coast that had been penned in and circled. It had to be Malaga. She did a rapid calculation the way her father had taught her. Two days, she decided, possibly one and a half with a good breeze, would get them there, and if he were no better in the morning—

"Aurora . . ." Lucian raised himself on one elbow, his eyes fixed on the vision in pale-green silk examining the map on the wall. "Aurora!"

Sarina jumped, startled, and hurried to him. She poured the fever water and held the glass to his parched lips. "Drink this down now. It will make you feel ever so much better."

He drank it docilely and sank back against the pillow. He had thought he was in hell, it was so hot and black where he was, but surely this was an angel. He tried to smile, but his eyes would not focus on her beautiful face. She was fading, disappearing . . .

"Help me," he muttered, and caught her hand so tightly that she winced. "I—might not come back from here . . ."

"You most certainly will come back," she said firmly.

He threw off his covers and sat up, his blue eyes wild. "Tell Aurora"—Lucian moistened his parched lips—"that I lied. Ryan will pay, but I'll not give her up to that bastard. I—love her."

"I will tell her." Sarina had nursed her father through high fever; she knew what it did to one's mind, but her voice trembled nonetheless. What if his words were true?

"Shane!" Lucian cried, for inside his head the drums had begun to beat. He had returned to a time and a place straight from hell. The fleet was gathered and waiting for the two of them. The lashes were waiting. "Shane, oh God . . ."

As the Ghost's low rasping sobs filled the room, Sarina stroked his hair and hands. She whispered words of comfort and encouragement, knowing that he was out of his mind with fever and didn't know what he was saying. When his anguish was finally spent, he rolled onto his side, his broad back to her, and slept.

She frowned and took up the lamp, the better to see his back. Her heart almost stopped. It was a mass of scars, hundreds of fine, pale crisscrossing scars. He had been lashed. She was brooding over it, wondering about it, when Donal came to relieve her . . .

Chapter 14

By the following afternoon, Lucian's fever had gone down and he was lucid. He wanted to be up and about, but to his disgust he was at the mercy of his weakened body. He was fit for nothing but sleeping, reading, and drinking chicken broth. He was also at the mercy of his thoughts. They churned constantly as he relived their last strike against a Douglas merchantman during which he'd taken a dagger in his ribs. He had been the first man over the rail, his sword drawn and his gaze sweeping the terrified crew. Hell, he had never even seen the knife coming at him. Luckily, it had only scratched him.

His thoughts boiled over onto his dreams of the night before, dreams of hell and damnation. And of paradise. Aurora had been in them, her soft, scented hands helping him to drink, cooling him, easing his pain; her sweet lips brushing kisses against his burning flesh. But were they dreams or had she actually been there? The uncertainty nagged him. Because if they were not dreams, then he had blurted out the truth about Ryan and, incredibly, gone on to say that he loved her . . .

He twisted his head on the pillow and grimaced. Love. God almighty. He had never loved a woman. Was such love similar to the deep emotion he felt for Shane? For his parents and Donal? He sensed instinctively, yet vaguely, that love for a woman involved much more. It was the lark singing at heaven's gate . . .

He shook his head. If he had to lie here helpless, he

might as well accomplish something. He took a thin book from his bedside table and was reading when a soft tap sounded on his door.

"Yes?"

It opened a crack and Sarina looked in. "I just wanted to see how you are. May I—come in?"

Lucian put down the book. "Of course. Come and sit a while."

He was always glad to feast his eyes on her, but he was not overjoyed at her seeing him in his invalid state. Damnation, had she seen him weak and raving last night?

"You're looking ever so much better than you did," Sarina said brightly. "Your color is good now, and your eyes are clear and alert." Even his hair was lustrous and vital again.

"I am feeling better," Lucian answered politely, carefully, but his heart was thudding. So she *had* been here. He hadn't dreamed it. Damnation, that meant he had probably said all of those things he remembered, and now he must make light of it. "To look at you, no one would know you were up tending a madman half the night." He sounded calm enough, but his thoughts were galloping. "You look as cool and beautiful as ever."

Sarina frowned. "You remember my being here? You were so ill, I assumed you were delirious."

He nodded. "Fever dreams. I had them all night long, and I remember every damned one. I was in hell, and then a beautiful cool angel in green came hovering over me. I recall giving her several messages . . ." His mouth tilted in a rueful smile as he added softly, "I hope you understand that it was nothing but fever talking—and I hope the rest of my ranting did not embarrass you." His grave eyes locked on hers, willing her to believe him.

Sarina's face grew hot, but she laughed lightly. "Embarrassed? Not at all. Not for one moment did I believe anything you said. I know fever talk when I hear it." But who was Shane? she wondered. He was no dream, for his name had been written in the book of sonnets, but she was not going to ask. Nor was she going to wonder if Lucian remembered her kissing and caressing him.

"How did you come to be with me?" Lucian inquired, concealing his irritation.

"It seems you asked for me." When he looked incredulous, Sarina smiled. Strangely enough, she was enjoying this exchange. "Really, Captain, why would I lie? Your lieutenant will tell you . . ." She refrained from adding that he was in this predicament because of his continued outrageous harassment of her fiancé.

"I see."

Lucian's thoughts were suddenly murderous. How could Donal have done such a damned stupid thing, knowing what fever did to a man's brain? Not only had this woman seen him ranting and babbling, but she had also seen him as weak and helpless as a day-old kitten. He got to his feet, wanting to find Donal and knock him down. He swayed. His head began to spin and roar.

Sarina was on her feet immediately, pressing him back into the bed. "Do lie down. You must not exert yourself." She frowned and felt his forehead "You seem a bit warm. Are you still taking the fever water?"

The door opened suddenly and Sky was there. "Aye, he's to take it, but you'll have to force it down his gullet."

Sarina's green gaze danced over Lucian. "I think not. I think he'll take it just fine." She poured out a half-glass and handed it to him.

Her lily fragrance and the nearness of her white arm teased Lucian's senses. Suddenly he knew he hadn't dreamed that she was kissing and stroking him last night. It had happened. He could still taste and feel her cool, sweet lips on his mouth and moving over his body. He cupped his hands around hers on the glass and allowed her to bring it to his lips. He drank, then smiled up at her.

"Somehow it tastes better when you do it . . ."

Sarina smiled back. "In that case, I'll be back tomorrow to give you more."

"I'll be loading the *Vengeance* tomorrow, but you're welcome to come and feel my forehead . . ."

"I shall. I promise."

Donal felt a twinge of uneasiness as he approached Lucian's bedchamber. Lucian had been asleep the two times he had stopped by earlier, and now he had just seen Aurora leaving. Did that mean he knew she had nursed him during the night and seen him pale and helpless as a newborn piglet? He gave a low, soft whistle as he rapped on the door. Holy hell, that would be a hard one for the lad to swallow.

"Come in." It was a growl.

Lucian was ready for battle. He glared angrily at the tall man who was his dearest friend and his strong right arm.

"Why did you bring her here?" Lucian's eyes glittered dangerously as Donal sauntered in and perched on the edge of the bed.

"Because it was Aurora you wanted," Donal said easily. "A hundred damned times you bawled for her."

Lucian gave him a black look and drew a deep breath, hiding the sudden, fierce pain that stabbed his ribs.

"Did it never occur to you that I was out of my head at the time?" When Donal didn't answer, Lucian went on, stiff-lipped with fury. "I talked in my fever. She knows Ryan offered to pay, and that I won't give her to the bastard. I fed her some pap about knowing I was dreaming and knowing exactly what I said, but God only knows if she believed me. She pretended to . . ."

Donal waved it aside. "No one takes fever talk seriously."

"Not only that, but she jumped like a scared doe when I caught her examining my wall map. Suppose she has discovered where this place is?"

Donal laughed. "Come, man, what would she know of maps?"

"You seem to think the situation is amusing."

Donal stroked his beard. "No, I don't think that at all. I think it's a damned serious business and is growing more so every day. I think it essential that you let the women go. All of them."

Lucian shot him a look of pure disgust. "We've been through this before, and my feelings haven't changed. Nothing has changed."

"Wrong," Donal said. "Everything has changed. It's not just between us and him anymore. These women and their families are being hurt." That Ginelle would never be his as long as she felt Aurora was in danger he kept to himself.

"Is it so easy for you to forget, then?" Lucian demanded hotly.

"Damn it, man, I'm not asking you to stop the vendetta, only to get the women to New York or back to England. I guarantee they'll not betray us." Holy hell, he had said this much; he might as well say it all. "Sky and I mean to marry our lasses, Lucian. There's love between us—but first, they must be returned to their people."

When Lucian stared at him, disbelieving, then threw back his head and laughed, Donal was stung. He said softly: "You find it strange that they would wed us?"

Lucian instantly regretted his tactlessness. "Not at all. Any woman would be lucky to get either of you. But damn it, man, you know the magic of this place."

Donal stabbed a dark finger at him. "You seem not to realize that that same magic has touched Aurora. The lass loves you."

Again Lucian laughed. "I think you need a glass of fever water, old friend." But his curiosity was piqued. "How did you come by this great wisdom?"

"It surprises me you haven't seen it yourself. The woman is like a dewy-eyed kitten around you, just waiting to be held and stroked."

When their eyes met and locked, Lucian saw that Donal knew he had made love to her.

"The lady is no scatterbrained chit, man," Donal chided him. "Surely you know she will be hurt if you take her again and again without loving her . . ."

Lucian's eyes glittered, for Donal's words angered him. It was the very worry he himself had had and managed to dismiss.

"So you are an authority on women?"

"Oh, aye," Donal answered. "And come to think of it, I'm not at all sure but what you love the lass and don't know it."

Lucian had had enough. He slid down into bed, yanked up the bed covers, and turned toward the wall.

"Go," he said.

"And if you haven't the sense to see what a treasure God has given you, why then, ship her up to Ryan. Give her back or make her yours. Free her or love her, old son."

"Lieutenant, you are dismissed."

"Aye, Captain, I'm leaving."

Ryan Douglas tossed in his bed in his fashionable house on Darcy Street. He could not sleep. But then, how could any man sleep who had his troubles? Ten of his cargos, two of them contraband, gone to the ocean floor since early April. And irony of ironies, he had lost Sarina and one of his valuable illegal cargos in one foul blow.

When he did sleep, he dreamed of pirates battering down the doors of his house and swarming into his cellar, where he stored the contraband that his uncle, Jon Gray, procured for him. He never kept it for more than several weeks, only long enough to get a good price from the wealthy buyers with whom he dealt regularly. Still, he could not suppress his nighttime fears that the damned Ghost would find his hiding place. And if the contraband was ever found in his possession—those precious jewels and perfumes concealed in the bales of tea and kegs of wine his buyers had purchased—all would be lost, for he was already an offender. Five years ago, one of his cargos had been confiscated and he had been fined in a run-in with the Royal Navy.

Ryan ground his teeth, thinking of his encounter with Lucian Thorne. That stiff and proper devil had not even bent an inch for old time's sake and accepted his bribe. After that, Ryan had been a model of propriety, at least on the surface. But easy money still intrigued him, as it had his uncle. He and Jon were two of a kind. They used only one vessel for smuggling, the *Stargazer*. Jon sailed the ship and secretly bought the goods on the far end; Ryan stayed on land and did the selling.

In winter, the *Stargazer* sailed to France and Spain and Portugal. Come spring, after selling all the goods that they'd stored in Ryan's cellar, they fared across the Atlantic where the run between New York and Florida was equally lucrative. And now the damned Ghost, whoever he was, was ruining everything.

Ryan savagely kicked the silken coverlet onto the floor and looked with active dislike at the bed in which he lay. He had bought it for his wedding night in hopes that it would titillate Sarina. It was a great Chinese-lacquered Chippendale piece, six feet by seven, hung with blue silk damask edged in gold orris lace. The lace alone had cost him well over one hundred pounds. He groaned. Now it looked as if he might not even have a wedding night—or a wedding for that matter.

Weeks ago he had put his response to the Ghost in the *Clarion* and the devil had not even acknowledged it. Now a message was on its way to George Fairburn. Ryan could no longer put off informing the old crotchet that his daughter had been abducted.

After bribing the *Stargazer* crew and Robert Quirk's crew to silence and attempting to solve the matter quickly himself, Ryan had finally had to admit that the time for silence was past. He needed more help than he could muster on his own. He shuddered thinking of the hell that would soon break loose: the old man's wrath, the outrage of the Crandall clan, and the fury of Joe Ward, that Rosie creature's coarse boyfriend, with his clutch of unwashed sailor friends. All of that in addition to the Ghost's continued strikes against him.

Ryan had at first suspected Lucian Thorne, but it soon became apparent it could not be he. Too many sources had reported back that Lucian was a ruined man, a drunkard living on some godforsaken island in the South Seas. No matter, whoever the fellow, the devil was ruining him financially. Somehow he must hang on until Sarina was returned to him and he could marry her and get his hands on her money. He rose, poured himself a brandy, and prowled his darkened bedchamber like a hungry bear. But the first thing he must do was stop dealing in high-priced contraband. Jon had just left for Florida, but when he returned, they would lay low for a while. The other thing he must do, and quickly, was convert the goods in his cellar to cash. Painful though it was, it would be better to take a hefty loss on the stuff than have it found on his premises. Maybe then he would stop having these damned nightmares . . .

Ginelle studied Sarina thoughtfully as they made a breakfast of Rosie's warm scones, jam, and tea. Was it true, what Donal had told her last night—that Sarina loved the captain? Ginelle was positively dying to know.

Sarina met her friend's solemn gaze over the rim of her teacup. "You must be having deep thoughts."

"They *are* rather deep," Ginelle murmured.

"If you'd like to talk, I'd like to hear . . ."

Ginelle patted her mouth with her napkin. Perhaps now was the time to bring up thoughts she had avoided saying. If she could just grasp her courage with both hands and plunge . . .

"I *would* like to talk," she said. "I've been secretive with you for too long, Rina, and I apologize. I thought it might make you more unhappy if I told you certain

things, but now I think I should tell you everything."
She folded her napkin and met Sarina's curious eyes.
"Last night Donal told me we will be here for a while
yet. I know you're desperate to leave, but the truth is,
I'm glad. Donal and I, we—plan to wed."

Ginelle looked so concerned that Sarina reached over
and squeezed her hand. "Ginny, I've been expecting
to hear of you and Donal for some time. I hope you
don't think I'm upset or—"

"He wants us to live as man and wife now," Ginelle
hurried to add, "and speak our own vows before God.
And I would, except I couldn't bear having such happiness when you have none. And so I told him that
we—you especially—must be freed before I will wed
him."

"Oh, Ginelle . . ."

"I was so certain he could sway the Ghost with such
an incentive as that, but, of course, he could not. That
man is as stubborn as a mule!" Ginelle swallowed; she
was just now coming to the hard part. How could she
ask Sarina if she loved the man who had stolen her
from Ryan? How could—

"If you love him, speak the vows with him," Sarina
said, interrupting Ginelle's thoughts.

"I cannot. I couldn't live with myself if I did."

"But you can. You can and you will," Sarina said
firmly, knowing it was time she made a confession of
her own. "I have been secretive with you, too, Ginny.
I can't explain it"—she clasped her hands tightly in her
lap—"and I don't understand it, but—I have made love
with the Ghost." When Ginelle stared at her, speechless, she managed a smile. "You see, what you have
done is not all that bad, whereas I—I have allowed myself to be seduced by a man I don't even like most of
the time."

Except that now, she thought, having seen his terrible scars and seen his weeping, she felt a certain tenderness for him.

Ginelle came suddenly to life. "Seduced? Sarina
Fairburn, you are not the sort of woman who gets se-

duced. You wouldn't make love without being in love."

"Ginny, I'm not in love, believe me. In fact, I'm so annoyed with Ryan, I doubt I love even him anymore."

Ginelle didn't show her delight at that news, for she had long since ceased to like or trust Ryan Douglas. She declared firmly: "Nothing you say will change my mind. Not only that," she added, giving Sarina a triumphant look, "but Donal says the Ghost called and called for you when he was wounded. When we are ill, we always want the ones we love."

Sarina laughed. "Abandon the thought. The only thing he cares about is my body."

Seeing a wistful look in those beautiful green eyes, Ginelle felt a thrill of excitement. Oh, fabulous day, Donal was right! Sarina loved the Ghost and seemed not even to know it.

"Since you're as annoyed with Ryan as I am," Ginelle said carefully, "perhaps we should rethink this whole situation."

Sarina tapped the table with her fingers and studied her friend, her lips curving in a smile. "Are you saying, perchance, that we should just enjoy ourselves here and not make such a fuss about being freed?"

Ginelle shrugged. "Does it not seem reasonable? It's clear to me that Ryan doesn't care a bean about us, and Donal has assured me that we'll be released eventually. In the meantime, here we are in paradise; I have Donal, Rosie has Sky, and you have—the captain."

Sarina looked pained. "Please, I don't 'have' the captain. There is a strange chemistry between us, nothing more."

Ginelle knew better than to argue. "I understand."

"And paradise or not," Sarina murmured, "our problem remains. The Ghost is a vengeful man who will not cease his attacks on Ryan—"

"—and one day, the captain and Donal will sail off and never come back," Ginelle added, her lower lip beginning to tremble. She bit it. "Is there nothing we can do?"

Ginelle didn't care a whit about Ryan and his cargos; she wanted only for her man to be safe. But she dared not share with Sarina the grand scheme that was forming in her mind. Not yet. Ginelle imagined Sarina luring and enticing the captain of the *Vengeance* until he fell so hopelessly in love with her that, to please her, he would do anything she asked. Then and only then would the *Vengeance* cease to sail.

"Could his injury have mellowed him, do you think?" Ginelle asked.

"I'll be visiting him today. I'll find out."

"Is he not going with the others then? Donal says they're setting out for supplies of some sort and the Ghost will go, too."

Sarina laughed. "Yesterday the man couldn't even stand! No, I fear he won't be going, no matter what he says. It's going to take him every bit as long as an ordinary man to recover from his wound—"

"And I suppose you'll be visiting him often?"

"I suppose—if he likes. Ginelle Crandall, what are you grinning about?"

Ginelle shook her head. "Not a thing."

Perhaps her grand plan would take effect sooner than she thought.

Lucian had arisen that morning, strong and ready to face the world again. Within seconds, his wound was burning like fire and there was such a weariness in his whole body that he muttered an oath and crawled back into bed. Damnation, when had he ever suffered such weakness? And to have it now when time was flying so quickly. Sky had come with chicken broth, forced him to drink more fever water, and complained that Lucian had reopened his wound. He had then slathered Lucian's side with a foul-smelling homemade ointment. All in all it was a bad beginning to the day.

By afternoon, Lucian had resigned himself to being in bed for at least one more day. But no more than one.

He was making use of his time by studying a technical book by Smeaton when there was a gentle tap on his door.

"Come in," he said, his heart leaping.

Sarina stepped into the room. "Good afternoon," she said softly.

"Good afternoon."

Lucian's eyes flickered over her sea-green lace and satin gown, the one he had bought in New York and not previously seen her wear. She looked like a queen and he felt his blood stirring. There was no doubt that her visits would speed his recovery. She moved to the chair beside his bed, the gown rustling, and sat down. The faint scent of lilies came to him.

"It seems you enjoy reading as much as I do." She tilted her head to see the book's title. "Smeaton—hmmm, that would be the diving-bell man, would it not?"

Lucian looked at her, astonished. As a man of the sea, he would naturally know about Smeaton's experiments on the diving bell, but this soft, delectable vision in her lace and satin . . . He frowned at her.

"How do you know of this man?"

Sarina's smile was mysterious. "Maybe someday we'll both know a bit more about each other."

He laughed. The little minx—touché. And when had he ever seen her so relaxed and easy with him? He didn't understand why it was, but he wasn't going to question it. He leaned back, gazing at her appreciatively.

Sarina's cheeks bloomed with color as his eyes moved over her. "I never thanked you for my gown . . ."

Lucian shrugged and instantly felt his wound protest the movement. It caused him to answer gruffly: "I never apologized for ruining yours."

Seeing a muscle tighten in his jaw, Sarina rose and lay a hand on his forehead. "What is it? Are you in pain?"

"It's nothing, believe me," he muttered through tight lips. He enjoyed her closeness, but at the same time it was agony. He wanted to pull her into his bed, stretch her out beside him, run his hands over her, kiss her all over, inhale her sweetness. Yet he could not even lift an arm without aching. He felt sweat pouring from his body.

"You're warm again." Sarina regarded him suspiciously. "Are you still taking that brew?" When he snorted, her eyes narrowed. She saw that the pitcher and glass were now on his bedside table. "I see. You've told Sky you will take it, but you aren't, is that it?" He looked so balky, she knew it was true. Immediately she poured a half-glass and offered it to him.

"Drink," she said.

Lucian blinked. He saw that she was going to pour it down his throat if he didn't obey. What was worse, he was too weak to fight her off. God almighty. Seeing the ludicrousness of the situation, he chuckled.

"Very well, She-Who-Commands." He clasped his hands over hers and drew the glass to his lips. He swallowed the contents, hiding a grimace, then kissed her fingers.

"Now, was that so bad?" Sarina tried to be firm. She wasn't here to crawl into bed with him but rather to learn more about him. "Promise me you'll take it faithfully."

"Impossible. I only make promises I intend to keep."

"Well, I'm sure you don't want me here every hour cracking the whip over you."

His eyes held a mocking light. "We might give it a try—it will be only for today, of course, for tomorrow I'm up and gone. That's a promise."

"Very well—" Sarina went to the spent hourglass on his washstand and turned it over. "I will return in an hour."

Lucian didn't want her to leave, but he wasn't about to ask her to stay. If she preferred going off to do whatever it was she did all day, then so be it.

"If my lieutenant is lolling out there on the veranda, tell him I could use a game of chess."

Sarina hesitated, her hand on the doorknob. "Would you—like me to play with you?"

"You play chess?"

"Why don't you find out for yourself?" Her green eyes were teasing as she came back to the bed. "The set is in my sea chest over there. We can put the board here on the bed.'

He watched, his gaze hungry, as she fetched the polished parquet board, set out the jade pieces, and pulled up her chair to face him. She smiled.

"You have the white," he said, low. "You go first."

Her slender fingers moved her king's pawn two squares forward. His reponse was identical. He leaned back on his pillows then, enjoying the sight of her contemplating her next move: her small white teeth catching her lower lip, her long gold-tipped lashes nearly touching her pink cheeks. She moved her bishop to queen's bishop four, one of several moves he had anticipated. His answer was immediate: queen's knight to queen's bishop three. Sarina blinked and bent forward, frowning, tapping a finger on her lips. It was some time before she answered: pawn to queen three.

Lucian smiled. She was a careful and thoughtful player, well-taught but not daring. Against his scruples, he decided to go easy with her. But that didn't mean coddling her. He moved his king's bishop to queen's knight five.

"Check," he said softly.

Sarina's eyes widened. It was so. Her king was in jeopardy, and he had done it so swiftly and easily that she had never even seen it coming. She didn't mind; it was only a game. She laughed.

"You play like my father. He taught me, but I simply can't think as fast as the two of you."

"Your own style reminds me of my brother's ," Lucian said. "Careful, solid."

"Indeed." That was all Sarina needed to hear. Careful and solid—meaning dull. "Queen's knight to queen's bishop three," she said sweetly.

As they continued to play, the light gradually grew

dim, and the fever water had long been forgotten by the time she made her last move. She patted a yawn and gave the Ghost a lazy look.

"Checkmate," she said.

Lucian frowned at the board and shook his throbbing head. "I have no excuses; I played my best. Your father is a good teacher."

Sarina was pleased with herself, but she didn't gloat. "Bear in mind, please, that I don't have a fever." She felt his forehead and found it was still hot. "We have forgotten your medicine." As she poured it for him, she asked, "Does your brother ever win when you play?" She saw his eyes flicker, as though he was seeing some distant scene.

"Shane has been dead for three years." His dry voice held no emotion. He lay back then, as if suddenly overcome with weariness. "Will you send in my lieutenant?"

"Of course, and I—I'm so sorry about Shane . . ."

Sarina did as he asked. She fetched Donal for him, then fled to her room. For some reason she would not understand, she felt wounded. Naturally, it was sad that his brother, who had given him a book of Shakespeare's sonnets and played solid careful chess with him, was dead. And it was sad that the Ghost wept for him still, but why should she, too, grieve so for him? And then she knew, and it did not seem at all strange for her to do so. She loved Shane's brother. She loved the Ghost . . .

Chapter 15

After four days Lucian's wound finally began to heal, but he still couldn't stand without dizziness, nor would his legs hold him. He would have cursed his fate but for the fact that Aurora was with him for hours on end. She read to him, played chess with him, laughed with him, teased him when he tried to catch and kiss her. Although his legs were not yet strong, his arms were. He kept drawing her onto his lap.

"I have a question, lady," he said. "That night I lay raving, did my visiting angel kiss and stroke me?"

Sarina laughed, but before she could answer, his mouth was on her lips, her throat, her shoulders. The Ghost was devouring her. Her own hunger was so great, she returned his passion in full measure as his hands moved over her, tenderly caressing and undressing her. But then, before she was fully unclothed, he began to tremble. His face and torso gleamed with sweat.

"Damn!"

Seeing how pale and taut his face was, she whispered: "It's all right. There will be other times. Shhh, don't fret, let us just lie here together for a little . . ."

Holding her soft body in his arms, her silken hair beneath his lips, feeling her heart beat against his chest and experiencing a warmth, a comfort he had never known before, Lucian was struck by a thunderbolt. Was this love? This wanting never to lose her, wanting to hold her and never let her go? He didn't have to wait for an answer. He knew. He loved her. God almighty, but he loved her. He could hardly believe the depth of his feelings, nor could he believe they were returned.

This was his enemy's woman, after all . . .

"You are recovered!" Sarina exclaimed when she saw the Ghost lounging on the veranda the next morning.

Lucian chuckled. "Even Sky noticed."

"How could he not? You're all better, I can see it!"

She was thrilled, for there had been many times when she had wondered if he would ever be the same again. Now he was as she remembered him, and a familiar fear tempered her joy. The same fear that plagued Ginelle—the thought that the next time the *Vengeance* sailed might be the last.

"There's something else I want you to see," Lucian said softly, so as not to be overheard. "Meet me at the dock after dinner. We're going for a little boat ride, you and I." He left then, striding down toward the *Vengeance*, before Sarina could ask what it was about.

When she stepped into the skiff that evening, she wore the green breeches and shirt she had made, and was ready for adventure. She had suspected the Ghost was going to show her the smallest isle in the Malaga cluster, and she was right. He rowed them down a still green channel with great trees crowding the sides to a white shore she had not previously seen.

"My lieutenant calls this isle the jewel of the five," Lucian said, beaching the skiff and stepping onto the sand.

He took Sarina's hand and helped her out, and soon they were walking down a bush-lined lane, the branches of the sweeping trees bowing overhead. When they came to a grassy clearing at the tunnel's end, she gasped.

"My goodness . . ." She lay a hand on her breast.

There were flowers everywhere. Great white trumpets; tall spires of blue, purple, and lilac; clusters of poppies; each blossom filling the warm evening air with its own sweet fragrance. Further on, like a picture framed in lushest green, was the foaming sea breaking on the white shore, a red-gold sunset touching it all.

Sarina had never seen such beauty. She felt her eyes brim with tears, felt the Ghost take her hand.

"I thought you would like it," he said, drawing her toward the creamy, foaming wavelets. "Come in with me."

"I—am not a good swimmer."

He laughed. "No matter. We'll ride the swells. Take off your clothes and come on . . ."

Sarina hesitated for only a moment. As she stripped down to her chemise and the cut-off underwear she wore beneath her breeches, Lucian also stripped. He took her hand, and side by side they walked into the bubbling surf, deeper and deeper. Sarina gasped in pleasure as a gentle swell lifted her off her feet. Lucian's arm went instantly around her.

"I—I cannot touch bottom!" she cried, clutching him in a death grip.

"You aren't going to sink. I'll hold you," he said gently, but still she clutched him. He kissed her fresh wet mouth that tasted of the sea. "Look, my arms are around you. Nothing will happen to you."

Suddenly she did feel safe; safe and free to enjoy the gentle swells lifting them, and to look at the glimmering beauty all around them.

"Look at the sunset on the water!" she cried, awed. "It's like a sheet of flame—and look, the moon is out already!"

Suddenly Lucian's mouth was on hers, his tongue exploring her lips, tenderly tasting their sweet saltiness. He lowered her wet chemise so that her breasts rose out of the water, white pink-tipped peaks, soft, gleaming, indescribably lovely. He pressed them together and tongued both nipples at once so that Sarina gave a low cry of pleasure. Lifting her, cradling her in his arms with the sea supporting them both, he carried her back to shore, kissing her face, her mouth, her hair, her throat, breasts, shoulders . . .

"Have you ever made love in the water?" he asked, lowering her beside one of the shallow tidal pools that pitted the coast.

"You know I have not."

He laughed softly, easily. "I guess you have not at that."

His urgent hands helped Sarina slip off her wet clothing, and when she finally threw the things to the sand, he drew her into the azure water, pulled her into his arms, and bent his dark head to her breasts.

"Little mermaid . . ." He tongued her nipples again.

Sarina closed her eyes, savoring the sweet spasm between her thighs, that warm, wet surrender she experienced in his arms alone. She wrapped her long legs around his and felt his hardness pressed against her.

Lucian drew in a sharp breath. The fast-deepening shadows emphasized her curvaceousness, the lush whiteness and smoothness of her soft flesh and plum-colored mouth.

"Do you like it here in the pool," he asked huskily, "or would you prefer the beach?"

Sarina arched her back, lifting her breasts closer to his mouth. Her voice was whisper-soft. "I like it here . . ."

He breathed in the clean, salty fragrance of her love-heated flesh and touched his tongue to hers. When had he ever wanted a woman as badly and as often as he wanted this one? It seemed he had an incredible hunger, and the name of that hunger was Aurora.

"You have cast a spell over me," he murmured.

He stroked her shoulders, and then slid his hands down over her ribs to her slender hips, lifting them, burying his face in the shadows between her breasts and in the silky fuzz between her thighs. He entered her smoothly and easily, lying quietly within her, quiescent except for a soft, almost impalpable throbbing. He closed his eyes, felt the warm walls of her sheath pressing in on him like a haven, a sweet shelter in a storm. He began rocking then, his eyes still closed, his swollen shaft filling her, slipping within her ever so gently, his face suffused with pleasure.

Sarina moaned softly under his mouth. How strange that she could not separate the Ghost from the wonderful gift he was giving her, the sweet, hot blossom of desire unfolding deep inside her.

Noting her gasping breaths and glazed eyes, Lucian knew he could unleash his mounting hunger. He began thrusting, no longer gently but harder, faster. When he felt the hot release of her own passion flooding her sheath and bathing his pulsing manhood, he reached his own peak. They lay on the soft sand, drained and somnolent in each other's arms.

Sarina stroked the crisp black curls on his arm. She had to tell him of her love; she could not wait any longer. She asked, softly: "Are you awake?"

"Yes," Lucian said softly, lifting her hand to his mouth and kissing her fingers. "I've been thinking of the best way to tell you—how much I love you." He rose on one elbow and looked down into her wide, wondering gaze, silvered now with moonlight. "It seems there's no way except this . . ." He gave her the longest and most tender of kisses, then cradled her close.

"I cannot believe it . . ." Sarina was stunned. "I was just about to tell you the same thing. I love you . . ."

"Do you now?" Lucian's eyes glowed, his heart thundering like the surf that had begun to rise. He tilted her face so he could look into her own shining eyes. "By the gods, Aurora . . ."

She laughed and sat up. "My name is Sarina . . ."

Suddenly she felt a white-hot burst of joy that Ryan had not responded to the ransom. If he had, this wonder between her and the Ghost might never have happened.

He spoke her name gravely. "Sarina . . ." He smiled. "It feels good on my tongue and it suits you. It's a beautiful name. As beautiful as you are."

"What about you?" Sarina asked lightly. "Am I ever going to hear the name of the man I love?"

Seeing his hesitation, she knew that nothing had changed. Now that he was well, the *Vengeance* would soon sail. But he surprised her. He said gruffly:

"You're right. It's time you knew my name. It's time you knew everything." He dried himself with his clothes, then pulled them on. Sarina, too, dried herself and dressed. They began walking up and down the small beach. Lucian took her hand, but his eyes were on the sea. "Have you ever heard of the Naipoor affair?"

Sarina searched her mind. "Was something stolen? Pearls, perhaps? Yes, I recall now. Pearls were stolen, and my father was outraged when the thief turned out to be a captain in the—" She stopped in mid-sentence, covering her mouth with her hand. "Oh, no . . ."

"It's all right," Lucian said, meeting her horrified gaze.

She stared up at him. "Are you saying you are—that captain?"

"Yes. I commanded the *Peacekeeper*. I'm Lucian Thorne."

"Lucian," she murmured, trying to shut out the rest of it by dwelling on his name. "Lucian Thorne. How beautiful . . ." A fine tremble began deep inside her.

Seeing her distress, Lucian added, "I'm not a thief, Sarina. My brother and I were betrayed."

Sarina saw that his eyes blazed. His mouth was a grim slash. She asked tonelessly: "It was Ryan?"

"It was Ryan," he confirmed harshly. "Donal learned of his treachery when I was in prison. We know how he got the pearls and what happened to the accomplice who procured them, but we don't know how he hid them aboard my vessel."

Sarina put her hands to her temples. "Really, I find this very hard to believe. Ryan has always been a perfect gentleman, a caring man . . ."

Lucian's laughter flew up to meet the night. "The bastard is a damned good actor."

She didn't want to believe him, yet how could she not? But she felt embarrassed after having defended Ryan for weeks now. She stiffened her shoulders.

"I simply don't see how my father and I could have so misjudged him. My father is a fine businessman. He has much experience dealing with people and is extremely astute."

Lucian's black brows drew together. "Then, of course, your father is aware that Ryan's vessels have been smuggling contraband goods through ports in the Isle of Man for the past six years. And he is aware that since New York began imposing duties on foreign goods three years ago, Ryan has smuggled there."

Sarina sighed. "No, certainly he is unaware of any such thing." She didn't want to believe Lucian, but he spoke with such conviction.

"The bastard is clever," Lucian said gently. "He's a fine, upstanding member of the trading world, and I know of his dark dealings only because of a chance encounter. It occurred five years ago when the *Peacekeeper* was on patrol in the Irish Sea. We were warned that a certain vessel was carrying contraband, and when we boarded her, we found it. I was damned shocked to discover she was Ryan's. I had known him as a lad on my first sea voyage but had lost track of him. I didn't know he had a fleet of merchant ships. There was nothing to be done about the loot we found—I had to confiscate it and report him—but then the bastard had the gall to offer a bribe if I would avoid his vessels in the future. For friendship's sake, he said. I told him to go to hell. We began watching his vessels with particular interest and confiscated other cargos." He drew in a deep breath. "Two years later, the pearls were discovered aboard my vessel. The bastard got his revenge."

"And you went to prison . . ." It was difficult for Sarina to take it all in. "It must have been unbearable."

Lucian gave a harsh bark of laughter. "Prison wasn't so bad. It was what put us there that I found unbearable. My brother and I, both innocent, were court-martialed; I was stripped of my command and my honor; both of us were flogged through the fleet . . ."

Sarina walked numbly, woodenly at his side, her heart growing heavy as she listened to Lucian's low, angry voice detailing the terrible event: drums leading a doleful parade of longboats carrying the prisoners to every ship, one after another, in the hastily gathered fleet. Shane, a slender lad of sixteen, dying after sixty lashes that tore his flesh from his bones; Lucian himself barely alive to take the final lashes on the fleet commander's vessel. By the time Lucian finished his story Sarina was weeping softly.

"After that, I had no reason to live, but Donal bullied me into surviving." Donal had damn well ordered him to live, he recalled, saying he had no business curling up and dying until the slime who had done this heinous crime had received his due.

"Was it then that you came to Malaga?" Sarina asked.

Lucian nodded. "It fell readily into our hands. Donal had been here before. He was friendly with the owner, an older man who had lost his wife and was yearning for civilization."

Sarina heard Lucian's deep voice describe his early days at Malaga. Sleeping in the sun and swimming and healing; Donal's far-flung net of men discovering who was behind the treachery; their scheming and plotting to find a suitable ship and the right men; conceiving the idea of the Ghost ship. Most seamen came from simple, superstitious backgrounds, and a ghost ship seemed a good way to terrorize the men on Ryan's vessel. If they were too afraid to resist, no lives would be lost. It was something Lucian insisted on.

Everything was working out as planned, Douglas suffering with the loss of many cargos, but it still remained for them to discover the warehouses or caches where he stored his contraband. It was thought that he had two caches, one on either side of the Atlantic, and it didn't matter which one Lucian found first. Either one would be conclusive proof of Ryan's guilt.

"I have talked too much," Lucian muttered as they walked up and down the beach, the tide rolling in, the moon glittering on the water, Sarina's hand held tightly in his. He looked down at her. "I have talked endlessly and you have been too quiet."

"I needed to hear and understand what happened." She looked out over the water, then back at his face. His eyes held the some bleakness she had seen there before. "I'm so very sorry about all that you've suffered," she whispered. "So sorry. Words fail me . . ."

She believed him, of course she believed him. She had painfully pictured everything he had described, but she was unable to put Ryan's face to the man who had caused such havoc. She could not. She could not even conceive of such a thing.

Lucian drew her into his arms and held her close, her soft, yielding body against his shutting out the leaden emptiness that overwhelmed him when he considered his loss. He buried his face in her hair, then his lips found her temple and the soft hollow behind her ear. His arms tightened.

"I need you . . ." His unexpected words surprised him. When had he ever admitted to needing anyone?

"I'm here," Sarina said, lifting her lips for his kiss. "I'm here . . ."

The next morning when the *Vengeance* sailed, there was no cause for grieving. It was merely a trip to replenish Malaga's depleted supply of meat and dairy products. The men would return that same evening. Sarina had spent so much of her time with Lucian that she welcomed the opportunity to visit with Ginelle. She had a lot to tell her.

They had gone to Sarina's favorite spot on the outer shore to see the ship's departure, and after her sails had disappeared from sight, Ginelle gathered her skirts and lowered herself to the warm sand.

"From the look on your face, you have news of some sort."

Sarina sat down beside her. "It's about Ryan—something we never would have dreamed of." She told Ginelle the whole story.

Ginelle was moved. "Donal said it was something awful, but he never would say what. He felt the captain should tell you first." She found a seashell in the sand and studied it, not looking at Sarina. "Do you believe him? The Ghost?"

"He has a name," Sarina said. "It's Lucian Thorne, and his story has such a ring of truth to it that, yes, I suppose I do believe him."

"Lucian Thorne? How utterly romantic-sounding." Ginelle gave Sarina a guarded look. "But what do you mean, you 'suppose' you believe him?"

"It's just that I know Ryan, and I don't see how he could possibly be the villain Lucian says he is. I never once saw that side of him, nor did my father." Sarina shook her head, her hands on her cheeks. "I'm so confused. I'm sure Ryan has his side to the story and I should try to keep an open mind."

"What are you going to say to him? If we ever do see him again, that is . . ."

Sarina's head was spinning, there was so much to think about. "It's clear that I can't tell him what I have been told. I wouldn't dare, and it's also clear that I must break our engagement. Neither of us is interested in marriage any longer . . ." She got to her feet and shook the sand from her gown. "Shall we return to the house?"

Ginelle's blue eyes danced. "Have you nothing more to tell me? You and Lucian have spent a great deal of time together of late."

"We played chess."

Ginelle laughed. "Indeed."

"In fact, why don't we play a game now? Lucian has offered the board to us any time he's gone."

"Let's do then. Perhaps I will trounce you this time."

The door to the Ghost's bedchamber stood open, and

the gleaming parquet chessboard lay where Sarina had put it the previous day, the jade chessmen already set up.

"Let's carry the king and queen and bishops separately so they don't topple off," she said. "The rest of the pieces will be quite safe."

As they left the room, intending to play in Sarina's chamber, Ginelle exclaimed, "A New York newspaper! I would love to read it—do you think Lucian would mind?"

"I can't think why he would. Bring it along. I'll glance at it, too."

As Sarina readied the chessboard and drew up chairs, Ginelle scanned the pages. She made a face. "It's hardly interesting. Shipping news, war news, and politics."

It wasn't until they'd finished their game and Ginelle had gone to her own room that Sarina sat down to read the *Clarion*. On the final page, her eyes were drawn to a small notice with a black circle around it. How strange . . . She carried it to the window, the better to see it.

I understand it read. *I await your instructions.*

She frowned and reread it, a terrible suspicion dawning. She looked at the date. June nineteenth. The *Vengeance* had left to deliver Lucian's ransom note to Ryan that same week.

Sarina sank into a chair, feeling as though she had been hit in the stomach. Lucian had lied to her. Ryan *had* tried to contact him! He did still want her, undoubtedly he did, and she, fool that she was, had believed Lucian and fallen in love with him, and all the while Ryan was waiting, waiting, still believing that she was his. And if Lucian had lied about this, had he lied also about Ryan's so-called treachery? And about loving her? She leaped up, pacing and twisting her hands together. Oh, God . . .

Just before dinnertime the *Vengeance* slipped quietly into the bay and tied up. As the crew began unloading

supplies, a soft knock sounded on Sarina's door. Heart
thudding, she opened it, so hurt, so furious that she
could not speak. She gave Lucian Thorne a blazing
look.

Lucian had never seen her so angry. He came in and
closed the door behind him. "What is it?" he asked
gruffly, grasping her shoulders. "What happened?"

Sarina snatched up the *Clarion*, opened to the last
page. She pointed a trembling finger at the small circled notice. "What is this, pray?"

Lucian looked from the paper to her furious green
eyes. "It's from Ryan." God almighty, why had he not
burned the damned paper?

Sarina hurled it to the floor. "How gallant and con-
siderate of you to say nothing of this when you knew
I was dying for word and every day seemed like a
week. H-how could you do such a cruel thing?"

His arms went around her, but she pushed him
away. She flung herself into the wing chair where she
sat trembling, so angry and empty that she could not
even weep. She looked up at his grim face. "And do
not dare to tell me it was to punish Ryan! I was hurting
just as much."

His voice low, Lucian said, "I could not send you
back to the bastard."

"That much I know," she said, breathless with fury,
"but would it not have been kinder to tell me so? Not
to leave me th-thinking that Ryan didn't care about me
or w-want me."

"God, Sarina—" He moved toward her, yearning to
comfort her.

"Don't touch me!"

"Damn it, I love you."

"Hah! Because it suits your present purpose to say
so?"

"By the gods, that is not so. Why are you complicating things?"

Sarina stood up, hands on her hips, cheeks flaming,
hair a gleaming red-gold cape tumbling over her
breasts.

"I am complicating things? *I?*" Her eyes glittered with unshed tears. "Oh, no Lucian Thorne, it is you who have complicated my whole life. Abducting me and then lying to me about so important a matter." She shook her head. "I wonder if I can believe anything you say."

"What exactly do you mean?" he asked softly.

Sarina saw his eyes go hooded, saw him become the Ghost, but she was too enraged to care. "I mean all of those terrible things you said about Ryan."

"I see."

Lucian clenched his teeth and strode to the window. Everything was falling apart. She doubted his word and now he was doubting hers. She had said she loved him, but what kind of shabby love was it if she had no more faith in him than that? Probably she didn't love him at all; probably it was Malaga working its spell on her, and that bastard Ryan Douglas was the one she would always love. The thought sat on Lucian like lead. Having just found her, was he about to lose her? Suddenly, surprisingly, he felt her hand on his arm.

"I do love you." Her voice was small, tight. "I'm confused and furious with you, yes, but—I love you. I'm just not so sure now that you love me . . ." Her beautiful face was pale and her rosy lips contorted as the tears came.

Lucian pulled her close and held her, tilting her chin so that her drenched eyes met his.

"I do love you. God, I do," he muttered. He gave her a hungry kiss, his hands moving over her.

But words and kisses were no longer enough. After keeping her prisoner for five weeks, it was time he made amends. He knew now that, more than anything, he wanted her happiness and he wanted it to be of her choosing. Even so, he was filled with despair, with an aching emptiness where before there had been warmth and gladness, for he knew now that he might lose her forever. He drew a deep breath.

"I'm taking you to New York tomorrow."

Sarina stared at him, blinked, dabbed at her tears with her fingers. "What?"

"Tell the others," he added crisply. "We will sail at sunup."

She had assumed that if the Ghost loved her, he would never allow her to leave him. Now she saw in his icy blue eyes that he was freeing her because he *did* love her, and he wanted her happiness. Her own love for him brimmed over as she gazed at his familiar face, the jet-black hair and winged brows and lean body. Teak and ebony. He was the Ghost, yes, he was excitement and danger and a fast, deadly, silent ship. But he was also blue seas and balmy nights, golden sunsets and hungry kisses. Paradise. He was the Ghost, and he was her beloved. They were one and the same. Sarina put her arms around him.

"Thank you . . ." She could have wept all over again, in gratitude and with love, but she kept her dignity. "We will not stay long. I must straighten out my situation with Ryan, and we will send messages to our families. We can return whenever you say." She looked up at his unsmiling face. "Wh-what is it? You *will* return for the three of us, won't you?"

"Of course. I'm just worried about leaving you with that devil." But the bastard would not dare harm her, he thought, and Donal would be nearby to keep a watchful eye on the three of them. Lucian kissed the tip of her nose. "I must help with the unloading now. We will talk more after dinner."

"Lucian, wait." Sensing his deep concern, she caught his hand. "Everything is going to be all right, I promise. There's something I have not told you. You see, my father is rather an important man back home."

Lucian grinned. "I rather thought he might be."

"He is George Fairburn, and when I see him, I'm going to tell him your story. He will inform the Admiralty. In fact, he will go to the king, if need be, to vindicate you." As much as she wanted to see Lucian's honor restored, she still could not put Ryan's face to that wretch who had betrayed him.

Lucian's laughter boomed. George Fairburn? Founder of a shipping empire that traded with the Far and Mid-East; a decorated war hero; friend to kings all over the globe. And Sarina was his daughter? By the gods. He had asked for a mere two thousand pieces of gold when he could have asked for the world and gotten it. But no, George Fairburn was not his enemy.

Sarina, too, was laughing. "I'm glad it amuses you so."

Lucian gave the tip of her nose another kiss. "As you say, cosset, everything will be all right . . ."

Chapter 16

D awn had not yet come when the *Vengeance* weighed anchor under a small high-sailing moon. She was lit with lanterns fore, aft, and amidships and her sails were furled. Oars propelled her through the still, green waterways of Malaga, through the vine-veiled cliff face, and then she was free, skimming windblown over the moon-kissed sea, a gray ghost, her gray-clad crew silently, competently manning halyards, tending tacklings, unfurling sails. Sarina hung on to the rail on the tossing deck, Ginelle by her side.

"I cannot believe we are actually on our way," Ginelle exclaimed, holding her cloak tightly against the beating wind. "And Donal says Lucian is not even asking ransom. How did it happen, I wonder?"

Sarina bent to Ginelle's ear. "Perhaps it was my telling him I loved him . . ."

Ginelle stared. "Y-you did? And you do?"

Sarina was laughing. "Yes. You were absolutely right, you know. I love him. I humbly admit that you knew it before I did, and now do close your mouth, Ginelle. It is impolite to gape."

Ginelle gave a happy gasp. "I want to hear all about it. I want to hear everything!"

As they talked, dawn came and the lanterns were extinguished. Pearl-gray yielded to lemon and then to gold as the great canopy of the sky split open and the sun poured out upon the sea.

"You love Lucian!" Ginelle exclaimed. She caught

and hugged Sarina. "Oh, Rina, does this mean you'll be returning to the ship with us after you see Ryan?"

"Yes." Sarina was enjoying her friend's delight.

"And I trust it means the Ghost will cease his attacks on Ryan . . ."

Sarina felt as if the sun had gone under a cloud. "We did not discuss it." Seeing Lucian approaching, she put a finger to her lips and pulled the hood of her green cape over her wildly whipping hair.

Lucian found the two women in the bow clinging to the rail, their heads close together.

"Will you ladies come with me, please?"

He led them to his cabin where Donal, Sky, and Rosie already awaited them. Taking a seat on the bunk where she had once slept, Sarina found herself remembering the glint of a knife, that silly sparring match between them, being chained to the bed, being chained to his soul . . .

"I want to discuss our plans," Lucian said. He remained standing, moving restlessly about the cabin. "Donal will go with you. He knows the area and will see that you arrive at your destination safely." He looked at Sarina. "Will you feel safe in that house?"

She was startled by the question. "Of course."

Lucian nodded, and resumed his pacing. It was doubtful the bastard would harm the daughter and friends of George Fairburn.

"At any rate, Donal will lodge nearby and contact you daily." Again his gaze locked on Sarina's. "It is understood," he said gruffly, "that you will not reveal to Douglas or to anyone our identities or the whereabouts of Malaga."

Sarina's eyes flashed. "You need even say such a thing?"

Ginelle cried, "Oh, I do hope you know we would never betray you!"

"An' may God strike me dead if I did such a dastardly deed!" Rosie protested.

"Fine," Lucian said curtly. "Now—you will be arriving in New York July twenty-sixth. I will return for you

August first. That gives you five days to complete your business.''

''Five days!'' Sarina exclaimed.

''Is it not enough?''

''It is—fine.''

''Good.''

Lucian did not want to be anywhere near the New York area when Sarina turned up on the devil's doorstep. He would head for a secluded cove he knew along the New Jersey coast, and there they would disguise the *Vengeance* and remain until they returned for the four of them.

Sarina was disheartened. Five days was forever when she had expected one day to suffice. But Lucian was right to give her that much time. Ryan might not even be there; she might have to wait for him. And she must arrange for messages to be sent to their families. Thinking of her father receiving her news made Sarina quake in her shoes. She prayed he would be so happy she was safe that he would not fuss about the rest—the cancellation of her wedding and the fact that she was not yet ready to come home. She would say only that the three of them were with new friends and would be in frequent correspondence. As for Ryan, she hoped he would not object to her breaking their engagement.

''Lieutenant, explain the rest of the plan,'' Lucian requested.

''Aye.'' Donal got to his feet. ''Tomorrow morning we reach Seabury, a fishing village, our first destination. Sky and one of the crew will row us ashore. From there, we will take a boat into the city.'' Seeing the women were completely confused, he laughed. ''Ladies, surely you did not expect us to take the *Vengeance* anywhere near New York?''

Sarina tried not to show her growing concern, but she had begun to think of all sorts of other difficulties.

''Once in the city,'' Donal continued, ''we will seek out Tom Chambers, one of our men. He will tell us where it is safe to lodge. The next morning, you three''—his black eyes lingered on Ginelle—''will attempt to see Douglas." He was not at all happy about her being anywhere near the bastard, but she had insisted on coming, as had Rosie.

"When will we see you again?" Sarina asked. Her heart was beginning to beat faster, for she could imagine everything going wrong. What if she never saw Lucian again?

"We will make those plans when we have to," Donal said gently, "but never fear, I will be close by."

Sarina's eyes sought Lucian. "What am I to tell Ryan? He will want to know everything. What shall I say?"

"Donal and I want to give it more thought. By evening, we will have decided exactly what we want you to say, including how you came to be freed. We are considering various possibilities."

Looking at her small, vulnerable form and angel face, the thick cloud of reddish hair cascading down her green cloak, Lucian felt an aching emptiness. Would she come back to him? He wanted suddenly to hold her, to cover her with kisses, to make love to her one last time. He sucked in a deep breath. No. It was impossible. They were aboard ship and while Donal and Sky knew what lay between them, his crew had no suspicion of it, nor did he want them to.

"That's all for now," he told the five of them, "except for you, Sarina. Please stay. Donal, leave the door open when you leave."

After the others had left, Sarina whispered, "Promise you will come for me."

"Have I not said I will?" he said in a low voice.

"I am uneasy . . ."

Lucian was well aware that she was still uncertain about Ryan's role in his past, that she found his villainy hard to believe. And while he wanted more than anything to trust in her love for him, a part of him was wary.

"Lucian, please, hold me tight . . ."

He wanted to do more than hold her. Wordlessly, he drew her to the side of the cabin, pressed her against the wall with his hungry body, and kissed her deeply, urgently. He lowered his mouth to her throat and shoulders, tasting her soft flesh, inhaling her fragrance, trailing kisses to her lips. His thoughts, his whole body reeled, electrified by her nearness. How could he let her go back to that devil? But how could he not? How else could he believe she loved him unless she were free to return to him willingly?

"Tell me everything is going to be all right," Sarina murmured between kisses.

"Everything is going to be all right, I promise. You are not to worry."

Sarina slipped her arms under his and pressed him closer. She loved everything about him—the way he looked and tasted and felt, the way he smelled of the sea and wind and sun. And what would she do if harm came to him?

"What is it?" Lucian whispered, his lips on her hair.

"I'm so afraid for you. I had no idea how dangerous this would be." She lifted her mouth to his, gave him a hungry kiss, and another and another. "I would die if anything happened to you."

"Nothing will happen to me."

"But your ship—anyone could recognize her and . . . and seize you."

He lay a dark finger over her lips. "No one will recognize us," he said softly. "You will go ashore in Seabury before sunup and we will hole up in a cove south of there until we return to Seabury for you. We will have added navy paint and extra ballast before then." He smiled down at her. "See, you are not to worry."

He heard a soft footfall nearing his cabin. With one last kiss, he thrust her into a chair and was sitting on his bunk talking to her when the tap came on his open door. His narrowed eyes went to the seaman who stood there.

"What is it, Garrick?"

Garrick looked from Lucian to Sarina. "I'll come back. I didn't know yer were busy." He turned to leave.

"Stay, man. The lady and I have finished." Lucian gave Sarina a nod of dismissal. "Be ready before sunrise."

She nodded. "We will."

After she left, Garrick said gruffly, "Cap'n, I hope yer ain't forgot—I regret that business earlier wi' the wimmin."

"I know it, Garrick. You took your licks and you've made up for it in other ways, so as far as I'm concerned, the matter is over. Forget it."

"Would yer let me help take th' ladies ashore? I want them ta know, too. I'm sorry I wuz a bastard."

Lucian regarded him thoughtfully. "Will this be the end of it then, man?"

"Oh, this'll be th' end of it, sir, I guarantee it. This'll put me heart at ease."

"Very well. You and Mr. Braden will row the party ashore before dawn and make sure all is well with them before you cast off."

Garrick smiled. "That we will."

Sarina stared out the window of the swaying coach as it made its way along the bustling New York City waterfront. She was taking everything in—the great ships tied up at the piers, the sounds of creaking masts and clanking chains, horse hooves on cobblestones, men calling to one another, the smells of the sea and frying fish and ale. It might have been morning in London, and she might have been on her way to visit her father's office or one of his ships newly arrived from India or China.

But she was not in London. She was in a strange land on a mission that had begun to frighten her. Now that it was too late to turn back, she sensed that Ryan might not give her up without a fight. Oh, why had she not stayed on Malaga with Lucian and sent a message to her father that she was safe and happy? She could have sent a message to Ryan, too, for that matter, but, no, she had felt she had to break their engagement in person.

"Rina—" Ginelle's voice was small and muffled, her cloak pulled up about her face despite the warmth of the July morning. "I am sorry to say that I'm afraid."

"Me likewise, mum," said Rosie. "Me poor teeth won't stop chatterin'."

Sarina sighed. "I admit I'm not looking forward to it either."

It was safe to talk. Donal had put them in a carriage driven by Thomas Chambers, one of Lucian's men. Sarina suspected his job was to keep a regular watch on Ryan's movements. She was reminded of Garrick, of how he had asked to help row them ashore at the fishing village. It seemed he was still trying to atone for his earlier crude treatment of Ginelle and Rosie, and Lucian had accepted his help—his own way of saying bygones were bygones.

"Would you listen to us?" Ginelle was giggling nervously. "At long last we are free and going to see Ryan, and Rosie and I are terrified and you are not looking forward to it! How things have changed in less than two months."

Sarina nodded. "It is hard to believe."

This was Ryan they did not want to see. Ryan whom she had once loved, a man she had loved enough to come all the way to New York City to marry. She tensed as the carriage slowed, stopping finally before a large elegant town house standing behind a high stone wall. The ornamental iron gate at the entrance matched the delicately wrought balconies on the tall narrow second- and third-story windows.

Ginelle gave a soft moan. "Oh, my, we are here, I fear, but it is a lovely house."

Rosie looked doubtful. "It's purty, all right, 'ceptin' fer them high walls an' th' gate."

Sarina said sternly, "Now we must remember, all of us, that we are not going to be here forever. Only five days."

"Rina, what if I cannot remember to—to describe the men the way Lucian told us—and h-how we came to be released and all? What if I do it all wrong?"

"An' me, I've forgot already what we wuz told."
Rosie's eyes were wide with anxiety.

Sarina's heart was thumping. "Shhh, hush now,
both of you. We'll all be fine. If he asks something of
you and you can't remember, say nothing. Act faint
and I will try to answer."

She herself felt somewhat faint as Chambers opened
the door of their carriage and helped them out.

"I will remind you again, ladies"—his voice was
low—"that as long as you remain at Douglas Hall, you
must take a daily stroll after your midday meal."

"Thank you, we will remember," Sarina said.
Chambers was lodging with Donal and would act as
their go-between.

"Tell Donal I love him," Ginelle whispered, "and
tell him not to worry . . ."

"My coffee is cold, Gilmore," Ryan Douglas muttered to his butler, "and I have had better scones and
eggs."

"I am sorry, sir. Let me take them back to Cook."

"No, no," he said with an air of injury. "They will
do. I will just pick at them anyway. I have no appetite
anymore."

There wasn't a thing wrong with his breakfast, he
mused, slathering butter and jam on a scone and biting
into it. He just wanted to grumble. He had received a
scathing missive from old Fairburn. The man had not
yet gotten Ryan's own message about Sarina's abduction, but he had heard of it nonetheless and he was
wroth. He had put a huge price on the Ghost's head
and raked Ryan over the coals for not informing him
immediately of the catastrophe. Damn. It was the
thanks Ryan got for trying to spare the old coot.

If he had had even a speck of luck, Ryan brooded,
Sarina would be in his house and in his bed by now,
and her father would never have been the wiser. But
maybe the tide was turning finally, what with the reward posted and the Ghost's being wounded ten days
ago. Since then, all had been quiet. In addition, Ryan

had managed to sell off his goods. He had taken a loss as he expected—damned bunch of vultures—but now he was well-fixed, at least for a while, and had nothing to worry about until his uncle returned from Florida with the gems he had gone there to buy. By God, this trip would be the last one until the Ghost was caught and hanged. Ryan could not stand such worry anymore. He frowned as the front bell pealed. Several moments later, Gilmore knocked and entered.

"Who was it, Gilmore?" Ryan asked, adding more cream to his coffee.

"Three young ladies to see you, sir. They decline to give their names . . ."

Ryan raised a curious eyebrow. Young ladies? Now what? He had cast a flirtatious eye on several wenches in several pubs during the week, but surely none would be so bold as to come to his front door in broad daylight.

"Put them in the drawing room, Gilmore. I will be there presently."

He took his good time about finishing breakfast, and when he had thoroughly wiped the butter from his mouth, he strode to the front of the house and flung open the drawing room doors.

"Now, ladies, how can I be of service?" He stopped, staring at them. His mouth fell open. "Sarina! Sarina, my God! And Ginelle!"

He was across the room in three long strides, caught Sarina up in a great hug, then held her at arm's length to gaze at her in disbelief.

"Hello, Ryan," she said gravely. She had not expected that he would seem such a stranger.

"Hello, Ryan." It was an echo from Ginelle.

Rosie dipped a curtsy. "H-hello, Mr. Douglas, sir."

Ryan nodded an acknowledgment to them both, but his gaze sought Sarina. He removed her green cloak and flung it onto the settle.

"My God, let me look at you!" He turned her about, running his hands over her arms and shoulders, tilting up her chin to see her face. "Where did you come from? How did you get here?"

"It's a—long story . . ."

She had never noticed how like chocolate his brown eyes were. They melted over her and suddenly his mouth was on hers. She was crushed hard against him as he gave her a long kiss, deeper than any he had ever bestowed upon her before. She stiffened, but he seemed not to notice.

"Gilmore!" he shouted. "Bring tea for the ladies. Will you take breakfast?"

"Thank you, we have eaten. And no tea, please. We are fine." Sarina was worried about the hungry way his eyes were moving over her.

"Darling, come and sit down." He led her to the settle and threw her cloak onto a nearby chair. "I cannot believe you are here. I have so many questions. Gilmore, you may go." He looked at the others. "Forgive me, ladies, sit down, please."

Rosie perched uneasily on the edge of the exotic chair closest to her. Ginelle made herself comfortable in a wing chair, pulling her cloak close and gazing about the room, her lips pursed. It was elaborately furnished with more money than taste, she decided instantly. There was too much of everything. Too much brass and crystal and velvet and brocade, rugs atop rugs on the polished floors, knickknacks and thingamajigs everywhere, treasures from all over the world. Most smuggled, no doubt.

She chided herself. She really must pay attention to what was being said, for Ryan was asking one of those very things Lucian and Donal had drilled them on. She stared at him as he spoke, thinking ruefully that, smuggler or not, he *was* handsome. A bit dangerous-looking, but handsome, and always so exquisitely dressed.

"—and you never heard his name spoken?" Ryan asked.

"Never once," Sarina answered. "His men called him captain, and the other man, lieutenant."

Ryan's chocolate-brown eyes went to Ginelle. "What did he look like, this lieutenant?"

Ginelle swallowed and felt her breath leave as she tried to remember. "F-faded blue eyes, sandy hair that was thinning, a—a scraggly beard, pockmarks." Oh, dear, *had* she remembered correctly?

"What of the Ghost?" he asked Sarina. "Describe him to me."

"Blue eyes, one with a cast in it, and the same coloration as the other man." Her eyes met Ginelle's. "We thought they might be brothers."

Ginelle drew a deep breath, seeing that all was well. It was almost turning into a game. "They had the same stubby little noses," she offered, "and the same unappealing, er, body structure."

"Brothers, by God!" He began to pace the room. "How tall?"

"I was careful to note that." Sarina stretched her thumb and middle finger in an approximation. "The Ghost was this much taller than me."

"And the other was shorter," Ginelle murmured.

Ryan stared. "You mean to tell me this scourge of the seas is no bigger than a midget?" Exasperated, he threw his arms toward a ceiling that was decorated with cherubs and gold leaf. "I don't understand this at all. My crews spoke of tall men . . ."

"Oh, there *wuz* tall men, sir," Rosie offered. "One wuz a quartermaster, I think he wuz called. He wuz th' lasher."

Ryan scowled. "The what?"

"Th-the man who used the lash," Sarina explained, heart flying. She had instructed Rosie to say as little as possible. "He was tall and dark-skinned and had no brains that I could see. He merely followed orders."

Ryan's dark gaze moved over his fiancée. She was delectable, more so now than ever before. She was rounder and softer, and her lovely breasts were fuller. Their white curves, heaped above the low neckline of her green gown, filled him with such hunger that he was hard-pressed not to bury his face in them and cover them with kisses. His manhood hardened. Surely the Ghost had not let this luscious little plum remain untasted. But go gently, he warned himself. It was a most difficult subject, and he did not want three wailing women on his hands.

"Eventually I want to hear everything," he said smoothly, "but for now, tell me just a bit more and then you must rest. The crew, for instance, what of them? Had they any distinguishing characteristics by which you could identify them? Ginelle?"

She blinked. "We—were afraid to look at them . . ."

Ryan laughed, but his eyes grew hooded. "You were with these men for nearly two months and you didn't look at them?"

"Ryan, you simply can't imagine th-the way they stared at us."

"What she is saying," Sarina said crisply, "is that we didn't dare look at them. They would have taken it as an invitation."

Ryan knew he couldn't allow the moment to escape. His gaze held Sarina's. "I must know. Were you—harmed? Any of you?"

Harmed? She had found paradise. Sarina lowered her eyes, the gold-tipped lashes brushing her flaming cheeks.

"No, we were not harmed."

"I am greatly relieved."

Seeing the blush suffusing her cheeks and spreading over her bosom, Ryan felt a swell of desire in addition to relief. At least two of his wishes had been granted on this day that had begun so miserably. He had Sarina once more, and he would be the first after all. He took her mouth hungrily, caring little that she did not respond, thinking only how sweet and fresh and succulent she was. But now was not the time nor the place for such musings, not with the other two looking on with avid eyes. He released her abruptly and patted her shoulder.

"I still have many questions, but they can wait until you have rested."

Having suffered his last kiss, Sarina knew she must tell him she could no longer marry him. She could wait no longer. Her worried eyes sought Ginelle, who nodded.

"Ryan," she began, "there is something I must—"

"You will stay here with me, of course," he interrupted. "All three of you must stay. My house is large, and I have a housekeeper and maids and a butler. Gilmore," he called, "come at once!" He was fingering a glossy strand of Sarina's hair when the butler entered. "Gilmore, instruct Mrs. Peel to ready two rooms and heat bathwater for the ladies. Show Rosie the servants' quarters."

"Yes, sir. You will come with me, Rosie."

"Yessir." Rosie bobbed a curtsy and was gone.

"While you are refreshing yourselves," Ryan continued, "I will send a message to Madame Bonnefleur, who makes my shirts for me. She has the finest dressmaking establishment in the entire city. We will order several fine gowns for you both, for I assume you do not have your trunks."

"Ryan, really, I must tell—"

He lay a stern finger across Sarina's lips. "My love, believe me, I know you are eager to tell me all the details of your abduction and escape, but later, later. I look forward—"

"Ryan, you will listen!" Sarina raised her voice and brushed his hand aside. "I am trying to tell you that I cannot marry you! In fact, I am wondering now if we should even stay in your house."

In the dreadful silence that followed, Ginelle slipped from the room. Sarina and Ryan stared at each other.

"Perhaps I have moved too swiftly for you," he muttered, "considering your ordeal. You are still upset." His own body felt as if it had been struck by lightning, but he recovered quickly, deciding he would easily overcome any objections she might have. "We will not discuss marriage now. Put it from your mind, Sarina. You will stay here to rest and recover—I will not hear otherwise—and one more thing—that devil is going to be caught and you women avenged, never fear."

He embraced her again, holding her closely and kissing the top of her head—God, that lily scent would soon drive him out of his mind.

Sarina allowed him to touch her only briefly before she stepped back a safe distance. How distasteful his intimacies were now—and had he always talked so constantly? She had been prepared to keep an open mind about him, at least until she could discuss the situation with her father, but now she saw that it would not be easy.

"Have you heard from my father? I trust he knows what has happened?"

"He knows. I will not go into the whens and wherefores of it just now, but he knows and has greatly augmented the reward I originally offered."

"I see." It was a new worry she had not considered.

Ryan could not keep his hands off her. He pulled her against him and caught the lobe of her ear between his teeth.

"God, but you are ravishing . . ."

"Ryan, you must not." Sarina placed her hands firmly against his chest and drew her head back.

Seeing that she was no longer comfortable in his arms, Ryan released her, but he could scarcely contain his irritation. Her slender body was as soft and sweet as ever, but what good was it when she was not melting, not yielding as she had when they said their goodbyes? He tried to imagine what the past two months had been like for her and why she should be calling off their wedding. He could not. Damn it, it was not fair that he, too, should suffer because she had had the misfortune to be abducted. Especially when she had not been harmed in any way.

Sarina saw Ryan's grim mouth and brooding eyes and grew more wary. She had four days to wait for Lucian's return, and it behooved her to tread cautiously with Ryan. While her heart reminded her that this was the man she had once loved, her head told her he was dangerous. If Lucian said it was so, it was so. But with Ryan blissfully unaware that she knew of his past, how could he possibly understand and accept her cool dismissal? She felt ill as she realized how careful she must be, what a fine line she must walk between reserve and friendliness so as not to put them all in jeopardy. She was responsible for Ginelle and Rosie's safety, after all. And in addition, there was the large reward to worry about now. It put Lucian and his men in more danger than ever.

She asked quietly: "Do you think Father need offer a reward now?"

Ryan's dark eyebrows met in a scowl. It was long moments before he said gruffly, "Why would you ask such a thing?"

He knew she was softhearted, he had seen evidence of it again and again, but to feel compassion for her captors was preposterous. And infuriating.

"It seems reasonable to me," she murmured. "We are here now and we are unharmed. Knowing Father, I assume it is ever so much money. I would hate for him to part with it when there is no longer a necessity."

Ryan walked to the window and gazed out, not allowing her to see the rage her words provoked in him.

"You feel there is no need to encourage and reward the capture of the man who is destroying me?"

Horrified, Sarina stared at his stiff, elegantly tailored back. In the marble foyer she glimpsed Ginelle's white face. Oh, God, how foolish she had been not to have more thoroughly considered the ramifications of her return to Ryan!

"Ryan, I—I apologize, that was extremely thoughtless of me. I never meant to imply—"

Ryan had regained control of his face and temper. He turned to her, his smile easy. "There, my sweet, it's all right. Of course it's a sensitive subject with me, and I understand your tenderheartedness, but you must not give this matter another thought. I speak for your father when I say the reward will stand as is. He would not hear of anything else, and it would be impossible to call off the hunt. It is now worldwide.''

''I—I see.'' Lucian's danger seemed so overwhelming that Sarina's legs felt weak. She swayed.

Ryan was instantly at her side. He called for his butler.

''Damn it, Sarina, I knew you needed tea and food. Gilmore, take the ladies to their rooms and see that Bess and Annie give them breakfast. Go, my love.'' He placed a quick kiss on Sarina's mouth. ''Have your bath and sleep for several hours. We will talk more this evening over dinner.'' When the doorbell jangled, he said, ''I will get it, Gilmore. You see to the ladies.''

Ryan flung the door open to find a rough-looking fisherman standing on his stoop. He looked down his nose at him.

''What is it, fellow?''

'' 'R you Douglas?''

Ryan gave him a withering stare. ''If you want work, apply at my office at the docks.''

''I got a message here fer Ryan Douglas.''

''I am Ryan Douglas.'' His eyes narrowed. ''Where did this message come from?''

''A sailor down at Seabury said you was to have it right away.'' He dangled a packet between two fingers but made no move to part with it. ''Said it was important.''

Ryan was immediately suspicious. ''What sailor was this? What vessel was he from?''

''Mister, I didn't care an' I didn't ask.''

Ryan's mind was hard at work. Who in God's name would be sending him a message from Seabury? Had it to do with Jon and the *Stargazer*?

''Is the fellow still there, do you think?''

The fisherman shook his head. ''I seen him an' his mate rowin' back to their ship right after. Soon's they boarded, she headed south.''

''When was this?''

''Yesterday. Dawn.''

''And you bring it to me a day late?''

"Mister, do you want the damned thing or don't you? I took time off from my work to come here."

Grudgingly, Ryan handed over several coins and received the sealed packet in return. He carried it into his drawing room and closed the door. He untied, unsealed, and unfolded it and then sat down in the Turk-worked chair by the window and read it. By the gods, it concerned the Ghost. He wiped his trembling fingers on his handkerchief and read the crude scrawl once again.

This is troo. August 1 in the morning the ghost sails north to seebery to get the Ladys you no. His Ships dark bloo and flying a english flag. The ghost is Loosian Thorn. Him and his men and the Ladys has been at his Island maloga. I trust all this is all satusfackury and i will get my reeward when i see you after you take his Ship. Trooly yours, J Garrick

For a long time Ryan sat staring out the window, his fingers tapping the arm of the chair. That Lucian Thorne was the Ghost did not surprise him, but what in bloody hell had Sarina meant by describing him as she had? He rose, got a glass and decanter, and sat down again. He poured himself a brandy and brooded.

He had suspected Thorne when this whole business began. He had had his men inquire in every port, but the word was always the same: Lucian Thorne was a ruined man living on booze and past dreams on Waa-paa-pau, some damned island in the South Pacific. The clever devil had covered his trail well, but it seemed he was not quite as clever as he thought. Now his days were numbered.

As for Sarina . . . Ryan shook his head and sipped the brandy gloomily, as disgusted as he was furious. He saw clearly that there could be only one reason why she had lied to him. She was protecting Thorne, which meant she cared for him. Loved him possibly. It was why she was calling off their own wedding. But had they been lovers? he wondered, seething. Would she have gone that far when kisses were all she had ever given him? God. And she was going back to Thorne, was she? Well, she was in for a surprise. Thorne would never have her. Never.

Ryan had hated the bastard since the day he'd first laid eyes on him. He himself had just been pressed into the navy. He was frightened, furious, sick as a dog in the wallowing seas, hating everything and everyone . . . And then he had seen Lucian Thorne, a lad his own age, calm, a rock, able to climb the tallest mast and accept the harshest discipline, laughing at danger, loving the sea and everything about it. The fool had thought they were friends, but Ryan had despised him as much as he despised the sea. Their paths had crossed again, disastrously, after he began smuggling, and not until two years later in Naipoor did he have a chance for revenge . . .

He poured more brandy, leaned back, closed his eyes, and smiled. Ah, Naipoor. What a triumph! Only a tiny, forgettable kingdom on the Bay of Bengal, but its treasury was magnificent. Even so, Ryan had never given it a thought, until one of the men guarding the vault, who knew of his former dealings, approached him in a pub. The vaults were inspected only once a month, he said, and if Ryan could get him and a small packet of pearls out of the country before anyone ever knew . . . Ryan had refused.

He chuckled thinking back on it, now, for the damnedest thing of all was that the *Peacekeeper* had just arrived in port and Thorne and his brother came into the pub as the fellow was pestering him. Seeing Thorne, Ryan had agreed to the proposition out of sheer perversity, in return for a half-share of the pearls. His regular cargo was legal, after all, and he would be gone long before the *Peacekeeper* departed. He had then pointed out to the fellow the delectable wench Thorne had with him. As he left, he saw the fellow approaching her and making advances and Thorne bristling. He did not wait to see the outcome.

When he saw the pearls the next morning, he knew he was not going to share them. Not bloody likely. He knew the very man who would buy them and they would assure his future. There was nothing to do but kill the guard. It was the first time he spilled blood, but the fellow was nothing but a common thief, after all. If he had left Naipoor right after that, he would be a wealthy man today. But he had not.

When it was discovered that the dead man was a vault guard, the vault was immediately opened and the theft discovered. Naipoor called on her larger neighbor, Hyderabad, to help find the thief, and a search was made of every vessel in port. The pearls were in Ryan's waistcoat pocket. When it became clear he would not get them out of Naipoor any time in the near future, he found the perfect solution: Thorne. If he could not keep them, he would use them another way, planting them on the *Peacekeeper* and leaking word to the authorities when he got back to London.

Ryan finished his brandy, musing that it had been simpler than he would have thought. A rainy night, a carousing crew, a few glib words, a bribe. It was unfortunate that the next day he had had to kill the young lad who had helped him, but then, what was one more death once the first blood was spilled? That had been in June. In September, the bastard was caught. Ryan had expected both Thornes to be hanged neatly and quickly. He had wanted Lucian out of the way once and for all, and had been unprepared for what had actually taken place, unprepared as well for the bastard's own revenge.

But enough of the past. He had to think, and quickly. Thorne must be caught. He would use three of his vessels, he would add extra arms, and he would hire men who knew how to use them. He would not trust his own men for this venture.

"Gilmore!" he shouted.

Gilmore appeared instantly . "Yes, sir?"

"Send one of the stable lads to my office for Hastings. I want him to come immediately. And bring me champagne. It seems I have many things to celebrate this morning."

Chapter 17

Sarina had agreed to eat breakfast only to placate Ryan but had found that she was ravenous. Afterward, she had bathed and slept the morning and the afternoon away. When Rosie knocked and entered to help her dress for dinner, Sarina discovered that her own gown was gone, in its place an elaborate creation that she was forced to don of necessity. It was ice-blue satin with a too-low neckline, a frilled collar, bodice and sleeves, and a voluminous frilled cream-colored satin underskirt. Viewing herself in the mirror, she wrinkled her nose. Undoubtedly, it was the work of Ryan's Madame Bonnefleur.

Ryan greeted her in the candle-lit dining room. After kissing her hand and seating her at the elaborately set table, he took his own seat at its head.

"Is Ginelle dining with us?" she asked, noting that a place had been set for her friend.

"I suspect she will be along shortly." Ryan's dark eyes moved appreciatively over her. "My dear, you are exquisite."

"I admit I am annoyed with you, Ryan. I cannot accept such a gift, and I am wearing it only because my own gown is missing. I would like it returned, please."

"Sarina, that rag has been thrown out. I bought this as a surprise for you when I was awaiting your arrival, and I insist you wear it. It is yours and I will hear no more about it. Gilmore, you may bring the champagne."

223

Ryan studied her with eyes veiled by the flickering shadows. Beautiful little liar, he thought, recalling her ridiculous description of the Ghost. But then, he must not be hasty. Perhaps the unscholarly Garrick was the one who lied. But he doubted it; he doubted it very much. He laughed aloud, contemplating the Ghost's dismay when he was seized by three armed ships.

Sarina regarded him curiously.

"Excuse my outburst, my love, but this is a joyous occasion for me." He filled their goblets with the bubbling champagne. "We must drink a toast." He raised his glass and touched Sarina's. "To our new life together."

Sarina's cool green gaze met his, unblinking. "Do you not remember what I told you earlier, Ryan? I cannot marry you."

Ryan's own eyes held nothing but amusement. "That is complete nonsense, Sarina. I will not accept it."

Sarina was growing warm. "I fear you must accept it. I am not going to marry you, Ryan. I am calling off our wedding."

He remained unperturbed. "Clearly we must discuss it later, in private and at length. Well, well, here is our sleepy Miss Crandall," he said jovially. He rose and seated Ginelle at his left. "Gilmore, you may tell Mrs. Peel she can begin serving."

As Gilmore departed, Ginelle gave Sarina an abject look. "I simply cannot believe I slept so long. I do hope I have not kept you waiting . . ."

"Not at all, lovely lady." Ryan poured champagne for her. "Sarina and I had several matters to discuss."

"I see." Ginelle took a sip and met her friend's eyes, but they were fathomless and told her nothing. At that moment, her complete attention went to the parade of sumptuous foods being carried to the buffet. "Oh, how lovely everything looks! My goodness . . ."

There began an endless feast: turtle soup, cold roast poultry in lobster aspic, savory patties, baby peas, all accompanied by champagne poured by the ever-present Gilmore.

Sarina ate, but she was furious, thinking how Ryan absolutely refused to take her seriously. And she was disturbed by his trappings of wealth. How could he continue to live so extravagantly after Lucian's many raids on his shipping? This huge house and servants, the damask-draped mahogany table aglitter with pewter and silver and crystal, expensive food, champagne—even her father did not drink champagne except on special occasions. It was all very strange.

Ryan speared a tender morsel of turkey endive with a silver fork, chewed it, and patted his mouth with a rose damask napkin. He was more than ready to hear how the three of them had escaped. Not that he would believe a word of it. Not after hearing the Ghost described as short, squat, and sandy-haired whereas Lucian Thorne was tall and powerful with hair as wild and black as the devil's own.

"I am most curious, ladies, how *did* you come to escape your captors?"

Sarina's green eyes widened, twin candle flames reflected in them. "We never said we escaped, Ryan. We were released."

"That is so," Ginelle agreed, her blonde head bobbing. "After weeks of our begging the beast to free us, he suddenly informed us we were sailing for New York with him!"

Ryan's eyes narrowed. "And why was that, do you think?"

Sarina drew a deep breath—this was the biggest lie of all. "From what I could gather, he was beginning to—fear for his life. I suspect he wanted to be rid of us . . ."

"Indeed." Lucian Thorne afraid? Not bloody likely.

Ryan leaned back in his chair, sipped from his goblet, and watched with lowered lids as Ginelle accepted another savory pattie and Sarina lay down her fork and knife. He relaxed his taut muscles and put his most winning smile on his lips. They were but two soft little birds in his cage. They were in his power. He could afford the luxury of toying with them, of seeing how far they would go with their lies. He asked smoothly:

"Does the fellow have some hideaway, or were you at sea most of the time?"

Sarina fingered the rim of her goblet. "There was one place where they dragged the ship ashore and careened her. We had been through a terrible storm . . ."

"But the rest of the time you remained at sea?"

"Yes," she replied tonelessly. "They took on supplies from time to time, but we were always forced to stay in our cabins." Suddenly she thought of Malaga, of making love with Lucian in a warm blue-green tidal pool on a silvery night.

"That is most interesting," Ryan said stiffly.

He had not missed the flicker of excitement in her eyes, nor did the candlelight conceal her blush, the rosiness spreading down her throat and over her breasts, revealed in the low-cut gown. She looked especially ravishing, but what he felt for her was not desire; it was rage. Everything was clear to him now. His fiancée and Lucian Thorne were lovers. The slut had given herself to his worst enemy.

Ryan rose abruptly, strode to the window, and stared beyond it, not seeing the faintly gleaming lantern on his lamppost or the beauty of the summer evening. The room behind him remained in silence. He heard the women's breathing, heard the watchman call the hour, felt the fury pounding through his body, tasted the hatred. He wanted to kill the devil.

And Sarina . . . He drew a harsh breath, knowing he wanted to kill her, too. But no, he would not harm her, not when he meant to derive a lifetime of ease and pleasure from the wench. No matter if she had forsaken him and given herself to the Ghost. No matter. Lucian Thorne would be a dead man soon enough, and she would be his. Fairburn Shipping would be his. He had merely to play this game right. He turned. Seeing the women's frightened expressions, he smiled.

"We are ready for brandy and coffee, Gilmore."

"Very well, sir. Will you have it in the drawing room?"

"Yes."

When Ryan drew out their chairs, Sarina found that her legs were trembling. Why had he been so angry? she wondered. Did he suspect something? And how could he change so quickly from fury to smiles? For the first time, he frightened her. It seemed she truly did not know him at all.

"Come, ladies." He took their arms and led them into the drawing room.

For an instant, he was tempted to tell Sarina that he knew everything. He wanted to watch her response. But he knew the greater pleasure would be in waiting until he had Lucian Thorne in chains and then telling her. Yes, he would wait. In the meantime, it would be amusing to see how far they would stretch their lies . . .

Propped up on pillows in the great mahogany bed with its damask canopy, Sarina sipped her bedtime chocolate and thought back over her three days at Douglas Hall. She could honestly say that the first day had been the hardest. After that, everything had gone smoothly. Ryan's eyes were still hungry, but he did not touch her. She had taken her courage in hand and spoken to him, explaining gently but firmly that she could not marry him because she had changed so much. And wonder of wonders, he had accepted finally that there could be no life for them together.

Now she was wide awake, still exuberant over her triumph and thinking that in two days, the morning of August first, Lucian would be leaving for Seabury. That same evening, she would lie in his arms. She could not sleep. In fact, she doubted she would sleep a wink until they were together again. She pulled a wrapper over her bedgown, both of them borrowed from the maid Bessie, and went to Ginelle's room.

"It's Sarina, Ginny. May I come in for a little?"

The door opened immediately, showing Ginelle clothed in the maid Annie's plain nightgown.

"I see you cannot sleep either," Ginelle whispered.

"No. I keep thinking about everything."

"So do I. I am wondering what Ryan will do when we do not return from our stroll Friday afternoon and he gets your note instead, explaining that we have left for good."

"I know. It will be a terrible shock, even though he seems accepting of everything."

Her message to Ryan would be the same as the one she planned to send off to her father. Both were already written and said how she was going away for a while to be with friends . . . Ginelle and Rosie were with her . . . he must not worry or look for her . . . She would write again.

She hated the deceit, but what else could she do? She walked to the window, pulled back the heavy brocade drapery, and stared out onto the quiet street with its flickering flambeaux. She hugged herself, thinking of Lucian—his strength like the sea in a storm, his tenderness, like the wing of a butterfly brushing her cheek. How she loved him. More than life itself. And what would she do if anything happened to him?

Seeing Sarina's face, Ginelle knew exactly where her thoughts lay. "He is not going to be caught," she said firmly. "Do not even think it."

"I could not bear for anything to happen to him."

"Nothing is going to happen to him!" Ginelle gave her friend a shake. "This is the Ghost you are fretting about, Sarina Fairburn. This is the scourge of the seas . . ."

Lucian walked about the deck of the *Vengeance*, examining every yard and sail, the spars and rigging, even the outer sides of the vessel for trailing ropes that might impede her progress. There were none. They had left the cove at daybreak and were making good time; he reckoned they would reach Seabury within the hour. Even though it was only a short run, he had insisted Donal give him plenty of time. Bad weather and emergency repairs had a way of causing delays, and Lucian preferred to be the one waiting offshore instead of the other way around. He knew the women would draw too many eyes and comments if they dallied too long in a village the size of Seabury. And so they had settled on a rendezvous this evening at six. Tonight Sarina would sleep in his arms . . .

But he was leaping too far ahead, he warned himself. He had no guarantee that she would be there waiting for him along with Donal and the other women. He had only her word for it and his own hopes. They were not enough. He slammed the door on his thoughts of her. He was at sea, and when he was at sea, his men and his vessel came first. He prowled the deck, spoke to the watches, inspected the *Vengeance*'s two banks of cannon, the swivel guns, the firelocks and sabers which had barely drawn blood, the half-pikes and boarding axes, the grapnels. All were in readiness. Now, should he change direction one degree to starboard to avoid any ship that might be lurking in the coves?

He looked past the larboard toward the misty coast, too distant to see yet closer than he liked. It was filled with inlets where ships could hide. Damn it, maybe they should shift course. But no, he was being too cautious. They were not on a strike, and his ship was disguised—she was dark-blue now and she sat low in the water like a heavily laden merchantman. His men wore ordinary seamen's garb, and the king's pennant flew from his mast. Even the vessel's name was obscured. None would know this was the ghost ship.

Lucian gazed downward, studying the swirling blue-green sea, its patterns constantly shifting and changing under the rays of the sinking sun. Like Sarina's eyes, he thought, imagining her beside him, her mermaid dress streaming behind her, her hair wind-whipped and lifting like a red-gold flag. Proud, defiant, brave, precious. So precious. He wondered when he had come to love her so.

"Captain!" the watch called from the crow's nest. "Sails dead ahead. Three vessels. They must've come from some inlet ahead."

Lucian looked up to see them loom abruptly out of the mist. They were only merchantmen and not armed. Even so, he regretted deeply not having changed course. What in hell had he been thinking? But it was too late to moan. His instinct now was to ready the cannon, but still he hesitated.

"What do ye think?" Sky was instantly at his side. "They're flyin' Spanish flags."

"I dislike showing cannon when they seem friendly."

But only because of Sarina, he thought. If it were reported that a merchantman bristling with cannon had been seen here, the area could soon be swarming with patrols. He did not want her endangered when he took her back to Malaga.

"I don't like it," Sky muttered. "When have you ever seen Spanish ships along this stretch?"

"I haven't," Lucian said. Realizing suddenly that he had made a deadly mistake, he ordered Sky: "Man the swivel guns and prepare to fire!"

"Man swivels, prepare to fire!" Sky bellowed.

The call was repeated throughout the *Vengeance*, but already the three vessels were moving in on her, closer and closer. One of the foreign crew climbed onto his ship's bowsprit and bawled, grinning: "Have your captain come aboard so we can talk."

"If you have business, come aboard my vessel," Lucian shouted back.

"Ay, that we will, mister."

A volley of small-arms fire sounded from the ship. Lucian shouted, "Win her and wear her, damn you!" To his crew, he yelled: "Fire!"

The swivel guns crackled and roared, thick black smoke filling the deck as they discharged their fire into the encroaching Spaniards. Answering fire came immediately from both sides, raking the *Vengeance* fore

and aft. In a cloud of dust and grime, Lucian saw a
tangle of broken mizzen and sagging sail.

"Cap'n," Sky shouted, "that bastard to starboard's
goin' to ram us!"

Even as his cry came, the enemy's bowsprit rammed
the *Vengeance*'s mainmast rigging. Lucian saw that her
crew bore halberds and pikes and swords. He roared:

"Arm yourselves for hand-to-hand fighting!"

As the Spaniards lashed their bowsprit to the *Vengeance*, and grapnels from their other two vessels clawed
her rails, Lucian's men caught up their own weapons.

These were not merchants, Lucian thought grimly.
They were fighting men. Pirates more than likely. He
had little time to dwell on the irony of the situation as
armed men swarmed up the sides and dropped on deck
from the spritsail yard, swords in hand, daggers between their teeth. There was a clash of arms, curses,
shouts, groans. His men, though they were the best
that could be had, were outnumbered; their position
was hopeless. He sprinted to the top step of the companion, sword drawn, narrowed eyes seeking the one
in command, but he saw none. And in the midst of the
pandemonium, he felt the weariness of sure defeat. He
himself would willingly fight to the death, but he had
not called these men to his side to die. Overwhelmed
as they were, he must give the order to lay down their
arms. Again he sought the one in command when a
decidedly English voice came from behind him.

"Mr. Lucian Thorne, is it not?"

Lucian spun, eyes guarded, heart hammering, every
muscle alert. This changed things. This was bad.

"You bloody sea-robber," the Englishman said,
"you've sailed too close to the wind for the last time."

"Who are you?" Lucian demanded. "What vessel
are—" He was felled by a sharp blow from behind. He
got to his feet, sent his attacker sprawling, and took a
fist in his face, in his groin and belly and back. He was
held by three men and beaten by the others, then his
hands were roughly forced behind his back and tied.

"Take him below," the Englishman said, wiping

blood from his mouth, "and divide up the rest of this scum on our three vessels. Mr. Douglas is going to be one happy man."

Douglas? Lucian blinked, shook the sweat and blood from his eyes. Even as he was dragged down the narrow companionway to the *Vengeance*'s black brig and shoved in, he could not believe Douglas was behind the attack. He sank to the damp planking, unconcerned for his bleeding body. Douglas? All right then, Douglas. But how? How in God's name had he known?

He stared at the blackness, at the awful vision that suddenly filled his mind: Sarina in the devil's arms, Sarina weeping with joy at being reunited with him, Sarina returning his kisses. It was as though Lucian had seen the unimaginable, the sun rising in the west or the moon falling from the sky. He shook his head. Sarina. Of course, Sarina . . .

Chapter 18

The *Vengeance* rode at anchor in the same gray waters that lapped at the distant docks and warehouses of Douglas Traders. Grapnels from one vessel clawed her rails fore and aft while two other Douglas merchantmen were anchored nearby. The *Vengeance* was captive, and in her black brig her captain sat on the damp floor and cursed himself for the hundredth time.

Lucian was chained at his wrists and ankles by heavy metal that cut into his flesh. He had no bed, no blanket, no warmth, only his disgust and fury to heat him. Although he could see nothing in the darkness, smell nothing but the sea and the ship's odors, he knew by the time spent en route that they had reached New York.

Now he heard only the slight groaning and creaking of the *Vengeance*, which told him that a skeleton crew was aboard her. His men would still be on the three other vessels, chained like himself no doubt. His rage mounted. He should have seen the trap—Spanish ships where none should have been. And of course they were not Spanish at all but Douglas Traders.

He rose, his body aching from the damp and the unforgiving hardness of the floor, the chains clanking as he pushed his hair from his eyes, and hobbled to the wall. He leaned against it. Damnation. He had ignored his own ironclad rule: men and vessel first. Instead, he had been deep in dreams, in hopes, endangering his ship and his men while he imagined Sarina returning to him, Sarina in his arms, Sarina loving him . . .

Sarina.

He grimaced, spat. He recited a litany of waterfront profanity from the harbors of the world and raised his locked wrists, defiant, toward a black heaven. The bitch. He had toyed briefly with the thought that Garrick had betrayed him, but hell, the fellow would have jumped ship at Seabury had he known what lay ahead. Instead, he had been trapped and led off with the rest of them.

No. It was Sarina who had betrayed him. He refused to think otherwise, nor did he wonder or care how she would deal with Ginelle's fury. But then, why should he think Ginelle was any better than she? God, he had been stupid. He deserved to pay for trusting a woman he had known was Douglas' from the very beginning, but his crew should not have to suffer for his stupidity. He smiled in the darkness, thinking how he would deal with Sarina when he was free. And he would be free again. He would hold no other thought in his mind but that of freedom. Donal would see to it as he had before. He could count on Donal.

Lucian raised his head, listening. There was activity on deck. Voices. Footsteps. It could be food coming, or perhaps they were changing the guard. It could mean the arrival of the Crown—or it could be the bastard Douglas himself. As Lucian pushed his hair from his eyes again, he smelled blood on his chained wrist. He had fought savagely before the enemy had taken him, and there were raw cuts and abrasions all over his body. Seeing the glow of a lantern through the barred opening of his cell, he straightened to his full height, eyes glowering. The bolt was shot back. The door creaked open.

Lucian narrowed his eyes against the light. Well, well. Douglas. He had hoped the Crown would be called in, but it seemed the bastard wanted to mete out the punishment himself. That was all right. Was it not what Lucian himself had done?

Now the game became a race against time. Either Donal would get to Lucian before he was tortured and hanged, or he would not. Worse, his whole crew might perish. Douglas would most likely ignore the letters of immunity Lucian had prepared for them.

Lucian watched, impassive, as his enemy imperiously waved in the guard and ordered him to hang the lantern overhead, place a small bench against the wall, and dust it. As the guard did his bidding, Douglas smiled at Lucian.

"Well, old friend, we meet again."

Lucian laughed. "Friend? We are enemies, bastard."

Ryan, too, laughed. "Agreed."

Lucian reckoned it was afternoon, but Douglas was dressed for a ball in silken breeches, silk stockings, a fancy foreign-made doublet with padded shoulders and embroidered sleeves, and a ruff around his smooth, smiling face. His scent cut through the stench of mold and sour ale that permeated the hold. Lucian watched, a sneer on his mouth, as Ryan sat down and made himself comfortable. He leaned against the wall, one leg flung across the other so that his double-edged sword could rest on his knee.

"You may leave us, Dobbs," he said.

"Aye, sir, but I'll be right outside th' door should yer need me." Dobbs gave Lucian a threatening look.

"So." Ryan gazed at his prisoner and waggled his knee with the gleaming sword on it. "How the mighty Ghost has fallen. You know, I wondered about you. I suspected you in the beginning, but it was said you were a broken man, a drunkard living on Waa-paa-pau somewhere in the South Pacific. That was clever. I appreciate the ruse." Ryan's brown eyes shone. "It is a pity, I think," he went on, "that you did not grant the small favor I requested those years ago. How easy to look the other way and accept the gift I was prepared to offer in return. Who would have been hurt, after all?

Merely the Crown, which is drowning in the gold of hardworking men like myself. But no, you had to be noble. Loyal.'' He shook his head. ''You will never know how easy it was to bribe another one or two of his Majesty's captains. Their families have many comforts now which they had not before, whereas you and I both know where your loyalty led. Such a pity, the Naipoor affair.'' He stroked his jaw. ''Tch. Such a loss. Your brother, I hear, and your command . . .''

Lucian wanted to kill him. He hated him with such intensity that he could feel it gnawing at his heart. He dared not look at him. He gazed at the flame instead.

''As for Sarina,'' Ryan said softly, ''I know you raped her.'' Seeing the steely flash of the Ghost's blue eyes, his mouth curved. ''No matter. She has told me all that she was compelled to do to remain alive.''

Lucian considered the time needed to take three steps and stretch his fingers around the bastard's beruffled throat before he took the steel point in his heart. He decided against it. He did not mind dying for a good reason, but death now would be senseless. He had too much to do still, the first being to escape.

''I grant you, she is exquisite,'' Ryan said softly, so his man outside the cell could not hear. ''I can't blame you, of course, but nevertheless, you will die most horribly for it. Bit by bit. But then, she has had her own revenge.'' Seeing those icy eyes blink, he smiled. He had got the bastard in the gut. Again he twisted the knife.

''Oh, yes, old friend, it was Sarina who told us where to find you and when to find you—and she has told us of Malaga. I look forward to seeing it later. In fact, I may well use the place myself . . .''

Ryan rose. He moved closer to Lucian, his sword up. ''Have you nothing to say?''

''You have said it all.''

''But I have not, old friend. The truth is, I have not yet decided what to do with you.''

Lucian kept his face expressionless.

''Oh, you will die, rest assured, but I must decide

when. Tomorrow, by my own hand, or next year after a trial by law, during which you will suffer even greater humiliation than you have known so far. The end result will be the same, of course—the gallows."

Still Lucian said nothing. Did Douglas not know about Donal Fleming? he wondered. That Donal, his lieutenant, had not been taken prisoner? It seemed he did not. Lucian felt a small flame of hope leap to life and begin to warm him. Time was all he needed now.

"I must return to Sarina," Ryan finally said. "She didn't want me to come, naturally, for she felt you would try to kill me, but how could I resist? Dobbs"— he raised his voice—"I am leaving." When the door creaked open, he added, "Give our prisoner six lashes. At your convenience, of course. Six more tomorrow." He left without glancing back.

"Douglas," Lucian called softly.

Ryan returned to the damp, stinking cell where Lucian stood, his eyes burning. God's bones, but the fellow had a frightening look about him. Ryan was grateful suddenly for the chains that bound him and for the burly guard by his side.

"You need not ask for mercy, old friend," he said coolly, "for I have none. It is at the bottom of the sea with my cargos."

Lucian's lip curled. "I would refuse your mercy were it offered. I merely wanted to tell you, *old friend*, that your woman was delicious, soft and ripe . . . and eager. More than willing."

Ryan's face flamed. "Lash this bastard now," he ordered. "I will send Johnson and Killian to assist you."

Lucian lay on his side in the blackness, feeling the fire—the stripes scorching his back, his throat burning from the cries he could not suppress, thoughts of Sarina searing him. His mind was filled with her: her gentleness, compassion, sweetness, breathtaking beauty. He groaned with rage and pain, thinking that everything about her had been a lie. She had betrayed him.

Fool, he cursed himself for the hundredth time. Gullible, trusting, credulous, lusting, lovesick fool.

He took command of himself then. This was not the time for black thoughts of revenge. That could come after he was freed—and he would be freed. Then he would decide how to deal with Sarina Fairburn. For now he must relax, place all of his thoughts and energy on the present. He must help his body to heal and maintain his strength for the torture to come. Feeling fingers of fire raying across his back, he noticed how like ice they were. If he could just think of ice, icy fingers moving over his back and his blood flowing to warm him . . .

Ryan stormed back to Douglas Hall, dark-faced and filled with rage. It was as he had thought. Sarina and Thorne had been lovers. Lovers! He wanted to strangle her. But not yet, not yet . . . He could make her trap herself, make her admit it first. Hearing hushed voices suddenly at the top of the staircase, he stepped into the drawing room and stood hidden, listening.

"Do hurry, Ginelle," Sarina was whispering.

"I'm coming, I'm coming. I couldn't find my brooch. Besides, are you sure no one is about?"

"Yes'm, they're all in th' kitchen. I jist checked. Awooo, I'm all pins an' needles!"

Ryan waited, hearing the rustling of their gowns and their muffled footsteps as they descended, then he stepped forward. He smiled, but his eyes were hostile.

"Good afternoon, ladies. Where are you going, pray?"

Sarina jumped. "Ryan! I—we are just going for our daily stroll after dinner . . ."

"Yes, it's such a lovely cool breezy day," Ginelle said, her voice quavering.

Seeing his slitted eyes and compressed lips, Sarina held her breath. What had happened? He never came home at this hour. She gathered her cloak about her more closely, hiding her small bag and worrying that he had overheard their whispers.

"I think you're leaving for more than a stroll," Ryan said grimly. "Why?" He wanted to see her squirm.

Sarina's heart plummeted, but she forced her face to remain placid. "That's not so. As I said, we're just leaving for our walk . . ."

Now she was certain he had overheard them. Oh, why had they not been more cautious? Yet he was not supposed to be there.

"I think you're lying, *ma petite*. Gilmore!" he shouted. "Peel!"

When the two servants appeared, he growled, "Gilmore, lock Mistress Crandall in her bedchamber." Ginelle gaped at him. "Peel, lock up the Coggins wench."

"Awooo, sir, yer can't do that!"

"I myself will take care of Mistress Fairburn."

Sarina watched, incensed, as the weeping Ginelle and Rosie were firmly escorted up the stairs by their stern-faced jailers.

"Ryan Douglas, do you dare to tell me you are going to lock me up, too?"

Dark-faced, wordless with anger, he grasped her arm and began dragging her up the stairs.

"Ryan, what is it? What has come over you?"

She clung to the railing until he cruelly pried her fingers loose and gave her a bone-rattling shaking.

"Come, damn you. I will not tolerate your disobedience."

He was forced to drag her the rest of the way. Sarina yearned to shriek that she knew every terrible thing he had done, but she did not. She knew it would make him even more furious than he was already.

"Just wait!" she choked. "Just wait until my father hears of the disgraceful way you are treating the three of us!"

"Silence!" Ryan shouted. The wench didn't know how fortunate she was. She deserved to be thrown into his black hole of a cellar.

Ah, but he would enjoy making her miserable.

* * *

It had been three days since Ryan had locked Sarina in her bedchamber. The first evening when Bessie had brought her food and tended to her needs, she had managed to slip out the door, but Gilmore had apprehended her immediately and borne her, kicking and screaming, back up to her prison. Since then Peel, a burly Englishwoman, had brought her meals and maided her, and Sarina was growing more and more outraged. Even the shutters on her windows had been barred from the outside! Hearing the key click in the lock, she spun and waited. The housekeeper entered with a dinner tray, locking the door behind her.

"Peel, I must see Mr. Douglas." It took all the effort she possessed to appear calm.

"Mr. Douglas is out."

Sarina gazed longingly at the key on the chain around Peel's thick neck. The woman was twice as large as she and as strong as a cow. There was no way she could wrest the key from her, unlock the door, and escape.

"Peel, this has gone on long enough. I insist that you release me this instant." The woman did not answer. She didn't even look at Sarina. She took the lunch tray, moved heavily to the door, and unlocked it. "Do you hear me, Peel? Release me! My father is a very important man, and he will be extremely angry and—Peel!" The door closed behind her, the lock clicked.

Sarina barely touched her dinner. Her appetite waned as her concern outdistanced her anger. Why on earth was Ryan keeping them prisoner and for how much longer? And was Donal still nearby or had he gone on to Seabury when they had not met him as planned? Surely he would tell Lucian that something was wrong. Perhaps both men were nearby even now, just waiting for a chance to rescue them. But if Lucian had come all the way into New York City, maybe he had been seized . . .

Terror gripped her. Was that what had happened? Had he come to help her and been captured? From the first moment she had realized she loved him, it had been her worst nightmare—that he would be captured and she would never see him again. It still was. But to dwell on it now would drive her mad, and what good would she be to Lucian if she were mad? She was so deep in her worries she didn't even hear the key turn in the lock or the door open until Ryan entered the room.

"Hello, my beauty."

Sarina leaped to her feet, her eyes flashing.

"You have much to learn about the treatment of houseguests, Ryan."

"Ah, then you would have me reward you for your treachery?" he asked softly.

She hid the fear that his words struck in her. "I cannot imagine what you mean."

His eyes stripped her of her green gown as he remembered Thorne's insolent parting words . . . *Your woman was delicious, soft and ripe . . . and eager. More than willing.* Would to God Thorne had lied, but in his heart, Ryan knew the bastard had told the truth. He had taken her and she had liked it. She had given herself to him. He drew a strangled breath, promising himself that she would pay. The way he meant to play this game, she would be his in the end and, sweet irony, all because of Lucian Thorne.

When Ryan did not answer her, Sarina stared at him. All of his charming, witty sophistication was gone without a trace. He was a stranger with icy eyes and a bitter, twisted mouth. What had he learned that had brought about this frightening change in him? What did he know about her treachery? Suddenly she was afraid to hear.

"I have seen your lover, Lucian Thorne, my sweet slut . . ."

Lucian? No! She didn't believe it. She didn't believe the bold dangerous Ghost could ever be captured by a man like Ryan. But, oh, God, if he were, did she dare admit what he meant to her? Her fear was like a fist squeezing her heart as she looked on Ryan's white-faced fury. No, she could not let him know. If Lucian truly were his captive and he thought they were lovers, Ryan would slay him without a trial. She must continue to lie. She must lie as she had never lied before and hope that the others would do the same. She forced a laugh past trembling lips.

"Come now, Ryan." She put her hands on her hips and gave him a mocking look. "I cannot imagine where you heard such rot."

"None of your lies, Sarina," Ryan said harshly. "I know everything. I know of Malaga—" He chuckled, seeing her gasp and the red flaring in her cheeks. By God, triumph! "So, Malaga rings a bell, does it? Now why would that be, I wonder, unless you have been there?"

It was as if the ground had gone from beneath her feet. Sarina straightened her shoulders and tried to cover her dreadful mistake, but it was too late. Her very love for Lucian had caused her to betray him.

"My three armed vessels took the *Vengeance*, and I have him in chains. He has told me all." He watched her through half-closed eyes, her beautiful face turning pale, her quick gasps drawing his eyes to her bosom. He stepped closer. "I fear the lash does that to a man."

Sarina's hands flew to her mouth. Lucian lashed again? Chained like an animal while the long, writhing snakes of the cat stung his poor scarred back again? Oh, no. No, no, no, no. She was with him, holding him, weeping with him, kissing and comforting him, dying with him. She did not see that Ryan was upon her until his arms were around her, pressing her close to him.

"Ryan, no! I will not—" His mouth took hers hungrily, harshly punishing. His teeth cut her lower lip— she could taste the blood—and he held her so closely, kissed her so violently and for so long, that she was nearly smothered. Finally he released her.

"Y—you beast!" She put her hands to her burning cheeks. She was truly frightened.

Ryan grasped her chin between steely fingers, hurt-

ing her further. "Listen to me, my love, and listen well.
We are going to wed and—"

Sarina struck his hand away. "No!"

"Yes. We will wed the same as we planned. Do you
think for one instant your father would give you to that
bastard sea wolf?"

What about you? she nearly cried. What about the
stealing you do? She choked it back, every instinct
warning her again that Ryan must not learn how much
she knew about him.

"I will not marry you!" Her voice rose. "No power
on this earth will make me marry you!"

But she was overwhelmed by all the things over
which she had no control.

"Oh, I am s-s-so unh-h-happy!"

A dam burst and months of misery and fear and uncertainty were unleashed.

Ryan peered at her and scowled. "Damn it, I cannot
abide a woman who bawls."

Suddenly Sarina's brain was at work as she fell onto
her bed, face down, sobbing. So he did not like women
who bawled? Hah! She sobbed all the harder.

"I know now that you never loved me!"

Damnation. Women! "Of course, I loved you," Ryan
roared.

"Th-then for old times' sake, for the love we once
had"—she sat up and regarded him piteously, her tears
still flowing—"let me see Lucian. Oh, Ryan, if ever you
loved me and if you have any mercy in your heart, let
me see him. Please."

Ryan toyed with his golden pomander, tapping it in
the palm of one hand. He saw instantly what she was
up to. He smiled, felt a quiet glow of jubilation. Step
into my snare, little bitch. Soft, ripe, satin-skinned little bitch. "You expect my mercy, yet you yourself need
exhibit none, is that it?" he said.

She blinked wide, wet eyes at him. "I don't understand."

"I am to be generous to your lover, but I, who love

you still, God alone knows why, am to receive nothing in return.''

Sarina shuddered. ''I—cannot marry you, if that is what you mean.''

Ryan studied her with hooded eyes, her lush mouth, fragrant red-gold hair, white skin, lush breasts, and rounded arms. Yes, he was going to wed her. Most definitely he was going to wed her, but like it or not, he knew he had to tread carefully for now. He could not keep her from her father forever, and when the time came for them to meet again, he didn't want her running to the old man weeping and wailing. No, he must plan carefully.

''I will let you see the bastard,'' he said gruffly.

''Th-thank you.'' Sarina was frankly surprised. She began to suspect a trap.

''Afterward, we will talk about marriage.''

And there it was. She might have known. ''Indeed, we will not. I have told you—''

''Silence,'' Ryan demanded. ''I am being extremely generous, allowing you to see the devil, but in return, we will talk. You will not close the door on me, Sarina. In the eyes of the law you are still promised to me. Never forget that.''

Sarina did not allow Ryan to see how much his words distressed her. She was through with tears for the present. Now she would concentrate on the only thing that mattered to her—Lucian. She was going to see her beloved. She was going to touch and hold him, kiss him, give him the hope she herself did not feel.

''Very well,'' she answered finally, realizing that for now, she must do exactly as Ryan ordered. ''After I see Lucian, we will talk.'' She did not meet his eyes.

''We will talk about marriage,'' Ryan insisted. ''Say it, Sarina. We will talk about marriage.''

''We will—talk about marriage . . .''

''Very good, *ma petite.*''

He did not miss the roses blooming so suddenly in her cheeks. Well, well, what did the wench have up her sleeve? Doubtless she thought she could promise him anything now and wriggle out of it later, but she would soon learn how wrong she was. No one ever got away with tricking Ryan Douglas.

"This has been quite productive, my dear, but now I must be off."

"One moment, please." Sarina's eyes flashed. "I will not stay a prisoner any longer. You will no longer lock me and the others in our rooms."

He could not help smiling at her audacity. "It is done."

"And keep that woman Peel away from me. She is dreadful. I insist that Rosie attend me again."

"You drive a hard bargain. But never doubt that it is a bargain, Sarina. You will be taken to see the bastard, and in return, we are going to get to know each other again. Do you understand?"

"I understand." She would have promised or told him anything just to get out of that room.

"And you are not to leave the house from now on. No more walks for any of you," he said curtly.

That was a blow. Sarina was about to demand an explanation, but considering his mood, she decided against it. Instead she asked calmly: "When may I see Ginelle and Rosie?"

"When it suits *me*," he growled.

Sarina saw Ginelle at dinner and Rosie brought her her bedtime chocolate, but it was two more agonizing days before Sarina was allowed to see Lucian. She died a hundred times over during the wait, but now she was actually on her way to him. Her heart raced as she wondered if he truly had been lashed. And how had he been captured in the first place? It was all quite unbelievable. She saw the *Vengeance* then, a swift gray proud powerful eagle chained to three squat merchant ships out in the sunlit bay. She shuddered, thinking of Lucian's reaction to his vessel's capture. He would be murderous with rage.

After a short, choppy ride in a longboat, Sarina clawed her way up the side of the vessel on a rope ladder, crawled over the rail, and was led by a man carrying a sword and a lantern down the companionway into the hold. It was black and damp and reeked of bilge water. Her flesh crawled. Oh, Lucian . . .

"Someone to see yer, Thorne," the guard bawled. To Sarina, he said, "I'll come in wi' yer, mistress. He's a bad un if ever I saw one."

"Thank you, but there is no need. I will be fine."

"Mr. Douglas thinks different. I'm to stay wi' yer."

She watched as the heavy bolt was drawn back, the creaking door shoved open, and the lantern hung on a peg in the passageway so that a bit of light reached the cell. She entered, faltering, her heart pounding and her mouth dry. Her eyes, accustomed to the sunny morning, could not see a thing.

"Lucian? It's Sarina." When there was no answer, she cried to the guard, "Bring in the lantern, I fear he is ill." The man complied, holding the light aloft and his sword at the ready.

Sarina saw him then. He was chained and standing against the wall, his jaw bearded, his eyes pain-dulled and half-closed against the bright light. When she caught the glint of heavy metal on his wrists and ankles, she died inside.

"Oh, Lucian . . ."

The dampness and stench . . . and he had no cot, no blankets, no light. She turned to the guard, outraged.

"What is the meaning of this? This man has no place to sleep, no way to keep warm! Who is in charge here?"

The guard lounged against the doorjamb, his amused gaze playing over her. "Mr. Douglas is in charge, ma'am. Yer can complain to him, but I'd say yer howlin' into the wind. He has this sea wolf right where he wants 'im."

Sarina was appalled beyond words. She simply had to persuade Ryan that changes be made. Gazing into Lucian's wintry blue eyes, she felt a growing dread. Was he not glad to see her?

"Please, can we be alone?" she asked the guard.

"I got me orders," he said, but went nonetheless to stand in the doorway, his back to them.

Sarina hurried to Lucian. She stood on tiptoe, her hungry arms slipping around his stiff, unresponsive body. She kissed his bearded face, his shackled hands, smoothed back his damp black hair.

"Beloved, I wanted to come as soon as I heard, but I could not. Were you lashed?" She ran her hands over his chest, his arms and shoulders. He was as rigid and unyielding as rock. "Lucian?" He made no answer.

"He gits six lashes a day," the guard said over his shoulder.

Six lashes a day! And he had been here four days at least. That was twenty-four lashes, and he had no bed or blanket or even a stool to sit on. She felt such hatred for Ryan that it sickened her. She stood on tiptoe, whispering:

"Why will you not look at me or speak to me? I know you are bitter, but I want to help you. Lucian, in God's name, what is it? What have I done?"

Finally, Lucian looked at her, all of his rage crackling in his eyes; his hatred for Douglas, his hurt and disappointment in her, disgust and fury at himself.

"It's too late for second thoughts, Mistress Fairburn."

Mistress Fairburn? Sarina was close to weeping. "What do you mean? Second thoughts about what?"

His eyes with their terrible light pinned her, pierced her. "Come, Sarina, you knew when you betrayed me to Douglas that he would imprison me. Why are you surprised?"

She stared up at him. "When I—betrayed you?" At first his words had no meaning, then she realized what he was saying. Her own green eyes shown wide and wild in the shadowy light. "You think I did this? You think I told Ryan? I? Lucian, my God! How could you ever think I would do such a thing!"

Who better? he thought, his fingers slowly encircling her throat. He felt the satin skin and slender, fragile bones before releasing her. Damn it, he could no more hurt her than he could crush a butterfly.

"Go ahead, strangle me," Sarina dared him. "How can I live, knowing you hate me? Do it and be done with it!"

Liar. Cheat. Temptress. He could not be near her without remembering her in his arms, how she felt and tasted, the fragrance of her skin and hair, her softness, her laughter, her words of love. And they were lies. All lies. He thrust her roughly away from him.

"Go. Go before I kill you."

Tears streamed down her cheeks. "How unfair you are!"

"It's strange that we should have the same thoughts," Lucian muttered, turning from her.

Seeing that the back of his shirt was blood-streaked, Sarina's hand flew to her mouth, stifling a cry. He *had* been lashed! Oh, the situation was hopeless. But no, one hope remained to them, only one—Donal. Thank God he, too, had not been aboard the ship.

"Does Donal know about this?" she whispered.

Lucian laughed. Did she actually think he would give her that kind of news to carry back to Douglas?

"I have nothing more to say to you."

"Lucian, tell me!" She wanted to shake him. "Does Donal know you're here?"

"Guard," he called harshly, "the lady is ready to go."

She was gone. The lantern was gone. Lucian put his hand against the damp wall and felt his way in the blackness to a corner. He slid onto the planks and sat, his back against the wall, remembering Sarina's smooth skin beneath his fingers and her soft breasts pressed against him. Detecting her lily scent clinging to his bare arm, he raised it to his nostrils, inhaled the fragrance, then supplanted his sudden, aching emptiness with fury. Damned if he was going to grieve for the treacherous wench when she deserved to be strung up beside Douglas.

Not that her tears had not been real. He knew they were. They were as real as her hunger for him. She could not have pretended such passion when he made love to her. But that was all it was—hunger, passion, not the love she had sworn. Hell, he'd been warned. In the very beginning, she had told him she would have her revenge; that she wanted him caught. Well, he was caught. Her revenge was complete.

Except that she was still not satisfied. She had wanted him captured and punished, but now her tender highborn sensibilities were bruised for she had not foreseen what capture and punishment meant. Once, she had said she could not bear to see him hanged . . . Lucian smiled at the memory. Hanging wasn't such a bad death—swift, clean. Doubtless she hadn't known of stinking black holds or chains or dripping water and sour food. Now she did.

He laughed, enjoying a bleak triumph. She wasn't going to sleep well tonight. She probably wouldn't sleep for a long long time, which was exactly what he wanted. He wanted her hurting, remembering; broken and weeping and drowning in guilt as she thought of his men and his vessel in chains because of her. He got to his feet, his heart pumping too hard, his blood running too hot and too fast for him to sit quietly. Jaw tightened, fists clenched, his entire body taut with fury, he closed his eyes and thought of Donal, Donal gathering a band and making swift plans. With every ounce of his being, Lucian willed him to hurry. There was not a moment to lose. And then, when he and his men were freed, he would crush Sarina Fairburn along with Ryan Douglas. It would be pleasant to consider the best way to go about it . . .

Chapter 19

Sarina was still shaking, trembling when she returned to Douglas Hall. But she shook with fear and grief, not anger. She had been in her bedchamber only moments before Rosie tapped on her door and entered. She gaped at her mistress' white face and red eyes.

"Oh, mum! Oh, my!" She fled and returned immediately with Ginelle.

"Rina! Oh, my goodness!"

Ginelle sat beside her friend and put her arms around her. "There, darling, it will be all right," she crooned, patting and stroking Sarina's hands. "Rosie, bring tea, please, and close the door after you." Rosie flew. "There now, love, it's all right. Everything is going to be fine, I promise. Donal will take care of everything."

"Lucian hates me," Sarina said, her stiff lips scarcely able to move. "He thinks I betrayed him . . . he thinks I told Ryan where to find him . . ."

"What?"

Sarina closed her eyes, only to see that black hole of a cell and Lucian in chains, blood on his back. She opened her eyes and saw the terrible images still. She would never forget them.

"He's so angry, he wants to kill me. He made me leave. He didn't want me there."

"Ryan did this!" Ginelle cried. "I will wager anything that he knows exactly who the informer really is, yet he lied and said it was you. Oh, he is such a dastard! He wants Lucian to hate you, Rina!"

"He is lashed every day," Sarina murmured tonelessly, "and he has no bed or blanket. He is in a damp pitch-black cell and he is ch-chained hand and foot . . ."

"There, there." Ginelle continued to stroke Sarina's cold hand, but her eyes were brimming at such terrible news. Donal surely already knew of Lucian's imprisonment, but he must be assured positively that it was not Sarina who had betrayed him. She had to get that message to him, even though they were not allowed outside the house. Her breath caught—oh, fabulous day, perhaps she could get out of the house . . .

Ryan didn't like her, he never had, and if she could just make him angry enough with her, pick a terrible fight with him, he might actually send her away! Her heart pounded at such a dangerous plan, but it might work. And as soon as she was out the door, she would go to Donal. From the windows, they had seen Chambers going by in his carriage, glowering at the house, and she would simply stroll the streets until she found him. Why, it was a wonderful idea, and she couldn't imagine why she hadn't thought of it earlier. But it needed refinement, and she must discuss it with Sarina. In the meantime, Donal must still be told. But how?

"Here's the tea," Rosie said, hurrying in and pouring two steaming cups. "It'll make yer feel better if yer kin jist take a sip, mum," she told Sarina. "It's ever so good an' hot an' black, an' Annie an' Bessie sends their love wi' it."

"Thank you, Rosie."

Ginelle blinked. Annie and Bessie. Of course, that was it—Annie and Bessie! She dried her eyes, took the cup from Rosie, and by the time she had added lemon and taken a first sip, her plan was made.

"Rosie, please bring Annie and Bessie to us," she ordered crisply.

Rosie looked hurt. "Ain't I enough?"

"You're wonderful, perfect. Now be a love and do fly. Bring them as fast as you can."

Sarina looked up. Seeing Ginelle's gleaming eyes, she knew instantly what she had in mind.

"Oh, Ginny, of course—I'm so befuddled I can't even think! We will contact Donal through the maids . . ."

"Yes. We will outfox that beast, Rina, never fear. And you're not to worry one more instant because Donal will hear the truth. He will know Lucian's condition and that you absolutely did not betray him. And he will know how to free him."

"But I doubt Lucian will believe him."

Ginelle held up a warning hand. "No buts. If Lucian chooses to believe that you could possibly betray him, then I say let him suffer a bit! Just a bit. And Rina"— she lowered her voice—"I have something to discuss with you when we're alone."

Donal had learned about the *Vengeance* the same morning she was captured. He was at the fishing wharf arranging for their afternoon passage to Seabury when he spied her in the bay. His heart sank into his stomach when he saw that she was grapneled to one Douglas Trader and guarded by yet two others.

Holy heaven, what a mess. What had happened? Had they all been on a grand toot and been surprised? But no, he couldn't believe such a thing. And how in the name of heaven had the bastard known where to look—or recognized the *Vengeance?* It almost seemed as if someone had told Douglas where and when to find the Ghost. Donal suspected her crew was being held in the three merchantmen with Lucian in the brig of the *Vengeance* herself. It was what he would have done, and it made rescue well nigh impossible, even if he'd had enough men, which he did not.

Now five days had passed with nary a sign of Lucian, the crew, or the women. They had ceased their daily walks, and while he was somewhat concerned, he felt they were in no immediate danger. Douglas wouldn't dare harm the daughter of George Fairburn, nor her best friend Ginelle.

Lucian Thorne, however, was another story, and Donal knew he had no time to waste. These past five days and many of the nights, he and Chambers had been scouring the docks and pubs for a rescue crew, but it was slow work. They had to be careful who they approached. Donal's face showed his grave concern when he met with Chambers that night, as usual.

"Any good word for me, man?"

"You have a message from your lady, sir. A maid from Douglas Hall gave it to me. She says she and her friend will take the same walk daily to exchange further news. I've already looked at it in case it was an emergency, and I would say it's strange news indeed. It's dated today, August sixth."

Donal took it, sniffed it—ah, God, Ginelle's wonderful fragrance—and carried it to a lamp.

Beloved, he read. *Ryan has shown his true colors. We could not meet you as we were locked in our rooms until two days ago. We are still forbidden to leave the house, but we trust the maids completely. Lucian is in the* Vengeance *brig, and being lashed daily. Sarina did not betray him—believe me. I love you with all my heart, my darling. If there is a way out, I know you will find it. Yours forever, Ginelle.*

Donal's black scowl was terrible to behold. "What in bloody hell is this all about? Locked in their rooms and confined to the house?"

"Aye, sir." Chambers was grim. "And that they should know the captain is being lashed . . ."

Donal shook his head and ran his hands through his black hair. "And what in holy heaven does she mean—'Sarina did not betray him'?"

"It's a mystery. And for Douglas to imprison them as he has—I wonder, could he have learned the truth?"

Donal nodded glumly. "It was my first thought. I fear we must assume it." He sighed. How in hell had everything fallen apart so fast? "Look, man, can you come back out with me tonight? Surely we can find some more men out there. You're tired, I know, but

maybe after a bite and a pint—" He was still confident
that the women were in no real danger, but the very
thought of Lucian being lashed again . . .

"Sir"—Chambers' eyes glinted—"he is my captain.
Say no more."

It was as though she was performing in some ghastly
charade, Sarina thought. Ryan at the head of the table,
darkly handsome in his burgundy satin waistcoat,
drinking glass after glass of champagne, eating pheas-
ant, making mocking comments; she at his right in the
ice-blue gown he had commanded her to wear, drinking and eating yet tasting nothing, silent for the most
part; the maids coming and going; Gilmore filling
Ryan's crystal goblet again and again. Sarina envied
Ginelle, who was eating from a tray in her bedchamber. She had been so angry with Ryan, she had refused
to come to the table.

"So I told them we would attend, *ma petite*. They are
charming people and eager to meet you, and I knew
you would greatly enjoy seeing their estate and their
collection of paintings and French sculptures."

Sarina gazed at Ryan in stony silence, but he seemed
not to notice. She knew he was drunk. He was behaving as if they were already married and she was not a
prisoner in this house; as if Lucian were not huddled
in that hideous black cell with strips of his flesh torn
off his back. Oh, she wanted to hurl her plate in Ryan's
smug face and flee. She wanted to go to Donal and tell
him that she had not betrayed Lucian—she feared he
had never gotten Ginelle's message.

"You will need a dress for the affair, of course,"
Ryan was saying. "I will have Madame Bonnefleur
come by to measure you and bring fabrics for you to
choose from. Perhaps a striped poplin or a lawn since
it is an outdoor affair."

Ryan was enjoying himself greatly. And why not?
His enemy was vanquished and suffering at his hands.
By and by, he would become one of the sadly de-
parted, for he would not allow Lucian Thorne to live

much longer. And Sarina. He studied her lazily. Little ice queen, those beautiful green eyes of hers cold and accusing. He smiled into his glass. It was of no import. She would learn very soon now that she was going to be his wife. There was nothing she could do about it. She was in his power.

"There is a concert we must go to Saturday night, *ma petite*. I recall how much you love chamber music."

He saw that she was growing more and more agitated, but he gave her no help. He wanted her completely, totally aware that it was she who needed his mercy, not the other way around.

"And then there is a play that I know you will enjoy. I will make reservations tomorrow and we—"

"Ryan—"

"Ah, I see that you need more champagne. Gilmore." He snapped his fingers.

"No, thank you, Gilmore." Sarina covered her glass with her hand and focused icy eyes on the man she had once loved.

"Lucian is being held under inhumane conditions," she said, wishing her voice were not trembling so. "I trust you are also aware that he needs medical attention."

"Ah, does he now? Gilmore—" Ryan raised his own glass for more champagne, his gaze not leaving Sarina. "I see you do not realize, my love, that pirates get no coddling in this country or any other."

"You wouldn't treat a dog the way he is being treated, Ryan. I know you would not!"

"Probably not. But then a dog would never sink my cargos with the specific intention of ruining me." Ryan regarded her narrowly. "Did the bastard ever say why he was bent on such revenge?"

"No." Sarina lied, knowing that the truth would put her in graver jeopardy than she was in already.

"I trust you will not forget the anxiety, not to mention the financial loss, his escapades have cost me."

Sarina lowered her eyes and said nothing. There was no denying it, yet he had brought it all on himself.

Ryan grunted. "I see you are too addled by him to care."

He covered her hand with his. Lovely, soft, white little hand, the fingers so slender and shapely, so rosy-tipped. He clasped them in his own dark hand, raised them to his mouth and kissed them, kissed her palm, the inside of her wrist. Ah, God, that fragrance she used. Desire flamed within him, fully and instantly aroused.

"Ryan, please—" Sarina tried to free herself as the kisses he was pressing upon her arm grew more impassioned. "Y-you must not."

Ryan's drink-glazed gaze slid over her face and bosom. "Must not, you say?" He chuckled, but without mirth. "You are hardly in a position to tell me what I must not do."

He kissed her other hand before finally leaning back in his chair. God, but she was ravishing. And she would soon be his. It was going to take great effort to wait . . .

Seeing the lust in his eyes, Sarina knew what he was thinking. She yearned to cry out that she would not marry him, not ever, but she dared not. It would only remind him that they hadn't yet discussed marriage. Now that she had seen Lucian, Ryan would certainly hold her to her promise to talk about it, and she wanted to avoid it for as long as possible.

Ryan's glittering eyes never left Sarina. He saw her resentment, sensed her defiance warring with her fear, and a smile touched his lips. It was time to begin the next phase of his plan to capture her. He would be magnanimous.

"Gilmore, we are ready for dessert," he said.

Sarina was not hungry for dessert. She could barely choke down the food Bessie had heaped upon her plate, but she didn't want to antagonize Ryan further. She accepted a bowl of berries and clotted cream.

"Perhaps I have been too harsh with the devil," Ryan said abruptly. Seeing her astonishment, he added, "Yes, I see that I have been unduly harsh. To please you, I will discontinue the lashing, my pet."

"Thank you." She was skeptical, wary, but she kept it hidden.

"And you say he has no cot or blanket?" He stroked her cheek and the silky skin beneath her chin.

"No, he does not."

Sarina's heart was in her throat. The glimmer in his eyes frightened her. It took all of the willpower she possessed not to push his hand away and run upstairs to her bedchamber and lock the door.

"Very well. Since it means so much to you, I shall arrange for a cot and blanket."

"Thank you . . ."

She whispered the words, fearful of interrupting his strange reverie. Better that his mind be on some distant thing than on her.

But Ryan's thoughts were on her. It was their wedding night . . . he was lowering her onto his great japanned bed with its satin sheets and pillowcases . . .

He smiled, imagining her struggles. There was nothing he enjoyed more than overpowering a beautiful woman, having her whimpering and writhing beneath him in her excitement. He saw himself pinning her wrists above her head and kissing her full red lips, plunging his hungry tongue between them, ripping the gown off that white, voluptuous body. He would have a hundred exquisite gowns made for her when she was his, but the first month, perhaps longer, she would not need any clothing. He was going to break her, and if that meant keeping her in his bedchamber, in his bed, naked, until she was tamed, why, so be it. Ah, God, to think that because of Lucian Thorne such a thing would be possible. How very ironic . . .

Ryan realized suddenly that Sarina was speaking. He focused on her with some difficulty. "I beg your pardon, m'love?"

Since her first day at Douglas Hall, Sarina had seen Ryan's unquenchable thirst for champagne. Tonight he was completely drunk. She decided it was a good thing to know and remember.

"I asked what you intend to do with Lucian," she said quietly. She was afraid to know, yet she was more afraid not to know.

Ryan nodded. "Ah. What will I do with Lucian? A good question . . ."

His head felt very heavy and he wanted to sleep. Maybe he would sleep tonight with Sarina in his arms. He reached out, stroked her cheek, and felt her stiffen. The arrogant little witch. He must go slowly, carefully, but only until they were wed. Then she would learn who was master. He tipped back his chair, rocking it gently and drinking the champagne that Gilmore kept pouring in his glass. Damned good man, old Gilmore.

"What do you think I should do with the Ghost, my satin kitten?" he murmured.

"I understand," Sarina said coolly, "that he must appear before the Crown and his peers."

"That is one possibility, of course, but there are others. The truth of the matter is, my love, that I have not yet decided what to do with the bastard. I find the subject a very dull one to discuss with so lovely a companion."

He leaned back, drained his goblet, and studied Sarina's beautiful eyes, his lids lowered. Cheating little bitch. What did she think he would do with the man? Of course, the Ghost was going to die. Most unpleasantly. And the lashings would continue, nor would he have a cot or blanket. She would never know the difference.

"My dear, do have another glass of champagne," he said, motioning for Gilmore. "And let us not discuss that wretched Ghost any more this evening."

Ryan visited the *Vengeance* the next afternoon. "Report," he demanded of the guard.

"The bastard don't talk, sir, exceptin' 'is eyes. I wouldn't want to meet 'im in a dark alley, I'll say that."

"How are his wounds?"

"Not good. Raw, but he don't scream. Shall I up the number o' lashes?"

Ryan thought for a moment. "No. Reduce them to three. I don't want him dead before he hangs, or unable to appreciate what is happening to him."

The guard grinned. "Right yer are, sir. Will yer be wantin' to see him?"

"Yes. You need not accompany me, just fetch me the lantern."

"Aye, sir."

As Ryan made his way down the companionway into the blackness of the hold, he knew that he himself would go mad if he were shut up in such a place for any length of time. What made some men crack while others seemed unaffected? he wondered. He recalled that Lucian Thorne had already spent one year in gaol under conditions not much better than this. How had he done it? Perhaps it was a lack of intelligence. If a man had a quick mind, he realized how much he had lost. On the other hand, the dimmer the intellect, the less he would worry. Yes, doubtless that was the case. Ryan hung up the lantern and slid the bolt.

"Thorne?" He peered into the shadowy cell.

No answer. Only the ship noises and the faint dripping of water. Ryan stood in the doorway until his eyes adjusted to the darkness. Ah, there he was, standing as tall and proud as ever, as though he weren't shackled hand and foot with his life's blood clotting on his back. Ryan shook his head in mock sympathy.

"What a shame you should have let yourself come to this end, old friend."

Lucian remained silent. He gazed at a spot over Douglas' head, his despair hidden, contempt flickering in his icy eyes. Was there some purpose for this visit, the third Douglas had made? Or would it be like the second visit, filled with prattle of meals eaten with Sarina, places visited with Sarina, passion shared with Sarina?

"I will never understand why you thought you would not be caught," Ryan said softly, "or why you

thought you could discover my cache. Oh, I know
you're desperate to find it, but you never will. Never.
And without it, who would ever believe the accusations of the dishonorably discharged commander of the
Peacekeeper? Your spies—you need better spies, old
friend—are inadequate, yet I humbly concede that
someone clever figured out what happened in Naipoor.''

Seeing the sudden shuttering of Lucian's eyes, Ryan
chuckled. Ah, it seemed if he wanted to see his enemy
rage, curse, despair, he should talk of Naipoor.

"Yes, Naipoor. I admit it. On the day I discovered
that the Ghost was Lucian Thorne, I knew you were
aware of how your downfall came about. Doubtless you
have learned some of the dreary details, but you cannot know how easy it was." He shook his head at the
wonder of it. "Bribes and brains, Lucian. It is all one
ever needs. And then, of course, those who have been
bought must be made to disappear. The coup de grace,
so to speak.''

It had been delivered to that nuisance, Garrick, for
instance. The fool had been demanding to see him,
wanting money for revealing the Ghost's identity and
whereabouts, but that would have interfered with
Ryan's own plans. Well, Garrick was gone now, food
for the fish, and Thorne would never know it was not
Sarina who had betrayed him. Ryan smiled at his enemy's furious face, noting that his act of indifference
had vanished.

Lucian growled, "You bastard. Rot in hell.''

Ryan laughed. "You will rot sooner than that, I
think. Hell will have to wait.'' He waggled the point
of his sword at the Ghost's lean belly. "Was it really
worth it, Captain? We could have helped each other. I
would have given you my approximate route on a given
day, you would have made sure you were at another
point entirely, and who would have been the wiser?
You would have gained much.''

Why was Douglas telling him all of this? Lucian
wondered. What were the devil's plans for him? Prob-

ably more torture before he was hanged . . . or would
he maroon them on some rocky, uncharted island to
starve? Or take their ammunition, let them sail off, then
blow their ship out of the water? Lucian lowered himself to the planks, his eyes impenetrable. He had already shown more fury than he had intended; now he
would not give the slightest hint that he was curious
about his fate. Besides, he was counting on Donal's
rescue.

"It's time I departed," Ryan said, annoyed at being
ignored. "Supper is early tonight. I have promised to
take Sarina to a chamber concert." Receiving only silence, he took the lantern and left.

Lucian sank his head in his hands. Damn the devil.
He was angry and empty and more desolate than he
wanted to admit even to himself. He was too aware
that Donal might not get to him in time; too aware that,
furious and hurt though he was with Sarina, he loved
her still and feared for her safety in Douglas' grasping
hands.

It was noon that same day when Donal, still looking
for a crew, stopped at the Black Ox for a bite to eat. As
he chewed, his practiced eye moved over every man
there before he saw one he liked. Royal Navy, big,
young, blond, open face, bold eyes. He took his pint
to the bar and stood beside him for a while before saying quietly, "I need a good man for some high adventure, sailor. Good pay for a couple of hours. What do
you say?"

"Sorry, sir. I'm just in from a year at sea." He
grinned. "Nothing's goin' to interfere with my drinkin'
an' my sleepin'."

"A year at sea, eh? That's a long stint. I well understand how you must be feelin', lad, but as I said, this
caper will last only a couple hours and—"

The seaman's blue eyes studied him. "Were you ever
in the Royal Navy, sir?"

Donal blinked. "Aye."

The other nodded, pleased. "It always tells. What ship?"

"The *Peacekeeper*." After all this time, Donal felt a thrill of pride in the admission.

The other took a long drag on his pint. "I know the *Peacekeeper*," he said.

"Do you now? And how is that?" Donal asked cautiously, dragging on his own pint.

"I was in the Bay of Bengal when she was there, three years ago." His eyes were dreamy. "Place named Naipoor. Were you on her then, sir?"

The hair rose on Donal's neck. "Aye. We patrolled the Bay of Bengal and the Indian Ocean then."

"Funny thing—I was on that vessel once."

"Come now, man, that's impossible unless you were visiting royalty. None but crew were ever aboard the *Peacekeeper*. What's your name, sailor?"

"Bascomb, George, sir."

"Well, then, Bascomb, suppose you tell me why you thought you were aboard my vessel?"

"Not thought, sir. Was. It was a teeming night and the streets were filled with seamen going back to their ships, all rowdy and bawling-like—you know, sir?"

"Aye. Go on, man." His heart had begun to thump.

"Well, we were tied up alongside your vessel, and this gent singles me out and asks me to take a pouch aboard the *Peacekeeper* and hide it—some kind of joke, he said. I said she wasn't my ship and he said, no matter, on such a night none would know. Well"— Bascomb gave a sheepish grin—"I was dead drunk, sir, and he offered me a pretty piece to do it, so I did. With the mob that went on, I wasn't noticed, and I stuck the pouch abaft of the back hatch, like he said, and I walked off and no one even so much as looked at me. I never thought of it again until just now."

Donal kept his face and his manner as calm as ever. "Did he have a name, this gent?"

"None that he gave me, but I remember him like my own brother. He was tall and good-looking with brown eyes and slick brown hair. Nice clothes. A real gentleman.''

Donal drew a deep breath. ''Mister, did you not hear about the pearls being stolen when you were in Naipoor?''

Bascomb halted his mug halfway to his mouth. ''Pearls?''

''Man, the Pearls of Naipoor, part of the national treasury, were stolen at that time. And you''—he poked a long finger against the seaman's chest—''were the one who carried them aboard the *Peacekeeper* in that pouch.''

''What!''

Donal looked skeptical. ''Man, I cannot believe you didn't know. Hell, every vessel was searched, soldiers all over. There was a huge stink about it.''

Bascomb looked amazed. ''I didn't know.''

Donal scowled. ''How could you not? Tell me that.''

The seaman, too, scowled. ''Maybe it was because of my condition, sir.''

''What condition?''

''When I came off the *Peacekeeper*, I was—robbed, sir. The gold pieces the gent gave me got stolen and I was near killed. In fact, if my mates hadn't come looking for me, well, I wouldn't be here tellin' you this. We were at sea before I was back on my feet again.''

Donal sighed and patted the young fellow on the shoulder. ''Laddie, come sit with me. I have a story to tell you . . .''

When Donal met Chambers afterward, he was grinning.

''It looks like you want to dance a jig, sir,'' Chambers said.

''That I do, and when you hear my news, you'll want to dance it with me.''

''I take it you found your mercenaries.''

''Aye. I would say we have nearly enough for a strike.'' Donal's eyes glinted, coal-black against purest white. ''And that's not all I found. Listen to this, man, and tell me if it's not the grandest stroke of luck a man could ever have.''

He related the whole story from beginning to end while Chambers listened, openmouthed.

"God's bones! I can't believe it—you've found him? The fellow who planted the bloody Pearls of Naipoor aboard the *Peacekeeper*?''

"None other.''

"Well, well, well, now, sir, isn't that something!'' Chambers, too, was grinning. "Will he testify? Do you know where to find him?''

"Aye. For the next month, he'll be sleeping at the Black Ox—and he'll testify. On a stack of Bibles, he says.''

Chambers sighed. "Amen. And now, we'd better get a move on if we're to meet the girl from Douglas Hall. She said they'd make a daily thing of it.''

Within minutes they were in Chambers' carriage racing down the cobbled street. Donal's black eyes narrowed. He stroked his beard, which had grown thick these last few days and gave him a forbidding look. He was dressed as a coachman in a green jacket trimmed in gold lace, navy-and-black striped breeches, and gleaming black boots. He had no hat on his glossy black hair, only a black patch over one eye, but his uncovered eye saw that every wench who was out and about felt compelled to flirt with him. Being Donal, he smiled back and winked at the prettiest of them.

"Ah, here we go, sir. Here is the one called Annie,'' said Chambers.

"The plump little redhead?''

"Aye. I had best drive on up around the corner. She'll know to come . . .''

They were examining a hoof of one of the mares when the girl approached.

Annie was frightened. Her pale-blue gaze darted about for any who might see her and report back to Peel or Gilmore or the master that she had been seen in suspicious circumstances. She was about to slip the coachman a note when his tall dark companion said:

"Hello there, little partridge."

Annie giggled as his one very wicked-looking black eye gleamed at her. Oooh, he was devilish handsome, and this was a different kettle of fish entirely from sneaking about with notes and such. The master surely couldn't complain about a bit of flirting! She beamed up at him.

"I ain't never seen yew afore, mister."

Donal jerked his head toward the carriage and its driver. "Been helpin' him out now an' then."

He drew closer and pinched her cheek for the benefit of passersby. Annie giggled again and turned red.

"Oooh, sir, ain't yew the wicked one!"

"Yer look a bit wicked yerself, missy." He added in a whisper: "Annie, I'm Donal. Tell the ladies I'm gathering men as fast as I can."

Donal! Annie gasped and struggled with her disappointment. He was so handsome and flirty that she might have known he was already taken.

"I—I'll tell them, sir."

"And tell them to be brave—it will take a bit of time yet, but they must not lose heart."

Donal's own heart was suddenly heavy, but he couldn't let anyone know, least of all the women. Despite his wonderful good fortune in finding Bascomb, he was well aware that Ryan Douglas' honor, his fortune, his very life depended on Lucian's silence. And on his death. There were only two reasons why Ryan had not killed Lucian already. Either he wanted something from him, or he simply enjoyed torturing him. It was Donal's great fear that he would be too late to save his captain.

"Tell Ginelle her note is next to my heart," he murmured.

Annie gulped. Oooh, not only was he handsome, he was romantic. "That I will, sir, an' here's another from both ladies. They said no answer is required." She slipped it into his hand.

"Thank you, lass. Tell them I'll try my best not to disappoint them."

"Yessir."

She blinked up at him, frightened, for he looked so grave. But then everything was all right suddenly for he was laughing, and his eyes were twinkling devilishly again.

"Yer a darlin' girl, Annie, an' I'll not forget yer help." He gave her a quick kiss atop her head and a pat on her rump. "Now, then, run along wi' yer. Maybe I'll see yer 'ere tomorry, eh?"

"Yes! Oh, yes," she said. "An' thank yew, sir . . ."

Chapter 20

Mealtimes had become unbearable for Sarina. It was then that Ryan took liberties with her and forced his plans on her. His drinking had also begun to frighten her—when he was drunk he regarded her so strangely. But at least he had not yet insisted that they talk about marriage.

"Good morning, ladies." Ryan took his chair. "How fortunate I am, seated between two such beauties. Ginelle"—he seemed amused by her icy stare—"you missed a rare treat last night. Haydn quartets."

Ginelle sniffed. "I find Haydn boring."

"Haydn boring?" He laughed. "Ah, well, I suppose I should have expected that. My dear"—he turned to Sarina—"I have procured those theater tickets I mentioned, and have I told you the dressmaker is coming this morning? I think you'll be pleased with her work."

Sarina bristled. It was too much, this being confined to the house, dragged to plays and concerts she didn't want to see or hear, and now—expensive gowns she didn't want and would never wear. She couldn't allow this insanity to go on another minute.

"Ryan, this must stop. I will not accept any gowns from you, and—and do not plan any more activities for me. Not only that, but it really isn't proper, my being here in this house with you. Surely you realize that. Already people look at me askance."

Ryan rose, scowling, from the table. "To hell with them! You are still my fiancée."

"I'm sorry," Sarina said hotly, "but I am not your fiancée!"

She stared, wide-eyed, as Ryan's face turned dusky-red. What had she done! How could she have forgotten why she was allowing him to control her? Oh, God, what might he do to Lucian if she disobeyed him?

"You are staying and that is the end of it," he muttered.

Ginelle jumped up, emboldened by Sarina's fury. "You cannot force *me* to stay, Ryan Douglas! You may have poor Sarina under your thumb because of Lucian, but you have no hold over me. I cannot abide the man!"

Her flashing eyes met Sarina's, letting her friend know that this was the moment she had hoped for—the chance to make Ryan so angry that he might tell her to leave.

"In fact, I cannot abide you either!" she plunged on. "I never have liked you, and why on earth you think you can lock us in our rooms and then forbid us to leave the house, I simply cannot imagine! Mr. Fairburn will skin you alive, not to mention my father and my brothers, who will hunt you down like the dog you are if you don't release us immediately!"

She felt so much better, having spoken out, that she forged ahead.

"And another thing, if it weren't for your incredible stupidity and conceit, none of this would have ever happened!"

Sarina held her breath. On first hearing Ginelle's plan, she had thought it crazy and far too dangerous to attempt. But Ginelle had convinced her it would be an easy matter to find Tom Chambers and be taken quickly to Donal. And so she had gone along with it. Now she wasn't so sure. Ryan looked as though he would break Ginelle in two. Sarina nudged her friend toward the door.

"Not now, love," she murmured, "not now . . ."

"Leave her be," Ryan ordered. "I would hear what the little viper has to say."

"I would say it in any event," Ginelle declared, breathless with anger. "I immediately saw the peril in your sending us on that stupid boat of yours, which had not so much as a slingshot on it to protect us! Did I not say that the Ghost might carry us off in the north when you were in the south seeking him?" Her face was red and her eyes flashed. The top of her shining blonde head came only to Ryan's breastbone, but he was stung by her fury.

"Sarina, did I not say that very thing? But poor Ryan, poor little boy, got all thin-nosed and huffy and hurt and had to have his own way. And look what happened! You are the cause of this turmoil, you stupid man." She pointed a shaking finger at him. "And you would be wise not to anger our fathers any further. Release us this instant!"

Ginelle put a hand to her pounding heart. Had she gone too far? Seeing the veins standing out on Ryan's temples, his brown eyes almost popping out of his head, she moved toward Sarina. The two of them stood, their arms intertwined, as Ryan approached. Ginelle felt Sarina's body tremble. She herself was quivering.

"Since you are so dissatisfied with the shelter I am providing," he said softly, "I suggest you leave it. Now."

Ginelle's heart leaped. Oh, fabulous day, her ruse had worked! But she mustn't let Ryan suspect. She blinked, wide-eyed.

"Now? Th-this instant?" She faltered, pretending to give a frightened glance at Sarina. "Perhaps I was hasty—"

"Damn it, woman, now! Throw your silly tantrums on the street from now on."

"And Sarina?"

"Sarina stays." Grasping Ginelle's upper arm between his steely fingers, Ryan separated the two women.

"You're hurting me!" Ginelle protested.

"You're fortunate I'm a gentleman, you little bitch,

or I would hurt more than your arm. And now, get out of my house.'' He propelled her rapidly toward the front door.

''Sarina!'' Ginelle shrieked, and dragged her feet. ''Oh, do something!''

But the look she gave Sarina over her shoulder was one of triumph. She was frightened, yes, but now everything was going to be all right. Donal would see to it, and Sarina's admiring eyes and silent applause were giving her courage.

Sarina was doing her own part in the charade. It would seem odd were she not to object.

''Ryan, please, do reconsider. You can't put her out—''

But she didn't dare beg too hard. She wanted Ginelle safe in Donal's arms.

''The bitch goes,'' Ryan stated. He opened the door and shoved Ginelle onto the stoop.

''My things!'' she cried. ''At least let me have my cloak and the bag with my things in it!'' Little did he know it was ready and waiting.

''Rosie!'' Sarina shrieked, ''fetch Ginelle's things quickly!''

''Mum, whatever is the—''

''Rosie, for goodness' sake, go! Fetch her things this instant!''

''Yes'm, right away, mum.''

Two minutes later, Ginelle's packed bag landed at her feet on the sidewalk and Ryan slammed the door shut, barring her return.

Sarina could scarcely sit still during the play that evening. Had Ginelle reached Donal or had some terrible fate befallen her? Ryan had hinted at the awful things that might happen to a woman alone on the street, and while Sarina was certain he said them only to frighten her, she was uneasy. As their carriage moved homeward, she peered constantly out the window.

Seeing her agitation, Ryan was pleased. If she ever did try to escape from him, she would think twice.

"What is it you expect to see, *ma petite?*" he drawled.

Sarina gave him a frigid look. "As though you need ask."

He chuckled. "I wouldn't worry if I were you. Such a delectable little morsel as Ginelle will have found a protector with no trouble."

Sarina knew his words were calculated to frighten her. She stared at him, catching glimpses of his face in the glow cast by passing street lamps. He was more of a stranger than ever. Cold, sardonic, cruel. She shook her head.

How could she ever have agreed to marry him? She asked herself. Sarina pulled her cloak around her and huddled in the corner, hoping Ryan wouldn't touch her. She felt about to fly into a million pieces with all the thoughts and worries crowding her head. Lucian, Ginelle, Donal, herself . . . The carriage stopped, and looking out, she saw the waterfront, and moonlight on the water.

"Why are we here?"

"See her out there, Sarina?" Ryan said softly "The *Vengeance*. It's a sad sight, is it not, to see such a swift vessel in chains?"

Against her will, Sarina's gaze was drawn to the great ship. Like a bird with its wings clipped, it didn't even resemble the *Vengeance* she knew. She would have given anything to free Lucian from the black hold, awaiting his fate.

"What will you do with him?" she whispered, her throat so constricted that it was painful to speak. "Will he—go before the Crown?"

Ryan toyed with his golden pomander, tapping it against one palm and filling the carriage with its scent. "I think not."

He rapped on the glass, motioning his driver to move on. "I want this over and done with, whereas a court trial would drag on forever."

"What do you intend to—to do with him?" Sarina asked, her hand on her pounding heart.

"Hang him—along with his officers."

He turned so that she wouldn't see his smile in the occasional flashes of light that filled the carriage. What had been an expression of growing concern on her beautiful face was now full-blown terror. She was going to yield to his demands . . .

"Ryan, my God . . ."

"It's what the Crown will do in any event, my dear, be assured of that. I'm doing them a favor."

Sarina could no longer control her panic. It swept over her like an icy black tide, and she felt as though she were smothering in it.

"When?" she demanded.

"Soon. Very soon."

What about the crew? Oh, God, she hadn't the heart to ask. But then, of course, he would do away with them, too. They knew too much. Oh, God . . . oh, Lucian . . . He had already suffered so much, and now he would go to the gallows thinking she had betrayed him. She began to weep, softly at first, then more harshly as despair overwhelmed her.

Ryan glared at her. "You would think I was killing you!"

"Y-you are! I will die when you kill him."

"I will never understand women," he exclaimed. "The bastard abducts and rapes you and thus gains your undying devotion. For that alone, he deserves to die."

Sarina didn't even try to calm her sobs. She fumbled in her bag for her handkerchief and mopped her drenched eyes.

"Ryan, I beg of you, do not do this. Let him have a trial."

"No trial," Ryan said. "Once and for all, no trial."

It seemed to Sarina that her weeping had cleared her head suddenly. Of course he would not want a trial, for then he would be exposed for the bastard he was. She saw, too, why he hadn't allowed her to leave his house; why he had insisted they were still engaged to be married. It seemed that Lucian's fate rested in her hands. She dried her eyes and pressed her arms to her trembling body.

"What must I do to—gain his freedom?" she asked quietly.

"Let us talk of it when we arrive home."

He was satisfied. She was responding exactly as he had known she would. He sought one small soft hand and raised it to his lips, slowly caressing it, kissing each finger, inhaling her intoxicating scent.

Sarina closed her eyes. She wanted to snatch her hand away from his disgusting slobbering and slap his face, but she forced herself to yield. If she absolutely refused to wed him, then what? Would he insist that she be his mistress? She didn't see how she could bear to do either, but if she did not, what of Lucian? What if Donal could not free him? Her mind spun with terrible thoughts: Lucian, chained hand and foot in that horrible damp black hole; Ginelle, going off bravely in search of Donal. Sarina knew that she, too, would do anything in her power to save Lucian Thorne. Even if it meant marrying a man she had come to loathe.

When the carriage arrived at Douglas Hall, Ryan followed Sarina into the foyer. He was jubilant, thinking how swiftly they had arrived at the heart of the matter—and for Sarina herself to have mentioned it first . . .

He handed his butler their cloaks. "We will have champagne, Gilmore."

"Not for me, Gilmore," Sarina said through tight lips.

"Pay her no heed," Ryan said lightly. "We are having a small celebration and Mistress Fairburn will certainly have some champagne." He led Sarina into the drawing room where a fire was crackling on the hearth.

"You have not answered my question, Ryan." She faced him, dreading to know the exact details of her fate, yet eager to have the matter settled and Lucian freed. "What do you want of me?"

He failed to hide his hunger as he caught both her hands. "You will marry me, of course."

Although Sarina had expected the words, she felt as though the room had tilted suddenly on end. The strength drained from her body.

"You would have a woman who loves another?"

Ryan laughed and gathered her into his arms. "I shall not be disturbed in the slightest. Ah, Gilmore, there you are. Very good, fill them to the top . . ." He kissed Sarina's rosy mouth until she was breathless, until Gilmore discreetly cleared his throat.

"That will be all, Gilmore."

Ryan released her and handed her the brimming goblet. He touched his own to it, his burning gaze never leaving her.

"To us, *ma petite*. To a new beginning."

Sarina placed her glass, untouched, on a gleaming mahogany table and stepped back. "But I have not said I would marry you," she protested.

"You will. You will marry me or your bastard lover will die. It is as simple as that."

"You are despicable! Evil . . ."

He laughed. "If you say so."

"I do say so."

She was completely repulsed by him and afraid of him, but she mustn't let it overwhelm her. She had to remember that Lucian would not be giving up, and that even now Donal was out there gathering men. Surely by now, Ginelle had found him and given him her all-important message. And she herself could delay the wedding by insisting that her father attend. Lucian would be free long before her father arrived from England, and when she told him everything, he would never give her to Ryan. Never. She felt such relief at the thought that she allowed Ryan to put his arm around her and lead her to the settee before the fire.

"We are going to talk, Sarina."

"What more could you possibly have to say?" Watching him quaff her champagne and refill his own glass before joining her, she said crisply, "You are turning into a drunkard, you know."

"And you have a sharp tongue which you will curb from this instant forth. Now"—he leaned back comfortably, sipping from his goblet, his dark eyes moving possessively over her—"as I said, we will talk. I have several important things to tell you. First, our wedding will take place next month—"

"Next month! But my father cannot be here by then."

"It is of no importance. Neither would he have been here for the first wedding we planned."

Sarina was devastated. In one stroke he had killed half her hopes. She felt like a lost child. Her lips quivered.

"I—want my father here, Ryan."

"Forget your father, Sarina. You are under my care and protection now. It is exactly as it was before. Nothing has changed."

She wanted to shout that everything had changed, nothing was as before. She would rather be under the care and protection of a shark.

"In return, I will allow the bastard to escape. But he is never to hear of your part in it. And be warned, my sweet, that I will blow him out of the water should he come near one of my traders again. Also, your father is not to know of your involvement with Thorne, or anything about him. Is that understood?"

"I don't trust you to free him," Sarina murmured.

"You will see him leave, I promise it. You will see the *Vengeance* under sail."

But she would not see the ambush that would be waiting, he thought. Lucian Thorne would never reach the open sea. "Speaking of trust," Ryan added gruffly, "why should I trust you? I am the one betrayed, after all."

"You have my word of honor. If you free him, I—will marry you."

Lucian would live, she thought. It was one shining hope that would keep her going. Once he heard of her marriage, he would never believe she loved him, but he would live. It was all that mattered.

Chapter 21

Donal, his spirits high, turned his steaming mare over to the stableboy at the Blue Onion and entered the pub. It was days like this that gave him hope—ten new men on his roster brought his band to thirty-five. Thirty-five strong, dangerous men who loved adventure and were hungry for money. Add to that Bascomb, who was willing to testify, and Donal was nearly ready to make his move. He sat down at the sturdy oak table, tipped back his chair, and yawned. Supper and bed, that was all he wanted now. He smiled up at the buxom barmaid who had been flirting with him all week.

"What kin I offer yer, sir?" Her eyes said that she herself was available.

"A pint and a bite of supper, lass. Bring me whatever's good tonight."

"That'll be the savory pie an' greens . . ." She looked wistfully at his gleaming black hair and broad shoulders. "Anythin' else . . . ?"

"Not tonight, lass."

He stared at the leaping fire in the hearth, but in his mind he saw the *Vengeance*, waiting, silent, chained to the merchantman with the other two vessels still guarding her; Lucian's crew divided and captive; Lucian himself in chains. Donal shook his head and sipped his pint. He had the men, he had the arms, now all he needed was the luck. It had always come

when he needed it, and he knew there would be no
rescue without it.

His task was to subdue the watches on the three
traders and the *Vengeance*, free the captives, get them
all on the *Vengeance*, and make sure she was armed,
and get her underway before anyone knew what had
happened. And all he needed was moonlight and a
bloody miracle. Ah, holy heaven, he was eager to
move, but so far, he wasn't quite sure how to go about
it . . .

He finished his meal, paid his bill, and, pleasantly
sluggish and ready for a good night's sleep, made his
way up the stairs carrying a spill for his lamp. As soon
as he entered his room, he froze. What in the hell—
someone was in his bed. Probably one of the wenches
who had been making eyes at him all week. He lit the
lamp and gently poked the blanket, marveling at the
change in himself. Since when had Donal Fleming ever
driven a wench from his bed?

"Wake up, lady. Have you not a bunk of your own?"

Sleepy blue eyes stared up at him, blinking against
the light. A full, rosy mouth pouted. He smelled the
familiar aroma of roses.

"Can I not sleep in yours, sir?"

Ginelle! Ah, dear God in heaven. He threw off the
covers, lifted her in his arms, and kissed her mouth
and face over and over as she laughed, wept and kissed
him back.

"Little dove. My precious white dove. Holy heaven,
lass, what are ye doin' here?" He stood her on her
feet, his suddenly concerned gaze moving over her.
"Are ye all right? Ye're not harmed? The bastard didna
touch ye, did he?" His black eyes flashed.

Ginelle giggled. "Never. I insulted him and he threw
me out."

Donal growled. "Are ye sayin' he threw ye on the
street thinkin' ye had nowhere to go?"

"Yes, but it was my plan! I taunted him on purpose—there was no other way to get out of the house."

Even so, Donal thought darkly, a woman alone and

a soft little beauty like Ginelle? It was one more score to even—the bastard had probably wanted his beloved to end up in a brothel. Fury flared up within him, but he doused it.

"All's well, at any rate. Ye got here all right."

He sat in the room's only chair and pulled her onto his lap. He buried his face in her sweet bosom and squeezed her hard. He wouldn't murder Ryan Douglas this evening. This evening he was going to make love to his lass.

"I-I must confess," Ginelle murmured, "that I nearly didn't get here." She hadn't wanted to tell him, but when he saw Mr. Chambers' black eye and cut lip—oh dear. "Donal, I, well, first of all, as you can see, I'm fine, but two men did try to—to pull me into their brougham, but just then your friend galloped up in his carriage and—"

"Men tried to carry you off?"

"Well, yes, but—"

"And the only reason you are here in my arms is because of Chambers?"

"I—yes . . ." Ginelle's eyes grew huge as she watched Donal's angry face in the half-light. "D-Donal, do not look at me so. You are fr-frightening me." She tried to pull away, fearing his terrible anger was for her.

Donal clenched his teeth. "There, lass, dinna be afraid. Ye're my sweet lass and ye're safe with me now. Ye'll never have to be near that bloody bastard again."

He would kill Douglas. As God was his witness, he would kill him with his bare hands, if Lucian didn't kill him first.

"Tell me about Sarina," Donal said gruffly. "Is he likely to throw her out, too? Or Rosie?"

"Not Sarina—she's still not allowed outside the house without him, but I'm not sure about Rosie. Oh, Donal, I have so much to tell you." She felt her body glowing, warming as his big dark hands moved over her breasts and cradled her face. She whispered, "But, love, can we not talk about it later?"

* * *

Sarina had spent a sleepless night. While she re-
joiced that Lucian would be freed, she felt hopelessly
trapped. Until she remembered that she was not alone.
Rosie was with her, and Bessie and Annie. She could
still send messages to Donal, and as long as she could do
that, there was hope for her—and, too, Ginelle was
free! Probably this very day she would get word that
she was with Donal. By breakfast, Sarina's spirits had
risen considerably.

She sat across the table from Ryan, her eyes on her
plate as he consumed quantities of scones, poached
salmon, and creamed eggs. Her mind was busy com-
posing a note to Donal. He must hear the wonderful
news that Lucian was going to be freed.

She nibbled her eggs and salmon, puzzling over
Ryan's promise to her. There was so much she didn't
understand. How could Lucian possibly be 'allowed to
escape'? He was in chains. She didn't even know if his
crew was on the *Vengeance* or the ships guarding it. She
didn't understand at all how it would be accomplished.

"I trust you have not forgotten the dressmaker is
coming again this afternoon," Ryan said to her. "More
coffee, Gilmore. And don't forget the soiree at the
French ambassador's this evening, Sarina. Madame is
bringing a gown for you to try. Possibly you can wear
it tonight."

Seeing the flush of anger on Sarina's pale cheeks,
Ryan again imagined her in his bed. He was obsessed
with the thought. He had considered the matter carefully. He could take her by force before they were
wed—God knows he was more entitled to her than the
damned Ghost—but then she would hate him even
more than she did now, and he preferred her gratitude
to her hatred.

He *could* wed her without pomp. In fact, he had considered sealing the bond as soon as the *Vengeance* had
sailed off into the rising sun. It could be done swiftly
and legally in his own drawing room with Peel and
Gilmore as witnesses, and then—then . . . He imag-

ined himself carrying her up the staircase to his bed-chamber, closing the door, locking it, removing her gown, carrying her to his bed, the bed he had bought especially for her . . . He had no doubt he would have to drag her there, the cheating little trollop, but then, he would greatly enjoy it.

As pleasant as it would be to take her sooner rather than later, a wedding witnessed by two hundred important townspeople and presided over by the bishop himself was more to his liking. It would bind her to him inextricably. Yes, he had made the right choice, and he would control his hunger and abide by it. Besides, a large formal affair was more fitting to his stature in the city.

"I do not want to go to the soiree," Sarina murmured. She was imagining Ryan's possessive arm around her all evening, his introducing her as his future bride, the congratulations, the laughter. She simply could not face it.

"Nonetheless, you are going, *ma petite*. There will be many such evenings. Now, do not sulk. And you have scarcely touched your breakfast. You must eat."

"I want nothing."

He laughed. "Then before you waste away, there are several things we must discuss." He went to his desk, found the legal document he wanted, and returned to the table.

"There are several things that I, too, wish to discuss," she answered coolly. "For instance, I don't understand about Lucian's escape. How can it possibly seem accidental when he is in chains? And are his men on different ships? If they are, will he not think it strange when he is suddenly unchained and they—"

"Why would you think he will be unchained?" Ryan snapped, losing all patience with her. "And yes, his crew is on the other vessels, but they will be herded onto the *Vengeance* in their manacles, fully expecting to be marooned or sunk at sea—"

After having given the matter considerable thought, he knew he could not risk their actually escaping.

Thorne was smart enough to realize what was afoot and would be wary of an ambush. Therefore he meant to unshackle only Thorne himself and three or four others. Sarina must see him moving about unfettered, but the remainder of the Ghost's crew would stay chained in the hold. His own men would then sail the *Vengeance* out of New York City and board one of his other vessels before sinking Lucian's ship.

"Marooned?" Sarina gasped. "Or sunk at sea? Oh, Ryan, you would not!"

Her terror for Lucian infuriated him, but Ryan kept it well-hidden. He said brusquely:

"Of course not. You must trust me more than that, my love. A key will be misplaced or dropped where one of them will find it. Several of my men must, of necessity, be knocked about, but then on Friday morning toward dawn, the bastard will be on his merry way and reveling in the thought that he tricked me."

Sarina didn't even notice the half-smile on his face, for her heart was soaring. She herself might be imprisoned still, but Lucian would be free the day after tomorrow! Oh, if only Donal could somehow get her away from here soon afterward and she could go to her love . . .

Ryan picked up the paper from the table. "Now, if you are satisfied, let us get down to some unfinished business. I want your name on this."

Sarina frowned. "On what? What is it?"

"An agreement which I had my solicitor put in writing last night." He brought ink to the table and handed her a quill. "Gilmore, fetch Peel. I will want you both to witness this."

Sarina quickly perused the document before looking up at him, her eyes accusing.

"You never said you wanted complete control of my finances." It meant she couldn't even buy a trinket at a fair without Ryan's approval. It meant he would control her inheritance.

"Now, now, my sweet, what does a little thing like you know about money? Every woman's property goes to her husband, as you well know. I merely chose to have it in writing.''

''And as you well know, my father would never permit it! He has already arranged for Fairburn Shipping to go into my hands alone.''

''You will therefore tell him you prefer it to be under your husband's control.''

''No! I absolutely will not sign this!'' she declared, as Peel and Gilmore stood waiting.

''You should reconsider, Sarina. Which would you prefer, your Ghost dangling at the end of a rope come dawn on Friday, or his heading to sea with the wind in his sails? His fate is in your hands. Which shall it be?''

Sarina gave him a look of the utmost loathing before taking the quill and slashing her name across the paper.

Afterward, Ryan said softly, ''If you are considering slipping away from me after he is free, my sweet slut, I do not advise it.'' His eyes were as cold and hard as marble. ''I will always know where he is, and I will not hesitate to kill him. I have killed before . . .''

''You bastard.''

She stormed from the room. She would decide later how to extricate herself from the terrible web in which she was bound, but for now she had no time to lose. She must get a message to Donal telling him that Lucian was to be freed. Rosie went for Annie while she was writing it, and, within minutes, was back with her.

''Annie, I cannot tell you how very important this message is to a great many people . . .''

''Yes'm.'' Annie's eyes were big. ''Rosie tol' me.''

''Have you any errands to run so there is a reason to leave the house now?''

''There's fish just in.''

''Good. Before you get the fish, Annie, you must find Chambers. Tell him to give Donal this note as quickly as possible. Can you do that?''

''Oh, yes'm. Yer want me ter go now, mum?''

Sarina nodded. "Please. And Annie, ask him about Ginelle."

It seemed no time at all before Annie was back with Rosie by her side. Sarina hastily drew them into her bedchamber and locked the door.

"Tell me what happened, Annie. Quickly!"

"Oh, mum, it was him," Annie exclaimed. "It was Mr. Donal himself driving the carriage. He's such a gent an' that handsome—"

"Do go on!" Sarina's heart was galloping. "What did he say? Did he read my note then and there?"

"He did, mum, an' then he give such a whoop an' he picked me up an' whirled me aroun' an' kissed me cheek an'—an'—" Overcome by the memory, she could not continue.

Rosie finished for her. "An' he said, mum, that it wuz the very miracle he was lookin' for. He thanks you from the bottom o' his heart an' says it's jist a matter o' time before they come for us."

Sarina's eyes grew damp with happiness. "And Ginelle?"

Rosie beamed. "Safe an' sound an' happy as a lark."

Sarina released a long sigh. It was more than she had ever hoped for. "Annie, thank you so much, and you, too, Rosie, and now, I think I want to be alone for a little . . ."

Donal was edgy. It was Thursday night, the night Sarina's note had said Lucian was to be freed, but when in bloody hell was anything going to happen? He and his men had been waiting in underbrush on the west shore of the bay for hours. He was stiff, hungry, and his eyes burned from staring out toward the *Vengeance*. He knew that the escape, as Sarina had so excitedly described it in her letter, was nothing but a sham to pacify her. Douglas would never let his worst enemy out of his hands; he would sail the Ghost ship somewhere and do away with her and Lucian and the crew.

But once they were all aboard the *Vengeance*, his own worst problem would be solved. Now he wondered uneasily if the charade would take place at all. But no, it was still too soon to think that way. He yawned, stretched, and tried to stay calm. He closed his eyes for a moment to ease their burning.

"Sir—" It was a low, excited voice on his right. "It's starting . . ."

Donal's eyes flew open. In the light of the waxing, near-full moon he saw that there was indeed activity. He smiled and wet his lips. "We'll just sit here and let them do all the work, mister, then we'll join them for the grand finale."

Silently, they watched as the other two vessels were rowed close and grapneled to the *Vengeance*, one on either side.

"There seem to be only a few of Douglas' men making the transfer, sir."

"Aye," Donal muttered, "and it means my mates are still shackled. Let's pile in now and be ready to push off as soon as they begin transferring."

"Aye, sir."

His men, hooded gray-clad mercenaries, quietly took their places in the three longboats. Each longboat would approach a merchantman, stealthily board her and, upon a signal, attack the *Vengeance* simultaneously from three different sides. They would subdue the enemy, force them back to their own vessels, bind them, and slash their sails. Once the *Vengeance* crew was in command, they would set sail, Donal with them.

"They've begun," Donal said finally. "Cast off, men."

Lucian stirred. Something had awakened him from an uneasy sleep. He raised his head and listened for some moments before climbing awkwardly to his feet. He was stiff and cold, but no matter. Something was happening on deck; he heard shuffling, angry shouts, curses, and then there was an unexpected flare of light from a lantern in the passageway. His cell door was unbarred, dragged open, and a man shoved in. God almighty. Sky!

"Bastard!" Sky shouted to his captor as the door slammed shut and the bar was driven home. He turned, his angry silver eyes softening as he saw Lucian. "Hello, Captain. I reckoned I'd find you here." He grabbed Lucian, gave him a fierce hug, and felt him wince. He held him at arm's length and was gazing at him when the light was removed. "Lad, lad . . ."

"Never mind, man, I'll live," Lucian said gruffly. "What's happening? Is it still night?"

"It must be near dawn. They're gettin' us all aboard, but God only knows why."

Lucian's mouth tightened. There were several possible reasons why, as Sky well knew, and none of them good.

"Have we lost anyone?" he asked. "Anyone lashed?"

"Garrick was troublesome right from the beginning. They took 'im out a while back, and I haven't seen him since. My guess is they killed him and threw him over."

Garrick. Damn. Lucian had not wanted to lose anyone. Well, he couldn't worry about him now.

"How many in chains?"

"All of us," Sky growled. "They took mine off at the last, me and three or four others." After some moments, he added. "You figure they're fixin' to sink us?"

Lucian nodded in the thick blackness. "Either that or maroon us." Knowing Douglas, he guessed they would be sunk.

Sky groaned. "By God, an' all of this because of that treacherous little Fairburn wench. Oh, lad, would I love to get my fingers around her neck!" He drove a fist into his palm and uttered a string of scorching epithets until Lucian lay a hand on his arm.

"Quiet, man, I hear something different. Listen . . ." He went to the door and peered out the small barred opening into darkness. "Sky, by the gods, that's fighting going on up there!"

There were muffled shouts and the clash of weapons, thumpings, and, at long last, ominous quiet. And then, hearing deep, familiar laughter ringing through the hold, Lucian himself began to laugh. A lantern shed its light on them, the door was hurled open, and there stood Donal, gray-clad, sword in hand, black eyes dancing. He clapped his two best friends on their backs and unlocked Lucian's shackles.

"It's about time, Lieutenant," Lucian said.

"Aye, sir. Now then, shake a leg, men, so we can get off by dawn. You've dallied here long enough. Sky, take this key and start unlocking the others." When he left, Donal said low, "Man, we owe this to Sarina. It was her message that told me of this sweet caper of Ryan's." Seeing the hope flare in Lucian's eyes, Donal hurriedly told him all he knew from Ginelle.

"I believe in the lass completely—I see you do, too," he said finally. "Oh, and I have a little something else to tell you, but not now. I must return to keep an eye on Douglas' activities. How about if you sail her up to Shoreham tomorrow night and we rendezvous there? We have plans to make . . ."

Chapter 22

I t was dawn, and Ryan, having promised Sarina that she would see the *Vengeance* underway, was in a suddenly foul mood. Damn her! The glowing look on her face was enough to destroy all the joy he had derived from his own cleverness.

"Is it not time we got out and watched for her?" Sarina asked. "Surely she'll be coming soon."

"Get out if you must," Ryan grumbled, "but I, for one, have no desire to wet my feet just yet."

He had chosen a vantage point downriver from the bay where he'd stopped the carriage. He could see all he needed from its comfortable confines, but Sarina was pushing through the tall dew-filled grass to the water's edge. She was correct in assuming that very soon now the Ghost ship would pass by on her last voyage. Once in the open sea, those who had been unchained would be bound again and thrown into the hold, his crew would be transferred, and the *Vengeance* would be sent to the bottom. Thus would end Lucian Thorne, Ryan thought sourly; an event long overdue.

Sarina gazed anxiously up the river for sight of Lucian's ship. For one wild instant, she even imagined herself calling out to him when it drew near, but she knew she would not. It would anger Ryan so that there was no telling what he might do. Besides, Donal had promised it was just a matter of time before they came for her and Rosie.

The thought had already sent her heart soaring

when, in the mist, she saw the *Vengeance* round a distant bend. Oh, God, it was true then! Ryan had actually done as he'd promised, despite her fear that he was up to trickery. All the sails were filled and she was flying, plowing through the green water with a churning, foaming wake behind her. She was drawing near enough now so that Sarina could see figures moving about on deck, and while she could not make out faces, one of the figures was so tall and his hair so black that she knew it was Lucian.

Her hungry eyes devoured him as he strode the deck, calling out orders. Suddenly she felt Ryan behind her. His arms went around her. His touch made her cringe, but she was grateful to him.

"Thank you," she murmured.

Ryan made no answer for it was then that his gaze actually went to the ship. He blinked, released Sarina, and stared hard at the blood-red pennant streaming from the highest mast. Hell and damnation, he did not believe it! He could not believe that the Ghost and his crew were making an actual escape. There was a splash as something was thrown into the water, another splash, plop, splash, splash, plop! Ballast. They were dumping the ballast. He ground his teeth as the *Vengeance* rose higher in the water and gained speed.

Sarina watched enthralled until all that was left to show that Lucian and his vessel had passed was the choppy water, the wavelets rushing up on the shore. She lifted her wet skirts and walked back to the carriage. Ryan followed her. Not until they were on the way back to Douglas Hall did he speak.

"I trust you are satisfied?" he said stiffly. He damned well was not. Heads would roll when he learned who was responsible.

"I am satisfied."

Sarina's thoughts and heart were still filled with the sight of the *Vengeance* when she returned to her bedchamber and found Rosie neatening it.

"Did yer see them, mum?" Rosie asked anxiously. "Did they git away?"

"Yes! Yes, yes, yes!" She wanted nothing so much as to open her windows and shout it to the neighborhood. To the whole world. Her beloved was free and he was going to come for her!

"I want to hear it all, mum, but not now. I'll pour yer tea, and Bessie will be bringin' yer hot water to bathe. Er, mum"—she lowered her voice—"there's only one thing—the master wants yer to come down now."

"Tell him I have taken ill—the dawn air has given me a headache."

"I done that already, mum, but he said if yer didn't come down soon, he'd come up an' carry yer down, ill or not."

Sarina stifled a scathing retort. "Very well, inform him that I will join him shortly."

As Sarina drank her tea, Rosie delivered the message and quickly returned. "Now, if yer sit yerself, I'll git the snarls out o' yer hair an' mebbe yer can tell me about it . . ."

Sarina obeyed, sipping her tea and recounting everything as Rosie brushed her heavy mass of hair. As she spoke, she wondered about Donal and Ginelle. Had Donal been on the *Vengeance*? Had Ginelle? She wondered, too, when she would hear about the plans to rescue her and Rosie. Or would she not hear anything until one night Lucian would suddenly appear in her bedchamber? She laughed at the thought, her eyes glowing. It wouldn't surprise her one bit if he accomplished such a daring feat.

With Rosie's help, she quickly bathed and dressed and arranged her hair, then went down to the dining room where Ryan was having coffee. Annie hovered near the sideboard, a conspiratorial smile on her face.

"Bring fresh scones, Annie," Ryan snapped. When the girl left, his unfriendly gaze settled on Sarina. "Are you always so late to breakfast, milady?"

"You know I am not," she answered calmly. "As Rosie told you, I have a headache. I did not sleep well."

"That will soon be remedied." His eyes moved over her. "Vigorous lovemaking is always a great inducement to sleep . . ."

Sarina caught her lip between her teeth. He was baiting her on purpose, but she was far too happy to snap back at him. She would not be here much longer, after all.

"By the way, have I mentioned that Madame is fitting you for your wedding gown this morning?"

"You—had not told me."

"And I will be buying you another ring . . ."

Sarina said nothing, but her eyes went to her left hand. The beautiful diamond and emerald band he had given her in happier days still lay in the bottom of her trunk where she had hidden it from the Ghost. Remembering her last glimpse of Lucian bold and free and in command once more, her heart flamed. How soon before she would be in his arms again? Ryan's quick eyes did not miss the curving of her lips.

"Ah, the lady smiles for a change. And since it cannot be the prospect of wearing my ring that pleases you, it must be some delightful memory."

"I am simply grateful that Lucian is free." Seeing a muscle jump in his jaw, she knew she was angering him further. She added quickly, "When will Madame be here? And will you need my help in planning the menu for the wedding or will Peel tend to all of that?"

Ryan studied her innocent face with narrowed eyes. Not for one moment did he believe she was interested in the coming festivities. In fact, he would be disappointed if she were. He much preferred that she suffer, especially since the devil had actually escaped. He had not the foggiest idea how it had happened, but there it was. He had just now spoken to one of his men who had witnessed the fiasco.

His plan had fallen by the wayside when his mercenaries were completely surprised by a swarm of hooded men who had then cracked heads, broken ribs, and slashed the sails of his own three vessels. Damnation, how many ghost crews did the bastard have in reserve? And how had they known when the captives would be transferred to the *Vengeance?* Was it a coincidence? It bloody well had to be, yet Sarina had known his plans. Had she somehow—but no, to think she was involved in any way was unthinkable. He was in a half-frenzy to question her about it, but how could he? It was essential that she believe he himself had freed the devil. What a tangle . . .

"Ryan?"

"Yes?"

Such innocence and purity on that beautiful face and in those sea-green eyes. The little harlot. What lies were about to pass her rosy dew-kissed lips now? He felt his body tighten with resentment, knowing that everything she had told him about the Ghost was a lie. Would he ever really know the truth?

"May I go outside for a stroll today? Just for a little? It has been so long and—and now that we are to be married, I—"

"No."

"But why?"

"Because I don't trust you."

Sarina told herself to stay calm. "Am I to be kept prisoner indefinitely then?"

"That is yet to be decided. You could improve your situation by telling the truth."

Sarina blinked. "I—do not understand."

Lucian's laugh was bitter. "Oh, you understand perfectly. I think. Tell me, now—the truth this time. Why did the bastard free you?"

Sarina saw that his anger was mounting. She moistened her lips. "I have told you. He was afraid. Hearing the great price that was on his head, he—" She jumped as his fist crashed onto the table and his coffee cup overturned.

"Woman, I warn you. I will not tolerate more lies!"

He remembered very well how Lucian Thorne had looked in that black hellhole on the *Vengeance*. Even in chains and with no hope of escape, his eyes had burned with hatred and defiance.

"I know only what I heard . . ."

"Bitch! The man fears no one and nothing. I will ask you one more time." He grasped her arm. "Why were you released?"

Sarina gritted her teeth against the dizzying pain that shot through her arm. She said defiantly:

"You are right. He fears nothing and no one, and it is disgusting to say that he does. He did it for me . . ."

Ryan wanted to knock her down and wrap his fingers around her soft throat. "Continue," he rasped.

"I—begged him to bring me here. Fool that I was, I was worried for you. For my father and for you."

He sneered. "Ah. You were worried for me. I am touched."

"Believe it or not, I wanted you to see that I was safe. I thought it had been hard for you, and I—felt badly about it."

"But you intended to return with him?"

"Yes." It was a whisper.

"You ate my food and slept under my roof, all the while meaning to steal away with him?"

"That very first day I told you I could not marry you or stay with you, but you insisted!" She tried to pry his fingers from her arm. "Ryan, you are hurting me . . ."

He did not release her. "You dare ask why I will not let you outside of this house."

Her own eyes flashed. "Yes, I do dare. Why am I still treated as a prisoner?"

"Because you are mine, damn it, and he is out there. He will return for you. It is why I have changed the day of our wedding to next Sunday."

"Wh-what? You never told me you had chosen a—a date."

Ryan smiled, pleased by the fright in her eyes. "Just as you do not tell me everything you know, beloved." It would be a nuisance, making new arrangements, he thought, but no matter. It had to be done.

* * *

After its flight, the *Vengeance* took refuge in a well-hidden cove along the New Jersey coast, one of several secret anchorages which Lucian had used in the past. His scouts had come shortly after their arrival, bringing fresh food and news, and returning again with materials to repair the damage done during their capture. Now it was sunset and Sky Braden studied his old friend as they ate a cold supper on deck in the fading light.

"How are you, lad?"

"That is the tenth time you have asked."

"I'll put more ointment on those wounds before we turn in." When Lucian nodded, his gaze distant, Sky added, "What a shock for the bastard, havin' us in his hands and then losin' us like that." He chuckled and gnawed a fresh turnip along with his heel of bread and cheese. "I reckon he's in a grand rage."

"Aye." Lucian's brow was lined. All he could think about was Sarina bearing the brunt of that rage. And what if Douglas should learn how she had helped? God almighty.

"I expect he means to blow us sky-high the next time he or one o' his traders sees us."

"He'll try," Lucian agreed. "The last thing he wants is for someone else to haul us before the Crown."

"Aye." Ale, not to mention the prospect of seeing his buxom little Rosie again soon, had put Sky in a mellow mood. "I wouldn't be in the bastard's shoes for any money. Us on the one hand an' the Crown on the other." Seeing that Lucian was still in a black mood, he clapped him on the shoulder. "Come now, lad, have a bit more ale and know that we'll get back to normal soon. We'll fetch Donal an' the two ladies an' let you recover a bit an' then—"

"We will be getting Sarina, too," Lucian said.

Sky's eyes glimmered like quicksilver. "Ah. An' that would be to teach her a lesson, I hope?" But he didn't like the idea one damned bit. It would be far better if Lucian never saw the traitorous bitch again—if he just put her and what she had done to them out of his mind. In fact, he couldn't be sure of his own actions when he saw her again.

"Simmer down, man," Lucian said. "Donal told me some things about Sarina that you should know."

"Donal did? An' when did he have time for that, pray?"

They had, all of them, Sky thought, worked like whirlwinds trying to get their vessel put to rights and underway. The bastard's men had damped their powder and they'd had to haul on fresh; his mates had needed to be unshackled; their small arms recovered. When in hell had Donal the time to engage in any discussion before he had gone off again with his men?

"Go on," he said. "Tell me. What did he say about the slut?"

Lucian was inclined to snarl back, but he saw that his friend's blood was running hot. "We were wrong about her, mister," he said, keeping his voice even. "Donal told me the truth when you left to unlock the crew. It was a message from Sarina that helped him free us."

Sky smiled and sipped his ale. "Oh, man, I don't doubt that a bit. Of course her heart was broken once her black deed was done. The lady has delicate sensibilities." His smile faded when he saw that Lucian was not amused. In fact Lucian appeared ready to mop up the deck with him. "Luc, hold on—" He got quickly to his feet. "Maybe you'd better tell me more . . ."

"There is little more to tell. Donal had only a minute, but he convinced me Sarina is innocent. Ginelle says she nearly fainted when she heard of our capture. That bastard has abused her, locked her and Ginelle in their rooms—"

Sky listened grimly as he finished, for it seemed his Rosie was not unaffected either. That bastard Douglas. Sky took a deep breath and drank the last of his ale. "I see now that I was wrong. I admit it."

"It leaves us with the question of who did betray us," Lucian said.

"Garrick?" Sky suggested without hesitation. "He was the first one I thought of."

"Aye, but it was easier to blame Sariña . . ." Lucian would never forgive himself for that. "We will learn sooner or later. Right now, it's a matter of getting those two women out of Douglas' house without his knowing it." He grinned. "We'll discuss it when we meet Donal in Shoreham. It shouldn't be too hard to figure out."

Not hard, no, Sky thought. Impossible. Nonetheless he grinned back. "Aye. We'll find a way, old lad. Believe me . . . we will." He yawned. The sun was down and the rest of the crew had already slung their hammocks on deck. "It's bed for these old bones, Luc. It looks like the rest o' the boys agree. No lights an' no noise don't leave us with much to do but sleep."

Lucian, too, rose to his feet and stretched. "I'm off, too."

In his cabin he lowered himself painfully to his bunk. It would be a while before he could move easily again. He closed his eyes, grateful for the bed, and tried to relax, but his body remained taut. He remembered Sarina. Sarina floating in his arms in the sea, in the moonlight; Sarina making love with him in a tidal pool, telling him she loved him. For two weeks, he had been cursing her, denying her, trying to hate her, and now—now he knew she was what she had seemed all along. She had not lied, had not betrayed him. She loved him. Loved him.

He groaned, rolled onto his back, and wondered what was happening to her at this very moment. Was she locked in her room again and had the bastard raped her? Was he raping her now? Lucian tossed his head from side to side at the terrible thought. God almighty, why had he ever let her go back to Douglas? His mind filled with his memory of her: a cloud of silky coppery hair spread over his pillow; eyes like the sea, deep, blue-green, shimmering . . .

He shook his head. He mustn't do this to himself. It helped no one. Not him, not his men, not Sarina. He needed to rest, to heal. He closed his eyes, but it was a long time before sleep finally came.

Sarina gazed stonily at her reflection in the tilted looking-glass in her bedchamber. There was no doubt that the wedding gown was a work of art; made of white silk, it had copious ruffles and frills, and a wide band of tiny seed pearls bordering the wrists and neckline. Nonetheless, she hated it.

"Mademoiselle, you are exquisite in this gown." Madame Bonnefleur's thick French accent was even less understandable because of her mouthful of pins. "Turn a bit, *s'il vous plaît.*" Sarina obeyed, her lips compressed as Madame fussed with the hem. "*Bien!* I have pinned and soon it is finished." She kissed her fingers. "Never will there have been such a bride!"

"I do not like the neckline being quite so low," Sarina said crisply. "Can you not insert another band of seed pearls here?" She pointed to where the bodice dipped, causing the full swells of her breasts to be exposed almost to the nipples. "I—I feel almost naked . . ."

"M'sieu himself has requested it, mademoiselle. In France, it is ever so fashionable, although I must admit, the style has not yet reached these shores."

"Well, it is entirely inappropriate for a wedding," Sarina snapped. It was just one more instance of Ryan's tyrannizing her life without the slightest concern for her own wishes. "I am asking you to correct the problem in whichever way you choose. With lace, seed pearls, muslin"—it could be a dishrag for all she cared—"but you will fix it, please."

"Mademoiselle has an exquisite bosom. M'sieu is quite correct in wishing to display it."

"But Mademoiselle does not wish to display it!"

Madame made a small moue, packed away her pins and scissors, and unhooked the garment. "I am sorry, it is m'sieu I must please."

Sarina was so outraged, she was speechless. She stepped hastily out of the gown and would have kicked it aside but for Madame's quick rescue of it.

"Rosie!" Sarina raised her voice.

Rosie hurried into the room. "Yes'm?" She stared, seeing her mistress' flaming face.

"You may help me dress, but first show Madame out."

"Yes'm."

After the woman had departed, Sarina threw herself face down on the bed and pounded her fists in frustration. She could not bear to continue like this, acting as Ryan's pawn . . . soon to be his wife.

"There, there now, mum," Rosie said as she hurried back. "I kin see she's a silly woman so let's git yer dressed an' yer kin tell me about it. How was the fittin'?" Her eyes were dancing.

"The fitting was fine," Sarina murmured. "The hem needed some minor adjustments."

Rosie stared at her. "Mum, beggin' yer pardon, but yer look so serious. Yer are playactin', aren't yer? Lovely as that there gown is," she said, tugging Sarina's own garment down over her head, "ye don't intend to wear it, do yer? Not wi' the Ghost comin' for us an' all. My, won't that give the master a turn!"

"Rosie, there is something we must discuss."

Rosie gaped at her mistress' grave face. "Yer don't mean to tell me yer goin' to marry him after all? Mum, I thought yer hated the brute!"

Sarina took Rosie's hands and pulled her onto the bed beside her. "Listen to me now. I want you to know that I would never marry him willingly—"

"Awooo, mum!"

"—but tell me, what am I to do if Lucian does not come before next Sunday? Then what?"

"Run! An' I'll run with yer. We kin find Chambers like Mistress Ginelle did an' he'll find th' Ghost for us."

"Do you not think I would if I could?"

Rosie's eyes filled; her mouth quivered. "Why can't yer?"

"Because Ryan will find Lucian and kill him, that's why! He has told me more than once that if I try to escape, or if I do not marry him, he will find Lucian and kill him.''

"Surely yer don't b-believe 'im.''

"I believe him. He is cruel. He had Lucian lashed, and he says he has killed before.''

"Now yer scarin' me . . .''

"I am scared myself—but he wouldn't harm you. I know he wouldn't.''

"It ain't fair,'' Rosie muttered. "A kind lady like you an' a brute like him.'' She got to her feet and blew her nose. "I'll fix 'im, I will. Even if yer do marry him, he'll not harm yer, mum. I'll get me some fairy flowers from the backyard fer his bedchamber an' I'll use them peacock feathers in the drawin' room an—''

Sarina was staring at her. "What good will those do?''

Rosie giggled through her tears. "In my part o' the country, everyone knows that fairy flowers—that's fox-gloves—an' peacock feathers in the bedchamber spells death to lovemakin'. He'll never know what happint, mum, an' he'll just be that aggravated . . .''

Sarina, too, began to giggle. "Then I will help you.'' The two of them laughed until their eyes streamed. "Rosie, how could I ever be gloomy with you around? Everything is going to be all right, I know it is.''

Rosie wiped her eyes on her apron. "Oh, my, that were a good laugh. I needs me a breath o' air now.'' She opened one of the double casement windows and gazed down at the street. "Bein' cooped up in this place all day without a breath o' air is—'' She gave a squawk and stepped onto the tiny balcony. "Mum, come to the winder, quick!''

Sarina hurried to do her bidding. "What? What is it?''

Rosie's brown eyes had grown huge. "It was the Ghost, I know it was! He's gone. He went 'round the corner. He din't look like him, not really, an' he din't act like him, but oh, mum, there was somethin' about the big bugger that made me think o' him. An' he was starin' at this house." She lay a work-worn hand on her heaving bosom. "He's come for yer!"

Sarina looked up and down the empty street, her heart pounding. "Do you really think it was Lucian?"

"Mum, it was him," Rosie insisted. "May God strike me dead."

Sarina laughed. "And since He has not, it was Lucian. He is here! Oh, Rosie . . ."

Lucian did not miss the excitement on the second floor of Douglas Hall. He saw Rosie and knew she had summoned Sarina, but not wanting the silly wench bawling to the world that he was in town, he turned the corner and vanished into a pub. Sitting in a dim corner with a pint, he tallied his accomplishments so far.

That morning before sunrise he had boldly sailed the *Vengeance* up to New York, borne to the right of Manhattan Island, and anchored in a cove at Shoreham on the East River. Donal, Ginelle, and Chambers had journeyed by carriage to meet with himself and Sky. The result was that he was going to pay Sarina a visit this very night while Donal and Ginelle stayed aboard the vessel to await his further orders.

Lucian finished his pint and called for another. The way things were falling out was cause for celebration. Donal had told him about finding the seaman named Bascomb. After three years, he was found and remembered everything, and was willing to testify to it. And then, on his own way to Shoreham, he had passed the *Gull* limping by, so poor in canvas she must have been through a great storm. He reckoned she was on her way to the government shipyard near the Kirkeby yard.

Lucian smiled. If the *Gull* were here, so was John Pomeroy, the man who had found the Pearls of Naipoor aboard his vessel. Before Pomeroy left New York, Lucian was going to rub his nose in Bascomb's words. He was going to get the two of them together even if he had to steal Pomeroy off the *Gull* to do it.

But for now, he had other things to think about. Sarina, and how to get her out of Douglas Hall . . .

Already he knew which bedchamber was hers. Before Rosie had spied him—how in hell had she recognized him, graying and stooped and with a limp?—he had spotted a ladder leaning against the side of the house. Some roof tiles were being replaced. And there were balconies on all the windows. He smiled, thinking how easy it would be to scale the wall and climb up to her room. And if he caught that bastard Douglas there, he would kill him. It was as simple as that.

Lucian was contemplating Sarina's surprise, and imagining her in his arms again, when he heard a mention of Douglas Hall by two men laughing over their ale. Tilting his chair back and listening shamelessly, he heard that on the twenty-fourth of August, the master of the house was wedding such a beauteous wench, there was not a man alive who did not crave her. As the jesting grew more coarse, Lucian paid and left in silent fury. It would not do to lay the bastards low and wreck the pub. Certainly not as the old limping seaman he was now.

He was raging as he returned to Douglas Hall to continue his study of the house and grounds. August twenty-fourth. One week from tomorrow she would belong to Douglas. What in the hell? He prowled the perimeter of the property like a panther, eyes narrowed, hungry, seeing all and remembering it for later use. He would leave nothing to chance, either in entering the house or in leaving it; he would not be caught unawares this time. Scouting the empty tree-lined alley that bounded the back of the property, Lucian smelled and heard horses. Stables.

On an impulse, he jumped, caught a branch, and hoisted himself easily and quietly into a tree. Gazing down over the high stone wall into the stable area, he looked directly into a pair of wide brown eyes.

"Oooh!" Rosie gasped, her hands over her mouth. "There, I knowed it was you under that gray an' wi' that weird limp. Oh, sir, oh, thank goodness!"

"Rosie, for God's sake," Lucian said, "go away." Of all the bad luck, having the Coggins wench gaping up at him with her mouth open. "Go, damn it. Scat!"

"But, sir, the stable boys is gone. When th' master's not here, the mice'll play, don't yer know?" She paid no attention to his terrible scowl. She knew exactly what must be done. "If yer comes ter th' front door a bit afore midnight, I'll let yer in," she whispered.

The front door? Lucian shook his head. "I'll go up the ladder. I know which is her bedchamber."

"An' break yer stubborn head?" Rosie shook her finger at him. "Ye'll do no sich stupid thing on that rickety ladder. Ye'll come ter th' front. Everyone'll be asleep, I promise yer." She gave him such a wicked grin that Lucian laughed.

"And just how will you manage that, wench?"

"Never yer mind, mister." Rosie rubbed her hands together. "I has me ways."

How lovely, she thought, that Cook had just ordered her to make bedtime drinks for the whole house from now on. She knew of a special brew that would assure everyone slept well tonight. Very well indeed. Oh, the good Lord did work in mysterious ways.

"Then I leave it in your hands," Lucian said low. "I'll be here before midnight, but everyone in this house had better be asleep. And you're not to mention one word to your mistress, do you understand?"

"Yessir."

His blue gaze swept over her so threateningly that Rosie was overcome by a delicious shiver. Oooh, what a masterful man he was! Almost as masterful as her own Sky.

"Is my man all right?" she asked, her eyes soft.

"Sky is fine. He misses you." Lucian touched his fingers to his forehead in a salute. "Until tonight."

It was midnight. Sarina couldn't sleep, nor could she read or do any of those things that usually made her drift off within minutes. She sat in her bed propped against a pile of pillows, the lamp flickering on the polished table by her side, eyes wide, heart pounding. Lucian was here. He had come for her, and before she bade Rosie good night, she had told her to pack her belongings. Although she had no idea how he would accomplish it, she had no doubt Lucian would take the two of them with him tonight. After all, he was the Ghost.

Instead of being forced to walk down the aisle in that outrageous dress, instead of waiting for a wedding night she dreaded, instead of spending a lifetime with a man she could not bear, she would be fleeing into the night with Lucian. . . . She was so excited, she leaped from the bed and stood in the middle of the room trembling. She looked around her and wrung her hands. Why did he not come? Had Rosie been wrong after all? She squeezed her eyes shut. No, she would not think it. He was here. He was coming for her. She froze when a tap sounded on her door.

"Mum?"

Sarina hurried and opened it. She gasped. The man beside Rosie was black-caped, a cowl covering his face, his height and the broadness of his shoulders filling the doorway. In the half-light she saw the glitter of blue eyes.

"Beloved!"

Lucian covered her mouth to stifle any outcry and pushed her inside the room. He quickly closed the door, locked it, and strode to the window overlooking the walled garden. He pulled back the draperies and tested the windows. They opened. The ladder was there should he need it. He closed the draperies and turned to Sarina, his eyes blazing.

Sarina gazed at him, suddenly frightened as he moved about her bedchamber on silent feet. She had expected this to be a joyous reunion, but he was angry and she didn't understand why.

Lucian steeled himself. His memory of her beauty hadn't come close to matching reality. The slender, curvaceous body; skin like cream; lovely flower-face, flushed with twin roses in her cheeks; soft pink lips parted; thick red-gold lashes wet now with tears; hair a silken coppery cape tumbling over her breasts, those full high breasts. He wanted to cup them in his hands, dip his head, fasten his hungry mouth on them, kiss and suckle them. But he would not. Not when she was marrying Ryan Douglas.

Sarina finally found her voice. "I'm so happy you are free . . ."

Lucian answered gruffly, "I'm sure you are."

"I—had hoped that Donal told you everything and that you were no longer angry with me." Seeing that his expression remained like granite, she cried softly, "Lucian, don't you believe me? Don't you believe that I did not betray you?"

"I know you didn't betray me."

"And you know that I love you?"

His mocking eyes answered her even before he laughed. "Ah, yes, you love me. Of course. That's why you're marrying Douglas next Sunday."

Thinking of her belonging to the bastard, Lucian felt his rage mount, his blood race. He was a volcano ready to blow. He wanted to crush her, destroy her as completely as losing her would destroy him. He couldn't believe it when she began to laugh at him. His blood ran hot at the sight of her head thrown back, her soft throat offered to him, her lips parted, beckoning. She gave a small shriek as he pulled her roughly into his arms and covered her mouth harshly with his.

Hearing her whimper, he knew he couldn't hurt her. God, he could not. He loved her. No matter that she had chosen another, he loved her. His hands, his mouth, his body grew gentle. He cradled her, caressed and kissed her. He was starving for her, his hungry hands moving over her face and hair, shoulders, throat.

"Lucian . . ."

"Shhh." He covered her lips with a kiss. He didn't want to hear that she was sorry. He just wanted to hold her.

Lucian's mouth and hands moving over her had ignited a sweet, hot flame within Sarina. She slid her arms under his and around his back, pressing him to her closer and closer. She stood on tiptoe, tasting his mouth and skin, running her hands through his thick black hair. Oh, she could not get close enough . . .

"Make love to me, Lucian," she whispered. "Please, just make love to me."

She shivered with sheer delight as his lips began exploring, tasting, kissing her starving body. When he entered her, when his fierce hunger lifted her from one breathtaking peak to another, Sarina knew that nothing had changed between them. Paradise was not on Malaga, it was within them . . .

Chapter 23

Sarina lay quietly, Lucian's arms still around her and her head on his shoulder. She brushed light kisses against the side of his throat and jaw and looked up at him. The lamp beside her bed still flickered, and in its soft light she saw that his eyes were closed. She stroked his dark arm, toyed with the hair on his chest.

"Lucian . . ." What they had done was complete madness—making love here in this, of all houses. They simply could not stay a moment longer. "Lucian, I know you're not sleeping," she whispered. "I know you are angry with me. I should not have laughed, but there simply is no time to explain now. Suffice it to say that I am not marrying that beast, and now can we go? You are in terrible danger here. I fear for you."

Now it was Lucian who laughed, a low chuckle. So she was not marrying the devil and she was ready to fly with him . . . ? Once again he had jumped to the wrong conclusion about her. When would he ever learn that she loved him and he could trust her?

"Lucian, please—" Sarina was on her feet and trying to pull him out of bed. "There's nothing to laugh about. You are in the gravest danger. We both are. Ryan could come at any minute . . ."

Lucian's eyes glittered as he surveyed her beauty and pulled her back into bed. He nestled her soft body close beside his, her head on his shoulder. "There is no danger," he said, his voice low. "Rosie has drugged the whole damned house with some brew of hers."

"Rosie! And she did not tell me? Oh! And I was so afraid she had been mistaken and you would not come."

"Nothing could have kept me away."

Lucian was at peace. When had he ever felt such peace? Certainly not for a long time, he thought drowsily, his dark hand moving absently over her hair and silken flesh.

Sarina caught and kissed it, stroked it, nibbled the crisp black curls on the back of it. She breathed in the wonderful aroma of his tanned skin: sea wind and earth and pine.

"How much time have we?" she whispered. She had seen that his thoughts were distant, but she had so much to tell him.

"At least an hour."

Lucian lifted her hand to his lips. What wonderful fingers she had. Long, slender, with such soft white skin and rosy nails. He wanted to eat them. He kissed the tips, nibbling them, kissed her palm and wrist, the inside of her elbow, moved up to the soft hollow at the base of her neck and behind her ear. Hearing her soft giggle, he knew he was tickling her.

"Lucian, stop. I want to tell you what happened—"

"I want to hear."

"—but first I want to tell you about the silly wedding thing . . ."

"Yes," he answered gruffly, "that I must hear." He continued stroking her skin, his fingers tracing her lush mouth, her slender throat, her small chin.

"Did Donal tell you I learned that Ryan was going to let you go free, and on what night?"

"Aye."

"Ryan wanted it to seem accidental, which is why he arranged for the key to be found—the key that unlocked the shackles. He didn't want you to know he had freed you."

Lucian's mouth tightened. "I see."

"I really didn't think he would do it until I saw you sailing away . . ." She slipped her arms around him and pressed her body tightly to his. "It was such a beautiful sight, you on deck giving orders, the sails billowing. And then you began throwing the ballast overboard."

Lucian sat up, his eyes suddenly hooded. "You saw us?"

Sarina nodded. "Yes. We were downriver from the bay where the *Vengeance* had been held."

"And did he tell you why he was doing this godly deed?"

Sarina, too, sat up, her expression grave. "It is what I especially wanted to tell you—the bargain I made with him."

Realizing instantly what bargain it must have been, Lucian groaned, shook his head, and felt the volcano inside of him gathering steam again. "You agreed to marry the bastard if he would free us . . ."

"How could I not? My choice was to see you hanging from the tallest mast or watch you sail away." Sensing his white-hot anger, she murmured, "That was the choice he gave me, Lucian, so yes, I agreed to marry him. I—died inside thinking of it, but I wanted you to live. It was all that mattered."

Lucian closed his eyes as rage pulsed through his body. God almighty, what a close call it had been. The cruelty of the bastard, the glib smoothness. He reached out and pulled her close, folding her in his arms.

"Sarina, I—would not have lived. None of us would."

She stared. "What?"

"Had his plan succeeded, there would have been no key, no escape."

"But—it did succeed! I saw you sail by . . ."

"Because Donal freed us."

"Donal!"

"He had been gathering men and planning a rescue all along. It was damned convenient for him, having all the crew moved aboard like that, but then his own band took over."

Sarina gasped. That must be why Ryan had been so

foul-tempered afterward. She put her hands to her suddenly flaming cheeks. "I—I feel such an idiot, a gullible idiot. A—a fool . . ."

"Never." Lucian caught her hands and kissed them.

"But I am. You are telling me," she said, her lips stiff, "that were it not for Donal, you would have been killed, all of you?"

"And without your note, my cosset, Donal would not have been there."

"And Ryan's men would have sailed the *Vengeance* out to sea and sunk her."

"Yes. I'm sure that was the plan."

Sarina's eyes glittered in the lamp glow as she considered the extent of Ryan's treachery. She snapped: "He should be keelhauled in shark water."

Lucian laughed. "Yes, that would be appropriate. Why don't we plan on it sometime? But not now. Now we should think about leaving. Get dressed, fondling." He rose and began to pull on his own clothes.

"Lucian, I know it's vital for you to find his cache . . ."

"We will talk of it later, Sarina."

"No, we will talk of it now." She got to her feet and drew on her wrapper. She met his eyes. "I have decided to stay here. I'm going to discover from him just where his cache is so that you can find it and end this whole ghastly business."

Lucian went to her and clasped her shoulders. He spoke low, as calmly and gently as he could. "You are going to dress. You are going to fetch your maid and we are leaving."

Sarina seemed not to hear or see him. "He wants to play games, does he? Then I will play games," she said softly. "I will play out this charade to the end."

Lucian shook her. "You are leaving with me if I have to carry you. Get dressed. That is an order."

"I'm not going."

He sucked in a deep breath. He had seen that mutinous look on her face before. Hell, he didn't want to carry a kicking fury down the street and end up in gaol.

"It's too dangerous for you to stay. Damn it, you've seen what he is capable of. He'll stop at nothing until he has you as his wife."

"He will never have me. Instead, I will have proof of his guilt. I'm going to clear you, Lucian."

His anger and impatience boiled over. "Thank you, but I decline. Now for the last time, put on some clothes unless you want to be seen in your wrapper!"

Sarina did not move. "Do you want to know where his cache is?"

"Why in God's name would he tell you?" Lucian asked sharply.

"He would not." She smiled, a strange light in her eyes. "Not knowingly."

Lucian's heart raced with fear for her. He shook his head. "Whatever you are thinking, I forbid it."

"Beloved, listen to me. He drinks heavily and he is the vainest creature alive. I have not the slightest doubt that I can discover the whereabouts of his cache with champagne and flattery. I'm not afraid of him now. I can do anything, knowing that you believe and trust me. By this hour tomorrow, I will have coaxed his secret from him. I promise you."

Gazing down at her beautiful face, Lucian's every instinct warned him to take her with him. Yet if he could put his hands on the cache and catch the devil there, he would have him. He would have him, and the thing would be over, and he and Sarina could be together. But the plan held grave danger for her.

"I don't like it."

Sarina laughed. "But you'll let me do it because you see that I'm right. It's the only way."

He pulled on his boots, strapped on his sword, and drew his black cape across his shoulders.

"You will not place yourself in any unnecessary danger . . ."

"I promise I will not," she whispered.

"And just as soon as you have the information, I'm taking you out of here."

"No. If you're to trap him, we cannot make him suspicious in any way."

He grunted. "I hate to admit it—"

She gave a teasing smile. "But I'm right. I must stay."

Lucian took a deep breath. Damnation! It seemed she had the makings of a general.

"All right then. You will stay, but you have but to call from your window if you need help. My men or I will be always within earshot. Do you understand?"

She nodded, eyes grave, smile gone. "I understand."

Lucian buried his face in her thick hair. He kissed her sweet, fresh mouth and wondered if he had suddenly gone mad to be leaving her there.

"I love you," he said gruffly. He claimed one last kiss from her eager lips, stepped through the window into the night, and was gone.

Sarina hurried to her window, but Lucian had already blended into the darkness, black on black. She felt frightened, empty. After holding him in her arms and making love with him, suddenly he was gone. It was like a dream.

But soon she began to gather strength from the thought that she need never experience such fright and emptiness again, not if she could help Lucian clear his name. And she would; perhaps she was the only one who could. She crawled back into bed, but she was far too excited to sleep. Instead she began to plan.

Everything she said and did this day, every glance, every gesture, every word must be coldly and carefully calculated to draw from Ryan where his cache was hidden. She must make him forget how angry she had been since he had forced her to sign away her inheritance. She must flatter and soothe and comfort him, get him to pour out his resentment and rage and hatred for Lucian. Especially, she must get him to boast of his cleverness.

She tensed then, thinking that she probably would

have to lie in Ryan's arms, in his bed, to accomplish her task. She steeled herself. So be it. Lying in his bed for one night was far preferable to being doomed to it for a lifetime. And it did not mean she would make love with him, for she absolutely would not! That was where she hoped the champagne would come to her aid. Her plan was a bold undertaking, but she was determined to succeed. Lucian would be proud of her . . .

Seeing that the sun was streaming through her windows, Sarina threw off the covers and hurried to make her toilette. This was one morning when Ryan would not complain of her tardiness. She had promised Lucian that she would perform a miracle before this night was over and there was not a moment to waste.

Breakfast was uneventful, as was the midday meal. Ryan, not surprisingly, had a bad headache and stayed in bed. Sarina was glad. She preferred to work her wiles over dinner. She requested that Cook prepare all of Ryan's favorite foods—beefsteaks, Yorkshire pudding, Floating Island—and she saw to it that the great mahogany table was covered with the finest pale-pink embossed damask and set with the best china.

She chose a new Bonnefleur gown for the occasion, a cherry silk creation with a low-cut neckline, and Rosie dressed her hair to perfection. Swept atop her head into a diamond and ruby circlet, it cascaded onto her bared shoulders and back and bosom in a cloud of red-gold ringlets. When she entered the dining room, ashimmer in the soft glow of many candles, Ryan's dark eyes glittered.

"I see you are finally using some sense," he muttered. He was already sipping from a goblet of champagne.

Sarina smiled and lowered her eyes. "The gowns you have given me are so exquisite, I can no longer resist them."

Ryan looked cynical, but he raised her hand to his lips. "If that is the case, you may throw away the blue thing. I am sick of it."

"Very well." Every gesture and gaze were important, she reminded herself. Every word. "I—am sorry if my silliness annoyed you. You have been wonderfully patient with me, I want you to know that." She raised her eyes to his, fluttered her lashes ever so slightly. "I think I was under some sort of spell . . ."

"Spell?" Ryan watched her, his own eyes narrowed. "Come now."

Sarina shrugged her shoulders, aware of his hungry brown gaze following her every movement.

"Looking back at the man and the way we were forced to live . . . I wonder now how we survived at all. We had only the barest of necessities, you know"—she gave a discreet shudder—"yet when one is in a situation with no hope of escape, one learns to live with it."

"This is more than you have ever told me before. Gilmore! Champagne for Mistress Fairburn."

Sarina daintily touched her handkerchief to her eyes. "Actually, I—have not wanted to think about it."

Ryan's eyes plumbed hers, but he saw nothing but the truth. God's bones, what was going on here? He watched as she raised the goblet to her lips and sipped. Such luscious pink lips . . .

"Let me assure you, Ryan, it's lovely to be back in civilization. I will never take it for granted again."

He watched her so guardedly that Sarina's heart was in her throat. She had always been dreadfully unskilled at lying, so why had she ever thought she could succeed now? If only she had escaped with Lucian. Oh, beloved, I will ruin it for us . . .

"It was primitive, eh?"

"You simply cannot imagine."

"I'm not surprised," Ryan muttered. "The bastard always was an uncultured clod, with no appreciation for the finer things in life."

"Exactly."

"Doubtless you ate from wooden trenchers and slept on straw under a thatched roof."

Sarina's laughter tinkled as he led her to the table and helped her be seated.

"How could you know!" She grew serious then. "I can laugh about it now, but at the time it seemed quite hideous. And too, I—I was certain you did not want me . . ."

Ryan scowled at her. Even had she been a hag, he would have wanted her, considering her worth.

"How could you have thought such a ridiculous thing?"

"He told me you had not responded to his demand for ransom." Again she touched her handkerchief to her eyes. Miraculously, tears fell as she remembered how bereft she had felt.

"The devil," he muttered. "I responded instantly, and when I had no word from him, I was wild with worry."

He began to sample the delicacies Annie served him from a silver epergne: potted meat, a cheese tart, a bit of lobster in aspic jelly, egg boiled in forcemeat.

"Superb." He touched his napkin to his mouth and took a great swallow of champagne. "Cook is improving."

"I made a few suggestions," Sarina said quietly.

Ryan's eyes shuttered. "By the gods, did you now?"

What was the wench up to? After behaving like a caged lioness for days, suddenly she was decked out like the queen and striving to please him. He wasn't sure he wanted to be pleased. He watched her sip champagne, close her eyes, sip again, sigh, smile.

"After all those weeks of moldy biscuits, moldy cheese, and rainwater, my palate suffered dreadfully. And my spirits. I fear I have been terrible company for you, and quite irrational besides."

"As a matter of fact, you have been," Ryan said crisply, unable to keep his gaze off her throat and bosom. He was beginning to feel damnably hot and tight in the crotch.

"And I have been unfair to you," Sarina murmured.

"I cannot deny it." He shrugged. "But then, all's well that ends well, I always say. By heaven," he addressed Annie as she approached his side, "is that beef and Yorkshire pudding you have there?"

"Yessir." She looked frightened. "If yer don't want it, sir, I'll—"

"Damn it, girl, of course I want it! Heap it on. Gilmore, more champagne, and more for Mistress Fairburn."

Sarina hid her smile. Perhaps the hardest part of this charade would be to keep her head. So far, she had taken nothing but sips of champagne, but Ryan seemed not to have noticed. By the time they had worked their way through the meal to the Floating Island, she had received his solemn promise that Ginelle was perfectly safe, and she had him raging over his lost cargos.

"—and I took more from him than any man should have to take," he muttered, his face flushed. "But for you, *ma petite*, he would be dead by now. Hanged by the neck until he was dead."

"Yes, I—I realize." Sarina stared at the table and shook her head. "All I can think is that my caring for him was part of some strange enchantment. Why, I feel nothing for the man now that he is gone . . ." She looked at Ryan with bewildered eyes. "But then, we were so helpless, so completely in his power. Our minds, our—very bodies were not our own. Oh, Ryan, can you understand?" she murmured. "Our very lives depended on whether or not we pleased him . . ."

"The devil," Ryan growled.

He began stroking her arm and the satiny skin under her chin, brooding all the while that what she said made sense. Had he not seen women in his own bed become fawning and eager to please him when their flesh was crushed and bruised? Had he not seen the awe, the adoration in their eyes? Women were made to be mastered. But it was exceedingly unfortunate that this one had been taken by another first. By Thorne. The blood fairly sang in his ears with the resentment he felt.

"How many times?" he said, his hand closing over hers.

"I—beg your pardon?"

"Come, come, my flower, how many times did your life depend upon your—pleasing him?" He refilled his goblet, having long since sent his servants from the room. "Twice? Four times? Five?"

Sarina shivered at the way his gaze was sliding over her. She looked down.

"Three . . ."

Ryan was pleased when she trembled. Well, well, it seemed she told the truth. She had been afraid of the devil.

"Have more champagne, my sweet." He filled her goblet to the brim and lifted it to her lips. "Drink, Sarina."

"I—I have had quite a bit, really."

"Drink."

Sarina drank. Her head spun.

"And now, I would like to hear how the Ghost treated you in his bed."

"Ryan, please! It is—a painful subject." She looked away from his dark, dangerous eyes.

"Ah, he hurt you. Sarina, look at me. Did he hurt you?"

Tears filled her eyes, but she obeyed. She looked at him, tried to blink them back, but they spilled down her cheeks. Beloved, forgive me . . .

"Yes, he hurt me," she whispered. "I was a virgin, after all."

"But after that—the other times?"

"Why are you asking me this?" she cried, her temper flaring despite her resolve to treat him with velvet gloves. "Can you not see that it—it pains me to think about it? I was mortified. Humiliated. Is that what you want to hear? I would hope that you—would be gentle," she added, looking down at her hands, clasped so tightly in her lap that her knuckles were white. "I have always known you were sensitive . . ."

By the gods but the wench was the most exquisite one he had ever seen. And she was his. She was finally his. He got to his feet, swaying slightly, and pulled out her chair. He took her into his arms.

"Let us go up to your bedchamber, Sarina. We can—talk further there."

Sarina's stomach tightened. "Yes, I would like that. You have provided me with a lovely room. I have never thanked you for it properly."

"And I have not told you how ravishing you look this evening."

So ravishing that he was going to take her, in fact. All he needed to accomplish the deed was to get another glass or two of champagne into her.

"I'm sure it's this lovely gown." As he grasped her arm tightly and led her from the room, Sarina murmured, "Oh, do bring your champagne along, Ryan, I know how much you enjoy it."

He stopped, blinked. By the gods, he had almost forgotten it.

"Gilmore," he bellowed from the hallway. "Mistress Fairburn and I will continue our conversation in her bedchamber. Bring a fresh bottle of champagne."

Chapter 24

There was no turning back. Ryan's hand clasped Sarina's elbow like a vise as he propelled her up the staircase and into her bedchamber. She was well aware of the reason for his urgency, but she was determined to forestall any intimacy with him, no matter how slight, for as long as possible. After Bessie had mended the fire and lit the lamps, and after Gilmore had opened fresh champagne and filled their goblets, Ryan sat down on the settee before the hearth and patted the seat beside him.

"You are too far away, *ma petite*. Come and sit beside me."

Sarina smiled. "Of course."

She felt in no danger. Lucian had promised that he and his men would be close by, that Rosie or she had but to call them from the window. She had instructed Rosie to wait in the hall just in case.

"You have intrigued me with your talk of Malaga," Ryan said. "I have more questions."

Sarina lowered her eyes. "If it pleases you, but I may not know the answers."

She felt a strange mixture of fear and exhilaration. She was certain that if she led Ryan far enough, she would get the information she wanted. But did she dare promise him more than she could deliver in the hope that he would be too inebriated to take advantage of it? At the same time she didn't want him so drunk that

321

he couldn't boast of his cleverness and reveal where his cache was hidden.

"I suspect the bastard has abandoned his hideaway now that I know of it and moved to another, but he still needs supplies. Where does he get them?"

"I have no idea," Sarina answered truthfully. "Once a week or so, he brought in fresh food, but I never knew where it came from."

"Did he ever talk about how many men he has scattered about the globe?"

Ryan had been frankly dismayed to hear of the crew of gray-clad cutthroats who had swarmed over the *Vengeance* and foiled his own plans for the devil. It had never occurred to him that Thorne had men other than those who sailed the ghost ship.

"Never," Sarina swore. That, too, was true.

She twisted Ryan's ring on her finger as she realized that she was walking a veritable tightrope, yet she was excited by the prospect of winning the game. How wonderful if this whole business could soon be ended and Lucian freed from danger. They could marry and have a house—they could even go back to Malaga in the summer. She was aware suddenly of Ryan's arm sliding across the back of the settee. His hand cupped her bare shoulder and his fingers stroked her skin.

"I have never seen you so beautiful," he murmured huskily.

"Thank you."

Seeing her pink cheeks and bright eyes, Ryan's hunting instincts were fully alerted. By the gods, the wench was excited.

Sarina sat straighter. She simply would not allow herself to shudder. "Do you remember the night when you and I first heard of the Ghost?" she asked.

"I will never forget it. You were ravishing . . ."

"Y-you never did get to see all of our maze or—"

She never finished her sentence. Ryan seized her, lay her back in his arms, and claimed her mouth in a passionate kiss, his hands moving hungrily over her bosom and thighs. She could not protest. She had led him to believe it was why he was there in her bed-chamber, but things were moving far too quickly. When he released her, she struggled to sit up, managing a light laugh.

"Ryan, you are extremely attractive to me, but, you are treating me as—*he* did." She smoothed the bodice of her gown, neatened her hair, and forced herself to remain seated at his side. "You will never know how I yearned for your—sophistication and restraint."

"Is that so?" Ryan answered gruffly, attempting to calm his heavy breathing and quell the heat in his loins. "Never fear, my flower, I was but taking a small sip of your charms. I would never allow them to overcome me."

Sarina blinked at his glibness. And to think she had once thought she loved him, had considered him passionate and sensitive and honest. How could she have been so wrong? She took up her goblet and sipped more champagne. She stroked Ryan's hand.

"Your charms, too, are hard to resist, my dear," she murmured. "Not only are you sophisticated and handsome and dashing, but you are, without a doubt, the cleverest man I have ever known."

"Ah, you think so, do you?" Ryan lifted his own glass to his lips and drained it in one swallow.

Sarina smiled. "I know so. Just look at how well you have done. This lovely home"—she looked around the room, thinking she would toss half of the furniture and knicknacks out if she could—"and the fact that your business is so successful despite your—great hardships."

He nodded. "The devil has made it somewhat difficult."

"I—I know." She touched her lips to her glass. "Oh, Ryan, what must you think of me?"

His handsome face darkened. "If you really want to know, I thought you were a damned fool who needed to be protected from herself."

"As indeed I was. I'm grateful that you cared." The words nearly stuck in her throat. Seeing his goblet was empty, Sarina raised hers to his lips. "Do taste mine," she whispered.

His hungry eyes met hers over the rim. "It is more delicious by far than my own, *ma petite*. Your rosy lips have sweetened it." He drank it all.

Sarina playfully tapped his mouth with two fingers. "How naughty of you. Now I need more."

"By the gods, you are adorable." He poured more for them both. "But let me finish what I started to say—"

"Oh, yes, do." She put the tip of her tongue to the golden brew, saw his hot gaze fasten on it.

"When you came to me with that foolishness about not wedding me," he said, "and when it was apparent you had been smitten by that bastard, I knew I had to protect you for your own good. Do you understand that finally? It is why I locked you in your bedchamber and had you sign our small agreement."

"I understand." She smiled, but her eyes flashed.

The small agreement that gave him total control of the business that was supposed to be hers. As she offered him her glass again, she saw the telltale glaze beginning to shine in his eyes.

"After all," she continued, "what does a woman know of business affairs and money?"

"Exactly, my dear."

"So it is only right that you handle it all for me, Ryan, since you are so very clever." She allowed him to kiss her again. She reached up, untied the bow in the cambric stock at his neck, and loosened it. "There, does that not feel more comfortable?"

He pulled off the stock, threw it to the floor, and unbuttoned his tight shirt collar beneath it.

" 'Smuch better. Let's make you more comfortable, too." He loosened the laces that held her bodice together. "There. Breathe better. Let's see you breathe better, my flower." He dropped a heavy kiss on her bosom.

Sarina did not protest. He would think it strange if she didn't let him touch her. She was detecting the first faint slurring of his speech, but only after he had drunk more champagne than she had thought humanly possible. How could the man even sit upright?

"I should've killed that devil for raping you," he muttered. "Should've hanged an' skewered the bastard." He pulled her close and kissed the swells of her breasts again and again.

"But I'm here now," she murmured, forcing herself not to cringe. "I'm safe with you." She held the glass first to her own lips, and then to his.

"I hate 'im," Ryan growled.

"I—wish you did not. It's bad for you." When he gave an angry snort, she said softly, "You have everything, you know. You have success, you are handsome, admired . . ."

"An' I have you."

"Yes, you have me. And you are clever . . ."

"More damned clever than you will ever know, lady."

"Oh, I have never doubted it."

Sarina stoically bore his fingers on her breasts, slipping between them, stroking, squeezing. She dared not antagonize him.

"Did I ever tell you I was pressed when I was a lad? No, I s'pose not—and who do you s'pose was on the damned vessel that nabbed me?"

"The Ghost, I suppose," she answered, imagining a young Lucian, strong, handsome, glorious . . .

Ryan nodded, his eyes half-closed. "I hated him even then." His sleepy gaze seemed glued to her bosom. He loosened the laces of her gown completely.

"Ryan—"

"Quiet, woman, you are mine an' it's time you learned it. I've been too patient with you."

As he forced her back into his arms once more, Sarina tried to hold the two halves of her bodice together, but Ryan captured her hands. Her breasts spilled out. She heard his harsh indrawn breath before he lowered his head, sucking on one nipple and then the other.

She was repulsed, but made no protest. And she had

to encourage him to drink more champagne. She whispered: "Ryan, my mouth is so dry—"

He kissed it. "Sweet as honey . . ."

"Please, may I have more champagne?"

He stared at her, threw back his head, and laughed. God's death, he had just been about to pour some down her throat. The wench was still too wide-eyed and tense to suit his purpose. He rose and got the bottle, noting as he did that the floor was tilting. He had had a bit much perhaps . . .

"Come, lie down in bed with me, my sweet. The drink's gone to my head." He grabbed her arm, felt her resistance. "Damn it, you silly wench, I'm going to be your husban'." He gave her a shake. "Get into bed—an' here is your drink." He put the bottle on the nightstand, stretched out and sighed. "Ah, God's bones, that's better. Now put your head on my shoulder, there's a good wench, an' let me tell you an amusing thing about your ghos'."

"He is not my ghost, Ryan."

Sarina was uneasy. He could scarcely stand and his face was red and damp with sweat. She feared he would doze off before she had a chance to question him.

"Beautiful, beautiful wench," he muttered. He opened the bodice of her gown again and gazed at her breasts, crushing them together so roughly that he hurt her.

Sarina stifled a cry. "You were about to tell me something amusing . . ."

"I was?" All of his attention was on her bosom. "By God, if you're not the loveliest thing. Take off your gown, and let me see just what it is I'll be acquiring through the holy rites of matrimony come next Sunday afternoon. Come now, S'rina—" He began to undress her. "Take off your little gown an' lie close, an' I will tell you about your damned ghos'." He watched as she rose obediently and stripped down to her chemise with trembling fingers.

Sarina was frightened. He was drunk, but he needed

to drink still more to be in her power. And then he might fall asleep without telling her what she needed to know—or he could overpower and rape her. Oh, why did everything important have to be so complicated? She had to make an instant decision, and she made it. She put her goblet to her lips and took several sips.

'It's so very delicious,'' she said, smiling at him, hoping to tempt him to further indulgence. "On Malaga there was nothing but ale. I could not abide it. Ale and those moldy biscuits . . .'' She offered her goblet to him and gave a prayer of thanks when he drank the remainder.

"Ah, yes, Malaga." Ryan's eyes, heavy-lidded, slid over her. "I want to tell you about your bloody ghos', S'rina—about when we were at sea. Lads at sea . . .''

"Yes, Ryan, I want to hear." She was almost afraid to move, to breathe for fear of distracting him.

"Bloody bastard," he said and shook his head. "I never did like 'im, I only pretended. Everyone thought he was so damned strong an' brave an' brilliant; destined for such great things." He began to laugh. "Well, let me tell you, he's as stupid as they come. I have bested him."

"I am relieved to hear that."

"Yes. I've confounded the mighty Ghost, the mighty commander of the *Peacekeeper*, the man who can do no wrong. He can dump all the cargos he wants, but he will never destroy me. Not that way."

Sarina masked her curiosity and confusion. What did he mean, Lucian could dump all the cargos he wanted, but he would never destroy him that way? She didn't understand. Knowing she had to draw him out further, she gazed up at him, her eyes dewy and admiring.

"How wonderful it must feel, besting him. If only I were a man, I too could have such satisfaction."

"Woman"—Ryan's gaze seared her—"you have me to protect you now, an' I swear to God, I'll see 'im dead in the end. You will have satisfaction. In turn, you will satisfy me. Is that understood?''

It took every ounce of her willpower for Sarina to remain docile. ''I understand,'' she said through clenched teeth. ''I am grateful for your protection. But now do tell me how you have bested him—can I give you more to drink?''

Without waiting for his answer, she poured the last of the bottle into her goblet, handed it to him, and watched, amazed, as he drained it dry. Seeing him fall back onto her pillows, she feared he was already asleep, but then he looked at her through lowered lids and smiled.

''I bested 'im for the first time in Naipoor. Remind me to tell you of the Naipoor affair, my sweet. An' then Garrick, alas, poor Garrick, helped me this time. Led me right to him.'' He shook his head, chuckling. ''Ah, s'wounds, but the fellow's dense. He thinks I have a trove in a cave somewhere for those few small things I buy on the side—as if I would be so stupid . . .''

''But then he cannot hope to match wits with you.'' Sarina's heart was pounding so wildly, she feared he would hear it. His news of Garrick was something she herself had wondered about.

''Match wits? Hardly. Ah, God, to think of it—him, a bloomin' thief, punishing me for doing a bit o' trading on the side.'' He laughed outright. ''He will never find my goods, S'rina. Never.''

He was quiet for so long, his eyes closed, that Sarina feared she had lost him to sleep. She patted and stroked his face until his eyelids fluttered open.

''My goodness, I had no idea you were doing anything so daring,'' she whispered. ''Is it not dangerous?''

He held her hand to his lips. ''S'easy. My only probably was the Ghost. Now he's no problem either . . .''

When his eyes closed again, Sarina wanted to scream and pound his chest and demand that he tell her where his stupid hiding place was. Shaking with eagerness, she traced his lips with her finger.

"Ryan?"

"Sweet bitch." He grasped her finger and put it in his mouth to suck on it. "Luscious bitch . . ."

"You are so brave and clever," she whispered, "and I admire you so much for having outwitted him. How on earth did you do it?"

He tried to pull her chemise down over her shoulders. "Take it off . . ."

"Soon. I will take it off very soon." Seeing that he was dozing again, his mouth open, she gave his arm a shake. "Ryan?"

"Hmmm?"

She lay close beside him, heart flying, fingers stroking his hair as his own hands moved clumsily over her.

"You are so clever," she insisted, "but do promise me the Ghost will never discover where you hide those things you trade on the side. Promise he will never find them, Ryan. They are ours, are they not? He has no right to them."

Ryan chortled softly. "What a greedy li'l bitch you are." He kissed her mouth. "Ah, God's death, what a sweet wench. He'll never have you, an' he'll never find my cache for there's none to find. Not anymore."

No cache? Sarina was electrified. She waited, afraid to move, willing his lips to form the words that would tell her where the treasure lay. Oh, Ryan, speak, she cried silently. You must hide your goods somewhere until they can be sold. Speak! She stroked his lips with her fingers. Speak, speak . . .

"No cache," he murmured. "S'all gone, s'all sold—except for the shipment this coming day." He grinned at her, and kissed her fingers again. "No one knows 'cept the cap'n. Uncle Cap'n. You know he is my uncle, S'rina? He has all my sweet gems an' tomorrow—" His eyelids fluttered and closed.

"Ryan!" She shook him again. Oh, God . . . "Ryan?"

"T'morrow," he muttered thickly, "I'll get them at the shipyard after crew's gone. Bloody crew doesn't know . . . no one knows . . . only me an' Uncle Cap'n . . .''

Ryan's eyes closed once more, the black behind his lids filling with beautiful swirling waves of white and red and purple. He felt himself sinking into them, but he would take Sarina with him. He was going to make love to her. He grasped her soft body tightly in his arms, took her mouth with his, felt her breasts yield to his hungry hands. She was struggling. Good. The more she fought, the greater his pleasure would be when she realized the inevitable—that she was his. All his. He was sinking more deeply, whirling, but it was all right. The little bitch would not escape him . . .

Sarina had hoped that Ryan's strength and passion would be diminished by the alcohol, but they were not. It was a struggle to escape him, but now he was finally asleep. Sound, dead-to-the-world asleep. To make sure, she gently pinched his ear.

"Ryan?"

She shook his shoulder, fearful that he might open his eyes and pull her onto the bed again. When he began to snore, she hurried to her desk for a quill and paper and wrote a brief message: *There is no cache now. Gems on ship arriving this day—his uncle is captain. He will get gems at shipyard.*

She had done it! Sarina thought, trembling with her excitement as she rolled the paper into a cylinder, tied it, and hurried to the front window. She had actually learned what Lucian needed to know and she was unscathed. She stepped cautiously onto the balcony, her attention divided between Ryan's sleeping form and the dimly lit street. She saw movement then, a form in a black cowled cloak directly beneath her window.

Lucian had been watching and waiting silently beneath Sarina's balcony for hours. He was wild with worry. What had he been thinking to let her do this dangerous deed? If the devil had harmed so much as her little finger or a lock of her hair, he had seen his last sunset.

The latch clicked. Lucian stepped away from the

house and looked up, his heart thudding. Seeing Sarina's white face and frightened green eyes, he went rigid. Ah, God, what had happened? Then she saw him and smiled, her face lighting up. Vastly relieved, he pushed back his cowl and held a finger to his lips. She was not to make a sound. She nodded, held up a small white cylinder of paper for him to see, and grinned.

Lucian's body was flooded with love for her. How brave she was, and what abuse she had taken from him. But now was not the time to think of it. He had work to do. And he was going to make up to her in a thousand ways for the grief he had caused her. He put his fingers to his lips and kissed them. He threw the kisses up to her until she laughed.

As Sarina watched, several other men materialized beside Lucian on the cobbled street. The hair rose on her arms and the back of her neck. Ten tall strong men. When two of them faded into the shadows of Douglas Hall, she knew they were staying to guard her. The others disappeared into the night with Lucian. She smiled. She would have been rescued in grand style had it been necessary. She was still smiling when she opened the hallway door to a sleepy-eyed Rosie.

"I'm going to sleep in your bedchamber tonight, love," she whispered. "Let us be ever so quiet and not waken anyone."

Chapter 25

When Lucian and his men were some distance from Douglas Hall, he took Sarina's slender scroll of paper to a lamppost, quickly unrolled it, and read it in the dim light. He frowned. There was no longer a cache. Instead, a shipment of gems was due this day and Douglas would claim them. In a shipyard? He shook his head and read the note again. There was no doubt about it. It said the shipyard—that would be the Kirkeby yard—and it said the ship was due today. And the bastard's uncle was the captain. His breathing quickened. There were two ships due today, the *Stargazer* and the *Breton*. Which one was it? He knew both of them; he had taken Sarina from the *Stargazer*.

"Sir, is somethin' wrong?" one of the men asked, peering up into Lucian's frowning face.

Lucian clapped the fellow on the shoulder. "Something may be right, Mr. White. Something may finally be right. We will soon know."

All eight men were members of his crew, but for the past several months they had been land-based, gathering information for him up and down the eastern coast. As they walked toward where their horses were tethered, Lucian began issuing commands.

"Jenkins, take three men and ride to Shoreham. Tell Mr. Fleming to take the *Vengeance* straightaway to Duck Creek and from there to the Hudson."

"But, sir, the Hudson in daylight?"

Lucian grinned. "We will not worry, mister. Only Douglas and his men know we have changed color, and they will have only two vessels in this area today—the *Stargazer* in the late morning and the *Breton* in the afternoon. Tell Mr. Fleming to take her to the cove above the Kirkeby yard and wait there until further notice."

"Aye, sir. If it's all the same to you, sir, we'll leave right now."

Lucian nodded. "Good."

"Watkins, Clives, an' Scott," Jenkins snapped, "let's go!"

Without another word, they were off. When Lucian and the remaining four men arrived at the Blue Onion, he sent them to bed. There was nothing more they could do until dawn, but he had some thinking to do—there would be no sleep for him tonight.

He pulled off his boots and lay down on his bed fully clothed, scowling at the ceiling. He had known so much, yet it seemed he had known nothing. He had been wrong about Sarina, and now there was this new idea to consider. No cache. It was damned strange, but no matter. The contraband would arrive today, and he would nab the bastard on the spot. And the captain was his uncle, was he?

Unable to calm his restlessness, Lucian got up and walked angrily, silently about the small room, brooding over what sort of torture Sarina had experienced to get this information for him. Had the bastard pawed her or abused her in any way? It was useless to speculate, but since she had seemed fine when he left her, he must assume she was. He wouldn't be able to do the work at hand otherwise.

He sent his thoughts backtracking over the past several months. He had begun his strikes in April, and while it had been impossible to hit every Douglas Trader in the fleet, he knew he had hurt the devil. But the cache had always been his main goal, finding it and linking it to Douglas, that undeniable proof of his illegal dealings. But wait—was it possible Douglas had had

no real cache to speak of since his first run-in with the
Crown? Lucian was certain the man had not stopped
smuggling, but he was clever, and gems or other small
valuable goods could be secreted in such a way as not
to be discovered. Like the Pearls of Naipoor.

Raging at his stupidity, Lucian slammed a fist into
his palm. That was it—it had to be it. And did he use
one ship? One man? That uncle of his, by the gods. It
would be interesting to see which ship had the contraband today, and who captained her. His eyes burned
into the blackness, a bright image blazing on his mind:
the vessel moving through customs, everything above-
board and shipshape, the unloading at the warehouse,
and then the captain leaving her at the shipyard with
a pouch in his pocket. But no, not the captain—Douglas.
Maybe both. They would probably share the loot.

Lucian's eyes glittered with excitement. One ship,
one man . . . There was great advantage in it. What
would the bastard care if the Ghost struck every vessel
he owned and destroyed every cargo when the most
precious treasure aboard was unsuspected, hidden
even from the crew? He had no cache to be discovered,
no treachery to worry about.

Lucian stretched out on his bed again and laughed
into the darkness. Well, well. It felt damned good,
knowing they need search no longer for some
hollowed-out mountain or abandoned warehouse,
some muddy cave at the base of a cliff that filled with
seawater at high tide.

At last everything was coming to a head—the contraband due to arrive, Bascomb willing to testify, a wedding to stop, the *Gull* in town. And an additional
boon—their inn was almost equidistant from those
places they would be watching: Douglas Hall, the
docks and warehouses, the Kirkeby yard . . .

The sun had not yet risen when Lucian, sporting an
eyepatch and bandanna, limped into the candle-lit Blue
Onion to meet his men for breakfast. They ladled their
own mush from the kettle in the fireplace and carried

it to a table some distance from where others sat. After a sleepy-looking barmaid had brought them beer, and hoecakes and molasses for their mush, White whispered:

"If this bugger has jewels on 'im, sir, does it mean it's th' end o' this whole caper?"

"The beginning of the end," Lucian answered, taking a long swallow of beer. He saw the four men exchange disappointed glances. "What's the trouble?"

"We'll be glad for yer, o' course, Cap'n, but we was all sayin' earlier we ain't never had such a good caper. We've enjoyed every minute. Yer a fair man, cap'n. Fair an' generous an' bold as they come."

Lucian laughed softly. "And you're good men. I've thought it many times, and as for this caper, the day's not over, man. Don't say good-bye to me yet." He took a bite of hoecake and washed it down with beer.

"Now here is what we'll do," he said. "Climpson and Mason, I want you at the Douglas warehouse out of sight. When the *Stargazer* arrives, watch for Douglas. If he boards her, stick to him like glue when he leaves her. If he goes back home, watch the house. See who comes and goes. If he does not appear by the time she's unloaded and leaves for the shipyard, ride ahead to the shipyard and wait there for us."

"Aye, sir."

"White and Campion, you'll come with me."

The men's eyes gleamed.

"An' where might that be, Cap'n?" White finished the last of his beer and wiped his mouth on his sleeve.

"The Mauser yards," said Lucian.

Campion looked doubtful. "Where government vessels is repaired?"

"Right, Mr. Campion. We're going to pay a little visit to the *Gull*. I saw her when she arrived in New York, and I suspect she's in for repairs."

Both men stared at him. White swallowed. "Ain't that a bit of a risk, sir, bein' as yer the Ghost?"

"I thought you liked my bold moves, mister." Lucian threw some coins onto the table and rose to his feet. "If you would rather, you can exchange places with Mason—except I picked you for your brawn."

White grinned. "Then I'm wi' yer, Cap'n."

As they rode through narrow cobbled streets that were just now filling with people, Campion said: "An' who might we be visitin' on th' *Gull*, Cap'n?"

"The commander, John Pomeroy."

" 'Struth!"

"Yer mean it, sir?" White goggled at him. "Yer knows th' bloke?"

"I know him."

" 'Struth."

Lucian had only to touch on any one of his Naipoor memories to stir them to life. He saw again the scene of his and Shane's court-martial; the great cabin of the *Gull* extending the width of her, and her quarterdeck thronged with officers in full-dress uniform. He saw the long table in the middle of the cabin and standing around it twelve men, one of them John Pomeroy. He had met his sharp gray eyes, but the captain of the *Gull* had looked away.

Lucian drew a deep breath. Not now, man. Now is not the time to delve into memories.

"We're going to persuade the captain to accompany us back to the Kirkeby yard," Lucian told his men.

"God's bones, how are we goin' to do that?" Campion demanded. "How'll we even get aboard to see 'im in the first place?"

"I have some ideas, but I want yours. Think about it, and we'll discuss it over a pint when we get there."

"Aye."

They rode in silence for a mile, having left the bustle of the city for a narrow dirt road that followed the shoreline. As they rounded a bend, the yards came into sight and Lucian's heart thundered. The *Gull* dominated the docks. She was so beautiful, so majestic even with her sails furled, that he halted his mount and gazed at her in silence, pride swelling within him and filling his throat.

Ah, God, what was more glorious than a first-rate

man-o'-war with her three gun decks bristling with a hundred cannon? She was an exact replica of the *Peace-keeper*, and he could still feel and smell what it was like to be aboard her, still taste the grand excitement of commanding a vessel that carried eight hundred and fifty men. He closed his eyes, unashamed of their dampness and grateful that he had good memories, too. In fact, he was tired of keeping the bad ones stoked and smoldering. Perhaps this was the day, at long last, when he would put them to rest.

Seeing their captain's face, Campion and White exchanged concerned glances. White muttered, gruffly:

"Sir, I sees an inn up ahead. The Mermaid."

Lucian nodded. "Good. Let's have a pint and make our plans."

Listening to his men gathered around a table in the pub, he soon concluded that his own first idea was the best of all.

"We'll go with the carriage," he said. "It's the safest bet."

"Aye, but how do we get the bugger off 'is vessel?"

Lucian smiled, remembering the stories he had heard. "I doubt that will be a problem. Pomeroy is a strutter. I wager he has given the locals a daily treat so far. We will take him right off the street."

The three grinned at one another, envisioning such a lively prospect.

"There should be a livery stable in the vicinity, Campion. Rent a brougham and bring it back here. White, ride into the village and see if our little peacock is out and about yet. I'll watch the *Gull* for him. Meet me back here at eight bells and leave the brougham behind the Mermaid."

"Aye, Cap'n."

Lucian chose a vacant field across from the Mauser yard from which to keep watch. He tethered his mount and sat in the grass, his back against a tree and his one visible eye closed. Passersby saw nothing unusual in a shabbily dressed stranger resting as he passed through town. None saw him open his one eye and gaze hungrily at the *Gull*.

Noting the repair activity aboard her and remembering how things had been in his own day, Lucian wondered if he would ever stand on the deck of a warship again. If things worked today the way he hoped they would, he would regain his honor and his command. And all because of Sarina, who had provided the missing piece to the mystery.

Thinking of her loveliness, her tenderness and bravery and suffering these past months because of him, Lucian was consumed by love for her. They would marry, of course. But what if he were offered the command of the *Peacekeeper* again? God knew he wanted it. In his happy dreams he still walked her decks. But then, so was Sarina in his dreams—having and holding her, taking care of her, protecting her, loving her. He shook his head. A married man had no business on a warship. He couldn't do that to Sarina.

Lucian tensed. A small figure was walking briskly down the gangplank of the *Gull*, crossing the road and heading for the village. Gold braid, gleaming boots, full regalia. John Pomeroy in the flesh, by God. Smiling, Lucian got to his feet, rode to the Mermaid, handed his mount over to the stableboy, and limped after the man.

"Cap'n . . ." White emerged from a shop and joined him. "I see yer found 'im. He takes two long strolls a day, mornin' and evenin', so I reckon this had best be it."

"I agree. Have you seen Campion?"

"Aye. He found a livery right outside o' town, but he had to track me down to borry some money."

"Hell, I should have thought of that."

"Now, sir, all's well," White said. "He'll be along any minute in his brougham. Tell me how yer wants to work this caper."

"We'll take him where there are few shops and fewer people. We'll stop the brougham, ask him directions,

and when he approaches to answer, you lift him in.
I'll be inside with the shades drawn.''

White rubbed his meaty hands together. ''Ah, Cap'n,
it's jist th' sort o' caper I likes. By the way, I has Campion's horse wi' me own.''

''Good. After we've snatched Pomeroy, you can
fetch mine at the Mermaid and follow after us to the
Kirkeby yards.''

''Aye, sir. Ah, here's Campion now.''

Lucian got into the brougham. White gave his mate
instructions before getting in beside Lucian. Campion
turned the carriage about, following John Pomeroy at
a discreet distance. As the shops grew scarce and the
people few, Lucian drew the shades. The carriage
stopped. White disembarked, unseen by their quarry
who was on its opposite side.

''Beggin' yer pardon, sir,'' Campion called down
from the driver's bench, ''but yer looks like a navy
man.''

''What of it?'' Pomeroy snapped.

''Me passenger has a question for yer, sir. Somethin'
ter do wi' a vessel called the *Gull*. Would yer know it,
sir?''

Pomeroy drew himself up to his full five feet four
inches, a magnificent sight in scarlet, white, and navy-
blue.

''Do I know it? Sir, I am commander-in-chief of his
Majesty's vessels in the North Atlantic, and the *Gull* is
my ship. What question does this passenger of yours
have?''

''Step right up ter th' carriage, sir.'' The door
opened.

Pomeroy stepped closer. ''What is it you wish to
know about the—'' White approached from behind and
lifted him off his feet. ''Here, what is going on? Un-
hand me, you hound!''

John Pomeroy was thrust into the carriage and into
Lucian's steely grip. The door slammed behind him
and the brougham gathered speed. Pomeroy was too
startled to open the door, cry for aid, or leap out. See-

ing the man on the opposite bench, he decided it would
be unwise to do any of those things.

The fellow was big and dark and disreputable-
looking, unshaven and dirty, with a black eyepatch, a
navy-blue bandanna hiding his hair, disheveled clothing. John Pomeroy didn't shudder as the man's one
good eye, blue and cold as ice, examined him.

"What is the meaning of this outrage, sir? I demand
to know."

"I mean you no harm, Commander."

Pomeroy stared. The fellow didn't sound as uncouth
as he looked. He had an educated voice and all of a
sudden his expression had lost its threat. He felt himself relaxing.

"I don't care for pranks, sir, and I must warn you,
abducting a commanding officer of his Majesty's navy
can have serious consequences."

He continued to stare as the fellow took off his eyepatch to reveal a second eye as clear and penetrating
as the first. He then pulled off his dirty bandanna. John
Pomeroy's mouth fell open upon seeing the thick black
hair it had hidden. Hair as black as ebony. By the gods,
he knew this man.

"Sir, I am Lucian Thorne, formerly of the *Peacekeeper.*"

"Thorne! Of course, the Naipoor affair. By the gods,
what is this all about?"

Lucian leaned forward. "I have very little time so I
will be brief. If you remember, I maintained all through
the court-martial that my brother and I were innocent."

"Every accused man claims he is innocent, Mr.
Thorne," Pomeroy snapped.

But in this case, he wondered if the fellow were telling
the truth. When Shane Thorne had been called forward
and Pomeroy had seen how very young and innocent-
seeming the lad was, he had wondered and worried.
But the evidence had been conclusive. And he had
badly wanted to be commander-in-chief. Recovering
the Pearls of Naipoor had been a decided feather in his

cap. But there was something about the damned affair that he had not liked. Why, he could hardly look them in the eye, either of them, during the trial, and then when the young lad had died under the lash . . .

"Sir." Lucian's voice held an urgency the older man could not ignore. "I now know who betrayed us and I know how it was done. The fellow was smuggling and I reported him. His revenge was to plant the pearls aboard my vessel. I have all the proof I need."

The captain of the *Gull* kept his face expressionless. As much as he regretted his part in the incident, this fellow could not go about abducting the King's officers.

"Where are you taking me?" he asked stiffly.

"To the Kirkeby Shipyards."

Lucian felt as he had in the brig aboard the *Gull*, body aching with tension, mouth dry, a cold sweat creeping over him as he watched the other's impassive face. He wanted him to go willingly, but he was prepared to use force.

"And what will we find there?"

"The devil is still smuggling. I believe he has brought precious gems through customs without declaring them. I hope to confront him and wring a confession from him regarding the pearls he caused to be placed on my vessel."

Pomeroy's gray eyes were wintry. "Indeed?"

For one terrible instant, Lucian saw that the whole scheme could end in disaster. Douglas would not show up, or if he did, he would be carrying no gems when he left the vessel. And then there would be Pomeroy's wrath to contend with. He straightened his shoulders. That kind of thinking would carry him nowhere but backward.

"Sir, I am sorry it was necessary to apprehend you, but there is no time for formalities. I respectfully request now that you accompany me as a witness."

Seeing Lucian Thorne's burning eyes, John Pomeroy knew that he was going to go with the fellow. Although he didn't like the idea that the Crown may have found an innocent man guilty, he couldn't ignore the possibility. He leaned back in his seat and gazed across at Thorne.

"Your request is granted."

Lucian blinked. "Thank you, Commander." God almighty. He could hardly believe it.

"Thorne . . ."

"Sir?"

"It would please me if you were right. I would like to see your command returned."

Lucian was hard-pressed not to give the little peacock a hug.

"Thank you, sir."

Chapter 26

Sarina was uneasy as she descended the staircase and entered the dining room for breakfast. What sort of mood would Ryan be in after last night? she wondered, seeing him at the window drinking coffee. More important, was the information she had coaxed from him the truth, or had he been so drunk that his words had meant nothing at all? Despite the knot in her stomach, she gave him a smile.

"Good morning, Ryan."

"I have had better," he muttered.

Ryan's head was about to explode from all that damned champagne she had poured into him last night. That plus his confusion. Had he taken her as he had intended? She had been pressed close to him, he knew that much, and he remembered kissing many delicious places all over her body. His manhood began to rise at the memory. But not now, not now, he told himself and quickly turned his mind to other matters. But it was a damnable thing, being unable to recall whether or not he had slept with her. When had he ever been so drunk that he didn't remember a thing like that?

"Are you ill?" Sarina asked, noting his flushed face and overly bright eyes. "I do hope you're not coming down with something. You cannot be sick for the wedding."

"I'm not 'coming down with something,' " he growled, "nor will I be sick for the wedding."

Now that he knew she could drink more champagne than any other female he had ever seen in his life, he wouldn't allow her to overindulge in the future.

"I suppose you have quite a few errands today," Sarina murmured, seating herself at the table. Rosie immediately presented her with a bowl of porridge covered with clotted cream and berries.

"Yes. Too many." A fitting for his waistcoat, appointments all over town, and two ships arriving, although he would meet only the important one.

He was filled with resentment over the appointments. It was woman's work, attending to flowers and food. But then, he had forbidden Sarina to leave the house until after they were wed. He wouldn't risk Thorne's carrying her off again. Once she was his by law and he had possessed her on their wedding night, he knew the devil would not abduct her again. Lucian Thorne had a certain stuffy honor that could be counted on. Now Ryan's curiosity about the night before rose again. Doubt was eating him alive. Had he possessed her already?

"I will have my eggs and sausage now, Annie. Put the scones over here, Rosie, and then you both may leave."

After the girls had hurried from the room, Ryan's gaze swept over Sarina. Seeing the rosy blush touching her face and bosom, he was certain she was his. He remembered the tantalizing texture of her soft breasts and arms beneath his fingers, the fresh taste of her, her intoxicating lily scent. He had much to look forward to . . .

"How was your night?" he asked, a suggestive smile on his lips. "Did you sleep well?"

He had wakened that morning just as she was tiptoeing from the room carrying her clothing and a hairbrush. Her side of the bed had been slept in. He had hurried to his own room, dressed, and come down for his coffee while she was still at her toilette.

"Yes, I—slept quite well." Sarina looked down at her porringer, her cheeks burning.

How much did he remember? she wondered. His greedy hands and mouth moving over her naked breasts? That frightening moment when he had nearly taken her? She would give anything for him not to recall a bit of it.

"How was your own night?" she murmured.

"Filled with delicious memories," Ryan lied, vastly annoyed that she hadn't complimented him on his prowess as a lover. Women always made mention of it.

He cursed his splitting head and blamed it on her. And despite memories of her luscious body, he had a vague sensation of dissatisfaction, of uneasiness, as though he had given more than he had received, although how that could be he could not imagine. Whatever, he had neither the time nor the patience to question her further. He had to hurry to be at his tailor's on time.

As soon as the *Vengeance* anchored in the cove above the yards at Kirkeby, Donal and Sky came ashore with Lucian's messengers and extra crew. Going immediately to Lucian's lodging in the Mermaid, they found not only Lucian, White, and Campion, but also John Pomeroy ensconced in an easy chair quaffing ale. Donal's mouth fell open.

"Come in, men." Lucian shook the hands of each of them as they crowded into his small room. "Sir," he said, addressing John Pomeroy, "this is my first lieutenant, Donal Fleming; my quartermaster, Sky Braden; and crewmen Jenkins, Watkins, Clives, Scott, and Andrews." He went on to name every crew member before saying, "Men, this is Fleet Commander Sir John Pomeroy, who has kindly agreed to assist us today."

"At ease, men." Pomeroy gave them a brusque nod before his gray eyes locked onto Donal. "I understand it was you, Lieutenant, who uncovered the perpetrator of this dastardly affair?"

"Aye, sir."

Donal was much surprised to see John Pomeroy

holding court, when he had expected to find him bound and with a gunnysack over his head.

"You are to be commended, Mr. Fleming."

"Thank you, sir."

Donal felt a lovely glow starting at the crown of his head and burning its way downward. Wait until Ginelle heard! Ah, holy heaven, never would he have believed things would work out this way. He still didn't understand Pomeroy's magnanimity, but now was not the time to ask questions.

"Mr. Thorne says you have also managed to locate the fellow who secreted the pearls aboard the *Peacekeeper*."

"Aye. George Bascomb. He is willing to testify, but I—uh—had to promise he would not be punished."

"So I hear."

"The thing is, sir, he had no idea what was in that pouch your man found. He was told he was taking part in a prank of some sort."

"I understand." Pomeroy continued to drink his ale. "I have already told Commander Thorne that I personally will look into this affair. Fortunately, the young lady, Rajeen, was released after several months."

'Commander Thorne'? And Rajeen released? Ah, holy heaven, what a grand day this was, Donal thought. There was a rap on the door then, and Donal opened it to admit Climpson and Mason.

"The *Stargazer*'s on 'er way, Cap'n, an'—" Seeing John Pomeroy in full regalia, Mason snapped his mouth shut.

"It's all right, Mason. This is Fleet Commander Pomeroy. He'll be helping us."

"Aye, sir." Mason blinked, swallowed, and saluted before turning again to Lucian. "Jon Gray's 'er captain, jist like yer thought, an' Mr. Douglas never boarded 'er at the warehouse. We figger she'll be here in twenny minutes er so."

Lucian nodded. "Now, Climpson and Mason, return to the warehouse. I want you there in case anything goes wrong. Jenkins and Watson, go to Douglas Hall;

if Douglas escapes, he may head there. As for those of
you who just joined us, three of you spot yourselves
within a mile of the Hall, and three within a mile of
the warehouse. If you see or hear anything wrong, in-
tervene. Failing that, report back to the warehouse. If
the bastard escapes, I'll be bringing the *Vengeance*
downriver. The warehouse will be our meeting place.

"A final word. Campion says the *Stargazer* has berth
seven. The vessels on either side of her are being careened, so drift into the yard one by one from different
directions and hide behind them. I want you close
enough to see and hear her crew when they disem-
bark—if this is a wild goose chase, anything you chance
to hear could be important. Commander Pomeroy and
I will remain in the brougham in front of the Mermaid
until Douglas boards. At that point, you, Carter, will
ride to the cove and tell them to bring the *Vengeance*
down . . ."

"Aye, sir."

"Ain't th' boatbuilders goin' to wonder who we are
an' what we're doin', skulkin' 'round the yard?"
Climpson asked.

Lucian grinned. "It seems they are all on a big job
down at the other end."

Donal laughed and rubbed his hands together.
"Fancy that."

"Yer luck has changed," Sky muttered, "an' about
time."

"Highly fortuitous, indeed," Pomeroy said, wiping
beer foam from his mouth with a snowy square of cambric.

"Climpson and Mason, take all of our mounts behind the Mermaid. Tell the lad to leave them saddled.
White, when the captain leaves his vessel, encourage
him to accompany you to the brougham and keep him
there. Sir John and I will already have left it. When
you see that we have Douglas, bring Gray to us."

"Aye, Cap'n." White's eyes gleamed.

"That's it, men, get going. Jenkins, one more thing.
Let me have your hat and jacket for now . . ."

* * *

Lucian felt a familiar cold sweat drenching him as he waited in the brougham opposite Sir John Pomeroy. The *Stargazer* had docked and her crew departed, but there was no sign yet of her captain or Douglas. Lucian moistened his dry lips, shifted his position, and peered toward the vessel through the crack at the bottom of the shade. Wild success or total failure were possible. To the good, Pomeroy believed him. That was a miracle in itself, and if the caper failed, he would start all over again. But first, he would get Sarina away from Douglas this very day. He regretted that he hadn't insisted she leave with him last night.

"Your quartermaster is right," John Pomeroy said softly after a long silence. "Your luck has changed, Commander."

Lucian forced a smile. "I have never been much of a believer in luck, sir."

Pomeroy's lips twisted into a facsimile of a smile. "Then consider that I shouldn't even be here. I was on maneuvers off the Canadian coast when I learned that I was needed in Belize."

Belize. The British Honduras. Lucian himself had fought the Spanish there on the *Peacekeeper*.

"If I hadn't sustained storm damage off Cape Cod, I would be well on my way there. I consider it a good omen."

Lucian grinned. "Maybe you are right at that, sir. Douglas has just ridden up."

Pomeroy peered out the slit with his sharp gray eyes, watched the man dismount and go aboard the vessel. "Do we move now?"

"Aye. And I'm going to ask you to wear this old jacket and hat."

Wordlessly, the fleet commander complied as Lucian donned his eyepatch and bandanna. They left the brougham, Lucian bent and limping, Sir John like a cocky beggar. After what seemed an endless wait behind the overturned vessel to the *Stargazer*'s left, Lucian heard footsteps—Gray coming down the gangplank. He crossed the yards, crossed the field, and had nearly reached the Mermaid when White appeared by his side. It took only seconds for the big seaman to encourage the smaller man to enter the brougham.

Lucian told himself over and over that this was it. This was what he had waited three years for. But it was too easy. It had to be a trick. What if the bastard had known exactly what Sarina was up to and had fed her false information? That had to be it—and all of this "luck" was a sham. At the thought, his heart began roaring in his ears. He was sweating again. Suddenly he heard footsteps. He didn't move or breathe; the men froze. He glanced cautiously around the upturned vessel and saw Douglas coming down the gangplank. Lucian moved swiftly, silently.

"Hello, old friend."

Ryan scowled at the crooked stranger standing between him and his mount. "Get out of my way, lout!"

When the fellow removed his eyepatch and bandanna and straightened his hunched body to his full height, Ryan's mouth fell open. Thorne!

"You!" he rasped.

"Aye, none other."

"Bastard, you must enjoy goading fate to the limit."

Lucian grinned. "I enjoy goading you, devil."

"I guarantee it will be for the last time."

What his worthless crews could not accomplish, he would, Ryan thought, raging. Here and now he would slay the fellow. He reached for his sword, but before it even left the scabbard, he felt steel at his throat.

Lucian put down his weapon instantly. "Draw, bastard. I will wait. I will gladly skewer you now even though I prefer that you die inch by inch for your treachery."

Having seen his enemy's lightning quickness, Ryan reconsidered. He muttered: "To think I spared you once, fool that I was."

"Did you now? That slips my mind." When Ryan glowered, he twisted the knife. "Ah, yes, now I recall. But I was never to know of your generosity, was I?

Only Sarina knew. And you never told her I was to go to the bottom with my ship and crew. And I was never to know how the pearls were smuggled aboard my vessel in Naipoor, was I? I was meant to hang or die under the lash as Shane did." Lucian threw back his head and laughed, but his blazing eyes were terrible to see. "It seems I have more lives than a cat."

"You are not only a criminal, you are mad to boot. Totally mad," Ryan declared, but his world was spinning. How had the devil ever learned about his agreement with Sarina—and that he had meant to sink him?

"Empty your pockets," Lucian said softly, "and bear in mind I am tempted to kill you now." He waggled the tip of his sword inches from Ryan's throat.

Ryan hesitated. Could he twist away from the steel so close to his throat and get to his mount? He knew he could not.

"Empty them, man. Now."

"Damn you."

By all the gods, how did he know so much? Especially how had he known he himself would be carrying a fortune in gems this very day? It was maddening. Reluctantly he brought forth one exquisite blood-red ruby newly removed from the wine in which it had been hidden.

"I had intended this for my bride," he muttered, "but I suppose you will plunder it as you did her."

Ignoring his words, Lucian took it and held it up to the bright morning sun. "Very pretty. Now let us see the whole lot."

"I—I have no more."

"Men, come out now," Lucian called. His prisoner glowered at the crewmen who appeared from behind the two careened vessels. "Empty his pockets," he ordered.

"Louts! Keep your filthy hands off me."

Ryan's own hands were shaking, but he did as he was commanded, turning out his pockets and emptying the gems into the pouch given him.

Lucian barely looked at them. His eyes were on the

captain of the *Stargazer*, now being led toward them by his crewman. Jon Gray's hands were bound, his eyes frightened in his white face.

"Wh-what is all this?" he muttered.

"Say nothing," Ryan ordered. "These men are pirates."

Gray's eyes opened wide.

"Ryan, have you—"

"Say nothing, damn it!" Ryan snapped.

"If you have something to say, Captain," Lucian drawled, "I suggest you say it. It will go easier for you." Gray stared at him and at the planking beneath his feet. Lucian shrugged. His icy gaze swung to Douglas. "No matter. We have Bascomb."

"Bascomb?" Ryan shook his head. "The name means nothing to me."

Lucian smiled. "Your memory will return when you see him. He will testify against you at your trial."

Ryan felt cold suddenly, and his head, aching since early morning, had begun to pound. Bascomb . . . Could that have been the fellow he had hired to carry the pearls aboard the *Peacekeeper?* He recalled some such name vaguely, but the fellow was dead. He had arranged it. He had seen him lying in an alley.

"A trial?" He forced a laugh. "Someone named Bascomb? What is all this nonsense?"

"What trial?" Jon Gray looked wild.

"Say nothing," Ryan ordered. "These men are criminals, all of them. You recognize the Ghost, I see, and you will recall the extent of his crimes. He has gone completely mad in his thirst for revenge against me."

Lucian turned to Jon Gray. He took the pouch from his own pocket and withdrew several gems, rolling them on his palm like marbles. He said quietly:

"I will also take the ones you are carrying, Captain. Did you happen to pay duty on them?"

"Well, I—" Gray began nervously.

Ryan's voice rose. "Of course he paid duty on them."

Looking from one hostile face to another, he wondered why he was lying, for Thorne knew, they all knew the gems were contraband. He had even boasted to the chained and helpless Ghost of his continued smuggling. Damnation, he talked too much. Now his only hope was rescue, but by whom? His crew were all getting drunk in the pubs surrounding the shipyard. The shipyard. That was it—the boatbuilders!

Where were the devils? he wondered. If only he could spot one of them . . . Ah, God, he must stall for time, say something, anything, any lie would do. He forced himself to calmness, let his gaze range coolly over the Ghost's motley crew of guttersnipes and ragamuffins.

"It would behoove the lot of you," he declared, "to abandon your lawless lives and come to work for me. I am always on the lookout for brave men." Ignoring the hoots and his enemy's mocking smile, he added, "I will pay double what *he* does, and I will see that you are not punished for your piracy. You have but to accompany me back to my office."

He glared at a small disreputable-looking figure who swaggered out from behind one of the careened vessels.

"I have heard enough to be satisfied," said the man.

"Now there is a man of sense," Ryan exclaimed. He disliked the fellow on sight, an ancient banty rooster strutting like a peacock, but at least the fool was on his side. "What do you say, men? Follow his lead and put all of this behind you." He bristled at their laughter. "Idiots, you are all idiots!"

"Ryan Douglas," said the banty rooster in a ringing voice, "I arrest you in the name of the Crown."

It was so preposterous that Ryan laughed. "Who the hell are you?"

"Men, seize this rapscallion. You have been misled by my unfortunate garb, sir. I am Fleet Commander Pomeroy of HMS *Gull.*"

Reacting instantly and blindly in his outrage, Ryan drew his dagger. He grabbed the little fellow and dragged him toward his mount.

"Stand back or I kill him!" he shouted. "He's a dead man." His head jerked up as he heard a distant cry.

"Mr. Douglas, sir, are yer all right?" It was one of the boatbuilders. Ten or more were coming at a run.

"I am beset by thieves," Ryan bellowed. "Hurry!"

Within moments, they charged Lucian's men, shouting, cursing, fists flying, and in the midst of the battle, Ryan mounted and fled. Galloping toward Douglas Hall, he wondered, still raging, how Thorne had known to be there. How in God's name had he known? And that beggarly-looking popinjay—Fleet Commander Pomeroy of the *Gull*? He spurred his horse sharply, angrily, thinking that the damned fellow had been disguised just as Thorne was. They had stooped to trickery.

It would have meant prison had they taken him, but they had not—nor would they. God's death, no, he would not be taken. He still had a trick or two up his sleeve. He would intercept the *Breton*, due in from London this very afternoon, and he would turn her around and head south. Once in Florida, there were endless places to which he could flee. But first he would get Sarina. He must not forget Sarina. But he suspected a watch had been placed on Douglas Hall. He decided on the instant to stop at a pub and hire four ruffians to go on ahead of him. He smiled. Thorne should know by now that no matter how clever he was, he himself would always be one step ahead . . .

Chapter 27

Sarina could not stay away from the drawing room windows. Every carriage that drove by, every man on horseback, was a potential bearer of tidings—good or bad. It was maddening, this waiting.

Rosie knocked and entered with a tray. ''Yer needs a bite o' somethin' to keep up yer strenth, mum.'' Seeing her mistress' white face, she quavered, ''Is anythin' wrong?''

''Probably not . . .''

''Yer holdin' somethin' back from me . . .'' Rosie's own face turned pale.

Sarina shook her head. ''I told you everything I know. It's just that I know so little.''

Rosie's brown eyes brimmed. ''They might be in gaol!''

''I doubt that very much''

Rosie gulped. ''They might be lyin' in gaol an' here I've been thinkin' how me an' Sky is gonna be together soon . . .''

''My pet, I'm sure you will. There, now.'' Sarina hugged her. ''You must not cry.''

''Mebbe ye'll have to marry th' master after all! Mebbe we'll never see our men agin and ye'll belong to Mr. Douglas forever.''

Sarina laughed, her green eyes blazing. ''You need have no fear of that.''

''But what if somethin' went wrong an' they're all caught? Oh, mum, I don't want ter stay here no more.''

"We will not be staying here, I assure you."

Rosie burst into fresh tears. "What else kin we do? Yer has no place else to go nor do I. We can't go out an' roam the streets, mum. There's all sorts o' wicked men out there jist lookin' fer tender female flesh like ours. Awoo."

"Rosie, for goodness' sake, you cannot believe that!"

Sarina took the girl in her arms again, stroking her hair and crooning comforting words, but she herself was growing uneasy. She would not marry Ryan, that much she knew, but Rosie was right. If Lucian didn't come back for them, then what? Where would they go? What would they do?

"Mum," Rosie gasped, "I—I hears th' master!"

"What!"

They hurried to the rear windows overlooking the gardens. The stables weren't visible, but now Sarina, too, heard Ryan's angry voice demanding a fresh horse. Within seconds he was standing in the doorway of the drawing room glaring at her. Sarina stared back. He was out of breath, his clothing disheveled, his face streaked with dust and sweat, and his always-sleek brown hair in wild disarray.

"You have three minutes to fetch your things, wench. We are leaving."

Sarina put her hands on her hips. "Perhaps you are leaving. I am not."

"Three minutes!"

Sarina heard him running to the back of the house, thundering down the steps to the cellar, but all she could think of was Lucian. Where was he? What had happened to him?

Rosie's eyes were wide, her fingers to her mouth. "Oh, mum, whatever do yer suppose happint? What's he doin' down there wi' all that crashin' around? Oh, me man's in gaol, I jist knows it! Mum, what'll we do?" She looked about, unseeing, then gasped, "H-he's comin' back!"

Sarina froze as Ryan returned to the room. His face was dark-red and swollen, his eyes glittering oddly.

"We are leaving, Sarina." He grasped her wrist and drew her after him.

"Ryan, I will not!"

She twisted out of his grip and fled into the foyer. He followed, caught her, and lifted her in his arms. Wordlessly, he strode toward the back of the house with her.

"Put me down!" She kicked and pounded him with her fists, but he held her tighter. "Damn you, Ryan! Rosie, help!" Sarina pulled his hair and continued to pound his chest with her fists. "Get Annie and B-Bessie!"

She heard Rosie shrieking for them as he carried her through the kitchen and out into the stableyard, then set her roughly on her feet.

"Hold on to her," he ordered the stable lad who stood at attention with a fresh horse. He mounted. "Now, lift her up here."

"Don't you dare touch me, you little whelp!" Sarina snapped at the frightened-looking boy.

"Lift her up here, damn it."

The lad obeyed with great difficulty, fighting Sarina's biting teeth and kicking feet, but finally she was settled tightly and firmly on Ryan's lap.

"Ryan Douglas, you are an utter bastard. A monster. You are depraved!"

"Silence, and stop your squirming unless you want me to throttle you. It will give me the greatest pleasure, I assure you." He applied spurs and whip, and their mount sprang forward and through the opened gate.

"I demand to know what this is all about!" she cried, but Ryan refused to answer.

He chose poorly traveled roads and they rode in silence. Sarina knew he was too enraged to speak. When he continued whipping his horse to greater speed, she finally grabbed his hand, tore the whip from it, and hurled it away.

"Madam, I will tend to you later," Ryan muttered, his voice thick with fury. "Never doubt it."

He sounded so threatening that she should have

been frightened, but she was not. She knew there was only one reason for their wild flight. Lucian was following them.

Lucian was in a black rage. The boatbuilders had caught them off guard just long enough for Douglas to escape. And when they had raced to follow him, they found that their mounts had been released and had run away. Two men eventually found their horses and rode off after the devil while Lucian and the rest of his crew boarded the *Vengeance* and weighed anchor. John Pomeroy returned to the *Gull*.

Lucian prowled the deck, oblivious to his crew's frenzied efforts to increase his vessel's speed as his thoughts raced. He brooded that he never should have boasted to Douglas of how much he knew; never should have let on he was aware that Sarina had bought his escape. He had been too cocky, his head too filled with the triumph of the moment. Now Douglas would have ridden directly to the Hall and seized her. He would have foreseen that the place was being watched and overcome the obstacle. At this instant he was probably carrying her into hiding. Or he had wreaked his fury on her and she was lying injured.

No! Lucian slammed the door of his mind on the thought. To dwell so negatively on her fate now would limit him as severely as dwelling on his own victory had limited him earlier.

"All sails set, sir," Donal said. "We should be nearing the warehouse in ten minutes." Lucian nodded, his face so grim that Donal added, "We'll find her, man, I haven't a doubt of it."

"Give me your thoughts," Lucian said, his eyes narrowed against the beating wind. "What will the devil do?"

Donal grinned. It was their old familiar game, and for Lucian to play it gave him heart. "He will get as far away from here as he can," he said, "except he has no ships in port."

"He is in flight. It would take too long to collect a crew."

"Aye, so would he intercept the *Breton*?"

Lucian nodded. "If he does not, he is a fool."

"He is a bastard, but he is not a fool. We will assume then that he will attempt to intercept the *Breton*?"

"Yes. If she is on schedule, she should be in the Narrows about now."

"How will he connect with her?"

"I myself would take the river road and look for a fishing boat I could hire."

Donal's black eyes had begun to dance. "As would I. And since neither you nor I are fools, nor is he, I think he will be on the lookout for a fishing boat. What else would the devil do? Ah, there is the warehouse ahead. Shall I slack our speed?"

"Aye."

"Look, there is a skiff coming out."

"It's Mason," Lucian said. "It seems we are not to stop, but he has a message."

Maston stood, bracing himself against the bobbing of his small craft, hands to his mouth. "He took 'er south on horseback," he bawled above the snapping canvas and slapping waves. "River road, half hour ago. Watson an' Jenkins was laid low . . ."

Lucian threw him a salute. He was a good man. All of them were good men.

After shouting the order to resume speed, Donal gave Lucian a broad grin. "Well, now, fancy that. The devil riding along the river road. There's not a doubt in my mind what he's up to. He will hire a fishing boat, hail the *Breton*, and if he succeeds in boarding her, he will turn her around and head south. I would! Holy hell, think of all the places in the Caribbean where he could hide."

"He will never get past Seabury," Lucian said. "Open ports and ready cannon."

"Aye," Donal said, his eyes glittering.

* * *

Ryan spurred his mount over and over; **he did**n't need his whip. The beast was tiring under his and Sarina's combined weights, but they were almost at Mallard Bay. He had given up all hope of finding a stray fishing vessel to hire, but Mallard Bay, a fishing village on the East River, could surely supply one. He was relieved when he finally saw the gleam of water through the trees and several fishing vessels tied up in the harbor. Now if only he had not missed the *Breton*. His other concern was that she might have been delayed and he would have an endless wait. But he would worry about that if he had to.

"What is this place?" Sarina asked sharply.

Ryan had been silent the entire journey and now, seeing the fishing vessels, she was frightened. He was going to take her somewhere by sea, and if Lucian didn't come soon, he might never find her.

"Ryan, I demand that you answer me!"

He grasped her jaw and jerked her face toward his. "You are in no position to demand anything, woman."

"You're hurting me!" She tried to pry his fingers away, but he held her tighter. "Ryan!"

"You will keep your mouth shut, do you understand?" When she continued to regard him with blazing eyes, he squeezed her jaw until she whimpered. "Do you? Do you understand?"

"Yes," she whispered.

He released her, but fury was boiling through Sarina's veins. Wait! Just wait! He wasn't going to succeed. When her feet touched the ground she was going to run and scream and tell the whole village that he was abducting her! She sat quietly, obediently, as they entered the main street, biding her time as Ryan turned his mount toward a fisherman readying his small craft for departure.

"In case you are contemplating an outcry or escape, don't," he warned. "If you make so much as one sound, this fellow gets my blade through his heart."

Sarina was chilled by his words. She had no doubt that he would do exactly as he said.

"Ho, there, fellow." Ryan raised his voice. "Has the *Breton* gone by yet?"

"Ain't seen 'er, mister, but then I weren't lookin'."

Ryan felt a surge of fury when the dolt didn't even raise his head from his nets. It was just his luck that he was the only man in sight.

"I require you to take us out to intercept her," he said stiffly.

"I don't run no ferryin' service."

"I will make it worth your while." Ryan's breathing had grown labored. "Damn it all, man, there is no time to waste."

"What yer mean, worth my while?" The fellow looked up finally. "How worth my while?"

Ryan drew two gold coins from his pocket and clicked them together in the palm of his hand. "This much."

The fellow's eyes widened. "Make it three of 'em."

"Very well, three," Ryan snapped. "But only if we leave now. Instantly."

"Aye."

As the fisherman looked at Sarina for the first time, she prayed that he would reconsider and turn down Ryan's offer. It was her only hope.

"Purty woman yer got there, mister."

"Never mind that, get a move on. Hoist your sails and hurry, for God's sake!"

"Aye."

Ryan pressed his fingers painfully into Sarina's arms. "Remember," he said, his breath hot on her cheek, "he dies if you make one sound or try to flee—my dagger in his heart."

As her feet touched the ground, Sarina warred with herself whether or not to obey. There was a change that Ryan would fail to harm the man in his haste to recapture her, but she couldn't risk an innocent man's being killed on her account.

"Make haste, damn it!" Ryan snapped. He had never seen such a slow-moving clod. "I will give you my mount in the bargain if we cast off in the next few minutes.''

He would have left the beast behind at any rate, but he was gratified to see the fellow's eyes gleam.

''Aye. Ho, Tom,'' the fisherman bawled to a distant figure crossing the beach, ''grab this here gelding for me an' tie 'im ter a post. I'll be back afore I goes out again.''

They cast off immediately. They had barely reached the sea-lane before Ryan spied the *Breton* coming toward the Narrow, her sails billowing.

''Run up your boarding flag, mister!'' he ordered.

''Eh? What yer mean? This ain't no man-o-war. I ain't got no boarding flag.''

Ryan glared at him. Why was he always surrounded by fools? He put his hands to his mouth and bellowed, ''Hallooo, *Breton!* Ahoy there!''

He stood, waving both arms at the approaching vessel and fearful they would be run down before they were seen. A figure came to the rail and scowled down at them. Thank God, it was Masters.

''Drop anchor, Masters, we want to board!'' he shouted.

The captain peered, blinked. ''What in hell—Mr. Douglas, is that you . . . ?''

''Yes, yes—'' Ryan shouted as the *Breton* ploughed by, ''drop anchor and lower the ladder, man!''

The orders were obeyed. Only after Sarina had climbed awkwardly up the dangling rope ladder and was aboard the vessel did she decide she could speak safely. The fisherman was gone and Ryan wouldn't dare harm her before a shipload of men.

''Captain,'' she spoke low, breathlessly, ''I am being abducted by this man. Please, I beg your protection.''

Ryan hastening over the rail behind her, took her arm none too gently and gave a harsh bark of laughter.

''This is my new wife, Masters, and we have had a tiff. I will calm her soon enough.''

Sarina's voice rose. ''He is lying. I am not his wife!''

Masters looked between them, confused. "Well, now . . ."

"Get going, Masters," Ryan ordered. "You know how touchy females are. She's just a trifle upset at the moment. I'll handle this." He snapped his fingers at a seaman who stood gaping at them. "Take my wife to the captain's cabin, crewman. I will be there shortly."

"Aye, sir."

"Captain,"Sarina cried, "he is lying. Why will you not believe me?"

"Get a move on, crewman," Ryan said. "Carry the lady if need be and confine her there."

"Aye, sir." The seaman looked nervous, but he took Sarina's arm. "Come along nicely now, Mistress Douglas."

Ryan watched as Sarina, furious, her head held high, entered the cabin and the door was closed and barred behind her. He shook his head, chuckling.

"What a tartar."

"Aye, but a real beauty, sir."

"Yes. All she lacks is taming, but then what is a honeymoon for?"

"Aye, sir."

Masters didn't know as he agreed with Douglas, but he didn't argue. For one thing, he didn't like the wild look in the man's eyes—as though he would draw steel at the least provocation. He shook his head. It was an odd thing, an odd thing, indeed.

"Masters?"

Masters started as his disturbing thoughts were interrupted. "Aye, Mr. Douglas?"

"Turn this vessel around."

"Sir?" He scowled at his employer.

"You heard me. Turn her around. We are heading south."

Masters squared his shoulders. "Sir, this is highly irregular. My men are tired. We have been on the seas five weeks and this ship is in need of repairs. We had heavy weather and—"

Ryan's eyes glinted dangerously. "Turn her around, Captain. We will put in for repairs farther south."

"But our food is almost gone, Mr. Douglas. All that's left has mold and weevils."

"Damn it, no one will starve if they don't eat for a day or two!"

Masters made no reply. All that he said was true. No one would starve and they could put in for repairs and food in almost any fishing village along the coast. But he didn't like it nor would his men like it. Yet he did not want to lose his position. He shrugged.

"Very well, sir. Uh, I might mention, we have a passenger who wants to get to New York as soon as possible."

"So put him ashore at Seabury and let him take a fishing boat back. I will refund part of his fare."

"Aye, sir."

"One other thing. My wife and I will have your cabin until we get to our destination."

"Of course, Mr. Douglas. My pleasure."

"And we are not to be disturbed today, if you get my meaning."

"I do indeed." From the hungry look in those glistening brown eyes, Masters knew the taming was about to begin.

"Under no circumstances are we to be disturbed," Ryan said.

"I understand, sir."

"Good."

Watching him stride off, Masters couldn't help but feel sorry for the woman. He shook his head. A man like that shouldn't be allowed to have a wife.

Sarina barred the door from the inside and sat on the edge of the captain's bunk, shivering and looking about her at the dreary cabin. How could this be happening all over again? It was insane. And where was Lucian? What had happened to him so that he had not come before this? Now that they were at sea, she doubted he would ever find her. She wanted to weep and scream and throw things. She wanted to take the cabin apart in her fury. Yes, she would do just that! But first, was there anything here she could use as a weapon? She was searching fruitlessly when there came a heavy thumping on the door.

"Sarina." Ryan's voice was muffled by the thick oak. "Unbar this door."

Hearing the outer bar slide back, Sarina stiffened. Lucian's men had broken through with a ram, and Ryan was angry enough to do the same. she slid back the bar with shaking hands. Ryan entered. He smiled and barred it again.

"You will pay for this, Ryan." Sarina still looked about the cabin, seeking a weapon. "I will see to it—my father will see to it."

Ryan laughed. "Your father will never find us."

"Lucian will."

"Lucian!" he spat. "This is quite a different story from the pap you fed me last night, you damned cheat."

Sarina gave him a scornful gaze. "Yes, I cheated. But what about you? Is a smuggler not a cheater? And what you did to Lucian was heinous. It was unforgivable."

"Or so he has made you think."

"Oh, come now!" she cried, furious with him. "Are you denying it? Are you saying you didn't arrange to have those pearls hidden aboard his vessel?"

"I'm the one who has questions, Sarina, but we aren't going to talk now. I have waited for you long enough, my beautiful slut." His hand shot out and caught her wrist. She gasped, twisted free, put a chair between them. Ryan chuckled. "You are more desirable than ever when you are afraid, *ma petite*. Your cheeks grow rosy, your eyes wide, and I can see your delicious little pink tongue . . ."

"Don't come near me, I'm warning you . . ."

"Ah, and what will you do, pray? Hurl me to the floor? Thrust me out the door? Come now, Sarina, don't be shy. I have seen your charms and tasted them"—her face flamed—"and last night merely whet-

ted my appetite." He caught her and pulled her
roughly into his arms. "You promised more than you
gave, I think, but now—"

"You were sickening. You were disgustingly
drunk."

Ryan's face darkened. "Because of you, you bitch."

"Yes!" she flared. "Because of me. I wanted you
drunk and I got you drunk. It was pathetically easy,
and you drooled and pawed me and babbled. Oh, yes,
you babbled. Believe me, it was the only reason I put
up with your repulsive touch. I wanted to know where
your cache was—and you told me!" She laughed at the
rage on his face. "You said there was no cache, but
you would receive a shipment of gems today—in the
shipyard. And I told Lucian—oh, yes, I have seen him
several times. He has visited my bedchamber . . ." She
shrieked when he grasped her throat.

"Has he now?" Ryan's handsome face was blood-
red, the veins standing out on his temples. "Go gently,
my sweet slut. Do not toy with me on this subject, I
warn you. The truth now. Did he come to your bedchamber? In my house?"

He was so cruel, Sarina wanted to hurt him. Suddenly she didn't care what happened to her."

"He did. We made love . . ."

"By the gods."

Sarina gasped as his fingers pressed against her
windpipe. She tried to pry them loose but could not.
Her head swam as smothering blackness enfolded her.

"I could kill you for that. Perhaps I shall. I shall consider it, but I will not kill you before I have fully enjoyed you."

When he released her and began to strip off his
clothing, she ran to the door. He caught her, gave her
a stinging slap on the cheek, and threw her onto a
bunk. She screamed.

"Yell your head off, my sweet. My men have seen
you are a tartar who needs taming."

He was about to remove his boots when there was a
wild thumping at the door.

"Mr. Douglas, sir?"

"Leave us," Ryan shouted. "I said we were not to be disturbed."

"Aye, but the cap'n thought ye should know—we're bein' followed. Chased. The men are sayin' it's the ghost ship, sir."

Sarina wanted to laugh, to taunt him, but she held her tongue, her breath. She had felt his fury. She watched as he sat on the edge of the bunk for a long moment, his head sunk in his hands. When he finally looked at her, he was white-faced, his mouth a grim slash. He rose, dressed, and strapped on his sword.

"I see you are amused by this," he said.

"Did you really think he would not come?"

Ryan shook his head. "No, I knew he would come, but I tire of this chase, Sarina. This is the last time he and I will meet, and I promise you, this time he is going to die."

Chapter 28

Standing in the empty cabin, Sarina was filled with a rush of memories. Lucian in gray, hooded, his angry blue eyes glittering . . . Lucian and Donal defending the three of them from his crew . . . Lucian kissing her for the first time . . . And now Ryan was going to kill him! Remembering his white-lipped fury, she had no doubt that he would, and terror swept over her. She couldn't live without Lucian! She couldn't!

Then she saw how foolish her fears were. Lucian's own fury towered far above Ryan's, and he was a fighting man. He was at home on the sea and with a sword in his hand, whereas Ryan was a merchant who was better at wielding a champagne glass than a weapon. She knew then that it was Ryan who would die. She had been so angry with him just moments ago, but now comtemplating his loss, she felt only sadness.

But it was sadness for the loss of a man who had never existed: a man she had thought was loving and gentle and compassionate but who was not. He was cruel and greedy and heartless, and his crime deserved punishment. Still, she didn't want him to die, especially not at Lucian's hand. Oh, why were men always fighting and killing each other?

She searched her mind frantically for some way to prevent the coming battle between them. Could she threaten to jump overboard? Hurl herself between them? She wasn't brave enough to do either, but something had to be done. She hurried on deck and found chaos, the crew hauling out guns and powder kegs, yelling, running into each other, not knowing what to do.

Ryan began shouting orders, but no one heard him for there was a thunderclap just then, and another and another. It was the crack of cannon, followed by cannonballs whizzing past and falling into the sea all around them. Sarina covered her ears and ran to the rail.

The sight that met her eyes sent her heart flying— the *Vengeance!* She was skimming across the dark waters, all of her cannon showing and her great sails filled, her flags flying with Lucian's blood-red pennant streaming from the tallest mast. Her eyes brimmed. Oh, God, Lucian was coming for her. Her beloved was coming . . .

"Them's only warnin' shots, Cap'n," a crewman shouted. "He wants us to stay where we are."

"And that we will, mister," the captain answered. "This is the Ghost and he'll not harm us. Our cargo's not worth a fight."

Suddenly Ryan was there. "So our cargo is not worth a fight, eh? You have just been relieved of your command, damn you. Clear the decks and position those guns!" he yelled to the crew. "Double-load them with shot and gun those bastards down when they board us."

"Aye, sir."

Sarina struggled to control her fear. She knew that Lucian would be one of the first over the rail.

"Mr. Douglas, th' powder seems to be damp . . ."

"What!"

"Must o' been th' storm."

"God's bones!" Seeing Sarina clinging to the rail, Ryan's full fury fell upon her. "Woman, you are to stay out of sight!" He caught her arm, dragged her to the nearest cabin, and hurled her into it. "Stay there until I come for you."

Bastard! she thought, anger sweeping over her. She

certainly would not stay there. She would go on deck again, only this time she would keep herself hidden. She jumped, startled to see that the darkened cabin was already occupied. A man lay in the bunk.

"Sir, I—I am so sorry! We didn't know you were here . . ."

He got to his feet and moved toward her uncertainly. "Sarina?"

Sarina blinked. "Father? Oh, Father! Oh, I cannot believe it!" She flew to him.

George Fairburn grabbed and hugged his daughter. "Where did you come from?" he demanded. "And what the devil is going on here?"

"Oh, Father . . ."

There was another explosion and then another.

"Under attack, are we?" he growled. "Well, then, I had best get out there. This tub sails like a haystack, and I'll wager this landlubber crew will defend her like one." He strapped on his sword belt.

"I'm so glad you are here." Sarina was nearly overcome at the sight of him. Now, finally Ryan would pay.

"Child, I am astonished, so grateful . . ." When another explosion rattled the ports, he strode to the door. "We will talk later."

"Father, wait, I must tell you—"

"Later, Sarina." He added, sternly, "Stay here until I come for you."

But Sarina had no intention of staying there. As soon as he had left, she crept on deck, virtually unnoticed, and hid amidships between two mountains of coiled rope. She watched, curious, as her father, assessing the situation, spied Ryan.

"Douglas! By the gods, how did *you* get aboard?"

Ryan whirled, his face dark with fury and frustration, his lips drawn back, the whites of his eyes showing.

"Fairburn! Wh-where did you come from?"

"From London," George Fairburn snapped. "I have some questions for you, sir, but not now." Seeing that the enemy was almost upon them, he called out to the crew, "Get those swivel guns loaded, and fast!"

"Do you think I did not order that?" Ryan lashed out. "These damned fools let the powder get wet."

The older man looked about the deck and riggings, his gaze like flint.

"For a man who's been besieged by the Ghost for four months, you seem to have few defenses. And your powder should have been stored in closed quarters."

Ryan's eyes blazed at the rebuke. He shouted to his crew: "Arm yourselves!"

George Fairburn saw that the enemy would cripple their ship with no effort. With no powder, there would be hand-to-hand combat with steel, and by the looks of the white faces and frightened eyes of the men around him, the battle would be lost before it was joined. He saw the grapnels fly then, the great claws jerking the two vessels together. He sighed and drew his own dagger, his thoughts going to Sarina and what might happen to her. His little girl . . .

Ryan's mouth was dry, his heart pumping. He had never met the ghost ship at sea. He had only boarded her when she and her master were safe in chains, but now she danced fiercely at their side, pulling, tugging at the *Breton* with her grapnels. As the wild music of pipes and drums burst from her like the voices of a throng of demons, he felt his hair stand on end. Suddenly his decks were aswarm, gray-clad hooded men leaping from their spritsail yards, climbing the *Breton*'s sides with boarding axes, daggers gleaming between their teeth, swords in hand. There was no stopping them. And the bastard—where was Thorne? he thought. Ryan was shaking, yearning to drive his own sword through him. Which one was he?

"Lay down your weapons and no one will be harmed," a deep voice rang out.

Ah, now he knew. Ryan retained his sword as his crew's arms clattered to the deck. Bloody cowards. He ground his teeth, felt cold sweat gluing his clothing to his body. Soon, soon his sword would drink the devil's blood.

George Fairburn, standing grimly next to two great coils of rope, slid his own dagger back into its sheath. Never would he lay down his arms, and never had he seen the likes of this—men giving up without a fight. What kind of lily-livered crew was this? Now it was Ryan for whom he felt pity and outrage. And his fear for his daughter was great. There was much he didn't know, but it was clear she had escaped from the Ghost and now he had come for her. Well, the fellow would have to deal with him first.

"Father . . ." It was a whisper from behind him.

His stiffened. In the name of God, what was the girl doing out here on deck?

"Hush," he rasped, "say nothing and don't move. You are in great danger." He couldn't believe it when she disobeyed and began to climb over the ropes. "Sarina, I forbid this!" He kept his voice low. "These men must not see you."

Sarina rose nonetheless and stood beside him. "Father, I tried to tell you—it's Ryan I fear. He is not the man we thought he was. Y-you must believe me."

He pressed his lips together. So. He had heard rumors for some time, and now here were these words coming from his own daughter.

"I believe you," he said, grimly. "I see the fear in your eyes still."

Sarina took his arm. "It is because there is going to be a terrible fight. How can we stop it?"

"I doubt we can."

"Where is Douglas?" It was the deep voice that had ordered them to lay down their weapons.

George Fairburn looked at the tall broad-shouldered figure in gray standing at the head of the companionway. So this was the Ghost . . . His dark-skinned face was partially hidden by his hood, and a great two-edged sword was clasped easily in one big hand. He strode to the quarterdeck.

"Damn you, Douglas, show yourself!"

Ryan pushed through his men. "I am here, you devil, never fear. My blade is itching to taste your blood."

"Soon," Lucian promised. "But first, where is she? Quickly now, before my men take your ship apart again."

Sarina leaped out before her father could stop her. "Lucian, I'm here!" she cried. "I'm safe."

Lucian pointed his long sword at her. "Stay there!" he commanded.

George Fairburn caught her wrist in an iron grip. "He's right. You will stay here."

What was this between his daughter and this tall sea wolf? he wondered uneasily. He had never seen such a glow in her eyes . . .

Lucian returned his attention to Ryan. "It's time to measure your sword with mine, old friend."

"I have been counting the hours," Ryan muttered.

Lucian tore off his hood and threw it to the deck, his cold gaze moving over the astonished crew of the *Breton*.

"Let me introduce myself," he said. "I am Lucian Thorne."

Ryan sneered. "Meet the thief of Naipoor."

Donal thrust a finger at him. "Ah, no, man, let the truth be known—" His black eyes traveled over the assembled seamen and returned to drill through Ryan. "You are the thief of Naipoor, you bastard. It is your turn to rot while Lucian Thorne returns to what you stole from him, the command of the *Peacekeeper*."

Lucian laughed. "Enough, Mr. Fleming." His feet were planted wide, sun glinting on the deadly shaft of steel in his hand. "Come, old friend, old enemy, let us get on with it. Death waits for one of us."

"Not for me, bastard."

Seeing them together and seeing the terrible hatred burning between them, Sarina knew that one of them was doomed. "Father, can you not stop them? Please . . ."

George Fairburn shook his head. "I would not even if I could."

She started forward, willing to put herself between them, willing to do anything to stop the bloodshed, but her father caught her arm.

"No, Sarina."

"Let me go!" The more she struggled, the more tightly he held her.

"Be still, child . . ."

"Lucian! Ryan! Please, stop." They ignored her.

Sarina feared to watch, but she couldn't look away. No one spoke. She heard only the men's breathing and the sounds of the sea and the ships: the whistle of wind in the sails, ropes squeaking, chains clanking, the rasp of metal on metal, the slap of water against wood.

Swords up, the two men began circling, each watchful for an unguarded opening, Ryan's lips drawn back in a snarl, a cold smile on Lucian's face, his eyes glittering. Finally there was the hiss, the first clash of steel on steel . . . From the first ringing contact between them, a current of awareness flowed between the two enemies.

Ryan, his heart sinking, knew within minutes that he faced a master swordsman whose skill was far greater than his own. He had suspected it at the shipyard when the devil's blade had come out of nowhere to point at his throat—so why had he allowed himself to get into this predicament? Ah, God, it was too late to wonder. Already he felt death breathing on him, laughing, waiting. He imagined he could taste his blood bubbling up in his throat to strangle him. His throat—was that where he would take the blade? In his heart? He tried to stop shaking, tried to swallow, heard himself gasping for breath as though his life's blood were already seeping away . . .

From the first, Lucian felt Douglas' fear through his blade. As he lunged, parried, ever circling, his keen eyes appraising and assessing his opponent's strengths and weaknesses, he knew he had won. The battle was hardly joined and he had won. Coldly, mechanically, with terrible speed and ferocity, he began to toy with his enemy, bringing him close to death again and again, only to let him escape so that he could torment him further. Seeing Douglas's waxy face and terror-glazed eyes, he wanted to laugh. He knew the devil was envisioning the kiss of the thin-lipped blade on his throat, slicing through his heart. Good. He had waited long for this moment and nothing could stop him now. He was tireless, his sword weightless, his lightning thrusts effortless. He had won. Douglas was a dead man . . .

Sarina had never seen a man killed. She had watched as death came on whispering feet to carry her mother away, but she had never seen violent death. She was horrified by the prospect; her body was shaking and wet with the sweat of fear, her fingernails driving into her palms.

At first she had feared that Lucian would be slain, but now even her untutored eyes saw that Ryan was tiring and beginning to slip on the wet deck, his sword seeming too heavy for his hand. Again and again she squeezed her eyes shut, but they always flew open again. She was afraid to watch but more afraid not to watch. Ryan was going to die. He was cruel and wicked and heartless, and if ever a man deserved a dreadful death, it was he. Still . . .

Sarina's breath caught as Ryan lost his balance and went down, his sword sailing through the air. Lucian's point flashed instantly to his throat. She saw the triumph in his icy eyes, heard his familiar low chuckle as a small red blossom appeared on Ryan's throat. Ryan dropped to his knees.

"Have mercy, old friend . . ."

Lucian's whole body and mind were prepared for the death thrust. He yearned to press his point to the bone, to hear the devil's scream and see his blood fly. He knew, were the tables turned, that Douglas would show him no mercy. But was that what he wanted—to be like Douglas? His hunger for revenge had already blackened his soul. Maybe it was time to consider mercy. He sought Sarina. Her hands were pressed to her mouth, her beautiful eyes wide and frightened. His heart melted. Having her, he had everything. He owned the world. The lark was singing at heaven's gate . . .

"Lucian, for the love of God . . ." Ryan muttered, the blood now flowing freely down his throat and onto his satin waistcoat.

Lucian lowered his sword and wiped the bloody point on his breeches. He looked toward Donal and Sky.

"Take him."

"Damn it, Luc—"

"Take him back to the *Vengeance* and toss him in the brig. The Crown can have him. Pomeroy will see that he gets back to England to stand trial."

Four days later, Sarina stood in the stern of the *Vengeance* watching as the setting sun turned the sea to a sheet of flame. So many times she had thought this moment would never come, but it had. New York was far in the distance, London lay five weeks ahead of them, and tonight she would sleep in Lucian's arms again. Dreams really did come true.

It was like the ending of a fairy tale. Lucian's coming at the exact right moment and her father's being aboard the *Breton*. He had been on his way to New York for various reasons—to question Ryan, to search for her, and afterward, to open an office there.

Sarina had done as she had vowed, telling him about Lucian and Ryan from beginning to end and asking his help in vindicating Lucian. She had been astonished to learn that his vindication was already assured and he would regain his command. And wonder of wonders, her father was buying Douglas Traders and would be staying on in New York for a while longer. How strange it all was, yet how perfect . . .

Sarina opened her cloak, threw back her hood, and raised her arms to the sky, laughing as the wind whipped her gown and her hair. Lucian was there suddenly, his arms around her.

"Is it real?" she asked, her face upturned to his.

He kissed her laughing lips. "No dream ever felt or tasted like you, fondling."

"Nor like you," she whispered.

He bundled her in her cloak and hood, for the late August winds were cool now and warned that winter was coming. He put his arm around her and snuggled her close, and together they watched as the fiery sea turned to copper and then pewter and the ship's lanterns were lit. Gazing up at the sky's vastness and the tiny points of light that were pricking it, Sarina cried:

"Oh, look! The moon is nearly full. Lucian, I just realized, I have not seen the moon since I left Malaga . . ."

She felt a sudden heaviness, thinking of all that had passed and all the terrible things that might have been but were not. Instead, this was reality—Lucian by her side in the windy night, the smell of the sea, the deck tilting beneath her feet, canvas cracking and slapping all about her as the *Vengeance* carried them back to England and to a life together. At least they would be together part of the time, she told herself. She knew Lucian would be returning to sea, and she absolutely would not interfere and go all wistful about it. The *Peacekeeper* was his very first love and he would have it. She would insist.

"Where are your friends?" Lucian asked.

"They've been primping ever since we left the harbor. This is a very special night, you know, and they wouldn't dream of getting their hair mussed . . ."

He met her laughing eyes and, lowering her hood, watched the wind lift her own thick mane of hair to whip behind her like a coppery banner. She was a marvel, a goddess, perfection—and she was his. He took her hand and led her to his cabin.

Sarina watched him lighting the lamp, and wondered at the mocking, mysterious glance in his eyes as he went to his sea chest.

"Close your eyes," he said.

"Lucian Thorne, what are you up to?"

He chuckled. "Close your eyes and hold out your hands."

She obeyed, laughing. And then she felt a cloud between her fingers.

"You can open them . . ."

She did. She gasped. It was a frothy bedgown of peach silk and satin and lace. Her mouth fell open. Lucian kissed it.

"Put it on," he said softly. "I'll be back in five minutes."

"I'll be waiting . . ."

Sarina held up the gown and gazed at it in the flickering lamplight. It was exquisite, the most beautiful thing she had ever seen. With trembling fingers, she tugged off her cloak and gown and chemise, kicked off her shoes, stripped off her stockings, and slipped the gauzy cloud over her head. It slid down over her heated flesh with a silky sigh—tiny capped sleeves that scarcely covered her shoulders, a high waist gathered on a peach satin ribbon under her breasts, a low scooped neckline that nearly exposed her nipples. She smiled, imagining Lucian's expression when he saw it.

She yearned to know how she looked, but there was no mirror in the cabin. She so hoped that Lucian would like it on her. She found her brush and had just smoothed her tangled hair when he tapped on the door and entered. She heard his sharply indrawn breath, saw the dark centers of his eyes widen as he gazed at her. Hungry eyes. The eyes of the Ghost.

"Is it all right?" she murmured. "I can't tell . . ."

Gazing at her, Lucian felt an instant deep thrust of desire, felt his manhood swelling. She was ravishing. The gown, a transparent veil clung to her soft body like mist in the lamp's yellow glow. He saw every delectable curve and valley, the taut pink buds of her nipples, the shadowy triangle between her thighs, the long supple legs. So fierce was his hunger that he trembled as he reined it in. He wanted to plunge into her, kiss and consume her, never let her go . . . But he would not. He would never frighten or hurt her.

"You're beautiful," he said, his voice low.

He lifted her into his arms and kissed her rosy lips, a gentle kiss that deepened as his arms tightened around her. He carried her to his bed, placed her on it, and began to take off his own clothing.

Sarina's pulse was beating so fast that she thought her heart would falter. She watched as he turned the lamp low so that there were only shadows. He slipped into bed beside her and pulled her tight against him, his warm lips and hands moving over her, tenderly caressing her and then slowly, expertly teasing her to an unbearable excitement. She wasn't aware of removing her gown, but suddenly her bare skin was against his, their lips and bodies sealed, and he was riding her to paradise. She was vaguely aware that she wept, but it was with joy and love.

Afterward, Lucian kissed her damp eyes and face. "I didn't hurt you, did I?"

"You were wonderful," she whispered. "You've never been so wonderful . . ."

When he smiled at her, she loved him more than ever. He had more charm in his smallest smile than any man she had ever known. She nuzzled his throat, kissed the deep hollow at its center, sniffed his skin that always reminded her of the wind and the sun. How she loved him . . .

"I want to care for you, Sarina," Lucian said. "I want to protect you, I want to give you the world. Whatever you want, I will give you . . ."

Sarina laughed, offering her lips again. "I have what I want, beloved. I have the world—it is you . . ."

Epilogue

May, 1794

The wedding was over. The young mistress of Kenley Gables was now the wife of Commander Lucian Thorne of HMS *Peacekeeper*. Sarina stood at her husband's side greeting the happy wedding guests who flowed through the drawing room and into the garden for refreshments.

"How many more?" Lucian murmured.

His collar was too tight, and he was too warm in his full-dress uniform. He wanted nothing so much as to be alone with his beautiful young wife. His wife. He could not believe it . . .

"Beloved, they've just begun to come," Sarina whispered. Seeing his frown, she added, "But let us move about. I'm perishing for something cool to drink."

"And here it is, Mistress Thorne." Donal was there with two cups of fruit punch in his hands. "My darlin' wife says we're to dance attendance on the two of you today. Your wishes are our commands . . ."

Ginelle laughed. "But only for today." She lifted Sarina's hand and gazed at the breathtaking ring on her finger, diamonds and emeralds embedded in a thick gold band. "It's simply too lovely for words, as was your wedding gown—and this green gown is even more so. My goodness, Rina, it's as if you're wearing sea foam!" She turned to her husband. "Donal, I ask you, have you ever seen a more beautiful bride?"

Donal's dancing eyes met Lucian's. "Only once, my dove. Only once."

Lucian laughed. "Wisely spoken, man, and I'll not take offense. Ah, here are my parents . . ."

It had been a happy thing for him, seeing the change in them since his command and his honor had been restored. They had begun to live again.

"Here's my father, too," Sarina exclaimed. "Do join us, all of you."

She had been fascinated to see that Richard Thorne had given Lucian his height and strength and darkness. Margaret Thorne had given him her own handsome features and brilliant blue eyes. During their weekend stay at Kenley Gables, Sarina had learned that they were caring and gentle people. She loved them already and was delighted that her affection for them was returned.

"Lucian had best treat you well, Sarina, or you come to me," Richard Thorne warned.

"And to me," Margaret said. "If Lucian doesn't know how to treat a lady properly, it's entirely my fault."

"But he does . . ." Sarina caught Lucian's hand and held it to her cheek.

George Fairburn clapped Lucian on the shoulder. "Be firm with her, son. Be firm—if you can . . ."

George Fairburn was content. He knew beyond a doubt that Lucian Thorne was the man for Sarina. He would make her happy. He would love her, protect her even die for her, just as he himself would. Not least, on that day when he decided to retire, Fairburn Shipping would go into strong and honest hands. It would not be for many years yet, for he had just doubled his empire with the addition of Douglas Traders, but when the time came, he would feel easy in his heart in handing it over to Lucian. Feeling a tap on his shoulder, he turned.

"Well, well . . ." He extended his hand, blinking at the dazzle of metal that met his eyes. "It was good of you to come, Sir John."

"I wouldn't have missed it," John Pomeroy said.

"You know Commander and Mistress Richard Thorne?"

"Indeed, indeed."

Not only did the Fleet Commander want to wish Lucian and his lovely bride well, but he intended to congratulate the elder Thornes on their son's acquittal. It was a fine occasion on which to display his uniform and medals.

"Congratulations, Commander." He shook Lucian's hand.

"Thank you, sir."

Pomeroy gave the bride a quick kiss on the cheek, surprising both of them. He straightened his shoulders and addressed Lucian.

"So, all's well that ends well, eh, Thorne? Speedy trial, everyone pardoned, and the real culprit in gaol."

Lucian nodded. "Yes."

Damn the fellow. He gazed down at Sarina, concerned that such talk on their wedding day would start her worrying over Ryan, but it seemed that she was all right. She knew such crimes as his had to be punished.

"I was most interested to see that the *Vengeance* is out of dry dock," Pomeroy went on. He smiled. "Planning to use it again, eh?"

Sarina didn't miss the hush that fell over their small group, or the annoyance in Lucian's eyes.

"How very interesting, Sir John," she murmured. "Lucian hadn't told me this news yet . . ."

John Pomeroy blinked, then said gruffly, "It seems I have said too much . . ."

Lucian forced himself to smile at the Fleet Commander. "Not at all. It's time my wife knew of the small surprise I have planned for her."

"A surprise?" Seeing Donal and Ginelle's glowing faces, she knew that something special was afoot. Something involving the *Vengeance*. She laughed. "Lucian Thorne, what are you up to? Tell me."

"Better than that, Mistress Thorne, I'll soon show you. Donal, any word yet?"

"Strange you should ask." Donal was grinning. "Here comes Manley with a gleam in his eye."

Sarina gazed at them, wondering what it was all about. Ginelle ready to burst with pink-faced excitement; Donal looking dark and wicked; Manley and her father and Lucian's parents pretending nonchalance; and Lucian—Lucian's eyes saying he loved her more than anything in the world and he hoped she liked his surprise. What on earth was it?

Manley stood before Lucian. "Sir, all is in readiness."

"Thank you, Manley." Lucian took Sarina's hand. "It's time to leave, Sarina."

"Leave? Now?" She was astonished. That wasn't at all what they had planned.

"Rina, I—I packed your trunk. It's in the carriage—and I put Rosie and Sky's gift in with it. They so wanted to be here, you know."

"Oh, Ginny!" Sarina went into Ginelle's arms, laughing, crying. It was all so wonderful and mysterious. "Thank you . . ."

She turned to all the familiar smiling faces, caught the hands of Richard and Margaret Thorne.

"Thank you all for coming to our wedding, and for the gifts and—" She went into her father's arms. "Goodbye, Father, I love you—and thank you for the wonderful wedding . . ."

Lucian took his bride out to the carriage, helped her into it, and as it clattered off, pulled her into arms. His hungry mouth captured hers. She was his. His wife. All of his life he had been moving toward this moment. He had sensed it only dimly at first, knowing that there had to be some shining thing to live and die for, but he had not known what. And then he had found Sarina. He offered up his silent thanks.

Sarina was in deepest bliss, eyes closed, Lucian's lips and hands moving over her, gentle, caressing, promising the heaven that was to come. She was almost sorry when the carriage stopped.

"Come along, cosset," Lucian said. "We'll continue our petting later." He laughed, seeing her delight as she opened her eyes and gazed out the window.

He lifted her from the carriage, keeping her cradled tightly in his arms, hearing her small gasp as she saw the handsome vessel at the end of the pier. The ship was gray once more and some of her sails were already filled, causing her to dance and strain at her anchor. She was eager to be off.

"I had hoped this was your surprise—a honeymoon on the *Vengeance!* Oh, Lucian . . ." Sarina gave her husband's cheek a resounding kiss.

Lucian chuckled. "It's not exactly the *Vengeance* anymore. There has been a slight change made . . ." He carried his bride to the end of the pier and pointed to the new name painted on the bow in gold.

"The *Sarina?* She is named for me?" Sarina laughed up at him, her green eyes glowing. "Lucian, I can't believe it!"

What better name, Lucian thought. His vengeance was a thing of the past. Now all that mattered was the future—and the name of his future was Sarina. In fact, he had some hard thinking to do. He wanted to spend every second of the rest of his life by her side, but he must also work as other men worked. Did he want to be at sea six months of every year, or was it time to enter his family's banking business? He already knew the answer.

His thoughts were interrupted, happily, as he carried his bride aboard his vessel and his men began cheering, shouting, giving him the victorious piping and drumming that always accompanied a strike while his slender wife, held securely in his arms, looked on with laughter bubbling from her rosy lips and tears in her eyes.

"Enough!" Lucian called finally. "Weigh anchor!"

The *Sarina* was immediately underway, her sails billowing, the crew manning her as swiftly and silently as if she still sailed under the hand of the Ghost. At the top of her tallest spar, where a blood-red pennant had once flown, there now streamed a sea-green banner emblazoned with a golden lark.

Sarina gazed up at it, wondering, her lips parted. "Lucian, how beautiful . . ."

His arms tightened around her. He wanted to tell her about the lark that sang at heaven's gate, but not now, not now. Tonight . . .

Sarina put her arms around his neck, brushed a kiss over his lips, and whispered in his ear:

"Are we going where I think we're going?"

Lucian laughed. "It depends on where you think we're going, my beautiful wench."

"Malaga?" Excitement sparkled in her eyes. "Are we going to Malaga?"

"Yes. Back to where the magic began."

She covered his face and his smiling mouth with kisses. "We can return every May!"

"You have but to say the word, She-Who-Commands."

Sarina laughed, then nestled in his arms, safe, loved, her thoughts filled with what was to come—the magic of blue skies and balmy nights, white sand, the soft winds that always carried the fragrance of night blooming jasmine, riding the warm waves in the moonlight in his arms. Malaga.

"What if I never want to leave?"

"That can be arranged," he said gravely.

"But your work . . ."

His eyes flickered. "Commanding a warship doesn't seem so important anymore."

She was shocked. "Lucian, I—would never ask you to give it up."

"I have given the sea years of my life, Sarina. Being with you, caring for you, is all that I want for now."

Sarina stared at his dark intent face, looking for a sign that he was teasing. There was none. Could he mean it? she wondered, her heart racing. Did he really mean that he wouldn't sail off again and leave her alone for month after month on end?

"I know how you feel about the *Peacekeeper*," she

murmured. "I know how much you love her and the sea."

Lucian laughed as he carried her toward his cabin. "And you know how I feel about you. Is it really so strange, my luscious bride, that I should prefer you to a warship?"

Sarina's mouth tilted into a teasing hopeful smile.

"There is no comparison," he assured her.

Seeing her husband's burning gaze moving over her, Sarina lifted her parted lips and felt his tender kiss. Apparently the discussion was over. Now and forever . . .

If You've Enjoyed This Avon Romance— Be Sure to Read. . .

THE MAGIC OF YOU
by Johanna Lindsey
75629-3/$5.99 US/$6.99 Can

SHANNA
by Kathleen Woodiwiss
38588-0/$5.99 US/$6.99 Can

UNTAMED
by Elizabeth Lowell
76953-0/$5.99 US/$6.99 Can

EACH TIME WE LOVE
by Shirlee Busbee
75212-3/$5.99 US/$6.99 Can